The Subtle Art of Spellcasting and Sarcasm

Airie Avant

A Conquest Publishing Original

Conquest Publishing

https://conquest-publishing.com

Copyright © 2025 Airie Avant

Cover Design: Abigail Baia

Edited by: Brandi Shaffer

Map illustration: Ria Designs

All rights reserved. No part of this publication may be reproduced, distributed, or transmitted in any form or by any means, including photocopying, recording, or other electronic or mechanical methods, without the prior written permission of the publisher, except in the case of brief quotations embodied in critical reviews and certain other noncommercial uses permitted by copyright law.

Any references to historical events, real people, or real places are used fictitiously. Names, characters, and places are products of the author's imagination.

To Alyssa, you are the sun.
And now, the truth of it is, I want to be like you.

Acknowledgements

In loving memory of Peter Brazas, my first best friend who always laughed the hardest. The world is better for having had you in it, and those of us who loved you are broken without your smile.

To Aimee, Angela, Cindi, and Nicole—you steel-spined, hard-assed, life-crushing women are a flighty writer's best friends. Thank you for never telling anyone I stole all my best lines from you four. Your uncontrollable laughter has always inspired my greatest insanity.

To Brittany, Abby, and the Conquest / Wild Ink family: You've built a strong, brilliant community of writers and collaborators. Thank you for showing so much love to my little story.

Special thanks to Sara Lunsford and Angelee Van Allman for the constant revisions, stunning art, unwavering support, occasional ass-kicking, and frequent hand-holding. Becoming co-workers was rewarding; becoming friends was a lifesaver.

To my mentor and friend, Scott Case—thank you for believing in me when I didn't deserve it, giving me a chance when I hadn't earned it, and carrying me through too many years when I couldn't handle it. No one has ever had a more steadfast, brilliant, or hilarious mentor than I do.

Jeff, Mark, Thub, and my incredible brother-in-law Joe—you are the men doing the work to make modern heroes good enough for the strong women I write. You inspire me. (I hope this acknowledgment suffices as payment for all the money I owe the first three of you.)

To my parents: You taught me that dedicating your life to something is always time well spent. You were right about everything. To my brother and grandmother: You inspired so many of the plot details and personality quirks that make this story sing.

To Pricilla, my little fallen star: I don't know what I did in life for heaven to drop you into my lap and show me everything that really matters, but I will protect your light with every bit of magic in my heart.

And Clint—every word in every language ever written is insufficient to describe how much I adore you, but I'll never stop trying. Thank you for being such an inspirational hero that I have to write around the clock to capture all your best moments. There is only you. Only ever you. Forever you.

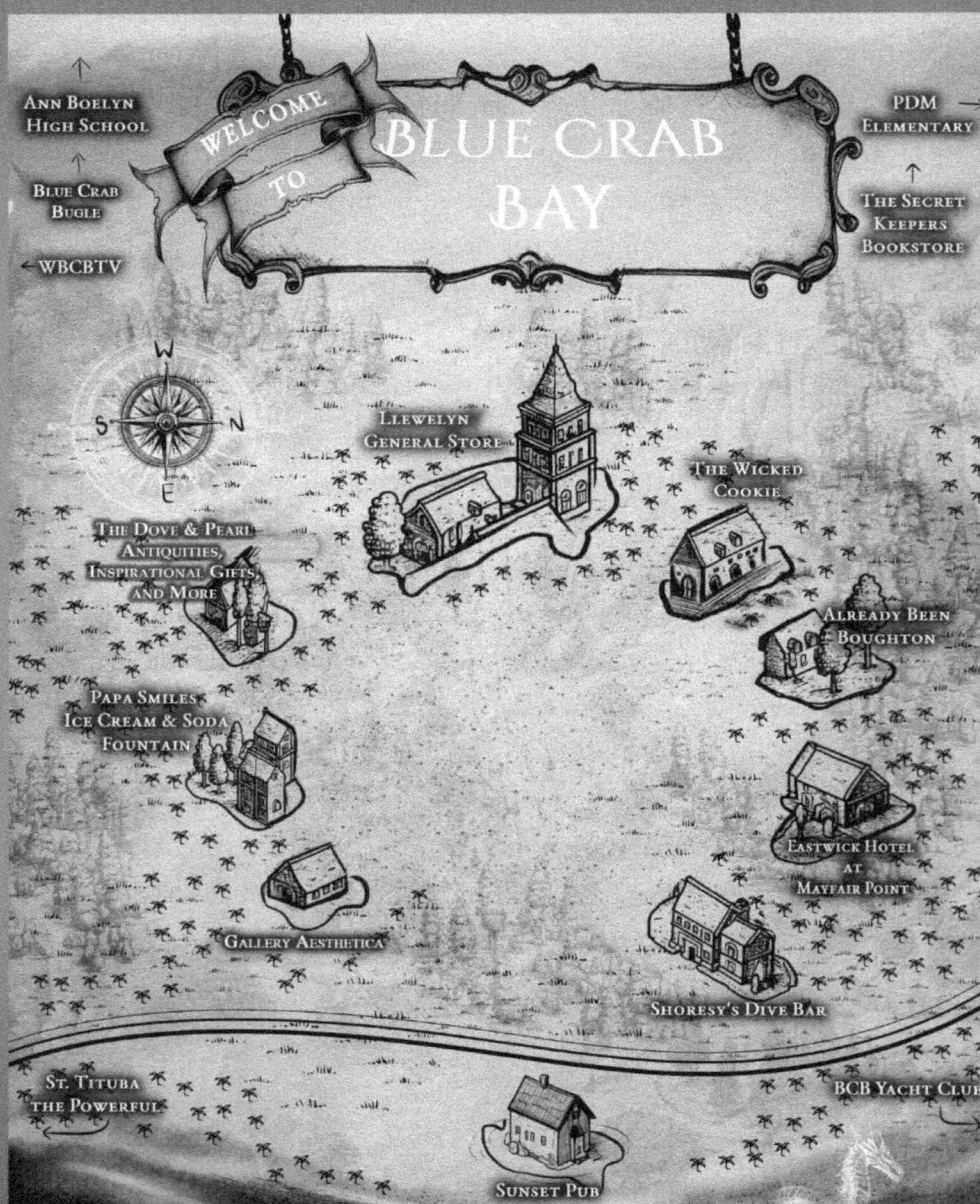

Chapter One

The prodigal daughter returns...

PHEME: *Welcome back! You're listening to* Blue Crab Bay After Dark, *the only podcast for witches, by witches, where we take a good look at the modern life, faith, and community of the oldest and largest concentration of witches in the southeast United States. I'm your host, Pheme, and as always, with me today is my co-host Eris and we're talking about Ostara, bunny legends, and how to celebrate with our coven even if you can't be on the coast!*

PHEME: *But first, a little raven told me a certain scorching hot teacher over at the elementary school got word her prodigal sister is headed back to the coast just in time to crash the family holidays.*

ERIS: *Is this the same daughter who's going to lose what little power she has if she doesn't make her ascension before the Frost Moon? Even though she's going to need more than eight months to learn twenty-five years of magic? It's literally a lifetime of magic.*

PHEME: *It's the daughter whose sexy ex has been seen around town with everyone's favorite ice queen. But yes, she's on a timetable.*

ERIS: *I was at the BCB Municipal Awards last night watching Mayor Dumpling pay homage to the ferret-faced fire chief for some last-moment, life-saving act of heroism. I ran smack into Old Lady Railroad Tie who told me the Prodigal One was finally finished with whatever vision quest she'd been working on and was finally coming to her senses and returning home to her parents.*

PHEME: *I have to be honest; I'm surprised she's headed back. Do you think she's finally over the embarrassment?*

ERIS: *Could you get over it if you were favored to win a state championship and based an entire speech on removing a tapeworm by starving yourself for a week and waving a piece of bread around your butthole until the tapeworm peeks out so you can snatch it?*

PHEME: *The jury is still out on whether that was an attempt at comedy...*

ERIS: *Comedy shouldn't end in tears. And I'll tell you right now, I know for a fact her father told her that story and she bought it hook, line, and sinker.*

PHEME: *Because he used to make that joke when he was in high school?*

ERIS: *Because he used to make that... yes, Pheme. Apparently, he walked up to her while the audience sat silently in horror, and she ran off stage saying it was a perfectly reasonable way to get rid of a tapeworm and everyone was just too dumb to realize it.*

PHEME: *There's nothing wrong with trying to make a kid feel better after losing something she worked so hard for.*

ERIS: *That man was a doctor. Capital M. Capital D. Doctor Slow Motion is what I called him.*

PHEME: *That's not going to help with our anonymity, Eris. Why do we bother with pseudonyms at all?*

ERIS: *Bahhh! Everyone knows who I'm talking about. There are like twelve families that matter in this town, secrets won't stay secret long. Your "scorching" sister comment was just as easy to figure out.*

PHEME: *Let's take a question! This one is from Ximena in Sedona. "Dear BCBAD, I loved your episode about Sanctuary homes. My question is: How do Sanctuary homes protect us from witch hunters?"*

ERIS: *There's no such thing as witch hunters; thanks, next question.*

PHEME: *Oh stop it, you! She took the time to ask, we owe her a better answer than that!*

ERIS: *You're going to tell people witch hunters exist?*

PHEME: *It wouldn't be historically inaccurate to see where witch hunters caused huge problems in the past, Eris.*

ERIS: *Fully designated Sanctuary homes are under the strongest anti-violence spellwork we have. In a properly warded Sanctuary house, there's a guarantee of both safety and acceptance. Houses operating as undesignated sanctuaries retain the ability to turn away those seeking refuge for various reasons. As safe and secure as it is in a Sanctuary, living there, operating one means you have to take in anyone who wants Sanctuary, whether they're the hunter or hunted.*

PHEME: *But witch hunters...*

ERIS: *Witch hunters don't exist! How is a human, even with all the training in the world, all the weapons, able to take down a fully grown witch? How?*

PHEME: *It's happened before.*

ERIS: *Bahhh! They deserved it. You'd have to be caught half-dead, broken, and smell blind for a hunter to get the best of a witch. They're not the same as we are.*

PHEME: *That's a painfully occultist ignorance you're speaking.*

ERIS: *Are we, as witches, not designated here to help them? Were they designated to serve our community? They need us. I know it's not the right way to be in this age, but they can't be a threat or there wouldn't be a full piece of the Trinity of Rules directed to serving them.*

PHEME: *Service before self is a fundamental tenet, but it's not a guarantee the help would be accepted or even wanted.*

ERIS: *Wouldn't a better, more equitable, tenant be—love them to death?*

PHEME: *What is actually wrong with you? Never mind, let's hear from a sponsor!* Blue Crab Bay After Dark Podcast *is sponsored by Bitty's Bat Shop. When I need a bat, I head down to Bitty's Bat Shop at 312 Heron Lane to find the perfect nocturnal spell partner. At Bitty's Bat Shop, buy your bat shit at batshit prices! And Wretched Gretchen's Emporium of Darkness and Lighting Solutions. Are you struggling to get the right lighting for your love spells? Do you feel like the darkness of your cellar is hollow instead of foreboding? Wretched Gretchen stocks only the most melancholy doom shadows in her store. Visit her showroom at the corner of Magnolia and Blue Crab Parkway...*

I pulled into the Llewellyn General Store, turned off the radio, and rolled my eyes so hard I almost saw my own brain tissue. Grabbing the steering wheel, I ground my back teeth until I could almost feel the enamel breaking down and let out a shaky growl. One good, full-body shiver hit me as my magic screamed to life now that I was home. As if the feeling of being slapped in the face by a billion ice-cold hands wasn't enough, I had barely crossed the city line into Blue Crab Bay and my return was already being broadcast across the whole community.

"Callie?" a deep voice drawled from the gas pump next to me. "You okay?"

"Oh, sure. It's just been a minute since I crossed that line, ya know?" I slipped out of my car and reached toward heaven, stretching and bouncing until my whole body shivered and relaxed. "How are you, Teddy?" I looked around the pump to make sure the face that flashed in my mind was accurate. "Oh, shit! How are you, Officer Mayhem?" I corrected after taking notice of his uniform and police cruiser.

"Stop it!" Teddy flashed a wicked smile and scooted around the pump to give me a brief side hug. "It's actually Captain, Callie, get it right," Teddy whispered.

"Captain?" I choked. Had it seriously been long enough for someone in my graduating class to become the captain of our hamlet's police force? "That's gotta be a record, right?" My color rose with embarrassment and a twinge of desperation. Was everyone here on some grand success journey, joyfully ensconced in their chosen calling, except me? But Teddy was a good, hard-working, smart guy from a solid family, and if anyone was prone to succeed rapidly it was Touchdown Teddy. I had a sliver of hope.

"Callie, the fact that I'm the youngest police captain in the history of Blue Crab Bay doesn't become a record until someone writes it down, so technically? No." Teddy tapped the nozzle against the rim of his tank and replaced it. "You need a fill-up? I'll put it on the town. Least we can do for the flutter it caused."

The flutter.

Such an adorable way to describe the way untapped magic came to life when an unascended witch, such as myself, crossed the threshold of town. It fluttered out to other witches, alerting them of my return.

"You're a gem, but I was on fumes when I got off Interstate Fifty-Nine and filled up there. I'm only here for a sack." Spicy crawfish dreams had followed me straight to stopping here first.

The urban legend that said the best food in any city was always found in the most inconspicuous places originated at Llewellyn's. It looked like an unassuming toothpick-legged shack with an enormous porch that reminded me of a scrawny kid holding a hula hoop around her waist. The cleverest trick about Llewellyn's was their undefeated record of always having exactly what the customer needed, when they needed it. Low, sleek, reclaimed wood tables were stretched across the store and stacked with opaque milk-glass jars, bottles, and flour sacks of all sizes and colors to hide their actual contents, giving witches cover if they needed to convert something for a special customer.

Barrels painted in a rainbow of neon colors separated the point-of-sale terminal from the rest of the store, each overflowing with locally grown produce that was always at the peak of freshness. Behind the old "crash-bang-bell" cash register was a dual-sided fridge system where they kept perishables, cold drinks, lunch meat, ice cream, and prepared foods like stuffed blue crabs and artichokes, and bags of the biggest, fattest, cleanest, reddest, straight-from-the-glorious-mud, crawfish in the whole world.

"Your grandpa bought two sacks yesterday!" screamed the ancient matriarch, Pippy Llewellyn, from her nest on the store's porch.

"Great minds then, I suppose," I called back to Pippy who sat wrapped in colorful layers of woven blankets. She looked over at Teddy who had only now finished filling a small gas can with diesel. "I guess I'm just getting orange slices, then. I'll see ya?"

"Saturday," Teddy finished the open question. "You staying?"

I nodded.

"Do me a favor and tell your sister to stop begging me to date her?" Teddy's eyes twinkled with mischief and sarcasm. "She's a sweet girl but it's really embarrassing the way she's trying to win me over by playing hard to get and not stalking me. I see through her game!"

Barking laughter erupted out of me. So loud and so long I saw a shimmer of insecurity flash over Teddy's face. It wasn't that the idea was ridiculous, though it really was, it was more the personal humor I had missed.

"I'll talk to her about it. Thank you for putting up with her obvious lasciviousness, Captain Mayhem."

Heaving my stiff carcass into the store, I heard Pippy, quieter now that I was closer.

"Big old honking goose. Such a pretty face but you got that noise coming out of it…" Pippy reached into her technicolor blanket swaddle and pulled out a folded white paper bag, jamming it between me and the door with an aged claw thrumming with magic.

Off-balance, I slipped backward, my worn-till-smooth flip-flops sliding around the freshly cleaned porch, and barely caught myself on the banister before I went ass-over-teakettle into the parking lot.

"You need better shoes," Pippy said. I felt the straps tighten slightly around my feet. Pippy's eyes twinkled cornflower blue and loaded with mischief. When I looked back down, my worn shoes were brand new again, the soft, bluish glow of Pippy's magic fading from around my feet.

I took the bag of candied orange slices and leaned in to kiss Pippy on the top of her downy, white head.

"Consider it a welcome home present. Come back when you're ready for your broom?"

"I'm not getting a broom, Miss Pippy. Scared of heights. I like my car anyway," I admitted.

"You wanna take forever while shitting on the environment, be my guest. I'll be gone in two hundred years, and you can roast on this planet with the rest of your generation," Pippy grumbled, leaning over to grab a stone before throwing it at me, missing by a mile.

"The village would collapse into the bay, Miss Pippy."

"Surprised ya came back, Callie."

"That makes two of us." I returned to my car ready to move on with my emotional support candy.

"You may call me Miss Pippy or Great-grandmother Llewellyn," she called after me.

THE SUBTLE ART OF SPELLCASTING AND SARCASM

"As long as I don't call you late for dinner?" I shot back.

"Never stop throwing stones in your glass house, Callie!"

I was a lousy witch. I should not have been, but I was. I came from two of the twelve oldest and strongest magical families in Blue Crab Bay, my father an Aigean and my mother an Eastwick. I was born Cailleach Osiana (and then **seven** more never-to-be-shared names because witches had a bitcoin-like need to make each of us highly individual and unique to protect us from evil) Aigean and in the genetic lottery... let's say neither my numbers nor my nome de blockchain had yet to come up, comparatively speaking.

Blessed with a glorious mix of blonde, brown, and copper hair that most people called "dishwater" and a warm, cheery complexion that was slightly too pink to be considered "peaches and cream" and looked more like a subtle shade of Oscar Mayer bologna. I had heard about my "such a pretty face" for decades.

I'd been told I was what people imagined Mrs. Santa Claus looked like in her late teens. It bothered me more when I was younger and became more offended at being likened to a woman whose entire persona was derived from her husband. She didn't even have a name! But at this point, everything that wasn't a direct insult got filed under compliment. I'd always been chubby, and granted, there were a few more pluses in my size since my late teens, but hey. Everyone I've ever met desperately wanted to hug me.

I should have been in a tiny candy-covered cottage making cookies for children and neighbors, humming Vivaldi, and curing sadness with a hug and a smile. I longed for nothing more than to be good and kind and gentle.

Now, here I was, inextricably drawn back home, my tiny bit of magic a magnet back to the South. Too much witch for the non-witch world and watching the clock run out on my chance to become fully ascended. I would have to open myself up, ask the universe for my witchy accouterments, and see what the future holds.

I parked in the back parking lot of my mother's store, The Dove and Pearl Antiquities, Inspirational Gifts & More, known locally as The Dove. Crystal sugar and orange gelatin candy occupied me while I worked up the nerve to go inside.

"Behold, the traveler has come!"

I whipped around to see the baby of my family, my younger sister, Orla *Gargamel* (**plus seven more**) Aigean crossing the street in a cotton sundress looking like Aphrodite made flesh. She was coming from Petronilla de Meathe, or PdM, Elementary, the town's only primary school where she taught, her dismissal time coordinating with my arrival almost too perfectly.

I didn't know her real middle name, because of that never-to-be-shared name power, so I'd been telling everyone, behind her back for about ten years, that it's Gargamel and nobody questioned me. Most people were always so taken aback I didn't know my own sister's middle name they'd argue with me, so I started saying Gargamel and poof, no more information needed. I was, of course, too polite to interrogate them as to why they shared their full and complete names so readily. Names had power. It's why witches were given ten of them. Plus, everyone had always called my sister either Sunshine or Sunny—I don't think anyone outside of our immediate family even knew she had another name.

It was the same for our brother, Aden; I knew he had more than just his first name, but it wasn't any of my business.

Sunny grabbed me around the neck, pulling me in tight to the smell of crepe myrtles, warm skin, and saltwater. In a way, she was the sun. When she completed her ascension in the baths of the water caves, her magic had been solidified as drawn directly from the energy of the sun.

I would need to reach my own ascension if I planned to stay home. I'd have to catch up on a lot of magical milestones I'd missed out on. And I'd have to meet all of those milestones before my twenty-sixth birthday on the Frost Moon at the end of the year if I wanted to keep my magic at all.

"I missed you."

I groaned under her. Sunshine was two inches taller than me and lean like our mother. Long hair, long legs, a golden ratio of visual perfection who could also make you feel like everything in the world would be okay, no matter what. She had our mother's hair texture, but Sunshine's thick, waist-length hair glimmered twenty-four-carat gold instead of the deep espresso color that our mother and brother had.

My mother and Sunshine were swans and I the chubby little pigeon flapping to keep up.

"Don't go near that table if you don't want to sit at the table, Callie." My sister stopped me before we walked into the store. "She hasn't let anyone touch it since you left. We took all the tarot information down and she only sells beginner decks on the rare occasion she finds one that 'speaks to her'." Sunny made air quotes.

"Tarot decks haven't ever spoken to her. It isn't her talent. Tarot is following memory cues and then filling in with body language," I explained the best I could.

"Being home will be easier if you try and see it her way." Sunny put her hand in mine squeezing them together. "You see so much, yet you remain blind." Her hand was warm and familiar, comforting even though I was the older sister and should have been the one comforting her.

"If it were magic—" I grabbed her hand when she tried to jerk away. "If it were magic, I couldn't read person after person without mistake. There would be confusion, shock, a missed prophecy, something almost artistic about it. I say the exact same stuff in conversations and people hate me for it."

"You're the only person who calculates an unbeaten winning streak as math and not magic. Nobody is that good. Nobody is that attentive. You don't have to like your gift or use it, but don't shit on it in front of Mom. It hurts her every day to see that table empty."

"Fine," I compromised, putting my hand up in surrender.

I opened the door, the chimes on the porch momentarily blinding me from the transition of sunny outside to darkened entryway. The store was cold; familiar smells of driftwood, parchment, candle wax, and vanilla cookies wafted around me.

The Dove was set up with a large front space filled with statues, collectibles, plants, specialty magic-imbued snacks, and bottled elixirs and tonics made by my father's father, Ruari. They were meant to spread comfort and harmony within the community and the various, possibly magic-related, items all scattered among one of the finest collections of antiques in the south.

The building faced east, and the south wall was floor-to-ceiling windows, some curtained, some stained glass, most painted shut from years of touching up. On the north end was a sunroom that ran the length of the building, bursting with plants and flowers. The sunroom led down into a small greenhouse, mirroring the big one at my parent's home. My father had retired from his medical practice the year before to "garden" full time.

My favorite piece in the whole store sat abandoned, tucked in the front of the sunroom near the front windows to glean in the morning sun. It was a small, mosaic table and three chairs, one only half the size of the other two, meant for a child, made for me. I spent hours in that chair watching my mother read tarot cards with my grandfather, learning what she could, getting frustrated, but still trying.

The tarot was the only magical intuition I had. Real spellwork is a complex mix of intention, balance, and reverence for the service you're performing. There's a ritual involved, especially with tarot, but I was good with rules and even better with books.

"Well, well, well if it isn't Calligraphy Jones, literary giant!" My mother bellowed my failed, juvenile, nome de plume when she saw Sunny and me. Mom strutted out of the storeroom with a tray of silver oddities that smelled like cursed objects and neutered love spells—the Tinman's sweaty balls.

"It's Callie now. That experiment is over. Callie. Not Haggy, not Cailleach, just Callie. Can we do that?" I asked.

"It's lucky when she says it!" my sister sang, turning suddenly and dropping into an overstuffed chair, the lines of her body collapsing like matchsticks as she sighed. "Those kids wore me out.

We finished making the bills for library day and I smell like paste and soggy felt."

"Do you need help with your outfit or are you settled?" My mother offered, ignoring the plea I'd given about my name.

"I'm seriously going to need a consensus on the name thing, Ma," I interrupted. My sister could make bills later. My nails dug tiny half-moons in my palms, waiting for her to comment that I'd gained weight. She'd say something complimentary like Zaftig, I'd take it defensively, and we'd devolve into sniping.

"I gave you that name, I'll call you what I like. The Great Mother whispered to me, not to you. When you have children, you can call them Dishwasher Cocktail Sauce or whatever the Goddess tells you." She put her hand up to stop me before I even thought to interrupt again. "I've never once called you Haggy. I won't be punished for an adorable mistake made by your sister. My mother named me Agrippa, but everyone calls me Aggie. Do you honestly think I've never been called Haggy by some rotten little kids?"

She made more sense than I wanted to admit. And she never commented on my body, to my very great relief.

"Call her Calligraphy Jones!" boomed my father, Osian, from the small greenhouse at the back of the store. He carried two large planters of young dogwood trees, one pink and one white, and set them on the counter near my mother. "Those are going to Anna Vienna Navarre." He pulled me into a hug and stroked my hair. "I'll call you whatever you want. My baby is home. You want a new name? We'll get you a new name. You can have whatever name you want," he cooed over me, someone finally making the fuss I'd craved.

"Callie is fine, Daddy." I hugged him and inhaled deeply, having missed the way he smelled, the way it made me feel safe. He was the earth and flowers, worn leather, a faint hint of pipe tobacco, and oranges. It was the smell of security, the warm happiness of acceptance, and I swallowed back a lump in my throat. He brushed a stray tear and ruffled my hair. My father had always been easily moved to tears and comfortable to let them flow when they came. He was a large man, taller than most, and without insecurity about his emotions or how they presented.

"How was the drive? Did you try that shortcut I sent?"

There was his tinker's heart, a never-satisfied, always striving need to improve on everything short of perfection. If my drive took sixteen hours, he would try to make it fifteen and some change.

"It shaved ten minutes off my trip!" I high-fived him and he beamed, thrilled someone had listened to his suggestions.

"I was worried you wouldn't see the highway," he said, knowing the detour was a little hidden from view if you were traveling without paying attention.

"I followed the mimosa trees. You've been busy." I gave him a pointed look and he blushed. "I swear I saw them in bloom seconds after I left the city, Dad."

"I know, I tried to undo all of them but they're totally out of control. I only planted a few on the property so we could harvest webworms—you know how much they love 'em—but they spread like wildfire. Back then, webworm webs were the key ingredient in the binding rituals which kept our kids from getting wild in school, until old Sunbeam showed up and they had no effect on her, but it was way too late and now they're everywhere. It's not like it's bad for the soil. You don't know how many spells I've tried..." He wandered off in his rant.

My father had a bee in his bonnet over non-native and invasive species adversely impacting local flora and fauna. He could go for hours on nutria rats, lionfish, kudzu, and if anyone mentioned Asian carp, we worried he'd get so heated his head would spin around and explode. His mimosa trees were a family joke masquerading as his secret shame.

Witches spent a lot of history trying to blend in without demolishing our magic and one of the most problematic trials for families was keeping magical children from casting in school since we didn't educate separately.

My father created a tonic for kids that would keep their magic quiet during the day, but not hinder their abilities later. Before then, parents had used spider webs which could permanently injure the witch and impair their abilities.

I always figured my sister decided to become a teacher to protect and shield our magical children from those afraid of their specialness. Considering she was a spitfire of magical talent that no potion, tonic, spell, or enchantment could dampen, she remembered the feeling of otherness that magical children could experience. She committed herself to protecting those children and helping them achieve their full potential while ensuring non-magical children feel accepted, loved, and special.

I watched my father disappear behind a large door and instantly recognized the soft, wispy, pink mimosa flowers that shook in the breeze he made when he walked by. He had a potted mimosa tree back there, and as soon as I realized what it was, he dragged it out of my view.

"Drive me home," my sister said. "I'm exhausted and starved. Grandpa has crawfish."

We were out the door and in my convertible before I could even sit. I needed to get home, get unpacked, stuff myself with crawfish, and figure out the rest of my life.

Sunny leaned forward and flipped on my radio, pointing and smiling when the podcast voices flooded from my speakers.

"You've heard this? It's my fan club!"

"Yeah, I passed the drive listening to it, but it reminded me of middle school," I admitted.

"They're obsessed with me. Every episode so far has featured a gossip segment centered around my life. I think it's Nymph Castleberry and Paris Arcola getting their catty nails out, personally." Sunny picked at her toenails after propping her dirty, bare feet on my dash.

"They didn't seem capable enough to make a mirror call, let alone host a podcast with modern tech and magical security, Sunny." That's when it hit me, and I stomped on the brakes as the clues rattled together.

"Hellfire bunny nuts, are you the scorching-hot teacher?" I yelled, flipping the radio back off. Sunny's face slid forward and almost kissed her grimy foot, which was still propped on my painstakingly clean dashboard.

My sister sat up, finally moving her feet back to the floorboard, and turned slowly to look at me.

"That I am," she smiled and turned up the heat on my steering wheel until I couldn't hold it.

"Oh, come on!" I squealed.

"You just tried to slap me in the face with my own foot!" Sunny reminded me.

"Well... keep your dirty paws off my dash. I cleaned the whole car so Dad wouldn't say anything about me living in a mess!" I didn't need to remind my sister how I didn't have her magical cleaning abilities.

"I can't help it. I see a clean dash and I *have* to rub it with my feet!" Sunny put her feet back on the dash and rubbed them back and forth so her toes would touch the windshield.

I thought I was going to break out in hives, but I had other questions burning. Fighting Sunshine when she was doing something she loved, like making an actual mess of something I owned, was too much work. I needed answers.

"So, you're the scorching teacher and I'm the prodigal sister, which means..." I couldn't even say it.

"Sounds like your ex-boyfriend and ex-best friend are an item, Cal." Sunny finished my thought.

"I ran into Teddy at Llewellyn's, and he didn't say anything." Teddy would have mentioned that.

"Fair enough, maybe I'm making the whole thing about me and they're talking about another ice queen and scorching hot teacher." My sister shrugged. "I'm sure Teddy would have been A-OK with being the bearer of bad news the moment you got home."

"Nope, don't want to think about that." I flipped on the radio, careful to put on music instead of hearing more news that made me want to immediately leave town again.

I took a deep breath and pulled away from the fading golden light of Pelican Square to head home and eat my feelings.

The gates were open when we pulled into the drive to my family's ancestral home, Dolphin House.

Dolphin House always seemed like a dumb name to me, invoking more zoo-like cement confines than such a brilliant, magical place, but nobody ever asked me.

The first sight of the house was designed to take your breath away, and I wasn't disappointed. There always seemed to be a swirling breeze beneath the sunshine in the entrance and today it was wilder and more persuasive than normal. Everything was awash in watercolors from the stained-glass panels and various crystals reflecting it, crystals my father charged in the garden, plants he'd cultivated for house growing, and thick, ancient rugs woven by the family over generations.

Sunny, our older brother Aden, and I lived upstairs. Grandpa Ruari was on the main floor right off the kitchen near his work, close to the warm center of our house as the tiny elevator was loud and slow. The kitchen was mostly original but supplemented with lower counters and easier access my grandfather told us was proof the universe told him the kitchen was his alone. My parent's room was up on the third floor, far from the melee of three rambunctious witch babies.

Everything smelled the same as when I left: warm cookies, cinnamon, vanilla, lemon sweetness, soft English roses, relaxing lavender, and the comforting sandalwood smell of father's hands. I slipped backward through time and felt like my absence had suspended the home in timeless animation, never changing without me here.

My vision smeared the present day against the decades past, and I watched three witch babies hiding at the top of the stairs waiting for Christmas morning. The whole of my family, cousins, aunts, and uncles, clustered around the oversized dining room table for Thanksgiving and the weekly harvest holidays we celebrated.

Everywhere I looked it was a special occasion, my brother was a toddler, adolescent, teenager, a variety of ever-larger suits following one after another as the bow tie and baby vest gave way to a sport coat as he grew up. My sister wore a million dresses from deep red velvet in winter to the palest orange chiffon on May Day.

Everything clenched tight in my upper arms, waist, and neck—like a poorly fitted frock in an unforgiving fabric refusing to give no matter how still I stood. I didn't remember sweating, but I was suddenly drenched and shivering under the vent, watching everything I loved, everything I willingly walked away from, my insignificance to the passage of time, and it was going to slice me to emotional ribbons before I finished it.

My memories became a noose of expectations.

Chapter Two

I may have more to learn than I imagined...

PHEME: *And you're back in the Bay with your hot, new podcast hosts, Pheme and Eris!*

ERIS: *We are neither hot nor new.*

PHEME: *But we are hosting, so let's talk about the rites of passage each witch must go through to finally come into power.*

ERIS: *We only have three hundred years or so... I don't think that's enough time.*

PHEME: *Not all at once!*

ERIS: *Where do you want to start?*

PHEME: *Scrying.*

ERIS: *We used to get mirrors, now we get crystal balls. What's next?*

PHEME: *Eris! That's the point. Why did we stop giving scrying mirrors in the 1960s or even divining rods in the late 1800s? We found a better way.*

ERIS: *It's largely symbolic, right? Mirrors were more common when the world was small. They were easy to hide, easy to use, and the silver was powerful for communication magic. It's a great conductor, and combined with water, we could communicate over ultra-long distances in a safe way.*

PHEME: *So why switch?*

ERIS: *We have cell phones.*

PHEME: *That cannot possibly be right!*

ERIS: *I'm not even kidding a little. I know how it sounds. Communication technology looks more magic than magic. Talking into a cell phone is less suspicious than screaming into a mirror.*

PHEME: *Why crystal balls?*

ERIS: *I think it's access and personalization. There's a message in the medium. The crystal speaks to the witch, providing a bump of power, a glimmer of introspection, and a primary nod from the Source that you're on your way.*

PHEME: *I was terrified the day I got my crystal ball. I don't know if my fear drove the universe to send a tourmaline or if it was the tourmaline that taught me to manage my fear.*

ERIS: *I don't believe you ever told me that. Red tourmaline?*

PHEME: *Quartz.*

ERIS: *Oh... I forgot you had a lot of trauma early on. Tourmaline was a true gift.*

PHEME: *It certainly was. For the listeners who don't know, tourmalated quartz is particularly effective for dealing with depression, suppressed memories, and other problems that can arise with a baby witch in trauma.*

ERIS: *Did you know that the oldest tools used by people are believed to be tourmalated quartz?*

PHEME: *That seems poetic, right? That the first thing we create to help us is here on this planet to help us alleviate emotional pain.*

ERIS: *My ball is also geared to alleviating emotional pain.*

PHEME: *You? I didn't think you had any emotions apart from anger?*

ERIS: *Au contraire, mon sorciere! I was much older than you when I received my crystal ball. And it was leaded.*

PHEME: *Lead? You got a lead crystal ball. What does that even mean?*

ERIS: *No, leaded. Leaded crystal. Like a decanter. It's full of whiskey and said to break in case of emergency.*

PHEME: *You are a truly bad person.*

ERIS: *So they tell me.*

PHEME: *On that note: Witches, are you looking for the perfect beverage to serve at your next soiree? Is your liquor cabinet lacking? Do you feel like your cocktails are more like worthy-of-being-mocked-tails? Diabolique Daiquiris and Draft is your one-stop shop for custom, costumed cocktail supplies! Throwing a masquerade ball that needs verve? Serve our masquerade mojitos that let you customize your disguise. Show off your patriotic side with Uncle Sam's Firework ale—now featuring your choice of Founding Fathe transformation. With Diabolique, our zombie daiquiri will turn you into a pile of rancid flesh with a zesty pineapple finish. Pick up your gallon from one of our six drive-through operations in the Gulf Coast area. Come to Diabolique for the daiquiris and draft beer, stay for the shapeshifting. Not responsible for stains or lingering smells.*

ERIS: *Did you just play your trauma to entice me to make a joke so you could pivot to a booze commercial?*

PHEME: *They're a sponsor. And you're predictable. Slainte!*

I dragged my bags up the stairs to put my luggage in the room I grew up in before hurrying outside to sit by the garden. I wanted the heavy smell of roses and gardenias to drown away the familiarity of the house and furniture.

"Are you ready to see what crystal ball the source sends you?" my mother asked with an excited smile. I'd been waiting for this moment, but a fresh zing of anticipation shot up my spine and tickled over my skin.

As witches moved toward ascension, we were gifted a number of witchy accouterments to guide us in the nature of our power. Any combination of woods and crystals could come up as we receive our crystal ball and wand, but they're each intensely specific to the witch and her journey. We usually had a really good idea of what to expect, but no witch I had ever known or heard of ever guessed the right crystal before the Source delivered it. Right or wrong, I wanted the crystal ball. The smooth surface would be a confirmation from the universe I was on the right path. The crystal type would give me insight to guide my studies.

I grabbed the hand she lay over my shoulder, the familiar touch of her rough, bony hands bringing back a flood of memories. My mother's hands were so unlike the rest of her, representative of her hard-working nature, and conflicting with her lithe, graceful stature. She stood tall, like my sister, with long limbs and few curves on her body. She was a willow tree, languid and fluid, moving like music in the wind. Her skin had the deep, velvety texture of an African violet.

She pulled me along behind her, not dragging, but not with any hesitation either. If her breezy walk and refined manner were the sloping branches of the willow, her hands were the bark. Shockingly rough and staggeringly powerful, they had a strong grip that felt safe yet foreign on someone so lovely. They were hands that could smash through a wall with little effort, grind herbs faster than a mortar and pestle, and glean the history and life from blessed and cursed objects with which she surrounded herself at her store. Her hands could grip us tight against any enemy and draw us back from the darkness and into the light.

Grandpa Ruari said her hands were aged by the magic she worked, slowly turning into the trees from which she drew so much strength.

On my parent's property was a large, ancient oak tree, almost shorter than she was wide and deeply connected to our family's history. She sat in the center of a small clearing, away from prying eyes and eavesdropping ears, and seemed to cast a preternatural silence over the space under her dense leaves. If you walked out the back door and past the yard, there was a moon door in the low stone fence that started a path which stretched a few hundred feet into the woods.

The clearing came up like a summer storm. A forest in one second and then bam, the path dumped you out into this meadow and standing there was a grand tree. I didn't always feel as reverent about her. As children, we climbed on her, napped underneath her boughs, swung from her branches, and treated her like a playground.

My mother squeezed my hand as my breath caught at the visual.

The oak didn't look like a playground. She looked like the Colossus of Rhodes, like I could sail through her trunk and enter a lost world, a demarcation of the points at which before, after, and never intersected. My mother laid out a blanket, weighted the edges with spherical crystals of various colors that looked too large to carry, and kneeled, patting the space beside her as she put her palms against the bark and bowed her head.

"Callie, it's time to ask the universe to give you a crystal ball. You can't just scry with tarot and expect to make any improvements."

I took my spot beside her, adjusted my clothes so they weren't snagged around my stomach, and leaned in. I placed my hands on the tree, took a nervous breath, and bowed.

My head rested against the rough bark, and I tried to center myself, but my brain was a beehive of thoughts that flashed in photos of fear and aggravation. I shivered a bit and tried to re-center.

Frustration bubbled inside of me, boiling my blood as another random thought slid into my brain, wondering if we'd have dessert with dinner. I opened my eyes slightly, checking to see if my mother was watching me try and fail to center myself enough to start a prayer.

No longer was I kneeling under the tree with my hands pressed against the bark in surrender. Without realizing it, I was sitting cross-legged on the blanket with the crystals around me in a circle, faint lights radiating from between each orb.

My mother stared at me, through me, her gaze clouded with magic and concentration, her wand at the ready. The spheres glowed with golden light as they levitated a few inches off the ground and spun, first in their spots, then rotating and spinning in a circle. I was the center of this odd universe as each orb crackled and followed a circular orbit around me, rotating like a Callie Solar System, flashes of vivid colors, each vaguely rainbow-bright under a golden glow of magic.

Spinning faster and faster, the orbs and their magic branched out between each other, each connected by a golden lightning bolt that pierced the center of my chest as they spun. For a moment I was awash with light, a Faraday cage of magic blocking out everything except my mother. One by one the spheres popped, exploding into sparks that rained down on the blanket but vanished before setting it on fire. I yelped at the sound, so engrossed in the colors and light that I forgot I was supposed to be praying quietly.

The glow became brighter and brighter until I had to close my eyes against the deep ache in my corneas, an ache I shouldn't have felt since I wasn't supposed to be watching. I pressed my palms to my eyes, trying to hold them against the lights that went straight through me, warm and comforting everywhere but in my vision.

My heart quivered with panic, worried the spheres waited for me to do something I didn't know, and thanks to my ignorance, my mother's collection exploded around me, shattering with unimaginable energy. I sat quietly, unmoving, waiting for my mother to tell me I could look, awaiting confirmation I was okay and wasn't ruining her prayer circle. I squeezed my eyes as tight as

I could and twisted my hands together, intertwining my fingers so tightly they hurt.

When I opened my eyes, my mother sat quietly in front of me, the crystals again weighing down the blanket, all the magic dissipated. She watched me with a most gentle expression on her face.

Between my hands sat my crystal ball. I'd never seen anyone go through the process of calling out to magic for either crystal balls or wands and expected to be far more involved. Didn't the Source need me to react so it would know what I needed?

The orb itself was nothing like the smooth crystals my mother used in the ceremony—instead, it was a spherical gray rock with zero magical energy vibrating inside.

Embarrassment and shame overtook me. Was this the representation of my witchiness: a sad, gray lump that wouldn't even work as a doorstop or pet rock because of the shape?

"There's a message there, Callie." My mother reached out and grabbed the rock, holding it up to her face, checking it for any veins or shimmer.

"Dumb as a box of…" I tried to be funny, but she wasn't amused.

"The universe wouldn't have given it to you unless you needed it." She handed me a cookie. The familiar scent of vanilla and cinnamon with a hint of something subtly lemon-fresh: the fopdoodle cookie, my grandfather's most powerful spell to cure a broken heart.

"I was expecting Moldavite, coming to terms with my emotions and all, you know?" I admitted, pointing to the rock.

Without responding, my mother nodded, a slight smile playing at her cheeks. She wasn't the sort to laugh at me for my lack of talent, but the smile sure felt like it. I was her embarrassment, her big, fat, stupid rock.

"I expected citrine for mine," my mom shrugged and took a glass bottle of water out of her basket and drank deeply.

"Your ball is amber, though?" I wasn't surprised she didn't see that. I was more surprised she was taking my ineptitude in such good spirits. Maybe she had more faith in my abilities than I did?

"Citrine is the merchant stone and your dad and I had just opened The Dove. When I got amber, it was a bit of a smack in the face, Callie." She offered me her water and I accepted.

It was bitter cold, the temperature where water actually hurts going down but satisfies a soul-deep thirst.

"What did the amber tell you?" I'd never really considered there's a serious reason we can't predict what we get, but if Mom could be so far off the mark, maybe this rock gave me some kind of insight into my busted magic.

"It's for tenderness," my mother said quietly and then burst into laughter.

"Well, that was a sign, huh?" I teased, laughing along with her. Of all her many outstanding qualities as a mother, witch, and woman, tenderness wasn't something I'd think of when considering my mom.

"Your dad said it was for restoration, that the universe was looking at the antiques and giving me a boost that way, but I knew why I got amber. Deep down we always know, right?" She shrugged and looked at me with my gray rock.

The sinking sensation that hit choked my breath right in my throat.

"Sunny seems to have come into her magic." I tried to change the subject toward something that would shift the focus off me.

"Well, she came into something! And it's not like everyone in the world can't see it," my mom laughed, leaning back against the trunk. "I wish I could take credit, but her magic is nothing like mine. Her ball is fluorite, but she expected sunstone, of course."

"You remember before she ascended? How hard was it to keep her from killing everyone?" I led her away from talk of my new rock.

"As long as she had the sun, she had magic."

"Remember the bunnies?" I asked.

"I remember your father had to make up a story there was an alligator in the woods that drove them into the schoolyard. Perfectly normal to have four thousand bunnies in a baseball field at recess. The Coppertone was a little harder to explain, Callie."

"She walked right out to those bunnies. She knew what she did!" My sister had only been in kindergarten a few weeks when the bunnies arrived. Her teacher had been reading the class a book that featured a bunny, and for some reason, it became the Holy Grail for little Sunny. The moment the class went outside they were waiting. Bunnies might be cute, but an army of rabbits numbering thousands was incredibly disconcerting for the rest of the school. I'd only been around ten at the time, and because my parents did such a bang-up job explaining my sister's magic to me, I thought if I covered her in layers of heavy-duty sun block it would stop her from casting. It made perfect sense to me.

"She looked like a baby werewolf! All that rabbit fur sticking to the thick layers of sunscreen as they crawled on her, the mothership of the innocent and precocious. It broke our hearts to tell you the sunblock trick wasn't going to stop it. You were so excited to help." My mother looked wistful in a way I hadn't seen before. Her eyes clouded over, and she shook her head. "You never could understand that magic doesn't listen to reason."

"She told me you don't have a tarot reader anymore." I changed the subject. I was drawing her into a conversation only she wanted to have, and I could feel her working on my mind, unraveling my loosely woven guard one strand at a time.

"Do you want me to ask you to read tarot?" She was pointed, looking me right in my eye, and I froze. That empty feeling told me maybe she wasn't pushing, but sincerely needed to know if I missed it.

A series of screaming crashes of metal on metal interrupted my response. Grandpa Ruari called us to dinner by repeatedly slamming the back screen door.

"You should get him a dinner bell." I only half-joked as we gathered the blanket and crystals.

"He had one when your father and I were young and bashed it to death with that old spoon." She leaned in and wrapped her free arm around the tree trunk resting her forehead against the bark. I knew she whispered her gratitude, her silent mantra of affirmation and surrender as thanks.

I left her to her moment, moving back through the field to the garden path that wound us to this place. I turned back when I stepped on the first stone and stopped short. I saw her, radiant in the field, the setting sun at her back, basket nestled in her elbow. Whether on purpose or not, she'd thrown the blanket over her shoulders, making a cowl around her neck that draped in the sun. The blazing, glowing orange ball of heat lit her up from behind and she was a shadow sent from heaven, a glowing halo of light bursting from behind her.

My first thought wasn't my mother's beauty. I realized if someone with no knowledge of witchcraft saw this, they'd think it was a Holy sign. She was the Great Mother, the divine spirit, the embodiment of love and creation bursting from a lithe woman wandering around a field with an artfully placed blanket.

If I didn't know any better, if I didn't know her as my mother, if it was the Middle Ages, if I didn't know for a fact that visions included body-wracking pain and terrifying memories, I would have thought I was having a vision. Fittingly, it didn't hit me until later there was little difference between me and that imaginary medieval peasant. She was a vision, but as was my way, I was blind.

Everyone but my mother and I sat around the dining room table digging through a platter of crawfish, potatoes, corn, and sausage—my welcome home feast.

Grandpa Ruari's mother, Cordelia, was a towering witch of intense green power. Family legend said she could choose herbs in the dark by the touch of a leaf to her cheek. When she died giving birth to Grandpa Ruari, he got everything his mother and father had to pass on.

His gift was charm spells wrapped in a delectable food delivery system.

Because he was powerful, he usually saw a need before anyone knew they had one and kept cures and potions ready to hand out. I often wanted to ask him why he was in a wheelchair when our kind was blessed to heal so rapidly, but in my heart, I knew my question would hurt his feelings. His pain wasn't my business. He'd always been adamant about his privacy and never using our magic to pry where we weren't wanted.

I heard his voice so clearly in my head, like he was repeating himself psychically, his cheerful voice turned serious and stern. When I was small, he had a way of teaching that felt so important I had no choice but to record it in my memories as though my magic depended on it.

"People in pain don't have time to waste, Callie. Their troubles aren't my business, and their time doesn't belong to me. If I made everyone who is suffering tell me a story every time they asked for help, I'd be hurting them even more. They'll tell me later if they want. And they're allowed their secrets if they don't," he explained.

I remembered I'd awakened during the night to a frantic tapping on the side door below my bedroom and investigated. I never knew who came that night, nor what my grandfather gave them, and part of me was terrified they'd use magic improperly if we didn't keep track.

"How do you know if they're going to use it for something bad?" I asked as he wheeled into the back lift to take me back to my room and put me to sleep. A bit of water and a few almond crescent cookies for sweet dreams he called Moon cookies in hand before he kissed my forehead and stroked my hair.

"I said I don't make them tell me. I didn't say I didn't already know. I'd never give out bad magic, Callie." He tucked me in and left my door cracked. My brain wondered how I'd know my magic until the cookie kicked in and happy dreams flooded my brain, driving the doubt away.

I shook off the memory and reached for the food, settling in between Sunny and Aden. Sunny reached across my plate, grabbed at a butter dish, and leaned over so far I thought she was crawling into my lap.

"Can I help you?" I asked.

"Hmm? Nope, just reaching..." She leaned further into me, crawling up the side of my chair. "A bit further..." I looked toward our brother Aden who sat on her other side. Her foot dangled in front of his face. She was trying to pick his nose with her toes, and he was rocking back dangerously far in his seat to avoid her.

"Did we raise wolves?" my father asked my mother.

"Only the one!" I shouted, tickling my sister, who curled into a ball and dropped into her seat, swiftly kicking Aden backward to the floor. Instead of crashing through the dining room window, he simply bounced against it and teetered back into place. I didn't know if he made the window rubber or had a soft squishy head to land on.

"More like hyenas," my mother agreed. "Or goats."

My father led us in the family prayer as my brother bewitched Sunny's food, turning her water to white vinegar and her fork into a handful of cooked spaghetti noodles. "We give thanks to the Source, the heart of the universe that which we serve in all acts great and small. We thank the Mother for her bounty, our health, and that our clan is whole again breaking bread as one, as all will be. With blessings and humility."

From the first bite, I was transported. My first meal home at my family table reminded me of an allergy commercial. The scene when a cloudy filter is removed right as someone ups the color saturation to garish proportions. I didn't fight it. The warm comfort spread through me, nostalgic tears pricking behind my eyes, threatening to open a well of feelings I'd been trying to keep sealed for years. Grandpa Ruari sat across from me and smiled softly, pressing his wand to his lips as if to shush the world.

I might not have given him all the credit for making me feel like I'd dozed off in a breezy summer hammock and awoken to Christmas morning, but when everyone else fell asleep sitting up at the table except him and me, even I had to marvel.

"Sunny told me you asked about the readings," he said evenly. "I left the cards in your bedroom, but I want a favor." He pointed his wand straight at me.

I don't want to say his smile faded because he was still the face of pure joy, but he became serious in a way that was unlike him.

"You know Sunny is much better skilled at…" I tried, but he cut me off.

"I know what Sunny is, and I'm still asking you. If and when… don't look away, Callie… but if and when anything happens to me, Aden will be fragile. I can't explain exactly why, but you'll need to pick up the slack in this family. You absolutely **must** make the ascension and find your power. I believe in you. Your place is here, and I want you to promise me you will find it." He stared at me, stern-eyed and serious.

I nodded quickly, swallowing the lump in my throat.

"Use the cards. Find your voice. Sometimes witchcraft can be gross and messy, but remember, I've always believed in you." His hand closed over mine and like a calm breeze, and a stillness slipped over me, a steadfast feeling of purpose conveyed by paper-thin skin littered with liver spots. "Now, do us both a favor and grab us that last chunk of bread before they come back and we don't get any." The twinkle in his eye was back, overshadowing the serious tone. The rest of my family didn't skip a beat as the conversation picked back up like the pause never happened.

"Aden! Do you remember the bunnies and the sunblock?" My mother smiled, pointing at Sunny and me.

"I remember greasy fur stuck to every plant in my greenhouse," my father laughed. "And I remember the litters of Bay lynx that grew out of control from all that food. Wait." He leaned over and looked at my sister. "Have you outgrown that trick?"

"We couldn't say the word rabbit or bunny for almost a decade, or she'd start calling them," Aden reminded us. "That's why we call it the Easter Floof!"

My sister wasn't bothered by the good-natured teasing, but behind her smile was a discreet sense of smugness. "Have I outgrown it?" she wondered aloud. She batted her eyelashes at our father, and the rhythm of her blinks was instantly matched outside on the garden stones. A fluffy rabbit had answered her call, beating his foot like a cavalry drum while waiting for my sister.

The deep, low hoot of a hungry owl snapped us all out of our stare and startled the rabbit so badly it left a tiny pile of poop nuggets on the stone before disappearing into the shrubs.

"You're going to clean that up. And you're going to heal whatever that rabbit eats in my garden, Sunshine," my father warned.

Hell hath no fury like an emerald witch defending his plants.

"You know, if that owl ripped apart that bunny, I couldn't handle it." Mom shivered.

The owl hooted again, louder and closer. The screens on the patio did nothing to stop the noise as the predator searched for the rabbit. The next hoot came from inside the kitchen and faded from the deep, low sound to a burst of higher cackling laughter, "*Whooooooooo* thought that was a real owl?"

My grandmother, Allegra, popped through the doorway, pie in one hand, shopping bag in the other. She was my mother's mother and passed on her abysmal cooking and domestic skills, hence the grocery-store dessert.

"Crikey, Allegra, you old goat, do ya wanna send me to an early grave?" My grandfather dramatically clutched his chest and flailed in his chair. "I don't have any recipes for owl stew!"

"Like you'd have a snowball's chance against a canary, let alone an owl, you ancient ruin," she scoffed and gave him the finger.

While Allegra looked like she was in her late sixties, my mother intimated she was closer to ninety. That wasn't a compliment. Non-witches might love to look thirty years younger than their true age, but our lives are long, and most witches look anywhere from twenty-five to thirty-five until they're damn near over one hundred. The fact Allegra looked older than she should was compounded by her trash personality aging her miserable countenance.

She stood in the doorway, late and unapologetic. Anyone else would have gotten a lecture and at least given a decent reason for their tardiness, but not her. It did not escape me that I regularly used an honorific for Grandpa Ruari but not for Allegra—it just felt and sounded wrong whenever I tried. Maybe I should have been troubled that my disrespect didn't bother her either. All things considered; I decided long ago Allegra preferred to not be reminded of our relationship.

Her cloying smile reminded me of powdered sugar on poisoned cookies. Sometimes, I forgot quite how much aversion I felt toward her, but when she looked at me, there it was, hot in my veins. I felt her disappointment with me, palpable in the air. Her stare appeared joyful but with absolutely no gentleness or affection. She stood haughtily, steel in her spine, and quicksilver in her veins. She struck me as battle-hungry. When I was fourteen, I added her picture to the high school dictionary under the word "judgmental", but nobody ever discovered it.

"Pippy said you're not getting a broom?" Allegra peered at me with hard, spring-green eyes as she took her seat next to Grandpa Ruari. Her smile bloomed when she set eyes on my brother and sister, flushed and lovely with pride and adoration.

"It's good to see you, too. I missed you. The drive was uneventful, thanks!" I said with all of the enthusiasm I could muster.

"I just want to know why you're telling people about this great fear of heights you have? Are we going around announcing our fears? You're planning to make your ascension and not fly? You've got another think coming, kid."

I glanced around at my family, waiting for someone to say something, anything. Maybe acknowledge her attack on me.

"You don't fly," I finally reminded her when it was obvious nobody was coming to my aid. Riding a bike made my girl bits hurt; I wasn't hiking myself up on a stick so both sides of my rump could flap in the breeze.

"I still learned how when I made my ascension. I can, even if I don't," she countered.

"You can't even drive a car. You never learned. You made that choice—can't I make mine?" I ripped the heads off my crawfish with a renewed passion.

"I didn't need a license because I learned how to fly, Cailleach."

Her use of my full name made me shudder.

"Allegra, that's quite enough. Callie has enough to learn for the time being and might decide differently when the time comes... something that will never happen if you badger her and sour the idea," my grandfather interrupted.

"You let her grow up with no discipline for our arts. Now her wand is a pen, and her broom is that foolish vehicle—what's next? Is her crystal ball a bean bag chair?"

"It's actually a rock. It's a plain, sad, gray lump of rock. Hell, maybe it's concrete?" I admitted. Might as well tell everyone at once.

Grandpa Ruari honked with laughter and slapped the table so hard the dishes popped up a good three inches from the tablecloth. As they settled gently onto the table, I saw my father wave his hand, his quick magic saving us a lot of shattered plates.

"Well," Allegra huffed. Leaning to the side she grabbed her pocketbook off the floor and placed it in her lap. She snapped it open, reached in, withdrew a wad of cash the size of her fist, and threw it in Grandpa Ruari's lap.

"Never doubt me again, Allegra. I knew it. I told you." Grandpa Ruari gasped, short of breath and pink from laughter.

The heat of embarrassment crept up my neck. They had a verbal sparring shorthand that felt like they were poking fun, but the vibe from my grandfather was warm and proud. I couldn't imagine why.

"I wouldn't believe it if I didn't hear it straight from her." Allegra steamed as she set her bag back on the floor.

"Faith, Allegra. I have it. You apparently need it," Grandpa Ruari kept on.

"Someday soon that luck is going to run out, and you know it." Allegra glared at me with glacial green eyes when she spoke.

All I wanted, from the deepest part of my soul, was to lock eyes with her and say, *But today is not that day!* but I didn't. Watching her lose money to Grandpa Ruari over something I did would have to be good enough.

"Have any of you told her what she risks if she doesn't ascend?" Allegra's words silenced the table.

"Banishment, ostracization, a life without magic?" I counted off. I knew the stakes. Everyone knew the stakes.

"Allegra, you're not helping," my father said.

"None of you are helping by leaving her in the dark about this," Allegra shot back, never taking her eyes off me.

"I know the stakes!" I tried hard to keep the pleading out of my voice. Why did she have to ruin everything? "But what's the worst thing that can happen if I fail? We live with plenty of non-magic people in this town. Will I have to move out and live in another home? There's enough magic in this family to spare, so why do you care so much?" I didn't intend to smack the table so hard the dishes rattled.

"It hits the whole line, Cailleach. It's not just your magic. There's no banishment. There's just nothing, for any of us," Allegra said. Her evil eyes twinkled merrily with the news of my fate. It looked like she took excessive joy in telling me I was going to be responsible for shattering my family. It was uncanny how lovely she looked during that single moment.

"That can't be real! You've all ascended!" Panic rose in my throat. I could hear my heart screaming, *They're all depending on you. It's all on your shoulders! Save the family, Callie!* and it blocked out the argument that exploded between my parents and Allegra.

"Deep down, she really *was* happy to see you, sis," Aden whispered.

"Yeah, she sure as shit seemed to enjoy that," I responded.

"It's not the whole line," Sunny explained leaning over to hold my hand. "It goes up through the generations, not down. It would hit Aden, but not me and not your kids if you had any."

I stared at her.

"Sunny, you're not helping," Aden said. "Nobody is worried or scared you won't ascend, Callie. We will all help you. You'll be fine."

"And it's not like this is an all-or-nothing situation," Sunny continued as though Aden hadn't admonished her. "If you don't ascend, then the elders can either lose their magic or, well, there's a reason the whole family attends the ascension, ya know?"

"I don't know, Sunshine!" I didn't want to scream but at this point, it should have been crystal clear I was entirely ignorant.

"That is a foul urban legend," my mother growled. "Nobody is going to drown my daughter if she can't ascend."

Her voice boomed with a siren strength as crosstalk faded to silence. She stood slowly, her breathing deep and strong as she locked eyes with each of us. I couldn't have looked away from her to save my life, but I didn't need to look away to know everyone was locked on her. She took control of the entire room and slowly walked around the table clockwise, touching each of us on the shoulder.

"Callie will ascend."

"Callie will ascend."

Everyone was desperate to repeat her words, to agree with everything she said. She had us hypnotized, bespelled with her confidence. We sat rapt, chanting, letting her will manifest through each of us, driving out doubt and fear and darkness. If she believed it, we believed it. If she was unafraid, we were unafraid. Her commitment was my commitment. I couldn't fail. I wouldn't fail. Any other option was laughable.

Gratitude overwhelmed me. The joy of being home, loved, surrounded by support and kindness radiated warm and soft around my heart, and the day drifted away from my thoughts, replaced by only harmony and my mother's exceptionally powerful magic.

Mommy magic was the opiate of families. It didn't so much remove the stress and anguish that settled like an elephant on my chest—I was still aware the entire future rested on my ability to learn a lifetime of magic in a few short months—but the terror itself was smothered under a soft blanket of acceptance.

My mother made me feel like success was inevitable. Was it the mists of magic that dulled my anxiety, or was I truly feeling the depth of my mother's belief in me?

The fear and rage that threatened just seconds before bubbled into the sparkling fizz of champagne, effervescing away in her magic.

Everything was fine.

Everything would be just fine. My mother wouldn't have such deep and total confidence in me if my success wasn't inevitable, right?

Right???

Chapter Three

Catastrophe around every corner...

PHEME: *Welcome back to Blue Crab Bay After Dark. Today's question comes to us from Xanthippe in Blue Crab Bay. "Dear BCBAD, my grandparents told me the witch communities in Europe are kept apart from the non-witch communities and they can do magic wherever they please. Why do we have to stay hidden in the Bay?"*

ERIS: *I'd rather serve a community who knew I was serving and could appreciate me for the benevolent witch I am.*

PHEME: *As compassion and service are a witch's highest calling, and we believe that's the reason we're all one soul, experiencing the world and each other subjectively at the same time. Compassion, that supreme lesson, gets easier when you can look onto another person or witch and feel in your heart that you're looking at yourself, living another life, learning those lessons. Be the person to them you will need to have by your side during that life. We don't have magic to enrich our lives and spend our days amassing fortunes and followers.*

Our magic is for the community and witches like to believe our incarnations are compassionately advanced enough to use it wisely.

ERIS: *Are you going to answer the question or wax poetic about how wonderful we witches are?*

PHEME: *We serve the community, so we remain part of the community. How can you serve people if you don't live among them?*

ERIS: *The question was why haven't we come out of the broom closet, not why don't we live in a segregated community, you dunderhead.*

PHEME: *Pitchforks and torches, anyone? Why wouldn't we hide it? Let's hear from a sponsor, okay? Charonte Cosmetics is offering thirty percent off of all full transformation sessions for all advance bookings this month. Swing by Salon Pandemonium to book your top-to-bottom redesign and walk a while in the sheer white specter of the Sidhe, or clip-clop down the cobblestone square as a noble Chimera. You can even spend a weekend in our bespoke vampire experience, where you'll wake with the moon and "feast" on our simulated "victims" at our Dead & Breakfast. Charonte Cosmetics at Salon Pandemonium—feed the demon in your mirror!*

ERIS: *Do you feel like these sponsors are getting a bit dodgy?*

PHEME: *I can't spend this much time with you for free. Someone has to pay, hon!*

The morning light in Blue Crab Bay was unlike anywhere else in the world. It's hazy without fog, crisp but not cold, the color of a day sprawled in front of you, blank and pregnant with possibilities. The convergence of the water, earth, sky, and salt made the area bubble with magic, feeding a strong and loving community of witches for centuries.

I rolled in my bed; the soft sheets still smelled of soap and lavender. Gentle breezes flowed over me, lightly swirling the sheer curtains on either side of my bed. We wouldn't have many more cool, beautiful mornings before the summer heat kicked in, and though I could easily spend the day drowning in the memories wrapped in my bed sheets, I could hear Sunny downstairs as a faint smell of pepper and egg sandwiches wafted up the stairs.

I grabbed the tarot cards from under my pillow and shivered, the weight of my return pressing in on me. What if I couldn't read anymore? What if I read with ease and everything I said was wrong? Desire, determination, devotion; all three were easy, but the actual doing? Doing and failing? How much shame could one daughter heap onto a family? A rumble from the center of my body shook me out of the self-doubt spiral.

"The rock ball means nothing. You'll make your ascension easily. You're good at tests. Look at all the people who made their ascensions. You have nothing to worry about," I reminded myself. "You will not shred the legacy of one of the oldest, greatest families since ancient magic manifested. You're an Aigean. No one in your line has ever failed to ascend. You cannot fail. You were born for this." My supportive, nurturing mantra was drowned out by a deep rumble from my empty stomach.

Hunger made me anxious, so I followed the aroma of breakfast, almost half-starved and dizzy from smelling something so delicious and so close for so long. By the time I made it to the table, Sunny had a sandwich in each hand, her cheeks puffy while she chewed.

"Grandpa left these. They went fishing," she said, motioning to the cookie sheet of sandwiches.

"And these!" I held up the silk bag and set them at a safe distance. If he came back to food-crusted tarot cards, I'd be ashamed. I bit into my sandwich and struggled to remember if I'd ever really eaten food before or if it was always dressed up cardboard. Nothing had tasted as joyful as some sweet peppers mixed with scrambled eggs and goat cheese.

"Are you going to read?" Sunny sprayed egg bits when she talked and then laughed at herself, spraying even more.

"I'm going to read," I promised, pushing the bag a little further away from the tiny hurricane of food spewing in front of me.

"Do mine first!" Sunny had always been a happy morning girl. I hated it.

"I'd like a little practice before I try to dole out any advice." I reminded her I'd been out of sync for a while. I didn't need to remind her I was unsure I'd ever been in sync.

"Scared you lost your touch?" my mother asked as she poured herself a large glass of iced tea.

"Isn't that the worst possible outcome?" I shrugged and pointed at her glass. She handed me her tea and returned to the cabinet to make herself a new one.

"Being right when it's terrible and nobody listening is scarier for me." My mother's eyes looked unfocused as she stared through the tea pitcher. Her voice was distant and soft. "I don't want to know when danger is coming."

"Long as she's right in the end, Callie doesn't care. She'd go full Cassandra if it gave her a few 'Told ya so' moments," my sister teased.

"You can be right, or you can be happy," my mother said as she turned back, the distance gone from her voice and expression.

"Neither would make me happy so, yeah, Sunny nailed it. I'd much rather be right." I shrugged and my mother briefly looked sad.

When they finished eating, my mother and sister scampered off to pray, leaving me with the cards to do, or not do, whatever it was I intended. I cleaned the table, washed my hands, washed my face, and sat, opening the silk knot at the top of the bag.

I don't know what I expected. Maybe part of me thought I'd touch flesh to card and be overwhelmed with a vision, voices from the Source, answers, and a flourishing rush of magic ability. What I got were thick, heavy cards—swollen with age, softly bare around the edges after years of use—and a queasy stomach.

Apart from the feel of cards in my hands, my other senses remained static: same kitchen, same soft breeze, same breakfast and baguette smell. I wasn't trying to dismiss the feeling of the cards, though. They were familiar and heavy, a bit too large to wield without care. Without much effort, I could still cut and shuffle lightning-quick, my fingers dexterous and nimble. Tarot was an oversized deck, but our family deck was bigger than normal.

The size was intentionally cumbersome. Muscle memory has a way of making a reader complacent, numb to the feel of a deck, almost robotic in the shuffle, and cut after years of practice. Our deck was precisely sized to always feel as though it's about to slip from the grasp, forcing the witch to focus their complete attention on controlling the deck and concentrating on nothing else.

As I shuffled, The Tower flipped out of the deck onto the counter.

Any movement from the cards is noteworthy. Cards don't usually slip around casually. They're made especially to fall heavy, demanding attention. These "accidents" can be just as important as the cards in a spread.

The Tower means doom, upheaval, so of course it fell out of my deck. I shook off the accident and replaced the card, dropping the Seven of Wands in the process. Family strife, sure. I set the cards down and tried to focus.

The next shuffle went splendidly, so I stopped before pressing my luck.

Three cards into the spread, I'd dealt The Chariot, representing the inevitable; The Tower, which symbolizes calamity and destruction; and the Ten of Swords in the third position, meaning innocence being lost.

I should not have stopped shuffling when I did. I gathered the cards back up, shuffled again, recut three times, and the Tower came first. Even I can't ignore that message of upheaval, brokenness. The shaken foundation, the destruction before rebirth, the most ominous card in the deck wanted my attention. The Wheel of Fortune crossed the Tower in the second position of the spread; the inevitable turning of luck, physical turning to spiritual. Next, I drew the Nine of Swords beneath the others in the third position. It represented passing knowledge, grief, and the hot, searing pain of waking up and remembering that despite your pleasant dreams, things were not okay.

I knew the fourth card would be The Hierophant before I turned it over. In our tradition, especially in my family, certain people have cards that associate with them, and The Hierophant had always been Grandpa Ruari. The ancient Greek priest, resting between two pillars; in our families, the pillars represented man and magic.

I don't remember turning over the rest of the spread, but the reversed Eight of Wands meant strife, the Five of Pentacles meant desolation, the Queen of Pentacles meant the hidden would demand attention, and the Eight of Swords meant that almost every move I could make would be the wrong move.

The cards took their positions on the table and the world went white around me. I saw Aden, my father, and my grandpa in that burning tower. I smelled the deep ozone in the lightning strikes, the sooty flames creeping up the sides of the stone walls of The Tower, and the sticky sweet smell of blood choking me.

A vision hit me in the chest, blocking out the foul burning smell and metallic tang of blood with the heavy stench of livestock. Someone, an indiscriminate figure, neither visibly male or female, sat on a dais in the base of The Tower, bedecked in thick robes and what appeared to be a zucchetto or skull cap of screaming neon, acid green. They were lit from the side by a gleaming white stallion, but utterly shadowed on the other by a black horse so dark it seemed to absorb any light that radiated nearby.

The figure stood and rushed me, and the sound of darkness spoke harshly as it grated against my soul:

"There comes an end to all things; the most capacious measure is filled at last; and this brief condescension to evil finally destroyed the balance..."

The shrieking darkness was drowned out, blocked by another scream, unrelenting in the distance. I could see lips moving on the face of the figure, but the only sound was high-pitched keening, desperate and sad, decidedly feminine and far away.

The screaming I heard wasn't coming from The Tower. It came from my voice, over which I no longer had control.

I don't remember my mother and sister returning, but they were there when I finally settled. My sister's voice was unbridled on the phone, frantic and desperate but still confused and trying to explain something that may not have yet occurred. Tarot is not an exact science but a tool witches use to focus our power and see whatever the Source wants to show us.

My ability had never looked like this. All I could see was disaster.

"Callie, look at me. What did you see?" My mother was snapping her fingers in front of my face. "What did you see? Where are you? What's happening?"

"I saw them in The Tower—Grandpa. DADDY!" I was screeching, sitting outside my own mind, panicking and useless. Why see anything if it didn't help anyone? I threw up hard on the tile floor beneath her feet. She reached over my shoulder to rub between my shoulder blades with one hand while easing me up with the other under my arm.

"Let's get you outside, okay?" She pulled me to my feet, and I found my legs floppy and ineffectual. I leaned onto her as she dragged me outside. She only appeared cool and calm, but I could feel the worry coming off her in waves and her hands shivered when she touched me. She helped me through the front door and onto the porch where I continued to empty my stomach into her shrubbery.

"Sunshine!" my mother screamed back into the house. Sunny fell out the front door and my mom grabbed her wrist and pushed her toward me. "Keep an eye on your sister. I have to do something."

She disappeared back into the house and Sunny got to work cleaning me up, which proved to be sisyphean. Every time her wand wiped away the mess, I'd rock back again and get sick. The image of the broken bodies of my father, brother, and grandpa kept swimming back in front of my vision, and the pain was too much for me to handle. When I had nothing left to get out, I sank into a wicker chair with an overstuffed cushion, putting my head between my knees so the world wouldn't pivot sharply on me as often.

"Something happened and I need you to go to Aden," I could hear my mom in the kitchen, talking to my grandmother via our two-way mirror, old magic that few people still have the equipment for. Astral communications were more popular, and honestly, the cell phone technology we had was far more convenient than mirrors.

The mirror was the only way to reach Allegra, who distrusted the government, phones, electricity, steam power, and anything else that made the world the littlest bit convenient.

"I won't let anything happen to him if we can avoid it. Damn it, try, Mother!" The panic in her voice tore at my heart.

Right as I teared up, my body calmed down, my panic retreated, and I heard my logical brain speaking. I needed to settle down;

hysteria wouldn't help anyone. We didn't know anything yet, and everything could be fine. I was making it worse, and I should relax and stop upsetting my incredible baby sister who loved me so much.

Sunny was such a good sister, a sweet sister. My baby sister never did anything wrong and only loved me despite my weak stomach and penchant for cheating at board games.

Sunny's golden magic held me close, whispering into my heart. Words that were not mine echoed in comfort, calming me. Protection and safety enveloped me, centering me back into myself as I took a deep breath and leaned forward, elbows on my knees, exhausted.

"I don't cheat at board games," I whispered at Sunny.

"Right. And I've never done anything wrong." Sunny scoffed.

The sound of tires on the driveway broke our connection and sent shivers back down my spine.

Chapter Four

I can't hear you over the sound of my heart shattering...

PHEME: *You're listening to Blue Crab Bay After Dark, the only podcast where no topic is off-limits!*

ERIS: *Except whatever topic I want to talk about, apparently.*

PHEME: *Oh hush, you old shrew! I had a flight this weekend.*

ERIS: *On your broom or just by flying ointment?*

PHEME: *Ointment. I needed a long, deep conversation with the Source.*

ERIS: *We're talking about illicit substances?*

PHEME: *That's right! Mimosa tea, flying ointment, moon drops, and the lover's knot.*

ERIS: *The first time I had Mimosa tea was right before my ascension. I was twenty years old and ready to come apart with nerves.*

PHEME: *I thought for sure I was going to learn the secrets of the universe.*

ERIS: *And?*

PHEME: *I imagined it would be like watching a movie, getting some kind of a message in flashes. Instead, it was just a flush of emotion, gratitude, connection, life, time—those things that really matter. I sat in a dry bathtub under these ancient wolf pelts that my great-grandfather collected when the area was young and laughed uncontrollably while my cousin babysat me.*

ERIS: *I saw a great web with pinpoints of light and connections that showed how interwoven the world is. At first, it looked like one of those super organisms breathing in time to the rhythm of the universe. It was the interconnectedness of people and how everyone has a place and a role to play in the grand plan of the Source.*

PHEME: *Have you taken the flying ointment?*

ERIS: *When I was widowed. It was wonderful and terrible.*

PHEME: *I've heard it's excellent for managing and expediting the stages of grief.*

ERIS: *Sure! If you think it's better to suffer all at once and speed through the stages of grief that we are supposed to navigate over time.*

PHEME: *You got it all out of the way?*

ERIS: *If you were to build a house by hand, you'd expect to smack yourself with the hammer occasionally, right?*

PHEME: *Sure, accidents happen.*

ERIS: *Flying ointment for grief is like having the house appear fully built in front of you so you can spend your day smashing your hand over and over with that hammer to balance out.*

PHEME: *Thank you so much for that visceral and vomitous description.*

ERIS: *It's not a suggestion that people need to jump on to scapegoat an important process! It's a tool used in very extreme situations.*

PHEME: *And under very strict guidance.*

ERIS: *You have to have a guide and an anchor. The guide will watch your experience to help you dig through the memories later as you parse them, and the anchor keeps you locked to the world, so you don't panic.*

PHEME: *The guide sees everything?*

ERIS: *Everything. They're watching it like a movie but through your eyes. Your feelings and thoughts are the soundtrack.*

PHEME: *Soundtrack! Brilliant! That brings up a good point! That point is that Blue Crab Bay After Dark is brought to you this week by Sounds & Senses, the first witch-only, telepathic music system! Are you tired of a boring old shuffle? Sick of your selection not making your heart skip a beat? Sound & Senses offers a full range of brain-reading musical programming to fit your taste, musical selection, and mood! Simply attach the discreet forehead apparatus and we will read your mind and play the exact song you need to hear at any given moment!*

ERIS: *Discreet forehead apparatus! New band name!*

PHEME: *WITH SOUNDS & SENSES YOU'LL NEVER SKIP ANOTHER SONG!*

ERIS: *That's a lot of words to describe a tinfoil hat.*

PHEME: *Are you still mad they just played The Macarena over and over when you tested it out?*

ERIS: *I know you sabotaged my experience!*

PHEME: *How dare you accuse me of...*

ERIS: *I can smell your deception.*

PHEME: *It's my new perfume!*

ERIS: *What's it called?*

PHEME: *Earworm, by Coty.*

ERIS: *I quit.*

I heard a car door close from the driveway and looked up from my knees. From an unmarked cop car emerged Declan Bradly, wearing plain clothes, a BCB PD badge on a chain, and carrying a well-worn dark-brown messenger bag clenched in his fist. His gentle and familiar face sent a chill up my spine. Teddy came from the driver's side as Declan hit the front stairs and dropped his bag on our porch.

I leaned back into the wicker chair and kept my eyes closed, begging my stomach to stop roiling.

My mom joined us briefly, grabbing Declan's hand. He pulled her into a hug, holding her head against his chest as he whispered horrors into her ear. I wanted her to escape his grasp, get away from whatever he said, but he held her too tight and spoke too slowly as she sobbed in his arms.

"Osian and Aden, they're alive. There was an explosion on the lake. Ruari didn't make it. Osian is in bad shape, and Aden's hurt but will be okay. Mrs. A., can you come with us?" His voice finally cut through the blood pounding in my ears.

Declan passed my mom to Teddy who helped her toward the car.

"Sunshine!" Declan snapped at my sister. She was lost in thought or magic, mindlessly running her hand over my back.

Declan put one hand on my shoulder, familiar and gentle, and then touched my sister to bring her back.

If there's ever a reason to be glad for traumatic events, they're a decent distraction when you're sitting with puke drying on your face, wild morning hair, and forty pounds heavier while seeing your first love for the first time in two years. Had I been capable of feeling anything, shame would have been low on the list.

"With your mom going to the hospital... I'll stay... Allegra's coming... meet you there. It's bad. It's better if I stay. She can lose her temper at me safely. You know how she reacts..." Declan's words came in snippets and before I could say anything, Sunny left in the backseat with my mother and Teddy. I don't recall how many times Declan offered to help me before it registered.

I only stood when Declan reached down to try and carry me into the house. I don't know why my brain focused on him throwing his back out by hoisting me out of the wicker chair, but it did, and I finally scrambled inside the house. I was bigger than the last time he'd hoisted me up and the slight chance he'd groan, or struggle was enough to send me straight to the grave in embarrassment.

I leaned into the kitchen sink, washing my face and arms, rinsing the foulness from my mouth; something to do in my helplessness. Declan moved behind me, taking his time, piecing the kitchen back together to stay busy. In the panic, chairs had been overturned and scattered, the back door to the garden stood open, and my tarot cards littered the floor. I kept rinsing; if my mouth stayed busy, I could avoid talking to him.

What was I supposed to say? *"I ruined my life, made a huge mistake, and was completely wrong. Also, all those years didn't count, and I was thinking of you the whole time, so wanna start over and just love me while I mourn my grandfather?"*

The sound of Declan's feet running up the stairs rescued me from needing to speak, but eventually, since he was a resident of Blue Crab Bay and a member of our coven via his family, we were going to have to have an awkward conversation. When he returned to the kitchen, he carried a wad of gray fabric under his arm and my small toiletry bag. He'd grabbed a new shirt for me, obviously because of the condition of my current one covered in vomit and soaked in sweat.

I took the shirt and changed in front of him but as I slid the gray tee over my head I caught his old scent, more memory than olfactory. It was enough to alert me he grabbed my whole bag of toiletries just to get me a single toothbrush and dug specifically into my drawers for the clothes.

"You knew where to find this?" I looked down at the tall navy letters across the chest. BHS, Boleyn High School. It was Declan's shirt once upon a time.

"Center drawer, center pile." He sat at the table, having done as much as he could without touching the scattered tarot. In our tradition, we handle tarot by invitation only.

"You didn't have to go upstairs, Deck." It wasn't a question. Declan was one of the most advanced witches in our coven. Even as a child, he had control of matter and manifestation with which even old witches struggled. He pursed his lips and crinkled his eyes, shaking his head no. I loathed how cute he was.

Seriously, how dare he?

"You understand the fundamentals and details of a toothbrush, the basic structure of toothpaste. You didn't have to go get that,"

I scolded. Declan could conjure anything. Why'd he need to get all up in my bedroom?

Conjure witches work with matter and energy in a specific way. While most any witch can produce simple items from short distances, especially in their own or other familiar spaces, conjurers by nature could tap into the matter and use that matter to manifest items. A master conjurer could reduce the matter of old and long-forgotten things, transfer it, and manifest it as a new item without breaking the universal balance. If Declan wasn't a master yet, he was closer than any other. Even the least transmogrification-inclined witches could pull a shirt they had seen from a place where they knew it was and draw it to them if they were in the same house. He shouldn't have been upstairs unless he wanted to be up there snooping around, making sure his shirts and our photos together were all unmoved. Briefly, I imagined he needed that reassurance.

"You needed a toothbrush. You needed a new shirt." He put his hands up when I tried to interrupt, already feeling my hackles rise. "And most importantly, you needed a minute without me standing behind you, looming bad news at you while you were trying to pull yourself together. If that act ruins my reputation in the coven, *pfft*." He waved away the idea.

I twisted my hair into a bun on top of my head and brushed my teeth in the sink, feeling bad I'd doubted him. Just because my magic was off didn't give me the right to question him. Declan could manifest a running vehicle if he chose to. He could get all the parts, all the fluids, incidental pieces even I couldn't name, along with a pair of fluffy pink dice to swing from the rearview anytime the desire struck him.

It wasn't as easy as drawing parts out of a junkyard or from a used car lot. Not all matter, even long-forgotten, was devoid of energy. Landfills, junkyards, any massive pile of detritus was an interwoven stack of matter, not unlike a Jenga tower.

If witches started snatching matter from precarious situations, collapses would happen, the matter would become energized, and, in the worst-case scenario, the collapse would wind up on the evening news and everyone would suddenly remember the long-forgotten parts and they could revert to their original form. This was in addition to the magical consequences of attracting undue attention, tampering with natural laws, and general conduct unbecoming a witch.

An uneasy, suspicious feeling growled low in my gut, but it could have been my earlier nausea and not the doubt. Was it more likely he went to give me a minute or he went to do something else, and if so, what was that something else?

Rooting through my drawers? He could do that from his house.

Looking for my diary? He knew I didn't keep one.

"You can be mad at me if it helps you right now, Callie. The only way out is through, so whatever it takes." Declan walked over to the hook on the wall where our keys dangled and grabbed my set. "I'm going to drive you to the hospital. If you're going to go into a rage, do it before we get near people who might be hurt by it."

"I don't think I'm mad," I stuttered.

"You, all of us, we're all going to have a lot to sort through with Ruari gone. I'd expect it to hit you the hardest. You were so close, and you just came back and now he's gone…" Declan's voice froze when his eyes landed on my face.

My heart burst into a billion shards of ice, painfully cold and sharp in my chest. My hero, the one person who never made me feel inadequate, was gone. The only voice that never said I wasn't living up to my potential, never expected more because I should be capable of more, was forever silenced.

The sensation of falling through time hit me, making me dizzy and sick again. I felt the warmth of Declan's arms around me, catching me, holding me on my feet though I wanted to collapse to the ground and disintegrate into dust to avoid the pain.

"I'm so sorry, Callie. I don't know why I said that. I've got you. I'm gonna get you to your momma, okay? I've got you. It's going to be okay. You're going to be okay." Declan's voice got further and further away as the darkness crept in around me.

My mother's normally glowing bronze skin was pale and sallow under the hospital lights. Lines I'd never noticed deeply etched the worry and stress into her face. Teddy had left her in a chair as he leaned over the counter, talking to the triage nurse.

"Your sister is in the back with Aden. They're releasing him shortly. He broke his wrist, but he'd already gotten far enough away he wasn't seriously injured. We're still waiting on news about your father," Teddy called to us as we walked through the emergency doors.

My mom grabbed my hand and pulled me down into the seat next to her, leaning against my shoulder and sighing.

"You don't have to stay, Deck," I told Declan. "We'll be here a while. I know you have other things to do." I nodded toward his badge, shining with the BCB PD Special Liaison sigil denoting the department we secretly called Magical Law Enforcement, and he responded by sitting on my mother's other side and dropping his messenger bag between his feet.

"I'll hang out until Aden gets discharged." He opened his bag and pulled out a roll of glossy papers wrapped with a rubber band and handed it to my mom. "I didn't know which you hadn't read so I grabbed them all."

She pulled off the rubber band and unrolled more than a dozen magazines, many of which had recently been scattered around her reading room at home. He followed that with a tumbler of iced tea, complete with ice and lemon; a package of crackers and garlic cheese spread; a napkin; and finally, her phone, charger, and purse.

"You are the biggest..." she swooned.

"Show off?" I offered and she glared at me.

"Sweetest, most thoughtful man, Declan," my mom chirped, ignoring me but snapping me out of my spiral.

I rolled my eyes so hard at her adoration I made my forehead ache. He'd always been indescribably considerate, but it was pretty much his calling. Nothing made him happier than procuring something special for someone who needed a break. His leather bag provided a clever way for him to conjure privately, in public. He could reach into the old bag, manifest whatever he needed, and produce it as though he was carrying it around with him the whole time.

When we were younger, students at Anne Boleyn High School, he would carry a backpack, but then told everyone he outgrew it and moved onto the beat-up messenger bag that once belonged to his grandmother, Fianna, a journalist and founder of the Pelican County Examiner, our local paper.

I heard more ice and realized he was trying to hand me a tumbler of my own. Raspberry lemonade, fresh berries, and lemons, straw instead of a mouthpiece; there were times I didn't like being transparent, but this wasn't one of them.

"You got any honey-baked hams in that bag?" I couldn't help myself.

"Spiral cut? Sugar glaze?" Declan leaned forward, locking eyes with me. If I pushed him, he would pull one out and make a ridiculous scene of it.

"You're still a brat," I reminded him.

"And your socks are inside out," he told me with a smug, smugly, smuggish tone as I felt the fabric around my feet change.

"Your magic is a menace!" I growled and kicked off my sneakers to fix my socks.

The moment I got my shoes back on my now properly socked feet, he did it again.

"For fairy's sake, Declan, knock it off!" I kicked my shoe toward him, but he looked right at my mother instead.

"That time it wasn't me," he pointedly spoke to me but stared at my mom who was deeply invested in her magazine.

"It's a brilliant punishment." My mother shrugged, never looking up, a slow smile creeping across her face.

"Declan, can you stay?" Teddy asked.

"Try getting me to leave." Declan put his arm around my mother.

"Can you get a statement? Go over the process while it's still fresh in Aden's mind?" Teddy sat across from us, elbows on his knees, his face a calm with blank serenity despite the current predicament.

"I'll do a reconstruction. That should help. I'll text you to send a black and white for me when we finish." Declan shook Teddy's hand, the slap between them echoing in the cavernous waiting room.

"I'll make an offering for Osian," Teddy promised my mother before turning his back and hurrying out the door.

"Someone's in a hurry," I pointed out.

"Callie!" my mother nudged me.

"You didn't pick up on that? He practically ran out and he never once made eye contact with anyone except Declan. Even when he talked to you, he never looked at you." I wasn't wrong.

"For fairy's sake, Callie. He's an empath and we're in a hospital," Declan explained.

"Mmm, something is off."

"Maybe you don't understand how deeply a place and a situation like this can hit an empathetic person," Declan countered.

"They're drawn to pain, aren't they?"

"Stop talking, Callie. Stop talking right now. We're all upset, and I know you think bickering will help but it won't. Stop talking or I'll soak your socks next time." My mother's voice was soft but terrifying.

An hour later, as I sat sockless, Aden finished up with the discharge process. Sunny pushed him in a wheelchair and his left hand was wrapped in a plaster cast. I absently wondered why our father hadn't healed him when it happened. The stabbing realization my dad was fighting for his own life hit me in the heart and I choked back a sob.

"Have you heard anything?" Aden stood and walked over to us as Declan rose to shake his hand. "Deck, it's really good to see you here with them, thank you."

Declan nodded, his expression turning sour. "I'm here with them and I'm here for them, but I'm also here for you."

"I know and I appreciate it." Aden smiled and sat next to Declan.

"I mean, I have to ask you some questions, Aden." Declan's words were heavy in the air. "You were a bit preoccupied when the first responders arrived. I only need to confirm your statement, fill in some blanks, check some reflexes... whenever you're ready."

It took another three hours of waiting, idle chatting, and a couple of uncomfortable naps before Sunny elbowed me awake in time to notice a doctor, dressed in scrubs, and coming toward us.

"Osian Aigean's family?" Dr. Cabotin, a neurosurgeon in the ER, asked, the exhaustion on his stubbled face turning to shock as we all rushed to talk to him at once. "He's stable," the doctor advised, taking a step back and defusing the panic racing toward him. "He'd been in the water when the explosion happened. We think he hit his head against the ship and the blow caused some swelling in the brain. It appears he stopped breathing for a moment, but until he wakes up, we won't know if there was any permanent damage."

"Can I see him?" my mother asked, quieter and more somber than I'd ever seen her. The doctor's stern, serious expression broke into a gentle smile, and I noticed he was much more handsome when he wasn't afraid of being trampled by a concerned family.

He took my mother's hand with a kindly expression. "I think that would be a great idea. Having you there will comfort him even if he's not awake quite yet. Let's get you some tea...." He led her back through the doors that separated the ER beds from the waiting room, almost guiding and supporting her. There's something inherently comforting about a stranger treating someone's mother with such gentleness.

Mother stayed to sit at my father's side and Declan drove us home, helping Aden to the kitchen table where he could give his statement in peace.

Sunny busied herself with food, occasionally interrupting them to ask Aden for advice on the recipes. We couldn't ask him to cook for himself one-handed, but if he wanted to eat anything healing, he'd have to advise her on what to add since he was the only one who inherited Grandpa's talent, and in what proportions and combinations, because, apart from a stellar hangover cure and period relief, my sister—for all of her glorious power—was a miserable kitchen witch.

Chapter Five

Fallout...

PHEME: *Once again, Blue Crab Bay After Dark has received five times as many questions about witches and familiars as any other topic. Perhaps it's because a certain someone keeps breeding their dogs and cats as instant familiars to capitalize on the idea all witches have a familiar but haven't found them yet! We want to caution our listeners, remember not all animal companions who adopt witches are technically familiars.*

ERIS: *Familiars are bound, sent directly from the Source to support a struggling witch. You can't just go find one, teach it to work a few spells, and consider it a familiar! But just because you don't have an animal companion sent by the Source doesn't mean you can't still have a strong magical companion work with you!*

PHEME: *And you can find many options for* **companion** *animals at the Greater Pelican County Animal Sanctuary across from Holland's Farm on Seagull Parkway. And you never know, your familiar might be waiting for you...*

ERIS: *Now don't you start that shit! You know that a witch who is destined for a familiar is going to find it—they don't need to go looking for it!*

PHEME: *It's a language technicality, Eris. We aren't the terminology police. I think we can consider animal companions and adopted pets among the creatures we discuss.*

ERIS: *Then we should keep them marked separate. For one thing, familiars are soul-bonded, and they will not survive the death of their witch. Does your shelter pup die when you do? No? Then you don't have a familiar.*

PHEME: *Familiars are the rarest of witch companions, especially those with warm blood. You can't make an animal into a familiar, regardless of the strength of your magic or the length of your training. Familiars happen. They bind to a single witch forever, or for the life of the witch, and act as both a guardian and guide.*

ERIS: *Even animists don't usually have them, because we're naturally against asking an animal to serve more than an occasional and exceptionally well-rewarded favor. Some witches believe that only inept practitioners receive a familiar as their lack of skill requires extra help.*

PHEME: *Eris, tell me, do you give any weight to the legend that familiars have a domestic form that hides their true identity?*

ERIS: *Cryptids? Rubbish. It's a bunch of weird, weak witches making up stories about their weirdly untrainable cat being the reincarnation of Bastet or every single horsey-girl witch who thinks her angel baby becomes a unicorn in the moonlight. If you're the only one who can see the transformation, it's not witchcraft, it's insanity.*

PHEME: *What about the legend of the Phoenix of Morgana Le Fey! There are hundreds of supporting witnesses to the magic of Morgana's familiar.*

ERIS: *Tales from seven hundred years ago that nobody can corroborate* or *maybe someone dyed her raven red and made a scene about it?*

PHEME: *My grandmother was...*

ERIS: *Busy telling people her own story of the minotaur, if I remember correctly.*

PHEME: *Before you get us shut down for blaspheming the old ones, let's hear from our newest sponsor, huh? Lost Island Getaways. Do you need to get away from the bay but don't want to travel more than a few miles? Do you need to make the most of a short trip and prefer to not spend the bulk of your holiday traveling? Lost Island, right off the coast of Pelican County, offers an all-inclusive vacation experience for you and up to one hundred of your friends. Lost Island, so close it must be witchcraft.... And as mentioned before, this podcast supports and acknowledges the hard work done by the Greater Pelican County Animal Sanctuary. Run by donations from people like you, the hard work of ensuring balance in the local fauna is a never-ending task as irresponsible breeders flood the county with domestic pets giving natural predators a buffet of food, leading to huge and dangerous spikes in the predator populations, endangering everyone, and throwing the ecosystem off balance. Donations can be made at any one of the GPC Animal Sanctuary Support boxes in and around the bay.*

I needed to be alone. I took my cards and prayer blanket into the garden, not wanting to disturb the coven members who'd be arriving to prepare the tree in the meadow for the morning Ostara worship. The weather was warm and breezy, hydrangeas around the patio blooming large and fragrant, a wall of gardenia on the edge of the property almost hazy behind the bumble and honeybee's fluttering wings.

I fanned the cards, splayed them face down, and ran my palm over the arc trying to remember a spell or charm for clues.

"Show me again," I whispered, trying to focus. "Rewind my vision, Great Spirit. Show me the vision you bestowed upon me in the thither and..." I stopped because, although it's okay if I make no sense, maybe doing weird shit in the yard while people around me suffered made me feel worse than not getting an answer from the cards. I shuffled again, cut, shuffled, and spread them in the arc.

Simple, direct spells are almost always the best to receive divine answers. Ask for what you want and be clear, concise, and genuine. Visualize, ask, receive, I thought and closed my eyes. I envisioned a card in my hand, the clue leaping from the deck, showing me exactly what I needed to know.

"Clue," I said. "Cluuuuuuuuue." Waving my hand over the arc slower and slower, giving the energy a chance to build, ignoring the tapping sound from the window in the back door of the house, and trying to speak my heart and trust my gift. "Clue, please, and thank you." I heard nothing but tapping. "Cluuuuuuuuuue, please, and thank youuuuuuuu," I chanted.

The door to the garden burst open, heat filling the space immediately. "Cal, are you missing a card?" Sunny flapped a kitchen towel over her head, trying to shoo something out of the house. "This stupid thing won't stop, uh, trying to fly out the door!" She jumped and snatched the card in the towel to bring it out.

Sunny gently carried the towel to me and opened it, careful not to touch the tarot card. In the towel was the eighth card in the major arcana of my tarot. The Strength card: steadfast, calm, an image of a woman and a lion most commonly, though in my deck, the lion was black with inky blue-black feathered wings, and the woman was strawberry blonde, bearing more than a passing resemblance to me in my newly Rubenesque body.

"I was trying to find a clue in my deck from the vision, anything I missed that might help dad." I took the card from Sunny's towel, noting she was extremely careful not to touch it. Her reverence touched my heart. If Grandpa Ruari was gone, the cards were mine. My sister would never touch them again unless I handed them to her. Grandpa left them to me. He believed in me. My chest ached as my heart thundered in my ears. Grief was by far the most uncomfortable emotion.

I tucked the card back into my deck but before I could gather it up to shuffle them, the same errant card blew out of the deck and back face up in the grass. Sunny met my eyes, and we watched the card blow toward the forest at the back of the yard.

We gave chase, following the card to the trees where it landed as the breeze gave way to a perfectly still silence. I heard a high squeak and gave my sister an expectant look. If she drove me out here for another damn bunny I was going to wash her pretty face in the toilet. She stepped back and put both hands in the air.

"I don't have wind powers, Cal. This isn't me," she promised.

I bent to grab my card, hoping whatever made the little noise was alerting her mother to a new being in the woods. The moment my fingertips closed around the card, an enormous, fluffy, black wrecking ball crashed into my bent-over body, knocking me to the ground. I expected it to push me out of the way in a fury to reach Sunny, but the heavy little beast, which smelled delightfully like puppy breath and clover, jumped on me and licked my face when I hit the ground.

"What the...?" Sunny marveled, crouching to get a look. "Did you conjure a puppy? Is this how slacker witches like you get a puppy? Is this how puppies happen for you?" We knew I had little animism talent, but the puppy was definitely for me.

"I was asking for a clue, and I think—" I pursed my lips to keep her from licking my mouth, "I think she's my clue."

The enormous puppy settled down immediately when I scooped her in my arms, floppy and joyful as her tongue lolled out of her mouth toward Sunny, a definite smile splayed across her muzzle. Sunny squinted at the baby Bernese Mountain Dog, a manufactured scowl hiding her smile. "Traitor," she snarked and stood up, helping me onto my feet. We walked back toward the garden, and I made myself busy scratching the soft, fuzzy belly of what seemed to be my new pet.

"She's not a pet, she's a *familiar*," Sunny said, though I hadn't asked. "She's a baby puppy but she's gargantuan. There should be a mark on her some place that matches your witch's mark."

"How do you know so much about familiars?" I knew of a few witches who had them but wasn't up on my lore and rationale. That the universe would send me one seemed like a waste of a good familiar for a crap witch.

"I have a little boy in my class, Thatcher Ingles. His mom, Tertulla, has an iguana familiar. It showed up when she was about twenty-one or so to help her stop drinking and straighten her life out. Her parents died when she was young, so she had a wild time of it. The iguana is named Buzzkill, so it was pretty obvious what his purpose is. Thatcher calls him Buzz and loves him, but you can see the irritation in Tertulla's face when it wanders up unexpectedly. She says they can communicate with each other and the lizard is a huge douche."

"Well, this sweet baby doesn't seem like a douche." I snuggled my face against her soft belly and saw her mark was indeed identical to my own, clear and precise against the pale skin between her back legs where the thigh met the ladybits. There was no mistaking it: she had the exact same triangle-shaped birthmark I did. Declan used to say it looked like a witch's hat.

I'd never felt so much love for something so instantly. "She seems like a proper little dumpling. My little doodle dumpling angel baby sweet puppy girl." I didn't even know where that came from—it just bubbled out of me. Sunny rolled her eyes. The bond was fast.

"She's cute for sure. What are you gonna call her?" Sunny asked, stopping at one of my father's favorite rose bushes. Bright cream with a lavender center that looked slightly gray in the early season, he used to spend hours tending that one bush, nurturing and loving it, splitting it into plants to fill the garden. "Hold up," Sunny called. "Aden asked for thorns."

"I'm going to call her sweet-baby-apple-dumpling-angel-shortcake-honey pie."

"I'm Clue!" I heard the puppy's little girl's voice in my head and almost dropped her right in the rose bush.

"Your name is actually Clue?" I asked, holding her at arm's length to get a good look. Clue was already extremely heavy and would grow into a massive dog. It felt like she weighed about forty pounds in my arms so I couldn't imagine where she'd go from there.

"I'm Clue. You're Callie. I could hear your heart calling me and I came right away. I love you."

More tears threatened to fall as I hugged her close to me. My sister stood frozen, staring a hole through us.

"You *can* hear her, can't you?" she gasped, sounding a little jealous she couldn't hear anything.

I nodded, rocking the puppy and responding with as many "I love you" thoughts and words as I could get out in one breath.

"Today keeps getting weirder and weirder." Sunny shook her head and stripped the thorns off of a rose bush with her thumb.

"I can hear her in my head," I admitted. "She said she could hear my heart calling to her."

"I'm going to call Grandma Allegra. Maybe she knows about familiars." Sunny traced her finger over the witch's mark on the puppy's underside. "And it wouldn't be a terrible idea to have her look over this one. Make sure everything is okay with her. It's not like you can take her to the vet and explain how she's the size of a teenage black bear. And..." Sunny lowered her voice and looked at me. "I don't want to draw the comparison to omens, but I'd feel better knowing for sure."

Clue didn't feel like a bad omen, and she wasn't entirely black. Her belly was a soft pink, and she had an adorable set of tan eyebrows and a white facial flash and socks that softened her deep fur, shiny blue-black in the sun.

"Do you want to see your house?" I asked Clue and carried her inside through the kitchen, trying to forget about my sister and her omens.

"*Water?*" Clue chirped in my ear.

I made Clue a small bowl of cool water and set her on the floor. She didn't so much drink the water as she fought the water with her face and front paws, spilling it everywhere. I sat down with her to help ease her nerves.

"What do you have there?" Declan saw me wrestling with Clue, trying to gently explain how to drink without trying to kill the bowl. His deep voice got Clue's attention fast, and she took off, her back paw landing squarely in the bowl and flinging it into my face with her mad dash. She jumped from the floor and landed in his arms, going limp for belly rubs and ear scratches.

"I think she's my new familiar," I said, standing up to dry off. I watched Declan move her tail and knew he saw the same mark I had when his eyes bulged in shock. He looked at me and I nodded.

Declan was one of only a few, select people who'd ever been face-to-mark, and it was hard to forget. I blushed at the memory and pushed it away since I didn't need my new familiar hearing my sexual history on our first day.

Clue took off inspecting around the kitchen, smelling, and standing onto her back paws to try and look on the countertops. Her bottom shook as her tail wagged her whole body with fresh excitement at each new smell. She bounded around, trying to take it all in and learn about her new surroundings, always with an obvious smile on her muzzle. She was all joy and excitement.

Declan placed his hands on the table and closed his eyes. A sudden breeze inside whipped up and disappeared in an instant. He was conjuring pet supplies: toys, food, bowls, collar, oversized, memory foam, pink-striped dog bed, and more treats than any puppy could eat, or so I thought.

Of all the things in my life I've been wrong about, and there have been many, the amount of food I assumed Clue could eat would be the biggest underestimation I'd ever make.

After a full can of wet food and a full bowl of kibble, the new ball of energetic love fell sound asleep in my arms. I laid her on her new squishy, pink bed next to the couch and she sprawled on her back, a tiny soft snore punctuating the silence of my adoration.

Leaving Clue to sleep, I turned my attention back to the table where Aden sat zoned out. Declan had conjured a small replica of the Bay, complete with marina, boat launch, the shopping plaza where The Dove sat, and a moving replica of my father's truck headed down our driveway. It was a fantasy world miniature version of our area, complete with sea birds flying across the water as the occasional dorsal fin popped out of the waves. I reached out to the birds and one curved around, landing on the tip of my finger. A gull the size of a fruit fly cawed; its small voice high pitched but unmistakable. I had never seen any spells like this before.

"So, you left at five a.m.?" Declan asked Aden and spread his hands apart, zooming in on the truck as the bird grew larger and bit my finger.

"Ouch! Declan, what the hell?" I looked for a cut, but there was nothing on my finger. He'd conjured that pinch on purpose.

"Callie, let me finish and I'll make the dolphin do flips, okay?" Declan smiled, but there was an irritation behind his eyes that made me feel a small twinge of joy.

"We were gone by five," Aden corrected him, glaring at me. "I don't remember the exact time we left. We drove to the marina…"

"You drove?" Declan asked, but Aden shook his head.

"Dad drove, Grandpa Ruari sat up in front, and I was in the back. We were on the boat and headed to the center of the Bay when the boat slowed and stopped. The engine was running but we weren't going anywhere. Dad tried stopping and restarting it, but it still didn't move. He could rev the engine, but we were stuck." Aden sighed at the memories.

Declan nodded as he swirled the miniature world around so Aden could see them on the boat. "Nothing unusual?"

"It was windy," Aden deadpanned.

"Cool. I'll write that you said the wind made the boat explode and we'll call it a day," Declan shot back a little too sharply.

"Boats break down, Deck. Dad tried to call for help, but we left our phones in the car. We thought we could use the boat radio to call ashore if anything happened. The boat would start but the engine wouldn't run, the radio wouldn't light up, no emergency lights. We were dead in the water. Grandpa offered to dive in and tow us to shore, but Dad asked him if he wanted us to toss in his wheelchair before or after we threw him in. We teased him that floating around was better than a drowned old-timer trying to show off his best Jack LaLanne impression. We were having a great time, cracking up at him, so sure and ready to drag us in."

Aden sighed and shrugged, exhaustion creeping across his face and making him look significantly older than his twenty-eight years. He briefly reminded me of Allegra, and I shuddered away from him slightly.

"But it wasn't that bad of an idea because we weren't that far out yet, so I pulled off my shirt and shoes and dove for the dock. I was maybe halfway back to the ramp when the explosion hit, and by the time I looked it was a white-hot fireball." Aden tried to hold back tears but failed.

"I didn't know what happened. I didn't know if they were dead or if it was a horrible backfire... I don't know what I thought. I wasn't trying to do anything but swim back to them. When I was about three-quarters of the way back, I swam up on Dad floating face-up with that gash on his head."

"You dragged him back and did CPR?" Declan asked and several dolphins came up in flips, splashing me with a gentle mist before he evaporated the teensy Bay. My stomach quivered rapidly at his attention. He knew exactly how to make me blush and I hated it.

"I dragged him up the launch ramp, slipped, and landed on my wrist, but I didn't even realize I was in pain until I did the chest compressions. I was leaning on him, one-handed, pushing with my fist until he threw up the water and gasped, I think. I remember I heard the sirens coming; someone must have seen or heard the explosion—I can't remember. Everything is so foggy and confusing. I kept pumping on Dad's chest and breathing for him until the fire department took over. They wouldn't let me help them. I tried, but they thought I was hurt so much more because of the blood from Dad's head wound everywhere. I kept trying to dive back in and get grandpa, but they strapped me to a gurney."

"How's that possible?" I tried to interrupt, but Declan shushed me with a deadly look.

"And that's when you realized your magic failed?" Declan offered. Aden folded his arms on the kitchen table and set his forehead on them.

"There's nothing. I can't heal, I can't conjure, I can't even feel my prayers in my heart. It's like being abandoned by everything that makes us magic."

"And still nothing?" Declan pressed him, but Aden didn't look at him.

"I can't even read our language. The first thing I did was ask Sunny to write something down in the hospital room. I wasn't even able to read our spells," he admitted with a shattered heart.

"I know this is hard, but we'll get your magic fixed. Trauma can cause magic to go wrong for a while. It's probably much safer if you avoid any kind of casting, at least for a week, Ade." Declan stood and moved to the seat next to Aden. "Do you have any idea why your father wasn't on the boat when it exploded? The amount of damage shows he was in the water when the boat exploded."

Aden shook his head. "My best guess is he jumped in to look and see if the prop was tangled. Maybe he thought he figured out the problem? I didn't even know he was in the water until I almost swam over his body. Maybe the explosion blew him off the boat? I can't be sure."

Without warning, Declan leaned in and pulled Aden's head to his shoulder, hugging him. "We're going to figure out what happened. I promise, your father is going to be fine. Dr. Cabotin is an outstanding neurosurgeon, and Osian is as strong as a team of oxen. Look at me." Declan waited until Aden met his eyes. "I promise. I swear by the Source, Osian will be fine."

I had no idea upon what Declan based that vow, but he was so stringent, his will solid, that even I believed him. He kissed my brother on his forehead and grabbed his messenger bag. "I have to go home and get ready for tonight. Callie, would you walk me out?"

I nodded and followed him onto the porch. A black and white cop car idled in the drive, the garish, cartoony blue crab on the side smiling joyfully and encircled by the words "Peace Officer".

"Declan, what was all that about?" I grabbed his arm and pulled him around to face me, instantly regretting the contact. He was so wildly familiar, his smell and the feel of his arm under my hand. Instinctually, I wanted to kiss him goodbye as I had so many times on this very porch.

I lost my breath when our eyes met, the moment coming when I tore them away and focused on his lips, catching his tongue drag across them before he pursed them into a soft smirk that set me on fire. Declan's casual handsomeness, a constitutional elegance typically reserved for men much older than him, ensorcelled me.

There was that Declan smell, a scent so faint, so intimate, I couldn't describe it accurately without bothering him. As well formed as my words typically were, it wasn't a naturally good smell like cologne or soap, though he did waft those pleasantries around with flourish. The smell that got me was deeper, musky, and rawly pheromone-based. It was complex and confusing, the way we smell our own body odors and feel embarrassed at the scent but remain compelled to keep inhaling the humanity of ourselves. Wicked, sticky, and a little too intimate for my own good, the heady smell and heat that swirled between us overrode my extensive shame and took over my every sense.

I leaned in, desperate to taste him, to force the clock to work backward and erase the day, take back the pain and uncertainty of the accident, and make me feel like a teenager again, even briefly.

My body against his, breasts, belly, hips, thighs all sliding into position, my shoulders, back, hands on his chest as I leaned into but away from him, familiar and desperate. Our courtship had been full of moments like this, drawing him to me slowly, but my better nature pretending to stop me as though I should possibly push him away despite my groin pressing against his. He would know, responding with dedicated precision, grabbing me around the waist as my arms came around his neck, our mouths crashing against each other. He would devour me, and I could pretend to try and desperately maintain my dignity.

Those were the rules. My role was to lean in, then lean out, teasing him but still clearly saying yes with every fiber of my being, giving him the clearance he needed to take me while maintaining the pretense I could resist him.

When he didn't melt into me, snatch me up, and pin me against the wall with his urgent kisses, I truly believed he didn't get my physical message. I never considered he heard my desire loud and clear but tried to ignore it to spare me the embarrassment of rejection.

In the way people continue to scream someone's name from a few feet away when they know they're being deliberately ignored, I mistook his gentle expression for unawareness, and my brilliant instincts told me to come on stronger because he's just not noticing. Soon, I was trying to pull his head down to mine. The more he resisted, the more I clutched at him. It never clicked in my mind he was fully aware of my flirting and was doing his best to politely ignore me until I got the hint he wasn't interested.

The blush I was faking to entice him into my arms became real, and the scorching shame of rejection flooded my skin. My internal monologue lost her mind in humiliation.

He's trying to get away from me!

He's pulling away!

Did I scratch him?

I clawed at his neck, trying to stuff my tongue down his throat. Hellfire bunny nuts, I assaulted him! Whoever is in that squad car is watching me go full Pepe LePew and maul him with my sexual frustration.

I should run.

I should just run back in the house, pack my shit, and take off. How'd I make this mistake? What made me think he'd want to make out on the porch when my family is suffering? Why the hell would my body choose now to try and rekindle our romance? Am I so desperate for attention and affection that I'm willing to manhandle the first person who stands close to me?

Just run, you complete idiot!

Throw up on his shoes. Fake a screaming fever and act like you're delirious with some encephalitis-style ailment!

"I didn't..." my voice croaked. I needed words, something we could laugh about. "Uh, oh! Uh. Coming?" I sounded like an old, sick frog as I tried to pretend I heard someone inside calling for me. Were I thinking at all in that moment, I could have played off the mental communication coming from my brand new familiar, but her loud snoring was audible even from outside.

"Callie, hang on. I've got a really bad feeling, and we need to keep a clear head right now. I have to go, but I'll be back with my parents later. Everyone in the area is coming by tonight to help your mom decorate the tree for tomorrow's Easter service. Don't leave Aden alone. I don't have a good feeling about his magic. I don't have a feeling this was an accident, Callie, and I want you to promise me you will not leave him alone. If he can't cast, he can't protect himself. Just stay with him until your mom gets home, please?" He had seized my wrist, and the weight of his words settled everything he both said and left unsaid. Of course, he warned me this way. I'd abandoned all of them and was now unreliable.

"I swear to the Source, I won't leave him alone," I promised and traced the triquetra on the back of his hand, a witch symbol for making a vow. If he didn't trust me entirely, he trusted our magic to keep me set to purpose.

A three-point Celtic knot, representing both sides of the promise and the promise itself between us; it was an ancient witch pinky-swear that would gently remind you to keep your vow if you wavered. It hurt like a bee sting if you forgot and would swell into a cursed and smelly boil if you broke your vow. It wasn't enough to do any real or lasting damage, but it did give the rest of your coven a good visual reminder that you were a vow breaker.

Every magical child has at one time or another, been covered from head to toe in open, oozing boils that reminded everyone around you were a little fibber of the worst kind. It's almost a rite of passage that we make promises we can't keep, give up secrets we never thought would be dragged from us, and witch parents loved to ask us to vow we were telling the truth. We would swear and instantly be found out in our foolishness. You'd think we'd learn the first time, but no. Only Sunshine remained unscathed because she was rare to *make* a vow as a child and would commit to her vow with a thunderous conviction until completion.

"I'll know more tonight. Have your mother call me when she gets home, give her my love, and tell Sunny bye from me." He kissed my forehead and jogged off to the cruiser, waving from the passenger seat as it turned and disappeared.

Sunny was in the kitchen with Aden applying a poultice to some scrapes he got when he fell. He carefully walked her through the recipes, leaning on her magic since his was seemingly nonexistent.

I slipped past them, scurrying past the sitting room and sliding behind the slightly open door at the other end of the entrance hall. Standing in Grandpa Ruari's room brought back the raging pain, now colored with shame, regret, humiliation, and mortification.

There was his smell, chocolate chip cookies, vanilla, and a hint of spices that usually gave me a warm, safe feeling but now crushed me with emptiness. His bed was made, creases fresh and stiff as he'd only made it this morning. The blinds were open, sunlight streaming through as though it were a normal day, a day without blinding loss and pain. How could he be gone? How did I come home and lose him immediately?

My chest ached and I wanted those years back. I needed another hug, another promise that everything would be okay. Nothing would ever be okay again. Even if it were good again, by some miracle, it would be without the only family member who loved me the most.

I leaned forward, resting my sweaty palms against my knees, trying to catch my breath and hold back the scream threatening to slash through my throat. I couldn't stand still. The anxiety, terror, and horror electroshocked my muscles, and I paced, shaking my hands as hard as I could until I heard the skin snapping as my thumb joints ached.

Feeling the frantic start to rise around me, I longed for an exit but couldn't go back near my siblings without them seeing the pain on my face. I sat on my grandfather's bed, picked up a heavy, mustard-colored throw pillow, and screamed into it, wishing it were an infinite void into which I could fall. Not a single sound left the confines of the pillow. Over and over, I unleashed the most wrenching howls I could muster, emptying the well of sadness and angst into the puffy silk square. Once I exhausted the embarrassment, fear, horror, and shame, I was just screaming to scream, to get it out.

It was disconcerting to screech at the top of my lungs and hear nothing, but then pull away from the pillow and hear the slow shiver of my wracked sobs echoing. I was holding a sound cloud. Ancient magic silencing the private sounds a person needed to get out but didn't want anyone to overhear.

They were wildly popular when I was a child some twenty years ago. Mothers would pass the spell to allow parents to let their frustrations out without scaring little kids, awakening babies who finally slept, or disturbing partners who needed rest. Soundproof and fully breathable, witches were careful to ensure the pillows couldn't be used to muffle the screams of a murder victim. They were less popular with younger parents who embraced their feelings and didn't feel the need to hide every scream or stuff down every powerful emotion until they exploded in a keening wail.

Currently, parents only kept a small sound cloud, often disguised as a tomato pin cushion. Small enough to carry on the body or quickly conjure in case of a stubbed toe or scared yelp. They were useful for unexpected, loud noises that could wake up or disturb their families.

Why did my grandfather need a pillow he could scream into without anyone hearing him?

Chapter Six

Hi honey, I'm hopeless!

PHEME: *Good afternoon, witches! You're back in the bay with Pheme and Eris! Today, we have a special letter, sent here by an anonymous listener.*

ERIS: *If they can't be brave enough...*

PHEME: *Shut your face and let me read this. Trust me, Eris. This is going to be worth it.*

ERIS: *Pshaw*

PHEME: *Dear Pheme and Eris, I keep hearing my parents talk about how difficult it will be for a fully grown witch to make an ascension late in life and it has me scared. I still have many years before I can even consider ascending, but should I start preparing? What happens? What can I expect? Does it hurt? Please talk about this topic. Sincerely, Anxious about ascending, Blue Crab Bay, MS, age eleven.*

ERIS: *Start a recording because this probably won't happen again, but you're right, Pheme. That's a great topic.*

PHEME: *I thought you'd be particularly eager to assist. Care to begin?*

ERIS: *An ascension is where a grown witch above the age of majority, but below her twenty-sixth birthday, makes a choice to follow the path of the Source, commit to our religion and magic, and take on the requirements that come with our abilities.*

PHEME: *Specifics, not beatifics. Everyone knows the theory.*

ERIS: *We drown you in water caves. Better?*

PHEME: *Stop scaring people!*

ERIS: *Do you have a better way to describe diving into a water hole and swimming into oblivion?*

PHEME: *When a witch makes her ascension, in our area, she finds a sacred space, somewhere full of elemental magic and history. We've chosen the water caves behind the northern falls on the Bay. We enter the water naked, our bodies prepared and cleansed, and we dip below the surface and swim down until we reach...*

ERIS: *Valhalla?*

PHEME: *Enlightenment!*

ERIS: *We run out of oxygen to hallucinate from the pressure and lack of food leading up to the event. The hallucinations are read as messages from the Source and we become imbued with a clarity of purpose and power.*

PHEME: *That started out a little rough, but I don't actively hate your description. What if a witch doesn't come up?*

ERIS: *It's never happened.*

PHEME: *Isn't that strange? That in all the thousands of us, for hundreds of years, not one casualty?*

ERIS: *The Source protects her wandering children.*

PHEME: *The Source does indeed protect her wandering children!*

ERIS: *Did your ascension hurt?*

PHEME: *Not at all. The colors were disorienting, and the power surge was a bit more destructive than my... uh, family was expecting, but we replaced the broken walls and carried on!*

ERIS: *Didn't you turn the whole back of your mom's house to sand?*

PHEME: *Several times.*

ERIS: *I had a really emotional ascension... Oh, don't look at me that way. I have emotions. I had to get really in touch with them once I ascended.*

PHEME: *It really does hit each of us differently!*

ERIS: *Sand, sobbing, same same.*

PHEME: *You know...*

ERIS: *Don't you dare...*

PHEME: *Our sponsor this week is none other than Papa Smile's Emotional Support Sodas. Are you feeling anxious about your ascension? Dreading your dream wedding? Is a presentation making you paranoid? Suffering from depression over a difficult defeat? Grab an emotional support soda. Fight your feelings with the fizzy, fruity flavors of our new and improved twelve-ounce cans of confidence! Sip away your sadness with a cheerful cherry cola or rein in your rage with a raspberry rhubarb tea! With Papa Smiles, we turn your frown upside down with a delicious drink especially made to drown your darkest days! Now available in Prickly Pear Patience, Cardamom Cucumber Melon Confidence, and the Limited Edition Leave Loneliness Behind Lemonade! Papa Smile's Emotional Support Sodas—find a flavor to fit your feels. Not to be combined with pharmacological supplements that impact serotonin or dopamine.*

ERIS: *There's a fine line between stupid and clever.*
PHEME: *B-B-B-Baby you ain't seen nothing yet!*

Our grandmother arrived first, having picked up our mother from the hospital. Despite her tumultuous relationship with Grandpa Ruari, his death had struck Allegra in a way I did not foresee. She looked exhausted, pale, and like the day had taken a century of her life force. She was impeccably dressed as always in a precision-tailored, linen pantsuit as pink as a carnation with blinding white tennis shoes. The massive, sparkling earrings and jeweled brooch in the shape of a hare with glowing with green eyes, much like her own. Her skin seemed thinner and her hair limp. She was showing her years instead of her power.

Allegra was from a time when women didn't leave the house undone. Pride and status came to her by appearance and carriage. Normally, she reminded me of a steel pole dressed in pastel fabric and sparkling ribbons, but today she was a rusted piece of rebar, the forge of her heart gone cold with worry and stress.

I don't want to say I shoved Allegra out of my way to get to my mom, but I probably did. I pulled my mom in close and clung to her, both trying to get a read on her emotional state and letting myself feel all the crazy swirling around my heart. I felt her gently start to stroke my hair, shushing me softly.

"He's okay. He needs time to heal and rest. He'll make it," she promised me over and over.

"What happened, Momma?" We made our way inside and sat at the table. Sunny passed out teacups, saucers, and a plate of cookies before grabbing the copper kettle off the stove and filling it from the sink. Not bothering with the cooktop, she smiled brightly as the kettle softly whistled while she walked to the table.

"He's not able to communicate at all. I tried to connect for hours, but it's so cloudy in his head. The doctor said there could be swelling on the brain, but he smells like brimstone."

There was nothing worse that could be connected to the explosion. Brimstone was dark magic, the hallmark of greed and rage work done by witches who didn't follow a code. Danger, terror, and every dark thing was predicated by foul smells, and even in my limited knowledge, it was crystal clear by the gasping reaction of those around me that brimstone meant evil.

"Witchcraft gone wrong or...?" Aden asked, smelling his hand and wrist.

"Deliberate," my mother said, locking eyes with Aden and he nodded, getting up slowly. "Later," she grabbed his good hand and pulled him back down. He would need a ritual cleansing and a blessing, the sooner the better. "I don't know what you'll need to get rid of it. I can't get a focus on anything specific. There's no sound or taste or anything visceral coming through in his thoughts and feelings. It's like the witch vanished without a trace."

Nobody said murder.

I didn't want to be the first to use the word, to speak it into existence. But it screamed soundlessly across my mind over and over, mimicking the voices around me as though we were all tapped in the same idea.

Grandma Allegra grabbed her chest. Sunny leaned over, cooing softly to calm her, breaking the silence. Witch work always left a mark. Magic has a fingerprint that lingers despite all attempts to wipe it away, but my mother was telling us that the fingerprint was missing. And that meant it was stronger magic than hers. We sat as the implication of such an obscene power settled around the room. A pounding knock on the door shocked us all out of our terror.

"Sun..." my mother nodded toward the door. "The Llewellyns are here."

Sunny opened the heavy front door and the family burst through, each one carrying a casserole dish, chattering relentlessly, and making a fuss over my mother and Aden.

Maya and Genevieve McDonnagh showed up next and made a beeline for Aden. Maya didn't bother with pleasantries and went on a wild rant about boat safety and how worried everyone had been until she finally burst into tears. My mouth dropped when I saw my perpetually single brother stand up and grab her tight in a hug. I picked up on the smell of roses permeating the air around them.

I hadn't known they were a couple. It made perfect sense, though, as Aden was calm and still, a deep well of thoughtful contemplation and intelligence, while Maya was a whirling dervish of emotions and senses. At five feet exactly, her small stature belied her furious nature, and if opposites attracted, they'd be together forever. She reminded me of a grave rubbing: ivory skin, raven black hair, big, seemingly tempestuous gray eyes. Maya, and her twin Genevieve by extension, were monochromatic in grays, black and white—little color variation in their features. Aden, on the other hand, was all color starting with deep olive skin that turned copper in the summer sun. His eyes were deep, rich brown, and glowed honey-gold in the light, but his hair was blue-black in an almost iridescent way.

Declan arrived moments later with his parents, Finn and Merriweather. Merriweather looked almost exactly like her Disney namesake. She was dark and plump with a heart-shaped face, icy blue eyes, and the softest hands I'd ever encountered. Finn looked like Declan plus thirty years. They shared the same ultra-thick chestnut brown hair and bright hazel eyes that mixed teal and gold like a rare star sapphire, although Finn had a little more snow on the roof and a few crinkles around his smile. They were so similar that one could imagine mistaking them from behind, except Finn was developing a robustness around the middle that Declan had so far avoided.

I often wondered how Declan's parents felt about their son's power to manifest things out of thin air when they were both tactile witches, he a carpenter (ain't no secret passage like a witch's secret passage) and she a... I suppose seamstress would be the nearest thing to call her, but it felt so weak. Merriweather did things with textiles that boggled the mind. From magically expanding sails and tents to making even the most unflattering garments precision-tailored.

The first story I ever heard about Declan's mother told me everything I'd ever needed to know about her and her son. When Declan was thirteen years old, his mother launched her own bespoke clothing house, Looking Glass Atelier. The grand opening of her atelier featured a fashion show and a live fashion museum where models walked a runway, and others wove their way through the streets with food and drinks while wearing masterclass reproductions of famous clothing from history and Hollywood. It was a bonanza of clothing, fabric, art, and witches; it was a behemoth of stress and preparation to get ready for it.

As the story went, the next morning after champagne was poured and the genius celebrated, Merriweather Bradley walked down the stairs of her home to join her family at breakfast, ready to start work on her first day as a business owner. Her mood was elated, but her patience had eroded.

The brilliant and hilarious Declan Bradley popped onto a chair at the kitchen table, grabbed two slices of buttered toast, and quipped, "Best thing about that party last night is knowing all that damn fabric is finally out of this house and I have my bedroom and bathroom clean again. Who'da thunk Mom's silly little hobby would ever be a real business?!"

When Declan came home that evening, he found his closet and drawers empty, not even a puff of fuzz left in the carved wood. Atop his bed lay a dozen different bolts of fabric, a snappy new sewing machine, and a note that said, "Enjoy your new, silly little hobby!"

The very moment his fingertips brushed against the note, his clothing evaporated, leaving him incredibly motivated to master his silly little hobby. To be fair, after a week she gave him his clothes back, but he never once pretended to talk down to another person after that. Merriweather was a savagely brilliant and creative woman.

The twelve ancient families arrived in time with some of the newer witches on the coast. Most, I felt, wanted a peek inside Dolphin House and a moment to look in on my family while we suffered.

My suspicion was temporarily distracted by the arrival of Bianca Aureliana, a friend of my sister's. Bianca owned an antique bookstore just outside of Pelican Square. A tiny shop of found things devoted to fiction and literature, The Secret Keeper's Bookstore was a warm and cozy den with a roaring hearth and myriad cushioned nooks and blanketed crannies to curl up with a long-forgotten tale and a cup of Comfortabili-Tea. Witches ooze cleverness from every pore.

Bianca's best friend and business partner (and possibly life partner? I didn't know and at that point, I was too scared to ask) glad-handed with other guests ten feet behind us. Ginger Arrietti was the owner of Exceptionali-Tea Company. Between the tea bar at the bookstore and her mail-order customers, Ginger's tea bags were making quite a name for our local apothecary witch.

Bianca hugged me tight, pulling me into her shoulder. Her wild, curly black hair perfumed with a mix of cocoa butter and a touch of vanilla, making me feel warm and safe when I inhaled. She squealed slightly in my ear, bouncing on her feet. I couldn't be unhappy in her light.

"I'm so happy you're back! Sun missed you so much. I brought you this!" Bianca pulled away and thrust a perfectly wrapped forest green box with a soft, golden pink ribbon at me.

"Oh, you didn't have to...." I grabbed the box and slipped off the ribbon to reveal an assortment of sachets filled with different teas. Responsibili-Tea for finishing tasks, Impartiali-Tea to see situations without prejudice, Carnali-Tea for amorous adventures, Clari-Tea for decision-making, Levi-Tea for humor, Sentimentali-Tea for nostalgia, and Sensitivi-Tea for unfeeling, heartless wenches, like me.

"Some old favorites, some new releases.... I thought you would enjoy catching up on what we've been brewing!" Bianca's excitement was palpable, and my smile got wider as she became more animated.

"Sunny used to send me jars of Responsibli-Tea while I was at school. I swear I only passed because of that!" I said.

"Don't let her pretend she thought of that gift, Callie!" Ginger joined us, bumping Bianca on the hip. "Whatever you like, let me know. We have a ton of tea in stock, and I need to make some room for the new brews coming this summer."

"She made Equali-Tea and Intersectionali-Tea for the college humanities department," Bianca sang, obviously proud of her partner.

"That's rather brilliant!" I'd never considered using teas or magic to let other people expand their experiences and perspectives.

"That's not the half of it," Ginger winked. "I'm working on Immuni-Tea and Luminosi-Tea for night-time games of tag. It brightens as you get further away so if anyone wanders off, they can be found in the dark."

"And the Immuni-tea?" I asked.

"It's coming along, but there are some widespread pathogens we're trying to account for," Ginger explained.

"It's actually immunity-boosting tea?"

"That was my intention, but..." Ginger blushed before yawning deeply, giving Bianca the chance to again compliment her partner.

"But it's looking like she might have a way to return an immune system to a witch with some tea and a little dose of magic. We're testing, but it's brilliant. It could really change the world. Your grandfather was instrumental in..." Bianca went silent as a pained look crept across Ginger's face.

Grief.

It made everyone tender. Tears threatened to break the surface so often that simple conversations could be minefields.

"He was a brilliant witch and I'm truly glad you are carrying on with his magic," I promised them.

My sister sidestepped around me, and the squeals of excitement reached a fever pitch between the three of them. Briefly, they reminded me of the Three of Cups: friendship, community, support, and feminine sisterhood.

As enticing as the conversation could be, the tone that came from them was too high, and I slipped out with my tea, backing away from the growing spread of people so I could get closer to the food.

I had fully leaned into my hunger when I walked slap into Rainbeaux Navarre—the numerology genius; a spiteful, bitchy witch who enjoyed looking down on me and my lack of casting ability, and my former best friend. She hadn't aged a day or gained a single pound in the years I'd been gone, and I found that incredibly disrespectful.

Beaux and I had grown up together, thick as thieves until around her thirteenth birthday. Were she not a witch, she'd have been some kind of engineer. Her sharp mind and analytical nature had been at war with her power her whole life until she developed a way to bridge those powers and connect magic to mathematics. She was also the person who discovered my name could be translated into Hagfish and decided to tell everyone. The nickname Haggy followed me for years and made my early teens a nightmare. Junior High isn't easy in the best of circumstances, and being called Haggy compounded my lengthy awkward phase.

I didn't expect her to grab me in such a tight hug. Her slender frame and dainty features belied a strength that felt like she could throw a Cadillac into the Bay. I choked briefly and gave in, hugging her back.

"I'm so, so sorry for Ruari." She held onto a sob, and I felt bad for my animosity. "He talked about you all the time while you were gone. He'd call me, have me tell him stories, memories of when we were little. We'd gotten so close."

I was shocked at her words. The Beaux I left was not an emotional sort. Granted, a witch passing was a shocking and sad experience, but this icy witch seemed truly pained. Her pain set me back and I softened toward her.

"Thank you for being there for him when I wasn't," I said softly, bewildered. I wasn't mad to see the years had seen her compassion grow but wondered if everyone who ascended was so much more evolved than I.

I held a lot of bitterness in my heart, and the memories of my former best friend were colored dark with pain and fear that overshadowed how close we had been and how much I missed having a best friend I could trust with my whole life. Maybe my own evolution could start with forgiving Beaux?

The children were put to work decorating the back meadow with hundreds of blossoms as their parents enchanted flower garlands to wrap around the tree. The meadow around the oak would hold more than a hundred people spread out on quilts, trays serving wine, juice, water, cheese, fruit, and cookies neatly placed in the centers.

We could, with the amount of magic in our coven, decorate the entire yard in a bewitching style, but it was more fun to watch the little ones pinning flowers to the tree limbs as their parents hoisted them on their shoulders and levitated them so they could reach.

The tree wasn't tall enough to be dangerous because the ground was enchanted to be a soft landing, a comfortable seat, and a gentle place to stand for hours if you wanted. We witches love our comforts.

When I came to offer help, I noticed a plaque on the ground behind the tree. It looked like a glass tile, gleaming yellow in the setting sun. I kicked at it with my foot, pushing grass off, and saw it was a circle.

There are some memories I didn't realize would hit me as hard as they did, and that yellow piece of glass was a two-by-four of joy upside my head. I crouched closer, running my hand over the top, and saw clearly as the forms in front of my eyes turned into my brother, sister, and me toddling around on the beach of Blue Crab Bay.

To keep us busy and help us find an outlet for our magic as kids, my parents would take us to the beach and let us make sea glass, a powerful, arcane magical item. Seaglass was made by separating sand into suitable colors, blowing it into a shape, and then heating it until it was a thick, flat, smooth, piece of glass.

The yellow circle under my fingers was Sunny's first piece. She was the heater that turned the sand to sea glass. Aden would separate the colors and a handful of seemingly beige and boring sand would give way to a rainbow of colors. It was my job to blow the small mounds toward Sunny who would light up and solidify the magic. My mother used to keep these in her bedroom window, but as I wandered around the perimeter of the meadow, I realized she'd embedded several around the tree.

Every color of the rainbow was represented, each corresponding to the elemental magic we channeled: yellow for the sun, orange for the spirit, red for fire, green for the earth, blue for the water, purple for the wind, indigo for the metal.

They were placed for protection, I realized. The oldest magic in the world, the base elements scattered to create a barrier around the tree and keep out anyone who might harm our sacred place. I looked into the shrubbery around the perimeter to see if they'd gone so far as to leave brick dust or a salt line, but it was regular dirt. It was possible my mother simply thought they were beautiful or that they made a pretty rainbow prism of colors in the right sunlight.

Clue stayed underfoot, reenergized by the adoration and business of the crowd. Grandma Allegra was immediately taken by the pup and didn't bother to hide her shock at my gift. I told her the story of the card and her eyes darkened slightly.

"Why do you look troubled?" I didn't want to know the answer, but I'd feel awful if something happened to Clue and I didn't pay attention.

"Familiars come to witches who are struggling. Everyone knows that, but they also come to witches who're in danger. It's rarely a guardian *and* a guide. It's one or the other, and I don't feel like you need a guide." Allegra grabbed my hand. "It wouldn't be a stretch to wonder if you need a guardian. Now that Ruari is gone, we are all in danger. None of you understood what he went through to protect this family." She blinked rapidly and shook her head, the thoughts in her mind dispersing with the motion. When she looked at me again, the vulnerability was gone, and she was back to the iron lady I was comfortable resenting.

We prayed in the garden that night, sending energy and healing to my father and gratitude to my grandpa for his years of service to our faith. There was no extended service or invocation besides the prayer and blessing of the tree and clearing, just a calm meditation and sense of reverence under a bright spring moon.

I wanted to try and focus my intention on the bizarre warning from Grandma Allegra, but I was drawn to the dynamic of the community in the meadow. It was a family to which I didn't realize I belonged, one that went on without me, seemingly weeding me out in my absence over the seven years.

I could hear the gentle singing of my sister and her group of toddlers softly purring an old lullaby that ranked number two on my list of "horrifying songs sung to children to make them feel better that are truly upsetting when you look at them with any sort of critical eye." It was titled "Shadow Moon" and was generally sung to the melody of the ABCs or Twinkle Twinkle Little Star tune.

"When you see the shadow moon, find your place to hide right soon.

Don't speak your name or tell your tale; hunters come by horse and sail.

They can't scare us one on one; entire towns must come undone.

Pitchforks, torches, ropes of silk; they blame us for their spoiled milk.

We give freely from the heart; from loving service we do not part.

Divine misfortune, where terror lies; blamed on witches' milky eyes.

Stand together to give your best; battle fear to make them blessed.

When they treat witches like a pest; lay that hunter straight to rest!"

The only song that was creepier than "Shadow Moon" was "You Are My Sunshine"—a horrible song that ended with a terrifying threat of someone taking your sunshine away? I loathed it.

Sunny was a beacon of angelic grace upon which the young ones could focus their attention. Lit with the light of heaven, they followed her prayers and sang as if she were their Pied Piper.

I was so compelled to watch her until my gaze drifted past her glowing countenance and over to where Declan sat with his back to his family, deep in conversation with Beaux. He seemed to be explaining something, almost negotiating with her as she kept shaking her head, wide-eyed and shocked by whatever he was telling her.

He grabbed her hand in a pleading gesture, and she relented whatever reservations she had and smiled. His face broke into a grateful smile, and he leaned in, kissing her hand and then her cheek. I broke into a rage sweat under my clothes, shaking slightly.

I'd forgotten the podcast. My ex and my former friend. The Ice Queen. There they were, so in love in my own home. I wanted—no, *needed*—someone to hurt as badly as I was hurting.

I was seconds away from a violent fantasy of revenge when Clue bro my concentration, streaking across the meadow in a flurry, howling at her prey.

"*GET BACK HERE AND PLAY WITH ME, FLUFFY RAT!!!*" she ordered the squirrel.

I don't think the terrified gray rodent was fluent in familiar because she ran like Clue had added her to the menu. My adorable familiar was headed right for Maya and Aden, but before she could crash, she leaped over them, soaring above their heads a moment longer than natural, landing softly at the tree and barking up toward its branches.

I jumped up as fast as the soft ground would allow and scrambled to distract her from the squirrel. I tried to grab her, slipped on the damp grass, and landed face-first in the mud, my front squishing deep into the wetness.

"Callie..." My mother called, but I put my hand up. I could not. I'd rather die in that mud than have help getting to my feet.

I knew my mother, or any other of the people sitting there praying, could help me clean up in seconds. To be honest, it was the straw that broke me. I stood, slipping twice more before reaching my feet, scooped up my puppy, and went back inside to clean us both up.

As I came through the back door of the house, Clue growled and wiggled, struggling in my arms. Slipping around the tile floor, I struggled to hold her as the wet mud I tracked in destabilized my footing. The puppy struggled out of my arms and took off barking toward the front door, losing her mind. For a moment, I stared into the darkness at the front of the house wondering how much worse the night could get. There would be mud to clean up for months.

I finally gave chase when I heard her nails scratching on the front door, her barking higher, harsher, sharper than before. She was frightened and my heart froze.

Every shadow seemed to be menacing me from inside the house. My mother's voice, bad magic, the smell of brimstone—all of it echoed in my mind, and for the first time, I was afraid to be alone in the house. I had a sense of being watched, someone looming in the dark. I told myself it was just my sister and her baby band of backup singers chanting that horrible tune that had me upended in the safest home on the coast.

Clue was frantic against the giant door, her scratching having all the impact of a feather brushing a rock. She spotted me and spun around a few times digging wildly at the threshold. Pressing my forehead against the wall, I tried to gauge the outside through the leaded windows, but it was all shadow and distortion.

"Please, shush. What's out there?" I urged Clue, my voice barely at a whisper.

She didn't answer, just growled and struggled.

I jerked open the door and stared into the yard, but it was silent and bright as the moon glinted off the cars parked in front. Shadows didn't creep in until close to the treeline, likely too far for someone to reach before being seen.

"There's nothing out there, baby!"

Clue sprinted past me and around under the porch, yapping at something I couldn't see. Her barking ceased fast, the frantic tone smothered under a slurping sound and muffled yummy noises.

She was nose-deep into a wet pile of dead animal when I finally caught up.

"Oh, for keening out loud!"

"It's so good! So fresh... seagull is my favorite!"

"You're going to get sick!" I couldn't wake up to a pile of puppy puke after today.

"I don't get sick."

"Then you're going to make *me* sick!" The soft, squishing nibble noises were starting to meet the foul, fetid smell in my face.

Clue looked back, the carcass hanging from her jaws looking more fierce than I expected. Plopping down on her tush, she flipped the shredded corpse into the air and ate it in one swallow like a pelican.

"Aren't the bones dangerous?" I hadn't had a pet of my own, but I was pretty sure there were cautionary tales of feeding dead birds to puppies.

"Not for me, I'm special. I don't even need shots. My own magic protects me, and it protects you too."

"I don't want to eat a whole bird."

"You'd feel different if it were a rotisserie chicken."

Damn it. She wasn't wrong.

Upstairs, I stood in my shower until both of us were drenched, and the last bits of dirt had rinsed from my clothes and her fur. I could hear Clue chattering excitedly about her new squirrel friends, her voice so joyful I couldn't even pretend to blame her for my folly. I'd been so swept away in jealousy that my surroundings were foreign to me.

I wrapped a towel around myself and dried Clue, letting her shake off the clean water while still in the shower stall. I offered to blow dry her hair and she jumped back and growled when I flipped on the hairdryer, so I gave up.

"Can I try?" Sunny asked from the doorway, holding a plate of fopdoodles and a bottle of milk. I shrugged and handed her the damp towel before drying myself off and pulling a nightgown over my head. Sunny squatted down, putting the towel under her knees and gently scratching Clue behind her ears. She pursed her lips and blew on the wet fur. I watched, astonished at how the hair dried almost instantly, no hard blast of hot air needed. Clue seemed to enjoy it, turning frequently to shove damp sections of her body toward my sister's face.

I plopped on my bed, stuffing a cookie in my mouth, desperate to taste anything but the bitterness of realizing Declan had moved on. Declan moved on and I threw myself at him. I was sick over it.

"Do I need to get another plate?" Sunny wasn't kidding. I kept trying to stop the pain and heartbreak by downing cookie after cookie, but nothing seemed to help.

"Did you know about Declan and Beaux?" I asked my sister directly. I knew there were rumors but had no idea it could actually happen.

Sunny shook her head and parted sections of my damp hair to dry them. I wanted to bat her away, but it was warm and comforting, and I needed it. "Of all the couples in the world, Declan and Beaux got together? What did I do to deserve this? Why does it hurt so much?" I whined, drinking straight from the milk bottle.

"She's not as awful as she was, but she's not around much," Sunny explained. "I was shocked to see her come tonight, but I thought it was to pay respects. I don't know what he sees in her."

"He sees the lack of an emotional wreck." I tried to laugh at myself. "The cookies don't even help." I set the plate on the bed and threw myself back, contemplating whether I should even stay here and be miserable while they were happy. "I know I let him go, but her? Of all people? You can say she's not as bad, but you know she only showed up here to ensure I saw her with him. I knew she always had a thing for him. They probably got together the moment I left."

"Maybe they didn't even wait that long," Sunny offered. She stretched out beside me on my bed. "They may have been seeing each other before you left. Maybe that was the unseen impetus behind your need to get as far away as possible?"

"You're not helping."

"I can turn her into a sea snake?" Sunny tried again to make me feel better.

"And risk her becoming a hydra and killing him? No, it was just a shock. No need to transfigure anyone."

"What if I hit her with my car? You can say you told me to say hi if I ran into her and I did, I just ran into her at about forty miles an hour?" Sunny, valiant little sister that she was, only half-kidded.

I cackled at the thought and caught the giggles from the cookies, laughing myself into hysterics. I laughed so long and so hard my face ached and my stomach cramped, but the joy turned to rot and soon I was sobbing over everything. In less than twenty-four hours I'd experienced every possible emotion, and I had nothing left but raw feelings of grief for my grandfather and dead embers from the only man I ever really loved.

I wanted the embers to be dead but seeing him with Beaux was proof they were smoldering, angry, and forlorn for myself while trying to be happy for him. I wanted to be happy for him, too. When I left, I released my hold on him and prayed daily he would find someone to love him the way he deserved to be loved. I didn't leave him because I stopped loving him; I left because I knew if I stayed, I wouldn't be someone worthy of being loved by him.

Realizing I had left, tried my best, failed, and still wasn't worthy of him, hurt more than anything. I couldn't live knowing he had a chance at real happiness, a family, a loving wife who would give him children to carry on, and he didn't get it because of my selfishness. Declan was the only person who knew my feelings because I made them clear when he proposed.

When we were seniors, Declan decided to forgo college and go into the Air Force, planning to use his magic to serve his country and assist in the National Defense Department of Witchcraft.

Declan was determined to rebuild and renew after Hurricane Katrina devastated our coast and left everything in ruins for so many of the non-witch families we loved. He worked with the teams of witches who set up rebuilding efforts and fell in love with the notion of giving back to the community through his magic. His talent set made him a natural reconnaissance soldier and his current career in magical law enforcement felt pretty inevitable from my perspective.

Declan always gave me a feeling of inevitability, a runaway chariot of emotions that would trample everything about me if I didn't manage to get a handle on it. He was a riptide of joy and passion, my own personal Calypso. I forgot about the world when he loved me, a distraction that always terrified me. I've never known magic to affect me the way Declan's presence does.

I do know that, had anyone else proposed to me when I was seventeen, I'd have laughed at them. I had no doubts I wasn't ready for marriage, cohabitation, or even college at that point, but Declan stole my better sense away from me, drowning me in love and adoration until I forgot myself.

Declan proposed on Samhain, or non-witches Halloween, but because we're in the south, we don't get the deep tones of changing leaves in Autumn. That didn't stop Declan from turning the entire backyard of his parent's house into a New England paradise of ruby red, golden yellow, and fiery orange leaves with harvest fruits scattered around. Thousands of twinkling lights flickered around us; he conjured fairies to dance around us as each individual blinked into and out of existence.

In addition to conjuring the fairies, hundreds of obsidian spiders engaged around us, spinning a sparkling, gossamer web between the trees while dozens of carved Jack-O-Lanterns lit around us. Animated skeletons rose from piles of bones on the ground and swayed gently against soft music that seemed to be coming out of unfurling dahlias.

It was, to be sure, a spectacle. He'd entreated the whole community to gather around and help him make it a perfect, ample, sparkling harvest romance representing bounty, harmony, and the fruitful life ahead of us. I was swooned, off my feet, and dizzy with love and promise. I spun around, looking at the entire scene, struggling to understand the depth of his planning to pull off such a massive event. I couldn't believe he thought I was worth that level of magic. When I finally looked back at him, he was beaming with pride. His smile was gentle and almost shy, visible nervousness masquerading as coyness.

"Did you do this for me?" I was flabbergasted.

"Since the day you sat next to me at the Yule feast when we were fourteen, everything I've done has been for you." He turned me, taking both of my hands in his. Witches stand before each other to propose—our marriages are based on equality, consent, and the idea two individuals come together of their own free will, making their own choice and speaking their minds. We don't kneel because we don't beg; instead, we respect the choices others will make.

"You are the whole of my heart, beyond time. I live this life to love you, honor you, protect you, and empower you. It won't always be easy, but it will be fun. It won't always be happy, but you'll always be held. We cannot promise each other everything, but I can promise everything I am to you. Wherever our paths take us, I walk with you, always." Declan held out his hand and wisps of green light coalesced into a spiral as though a cosmic funnel of space dust formed in his palm.

He held an emerald of the deepest green and shimmering in the fairy lights. Engagement rings are very specific to the witches. The stone was as unique as the lovers and rarely diamonds, which traditionally symbolize spiritual power and the infinite fire of the Source. The emerald represented timeless patience and successful love which was an interesting promise from someone with respect to binding our lives together for as long as we could.

Looking back, I almost feel like he knew, or at least felt it coming, that I'd disappoint him. When I told him I was leaving and wouldn't be accompanying him to Texas, he just hugged me, told me he was proud of me, and told me it didn't change how he felt about me. I hate to admit, I thought he meant he'd never stop loving me, that he'd wait forever.

"I thought he'd wait forever, too," Sunny said, sliding down next to me. She put her arms around my neck and pulled my head into her shoulders. "I'm so sorry this hurts so much."

Chapter Seven

I saw that going better in my head...

PHEME: *This week, we're talking about the municipal push to make the northwest side of the Bay into protected magical areas that will be sheltered and restricted from any mixed-living developments.*

ERIS: *It's a bureaucratic restrictive covenant to ensure the divide between witches and non-witches, because let's face it, non-witches are so much more likely to create ecological trauma. It's no secret this area has been negatively affected by the actions of non-witches...*

PHEME: *So much of that area is already protected land though, Eris. The water caves on the north side of the Bay are fully warded and loaded with deterrents to keep non-witches away. The southern beaches are protected. All the way from the spot where Anne Dieu-Le-Veut came ashore while running from French authorities and down another three miles inland where her crew was hanged by the same authorities a day later.*

ERIS: *Those places grant us a wealth of traumatically usable and emotionally charged ingredients. It's our duty as witches to turn the pain of the past into the joy of the future.*

PHEME: *I think it's because so many of our sacred sites have been sites of intense tragedy and bloodshed, so maybe we can tap into that magical energy and use it to manifest incredible change.*

ERIS: *And the whole northwest side of the Bay isn't THAT! It's a land grab!*

PHEME: *Why don't you settle down while I mention our sponsor?*

ERIS: *Some spells and potions require more robust elements! It's less sacrificial and more situational in almost all cases! We might need bat bone dust but come on! Just get it from an animist who recently found or nursed a bat whose life ended; ergo, the bat gave, and we accept. This isn't complicated—we have RULES!!!*

PHEME: *Are you looking for the perfect jewel? Do you need a wearable piece of supercharged jewelry at a fraction of the cost and with none of the misery of mined gems? Crystal's Ball is the largest magically charged gem creation lab in the bay area! Are you looking for passion, romance, and physical purification? We've got the perfect garnet to get your gonads going! Are you in the doghouse over a little white lie? A flawless topaz will tell your partner that you're ready to take on enhanced truthfulness and ask forgiveness, plus it comes in dozens of colors, cuts, and settings. Bespoke stones by appointment only. Crystal's Ball, 428 Coral Drive. Now open on Fridays!*

ERIS: *You know, I was almost reluctant to come into the show today. I had this feeling you were setting up sponsors to get me to talk about trauma.*

PHEME: *Oh Eris, I would never do that. I don't think I know about your history to use a sponsor to entice you to share with our listeners.*

ERIS: *No, Pheme, I know I'm so paranoid in my old age. The young witch at the clock repair shop asked for my surname and I screamed at her. I actually told her it was Dickering, like how you're dickering around with my watch! Which was funny, but not. She was really surprised about it, actually.*

PHEME: *Surprised an ancient ruin like you would use profanity?*

ERIS: *No, apparently, they have a trinket exchange storefront with a similar name, and she thought I was there to do a secret shopper review.*

PHEME: *Which is why you felt set up here?*

ERIS: *Exactly! Then I realized you give the sponsors after I share, so how are you setting me up? You'd have to be ordering sponsors based on situations you know are critical to me.*

PHEME: *Like how, if right now, I threw out a sponsor for Nermal's Name Change or Stop Screaming at Service People Seltzer?*

ERIS: *Precisely. But, since I've already told the story, and that sponsor didn't correlate, I admit I stand corrected.*

PHEME: *We have a second sponsor.*

ERIS: *You can't possibly...*

PHEME: *Unless I did.*

ERIS: *Okay, Nostradumbass, let's see what you've got.*

PHEME: *Today's second sponsor is Normal Dickory's Clockworks Exchange. Does your watch need a new battery? Anniversary clock no longer measuring the passage of the obnoxious human yet inhumane concept of time? Don't bother with fixing that old junk! Come to*

Dickory's and get some new junk! Our junk works and we'll swap your broken junk so we can fix it and pass it off to another glorious patron! When you want to stop looking at that broken piece of crap, bring it to Normal Dickory! No longer accepting cursed items and death clocks.

ERIS: Is that the place over on...

PHEME: Driftwood Parkway, right next to...

ERIS: The Tick-Tock Tinker: Tune-Ups and Troubleshooting for Traditional Timepieces?

PHEME: Oh... you've heard of it.

ERIS: Is this why you've been up my ass about getting my watch fixed?

PHEME: Timing is everything.

I woke before the crack of dawn feeling even worse than I expected. Sure, my heart was tender, and every other thought was about Declan and Beaux, but I wanted my grandfather with a pain I couldn't rationalize.

The thought of wallowing in self-pity was attractive, but it would be noticed and attributed to Declan, and something inside me loathed letting that happen. Declan gave up his happiness to try and help me achieve mine when I left, and I tried to give him the same. In my preposterous little heart, I was incapable of dealing with anyone knowing I was eating my heart out over my ex, though I was.

Clue snored gently, her lengthy frame taking up more than half of my bed, her little face more adorable than I realized.

I dressed quietly in the white cotton gown my mother had left on the door. Religious events had specific forms of dress that were universal among witches, and natural fabrics were non-negotiable.

The drape of the gown was pristine, hiding all of the extra weight I carried, and with my hair dried by my sister the night before, I didn't actively dislike what I confronted in the mirror. I'd recognize Declan's mother's handiwork anywhere.

Slivers of light from the rising sun stirred Clue from her sleep and I sat, scratching her awake. She yawned and stretched deep before jumping down and racing around. I shushed her slightly, not wanting to wake up everyone in the house before I had a few minutes to myself. Clue settled and followed me downstairs, and I let her out to eat on the patio while I stepped into the garden.

The first lesson that everyone had always tried to drill into me was that I needed to master was listening to the elements and finding which connection felt strongest. Even small kids start with the first four elements to begin identifying their magic. The problem with being gone for seven years is that you don't feel connected to anything after that. So, I'd go back to basics. Listening to the earth, air, and water. If that didn't work, there was always standing too close to an angry Sunny to see if her fire liked me more.

I tried to clear my mind and think about the early morning sun, the radiant heat, and the warmth above me. I focused on the new spring season and the flowers blooming around me.

The problem with spell crafting is I didn't always know what I was looking for. Things were supposed to happen, supposed to react to my spirit and power, but the sun kept rising, paying no attention to me. Maybe all the sun's magic was dedicated to my sister?

None of my other family had such a dedicated element or any elemental control the way my sister did. Elemental magic was the earliest training because it didn't usually cause a stir. Witches were supposed to be able to draw power directly from the elements, not feed off them like vampires.

I dug my toes into the soft ground and forced my thoughts to the grass and soil beneath me. I thought of the trees and the leaves, all turned toward the sun, basking in the spring rays, waiting for rain. I contemplated life and ages in each bit of soil, the beginning and end of life. I silently called to the spirits, wishing them to communicate, trying to make something happen.

No sun, no soil, nothing but a gentle breeze and the call of a bird I couldn't identify far in the distance. The more I concentrated, the more frustrated I became. The lack of response from the world around me made me feel useless.

Beaux's high cheekbones popped into my mind, and I knew without knowing that she'd never struggled to find her place. She could see patterns in the world few others could find with a million years of study. It was as much earth magic as the seeds of a sunflower or the shell of a nautilus.

Center, deep breath, calm power, and intention, I thought, pushing my rage aside. I brushed my fingers absently over a nearby hydrangea and felt the morning dew's droplets on my hand. I focused on the nearest bloom and tried to bring the drops together, trying to create a small bit of water from a collection of smaller bits. I focused so hard on the hydrangea it almost became burned into my vision. My head was splitting, and no water was moving. I was furious, the world ignoring me, the water, the soil, the sun, all refusing to heed my commands.

"What in the Goddess's name are you doing?!?" I heard my mother yell, but she sounded miles away. I turned, looking away from the shrub, and froze. Trees were bent almost half over, flower petals littered the yard, and my poor baby Clue was gripping the ground with her claws to keep from flying away, her fur fluffier than usual as wild gusts of howling wind battered her and destroyed the yard.

The moment my concentration broke, the wind stopped.

My sheepish instincts crumbled when I saw the disappointment on my mother's face. She stormed past me to the back garden path and found the clearing and the tree wrecked. The floral garlands had been ripped off the branches, decorations mangled, branches scattered across the sacred space. I caught up to her, the chaos spread out before us.

"Momma, I didn't know…" I tried, but she cut me off.

"We can fix it." She tried to smile but exhaustion overtook her face when she pulled out her wand. "Don't worry, your sister and I can fix this. You should go visit your father."

"We won't have much time. Service starts soon," I said. Then I knew. She didn't want me at the church service. She wanted me out of her reach and away from her people. My mother wanted the spectacle daughter to give her a break for the day. I felt the hot burn of tears and fought them back, swallowing hard, and returned to the house to change out of my church clothes.

I grabbed Clue and we left.

The hospital was quiet so early on a holiday. The parking lot was almost empty so I left my car running with the air conditioner on for Clue and promised her I wouldn't take too long.

"Music?" she chirped before I could leave.

"Yeah, you want music? I can put on music." It was nice to feel useful for something.

"Motown?" she asked, panting.

"We can do Motown!" I turned the radio to a station playing The Temptations and ruffled the fur on her head. "I'll be right back, promise."

"Take your time," she replied and howled about her papa being a rolling stone.

My mind was lost, swirling with wind magic, my mother's disappointment, a Motown-loving familiar puppy, Declan and his perfect Beaux, the super couple.

The soft whirring machines that surrounded my father provided a near-fatal ambiance to my afternoon. The tall, broad, thundering man I knew looked frail and old in his bed, plugged into his medical matrix, pasty and chalky with almost no magic luminosity or sparkly cyan aura flowing under his skin. Holding his hand felt sour, sad. When the grief bubbled in my chest, I dug my nails into my palm until the faint burn of oncoming tears faded from my nose.

I couldn't spend time sobbing. That big gray rock was proof I was woefully unprepared for my ascension and eight months would be cutting it close. My grand fallback plan had been Grandpa Ruari. He knew how to explain concepts in a way I could understand. His patience made me feel competent. With him gone, I needed my father. The only way I was getting my father back was to figure out what happened.

I needed to gather my thoughts. Having a familiar who could read my mind had inadvertently made me less inclined to fixate on the problem at hand. This was a perfect time to do just that. I pulled out a pad of paper and a pen. I had no idea what to write down.

~~Dangerous things afoot~~
~~The case of the comatose father~~
<u>What the hellfire happened?</u>
Brimstone - dark magic
Electronic interference
Aden's power is gone
Dead seagull? Poison?
Dad poisoned?
Ask Mom if Sunny cooked recently

> CRYSTAL BALL MADE OF ROCK
> DID PIPPY CURSE ME SO I GET A BROOM (PICK UP MORE ORANGE SLICES)
> WHY DO I NEED A GUARDIAN?
> WHY WOULD THAT GUARDIAN BE A PUPPY?
> COULD IT ALL BE AN ACCIDENT?
> NO, BECAUSE THE BRIMSTONE AND ADEN

The truth was, I had no idea if there was a connection, but I didn't see how there couldn't be. Ruari was dead. My father was in a coma. My brother had no magic. Each one was attacked differently and two were still... they hadn't recovered. I could imagine an accident—but for Aden being stripped of power? There's no force I've ever heard of that could do that and leave the witch alive.

If it wasn't an accident, then it was murder. If murder, who was the target? Was it Grandpa Ruari and my father was a bystander? No. Aden was impacted. Would my father wake up without magic? My mother couldn't feel his magic. Could she feel his magic through the coma if he had it?

> ASK MOM ABOUT DAD'S MAGIC. SAME AS ADEN'S?
> CALL TEDDY (BETTER THAN GOING TO DECLAN)
> LEARN ABOUT YOUR BIRTHRIGHT YOU COMPLETE TOOL.

"Good morning!" Dr. Cabotin made his way into the room, smiling gently at me.

"Good morning," I set down the pad and straightened up in my seat.

"How's our guy today?" The doctor grabbed my dad's chart and wrote quickly, glancing at the machines, translating their information without any emotion on his face from which I could try to discern meaning.

"Unreasonably quiet." I wasn't wrong. My father was not a man of few words.

"That's to be expected. Your mom was here yesterday, and she didn't get anything out of him. He's got a long road, but we're staying positive." Dr. Cabotin looked up at me and winked, bright green eyes crinkling at the corners as he smiled. He was more handsome today than when I first saw him, less stressed, and not as exhausted looking.

"Do you think he's going to be okay?" I choked on the words, the idea of anything else breaking my heart.

"Oh, of course. That's what we do..." He rushed over to my chair and crouched beside me, laying his hand over mine and my father's. "We make people better. I'm going to make sure he gets better."

I couldn't help myself and hugged him, embarrassed to be pouring emotions over a stranger's shoulder.

He didn't pull away but slipped an arm around me and stroked my hair, shushing me. "You have to be strong. Being here with him is good. It helps. We're going to do everything we can."

I wanted to believe him. I wanted my heart to stop breaking and my father to be well. "It's nice to know there's something I can do to be useful." I snorted, trying to make light of his words, but honestly, my whole body felt better when the doctor told me I was of some use.

"What are you drawing?" Dr. Cabotin pointed to the pad in my hand. "Is that just... filigree?"

"Oh, yeah, um, I was doodling. I was going to write him a letter, but the words didn't come." I'd completely forgotten I'd been making my list in witch writing, Lineara, an ancient alphabet that looks to non-witches like filigree. I tore off the top sheet and crumpled it before stuffing it in my pocket.

"Letters help! Having his family visit, talking to him, reading to him, anything like that really will help. You know, if you want to help on a broader scale, we're always looking for blood and plasma donations and trying to get people signed up to be organ donors." He smiled again and stood, keeping his hand on my shoulder. "Doctors can't do it all by themselves. That's a way everyone can help."

"Anything I can do, Doc." I nodded with a simpered smile. That wouldn't ever happen. If my father and brother suffered from magical maladies—my blood wouldn't help. Sending blood out into the world was asking for trouble in the witch world. Keep your name short and your blood in your body.

"Call me Noah, please." He reached out and I shook his hand. He was warm and soft, immaculately manicured, a dexterity in his fingers belied in his grip.

"Callie, I'm Callie." I silently prayed to the universe he wouldn't ask the inevitable.

"Short for?" He smirked and I could see him trying to guess behind his eyes.

"Calpurnia," I lied before I could stop myself.

"Another bronze age name! I love that," he said, and I nodded. If he wanted to think that was the theme, it was fine by me. Calpurnia made so much more sense than the reality.

"I do prefer just Callie if you don't mind." The last thing I needed was him using my newest pseudonym around my mother and father and finding out how ridiculous I am. It felt good to have someone in town who didn't think I was a catastrophe.

"Callie is a lovely name. It's nice to meet you, Callie." He seemed less assured suddenly, his face more authentic with nothing hiding behind his position.

"It's nice to meet you too, officially. I appreciate you taking care of my dad." I wondered how my father would feel, his life hanging in the balance while non-magical doctors worked tirelessly to return him home after his ordeal.

"He's so strong. I'm sure he'll pull through. I'm truly sorry about your grandfather. Your mother and I talked a bit about him, and he sounds like he was a special man." Noah had a kindness and bedside manner that was severely lacking in most professionals. I understood they saw terrible things and dealt with death and the only way to manage that was to toughen up, but there was a gentleness in him that made me feel safe and free to have feelings in the face of a stranger.

"He was a riot, that's for sure. Always happy and energetic. We used to tease him that whenever he got angry it was like watching a leprechaun go into a rage. It's a terrible loss for my family." I didn't want to think about how much I'd miss him, or how I'd just come back to them and was looking at losing the most important men in my life.

"Can I ask you a question?" Noah set his clipboard back in the bed slot. I nodded and encouraged him to continue, because at this point, what did I have to lose?

"Your mother told me your grandfather put your dad through medical school by selling cookies. Is that true?"

"It's true. I think he ended up selling a few million cookies by the time my dad was done with everything. It took him twelve years and my mom said it almost killed him with exhaustion, but my father really wanted to help people."

"She said Tulane, Feinberg, and then National for his Naturopathic Doctorate, right? That's a combination you don't often hear in medical schools! I'm an UNO / Vanderbilt man myself. I didn't even apply anywhere else because I don't want to deal with the winters." He kept smiling and raked his fingers through sandy blond hair. "Did you ever consider going into medicine?"

I shook my head. "I don't like sick people."

"Well, that *is* a big part of the job." Noah shrugged.

"I never had the calling. I'm still exploring." I tried to be charming, but everything felt hollow.

"Apologies, I thought your mother told me you were a writer." I know he wasn't saying it intentionally, but I heard the echo of the words in my head long after he finished.

"I tried to be, and maybe I was at one point, but now it's a hobby. I don't have a story to write currently. I'm coasting until I find my place."

What was it that made me want to keep talking to him? Granted, he wasn't hard on the eyes, but corn-fed good looks were no excuse for oversharing.

"I don't know much about being a writer, but I do know about finding your place, and for some reason, I think you'll manage." He smiled again as though he was nonplussed at my disregard for my chosen career. "You know, we all have a calling." That phrase shook me out of my doldrums, and I felt better.

"For now, my calling is to hang out with my dad for a while." I felt settled and relaxed. I wanted to thank him for the banal conversation, but that would likely break my bliss.

"I'm finished with rounds at eleven; I'll swing back by and check on him before then. Enjoy your hang out." He left and again I was alone with the beeps and whirs of the machines strapping my father to the bed. It was a soft, melodic white noise that sounded like the sea lapping at the shore as if the world was following the rhythm inside a rhythm.

When I left him with a kiss on his forehead, I made my way back to the parking lot. The music was playing at a much higher decibel than I set it. I raced over and froze.

If you've never heard an oversized puppy singing Otis Redding at the top of her lungs, you haven't lived. Clue was having the time of her life, rolling on my seats, chewing on her leash, and going ham on the music, her singing a distinct howl around the words. She swayed and pawed the air, dramatic and adorable.

"I'm going to need a car camera for you, huh?" I slid into the cool car and turned down the radio. Clue jumped into my lap and nuzzled at my face.

"Chicken livers?" she asked, licking my face.

"I taste like chicken livers?" Maybe I was going deaf from the wind earlier.

"Chicken livers for me!" she chirped. *"I protected the car and for my reward, I would like chicken livers."*

"Well, I certainly can't argue with that. Let's try and find you some chicken livers." I pulled out of the parking lot to go on our first apparent quest. "I'm a little surprised you don't eat wolfsbane or mandrakes."

"*I can't grow up big and strong eating flowers alone, Callie,*" Clue said.

Chapter Eight

Where I really try to get it together...

PHEME: *Overwhelmingly our listeners want to talk about the rumor coming from last night's memorial for Ruari Aigean.*

ERIS: *From the moment witches left Dolphin House, I've been hearing about a lot of rumors...*

PHEME: *There could be an engagement on the horizon!*

ERIS: *There could also be a scandal on the horizon.*

PHEME: *True love doesn't care about scandal...*

ERIS: *But I care about scandal! We have a familiar in our midst! Hot on the heels of our last broadcast, Blue Crab Bay is now home to a rambunctious puppy. Like most fortune, the familiar seems to have landed herself at Dolphin House, where it will most likely be pampered and adored.*

PHEME: *You say that like it's a bad thing! We just talked about this and now we can actually interact with a familiar and give our listeners our opinions! This is primary witchery at its finest!*

ERIS: *There was a time when familiars were common, and now witches have outgrown the need, I'm sure. Have you ever known any witch to have a familiar if she didn't need some help in the spellcasting department?*

PHEME: *Neither of us has ever known anyone with a familiar! That's the point!*

ERIS: *I hear stuff!*

PHEME: *Did you just say, "I am horrible"?*

ERIS: *I said I hear stuff.*

PHEME: *I'm pretty sure you said horrible.*

ERIS: *No, I just said I hear stuff.*

PHEME: *What?*

ERIS: *I said I hear stuff.*

PHEME: *What?*

ERIS: *I SAID I HEAR STUFF!*

PHEME: *What?*

ERIS: *You're a juvenile. You hear me. You're a juvenile. Fine, I don't personally know anyone with a familiar, okay? But when I'm proven right, I'm coming over there and punching you right in your mouth. Go blow it out your cauldron!*

PHEME: *Perfect transition! Listeners, do you need a new cauldron? Can't afford precious metals but want to avoid the magical metallic tang of plain old iron? Try Malarkey's Mystery Metals! Each new cauldron comes with a free trial of pseudo-soulfire! When you can't conjure your own heat, try pseudo-soulfire! Might save your life, might melt your knife! Only at Malarkey's!*

When I finally arrived back home, the last of the cars were making their way out of the driveway, leaving my family alone in the house. My mother sat on the front porch, waiting for me.

"You have to put in the work." She didn't look at me.

"That's what I was trying to do." I sagged against the pillar at the edge of the stairs.

"Callie, you can't ignore magic, mock it in disbelief for years, and then expect to be able to work it the moment you get home." She rolled her eyes at me.

"You told me to start with the elements. I was trying to connect with the Source, but I didn't feel anything, so I tried to connect with the ground and then water, and nothing would happen, so I got frustrated."

"I told you that when you were *sixteen*! If you would have listened, it wouldn't have destroyed our property. You've let the muscle atrophy. You need to learn to focus. Can you learn to focus?" She was more furious than I expected. I must have done more damage than I assumed.

"I was trying that on the patio earlier..." I tried but she snapped her fingers, and my voice failed. Mommy magic.

"Focus!" she barked.

I took a deep breath and envisioned a warm orb of opalescent light, all of the love and experience of lifetimes lived, and love shared. I thought about the breeze and tried to bring it around myself again, but my mother stopped me.

"No. Just focus."

I was getting exhausted trying to block out the world. My feelings were hurt, my heart was cracked, my father hanging in the balance, and the key was focusing, and focusing felt impossible. The longer I spent staring at the imaginary ball of swirling light, the more I noticed the colors start to separate, blend, and twirl around each other. It was a myriad of impossibly thin strands of brilliant pastels, warm and languid and interacting in a fluid dance.

My hands grew warm and the stress and shame I'd been carrying slowly lifted off my shoulders. Petty though the comparison might be, the clarity of the strands continued to develop like I was staring at a puzzle that only made sense when you relaxed your eyes, and they crossed. The closer I looked, the clearer the strands became, and I realized they were less gathered around the light as they were radiating the light as one.

"Now, open your eyes but don't lose focus." My mother's voice was impossibly soft, a whisper guiding me.

I slowly opened my eyes, still concentrating, and could see the strands of color over the world around me. Thunder pounded in my ears as I struggled to comprehend the minute connections between everything. The energy passed between every blade of grass, between my mother and me, mesmerizing me.

I could see the foundation of the Source and the vast connections in the world. The moment it dawned on me I could see it; the vision pushed me out as though I realized I dreamt within a dream.

I couldn't hold it, and the colors faded from my vision.

"That's what you need to master." My mom leaned forward and handed me an icy glass of water. "We're going to do a crash course. Starting Monday, you'll visit your father in the mornings and then meet me at the store. We'll practice and I'll go see him in the evening while you study. Tomorrow, you're going to the cages. No spectacle, no running out in disgrace. You're going to go, find your wand, and come home without incident. You will not be the first witch in this line to fail!"

Terror rose in my stomach. Nothing about her countenance suggested she was being hyperbolic. Deadly serious was the description that came to mind.

"Momma, I'm not going to fail you..." I tried to smile charmingly but probably looked like I had a sharp fart coming.

"You do the work, and you'll ascend. You listen, you follow instructions, and you put in the work, and you'll get there. Or die trying," she promised.

I nodded in agreement and realized I couldn't talk myself out of the work I needed to do.

"It's still early, Callie. I think it would be a good idea for you to have some mimosa tea," my mother said, leading me into the house.

"Even with all the drama I've created?" I was a little surprised at her suggestion. Mimosa tea was strong magic that I'd never even tried to use. If my memory served, it could make a witch incredibly sick if brewed incorrectly and even brewed correctly, the magic was strong and psychedelic in nature, providing visions, dreams, connections with the Source, and messages. Traditionally, mimosa tea wasn't taken until right before the witch made her ascension.

"Callie, I can think of a million reasons you shouldn't have mimosa tea. But you need a long conversation with the Source. You need a connection and inspiration to give yourself over to the magic, and nothing can do that faster than mimosa tea." My mother grabbed the kettle while I gave Clue fresh water.

The kettle whistled high and shrill before she reached the table. I wondered if I'd ever gain control over my magic the way she had it. She poured the hot water into my cup and let it sit a second while she summoned a small crystal vial out of thin air, probably because she kept the mimosa tea hidden from the family lest we all decide to spend our lives day-tripping. She sprinkled a pinch of tea in my cup and added a lemon wedge, a little honey to mask the bitterness, and it was ready.

"Drink up, sweetie." My mother handed me the cup and went to the large armoire next to the cellar door and grabbed a rosewood box. She brought it back to the table and opened it. She had an old-fashioned cassette Walkman, a sleep mask, and a large amulet known as the Dragon's Cross. It was a large square diamond for spiritual clarity, dispersing energy and providing an anchor during star walks. It was surrounded on each side by square labradorite which deeply amplified spiritual messages and psychic abilities. The size and weight of the amulet would prevent my soul from astral projecting as the tea could make me confused about whether I was seeing visions or reality—witches could get lost if that happened.

I slurped the sour liquid and clicked my tongue at Clue so she would follow me to the yard.

"Your momma left you a surprise for your experience," Clue chirped as we made our way through the stone gate and toward the oak tree.

"Do you know anything about what I can expect from this?" I had a vivid imagination and worried that losing control would horrify me by bringing my worst nightmares to life.

"Nope, but don't be scared. I'm here to protect you."

The surprise was beautiful. My mother had left a hammock in the branches of the oak tree, swaying in the breeze. She knew that being outside when the tea kicked in would enhance my experience and comfort would relax me. I slipped the amulet around my neck and climbed into the hammock, careful to keep from flipping over onto the ground.

I gazed up toward the leaves and put the earphones over my head. A slow hum buzzed in my right ear, its echo in my left, switching back and forth slowly until it matched my breathing precisely. Once I was breathing in proper time, I could no longer discern the change in which ear could hear what, and the sound, a soft, gentle tone that ebbed and flowed like the sound of the universe being uncovered.

The leaves shimmered in the sun, the dappled light falling across the trunk as the breeze shook the branches. Something was fascinating about the way the wind swept around me. I could feel every separate and individual hair on my body blowing in the breeze and soon they too moved in time with my breathing and binaural music. The bark on the tree wiggled slightly, the light moving between the leaves making it look like faces were watching me. Gentle, ancient figures in the tree were welcoming me to their presence, kindly changing from one form to another.

Faces gave way to wood sprites, nymphs, fairies, and gnomes running across the trunk, up into the branches, and disappearing as soon as I could notice them. Their laughter tinkled in my heart, their spirits completely in the moment, thanking the Source for the blessing of a perfect day, for their joy, the bounty of the tree, and their loving community.

The sight of so many different natures living in harmony pricked my heart. Witches worked so hard to live at peace with mankind—what if we could all connect the way the mysteries lived in this tree?

The longer I stared, the sadder it made me feel, a whole world of joy I'd never been able to experience, both real and unreal at the same time. A tear slipped out of my eye; I was so full of longing that it overflowed out of me.

I slipped off the headphones and put the sleep mask on my face, ready to look inward and see what my cracked mind would show me if I wasn't distracted. I returned the headphones and drifted into the darkness.

It's hard to describe the darkness when it isn't exactly dark, but blackness filled with shapes and fractals stretched out forever in front of me. It reminded me of the drawings of the universe from physics class, a large grid formation dipping and swirling where planets would settle, space-time floating across huge swaths with swirling black holes appearing and disappearing in my vision.

I felt like I was flying through the cosmos, but it wasn't finished. It looked like a dark sketch before some CGI animation. I could see in every direction. I was there, deep in the abyss, watching the universe move around me, a wisp of space dust, insignificant.

I stood on a platform, looking out over the darkness. Behind me was the warmth of the Source, an infinitely huge, white ball of gleaming opalescent light. That was where my journey began, deep in that light, part of everything, warm and content until I came here, alone, so small and scared of being so alone. I could hear a voice telling me to move forward, but I was frozen.

"Agrippa?" I asked the voice that directed me. "I'm supposed to go to Agrippa?"

"Move forward," the voice confirmed. I didn't hear a yes, but I knew it was sending me to the right place. I've never been more worried about making a mistake. I stepped forward and found myself perched on a ledge, the deep abyss swirling around me, whirlpools opening and closing as they passed.

"Continue," the voice commanded, and I confirmed again.

"Agrippa?" I couldn't move until I knew.

"Continue." The voice was calm and gentle, but insistent. I tried to step forward and couldn't move. "Think your way in," the voice advised.

I didn't know what that meant. Think my way into what? The whirlpool opening?

That one, I thought, and suddenly I was in the whirlpool, sliding through the fabric of the universe, surrounded by blackness. The tunnel got tighter and tighter as I moved through, and I wasn't moving of my own volition as much as I was thinking about continuing forward and the tunnel opened and closed to push me through like I was being digested.

"This one is for Agrippa. I'm supposed to go to Agrippa," I confirmed again, worried I'd chosen the wrong passage.

"Continue," the voice said quietly. I could feel it giving commands to others, communicating and directing those who came after me.

The sound was garbled, growing softer and softer until all that remained was darkness and silence.

"Agrippa?" I tried again but heard nothing.

I briefly panicked, feeling alone and lost. I couldn't go back because the tunnel was closing as I moved closer and closer to whatever ending awaited me. I tried confirming again and again but the silence was all around me.

The tunnel ended in a small space where I could barely fit, pushed against a flexible wall that had a soft green hue in the center but darkened to black nearer the edges. I couldn't remember how long I waited, slightly irritated I was waiting for her, for someone else to be ready, nothing but this soft space to occupy me. Ever so slowly the green membrane got lighter, brighter, turning orange and then peach as the light grew around me.

I knew instinctively I was going to be born. I didn't remember my father or any other person; there was nobody but Agrippa, the one who called for me. I knew her intrinsically, understanding that my journey from the Source was for her, to be her daughter above all things.

This was where I came to be. This was how life began. I heard a voice deep in my heart, "You shall not be afraid. You were born to do this."

I sat up with a start, pulling the blindfold off my eyes, shocked at the darkness around me, the Walkman long since finished with the soundtrack of my star walk. I could hear Clue snoring like a freight train next to me, her belly up, legs spread toward the moon.

The laughter came over me like a tidal wave, relief exploding from my heart as I realized I was back in the hammock and safe. It felt so real, like I was watching a memory instead of having a dream. Was it a dream? It felt like I was awake, watching, but knowing it had already happened.

I laughed so hard I woke Clue who snorted and jumped to her feet. "*Star-spangled Ding Dongs!*"

"What?" I laughed even harder, unable to stop until my stomach hurt.

"*Squirrel dreams, nothing new.*" She stretched deep and yawned, shaking herself awake.

"I saw my birth journey, from the Source to the womb," I explained as I gathered up the Walkman and sleep mask, heading back to the house.

"*You kept repeating your momma's name,*" Clue told me.

"Yeah, it was like she was the reason I was being born. I felt like I had to make sure I was going to her, that it was all about her." The vision was still so bright in my mind, wanting to talk about it so it didn't fade. "How long was I out?"

"*About five hours. I was wondering if we were going to sleep outside.*"

"I wouldn't make you sleep outside!" I promised my familiar.

"*I wasn't sleeping. I had to get rid of that seagull and I found a turtle that got trapped behind the rocks close to the pond.*"

"Ugh, how bad was the seagull? Wait, did you have to get rid of the seagull to eat the turtle?" I wasn't sure what all Clue would consume if given the chance.

"*No, the turtle is my friend and the seagull came out like a sad gray mist that became a patch of carnations, over there.*"

Clue nodded with her head, and I followed over to a rather dense patch of carnations that looked lavender in the evening light.

"I don't think I've ever seen gray carnations."

"You should probably get used to it since I'm going to be eating a lot of seagulls around here. They can be bullies and Ellerie said he was picked up from the river and they tried to drop him on the rocks. That's why I told him he could live here at the pond. I'll keep him safe from seagulls." Clue stopped and stretched back on her haunches, pulling her front legs out and sliding them to her body. Her claws left deep scratches in the grass—scratches that soon filled in with thick, ultraviolet geraniums.

"Those are a choice?" It hadn't occurred to me Clue could choose how her magic manifested.

"How'd you figure it out?" she panted at me.

"Turtles eat geraniums. You should have stuck with roses if you wanted to fool me."

"They eat roses, too."

"There are roses everywhere. They wouldn't have stuck out as much." I don't know why I guessed she was in control of her magic. Something in the geraniums just made it clear.

"Maybe you're just getting in better touch with your magic?" Clue offered.

"If that's true, I'm sure it's thanks to you, Clue." Everything about her made me feel better.

As I pulled open the back door I briefly wondered if Clue gave the turtle the name Ellerie or if it came with a name the way Clue did?

Inside the house, my sister and brother were sitting at the kitchen table, poring over small charms that were no bigger than my thumbnail. They were surrounded by tall, corked bottles full of flowers, purple-swirled fluorite crystals, and shimmering with liquid. A seemingly empty jar was sealed alongside them, and I glanced at the yellowed, handwritten label.

"Butterfly wind," Aden said. Advanced magic for anxiety and panic. The charms would be enchanted and sold as a child's toy, something the kids could fiddle with to rid themselves of excess energy.

"How do you get that out of the jar without losing it?" I imagined the wind would spill out everywhere when the jar was opened.

My sister grabbed the jar and waved me over to her side. She pointed at the jar, and I saw wisps of orange smoke swirling around the top of the lid. She turned the jar upside down and the wisps flew upward to the top of the jar, still swirling. Sunshine unscrewed the lid and gently set it down. She picked up her wand and reached it up into the upside-down jar. A wisp swirled down and attached to the tip of the wand and clung tightly while Sunny pulled the wand back out. She set the jar back on the cap and uncorked one of the bottles and repeated the process in reverse, recorking it with a hardy shake.

"Clever. Where's Mom?" I asked.

"She's in the cellar working on cauldrons." Aden pointed to the door, which was cracked open, revealing the old wooden stairs.

"Did you go star-walking?" Sunny asked, pointing at the amulet I still wore.

I nodded yes and moved toward the cellar. "I'll tell you about it after I talk to Mom. I wanna get her opinion," I admitted. I slipped down the stairs and announced myself.

The cellar was a solid stone room, the floor an ancient altar long sunk beneath the earth and carved by magic where the water made digging impossible. Many witches in the area had constructed subterranean areas and safe rooms. Our cellar was ancient when time was small, and when the stone room was uncovered during the building of Dolphin House, it was taken as a sign from the Source that witches should make our home here. Functioning as a mix of a workshop and a laboratory, it was my mother's domain. Long wooden tables were covered in candles and dry herb bundles. Parchment was strewn around, some piles a foot high. In the center of the room was my family cauldron, passed down through the generations, solid tungsten, two inches thick, and weighing a trillion pounds. It was the largest on the coast, over five feet across at the rim and four feet tall holding almost six hundred gallons when full. Incidentally, it could also fit five children playing hide and go seek, not that I would admit to anything.

"How was your journey?" my mother asked, looking up from her soldering iron. She was fixing problem areas in a small three-gallon cauldron that had a front plaque reading *Merriweather*, letting me know it belonged to Declan's mother.

"I saw my birth. I saw myself leave the Source and travel through space and time to my body," I explained, but she didn't look up.

"As long as it was good, pleasant, peaceful, and you're feeling better, that's all I need to know. The less you tell me, the more of the story you have to decipher without my input or influence. But I am really happy it was positive." She kept working on the cauldron, softly chanting magic back into every patch.

"What did Merriweather do to that cauldron?" I asked. It took some intention to crack an ancient titanium cauldron.

"She was responsible for the fireworks during our Lunar New Year celebration. The vessel was too small for the spell she cast. She tried to get a dozen eighteen-foot-long dragons and forty ten-foot-tall lions out of this." My mom was snickering at the memory. "I should say, she managed to get them out, but she couldn't get them back in and they ransacked the town for hours until we had to bind them and force them back in, which cracked her cauldron."

"That sounds exciting," I murmured. Lunar New Year was one of my favorite celebrations, because of the huge fireworks and street celebrations.

"It was terrifying. We had fire monsters running wild in the streets, chasing people down, and dashing up the sides of buildings. We tried to drive them into the Bay, but it didn't stop them. We finally had to use the double binding and cast that my mother says is only for demons." My mom looked up, laughing at the memory. "We cleaned scorch marks off the streets and buildings for a month. I told her to get rid of this thing, but it was her first cooker, and she won't hear of it, so here I am." My mom stretched up, rolling her neck and shoulders to loosen up after sitting hunched over for so long.

"Can I have a cauldron?" I asked, eyeing the few she had on a shelf. Most were either copper or silver, with one that looked like pink marble holding potions and scrolls.

"I'm all out of size two in pewter," my mother teased. "But when it's time for cauldron work, I'm sure we'll find something for you to use to raise a little hell and blow some stuff up. Sadly, today isn't that day. Come kiss me and get some sleep. You've got a big day ahead of you."

I kissed her on the forehead and took off the amulet, setting it next to her. She waved her hand over it, making it disappear as it returned to the box whence it came.

"Is it going to hurt?" I asked before heading back upstairs. She whispered only loud enough for me to hear.

"Only if you're doing it right."

Chapter Nine

"There's gonna be a montage..."

PHEME: *Let's start with an easy topic today, Eris. Language is the great unifier. Why do witches have their own language apart from their communities?*

ERIS: *Every single society that has ever existed has had a language. Why shouldn't we have one?*

PHEME: *It's not about should, but language develops as children develop—Lineara is not like that. It's inherent knowledge. We learn to speak but we know the words inside of us.*

ERIS: *It's the benefit of being born into the magic that we don't have to learn to communicate safely.*

PHEME: *So how do we develop that knowledge? Does it manifest with our magic?*

ERIS: *Kids have command without magical manifestation. I think it's in our blood.*

PHEME: *I have to disagree. If a witch is stripped of magic, they're stripped of the ability to read our language.*

ERIS: *If someone is stripped of magic, they shouldn't be able to read our language.*

PHEME: *What if they're stripped by accident?*

ERIS: *How, in the name of the Source, can someone's magic be stripped by accident? It takes twelve witches working in conjunction to pass that sentence.*

PHEME: *Surely, you've heard about a witch who lost magic...*

ERIS: *I believe that will prove to be temporary. Temporary displacement of magic is very different from a ritual stripping.*

PHEME: *You seem to be more mindful of your words today, Eris. Have you taken the listeners' feedback to heart?*

ERIS: *I have not. I refuse to give you a comment you can use as a segue into some trashy commercial.*

PHEME: *Speaking of segues! This episode is brought to you by Cloud & Company Water Storage! Summer is coming and Cloud & Co. has all your water storage needs. From full-acre storms in a blanket stratus to square-meter sections of cumulus, you never have to worry about overwatering or underwatering again. Stitched cloud quilts are sewn to your specifications, so each section of the garden gets the exact rain it needs all season long. From the company that brought you the biggest hit of April Fool's Day—the Sadboy Single Storm. When you want to send a storm cloud to a sad boy to follow him all afternoon, Cloud & Co. delivers.*

ERIS: *Okay, that is a bit of a stretch on the connection there. I didn't exactly link you back to the commercial with the word segue. Segue isn't part of the cloud storage.*

PHEME: *Remember when you went on that Segway tour in the French Quarter, and it poured down rain on you the entire time?*

ERIS: *STOP TALKING!*

PHEME: *Cloud & Company Water Storage! They're not only our sponsor, they're also my supplier!*

I didn't get too far into my journey before I lost my temper with the difficulty of relearning magic and grew three-inch-long black claws.

I stood, moderately crouched over a pentagram, sweat pouring down my body on a muggy, overcast day. Around me, batting cage after batting cage after batting cage, all full of witches younger and yet more magically advanced. Loud, distinctive cracks rang out around me like rifle shots followed by a thump and sliding noise that sounded both wet and gritty. The cracks had no timing synchronicity; several would come quickly on top of each other followed by silence for long seconds as they ramped up.

To connect with the wand inside the wood, a witch forced all of her magic, all of her will, and all of her strength directly into the bat just before it connected with the ball. If the magic matched the wand, the bat would shatter, spraying sea glass in all directions as the wand sat in the hand of the witch. If the magic didn't match the wand, it was forced back up the arms in a rage of fire and electricity to be repeated until successful. At least, that's how it felt. There was a strong possibility that there was no pain, and I was being a drama queen.

The only solace I had was when I heard the shatter of glass, the peal of laughter, and the cheer of families as the cages finally bestowed a witch their wand. It would be worth it. As far as I knew, no witch ever died in the cages—but if I was the first, it wouldn't have surprised me.

I couldn't see the witches in the cages to my left and right as thick, black metal slats were woven between the fencing to allow privacy. I wasn't even sure they were experiencing the same torture as me—and for their sakes, I hoped it was easier for the young ones.

"I can't go again. My arm is going to break. Momma, I cannot..." I begged but she laughed, a reedy screech that lingered over the top of my sister's guffaws. Screaming, blinding pain shot from my elbow to my shoulder in both arms as I rested them on my knees, resting my thighs against my calves to take the pressure off my muscles.

"Another one, please!" my mom called to my sister, ignoring my pain.

"How many even is that? Seventy-five? Eighty?" I stood to meet Sunshine eye to eye, abhorring the feeling of someone looming over me.

"*Six, Callie,*" Clue chirped in my head.

"It took me almost twenty whacks to find my wand, Callie. Keep swinging," my sister said. She handed me another bat and backed off toward the fence, slightly behind me so if I went wild, she'd avoid taking the softball my mom had in her hands to her face.

My mother wound it up and beamed a softball straight into the bat I was holding, the collision again jolting my shoulder painfully. The softball plunked off the edge of the bat and fell to the ground weakly. I was way too old for this shit. We had to direct all of our power into that swing, but no matter how hard we hit, if the magic wasn't a match, the ball just flopped, all of the magical intention sent with the softball released back into the witch's body.

"No on the holly, Ma!" Sunny called and handed me another bat as I dropped the most recent into a return bin at the back.

"Try the mahogany!" my mother called back toward us. She bounced slightly on her toes and rolled her shoulders.

Sunny tossed me another bat and I took another swing, felt another jolt, and this time actually cried out in pain. My mother threw softballs like guided missiles like she figured she could help me find my wand by applying the pressure herself with the ball instead of relying on me with the bat. She probably wasn't wrong, and I could use all the help I could get, but damned if it didn't jolt me into uncomfortable awareness with every pitch.

I tried bunting with the mahogany. My mother threw the ball with everything she had and I, in my great wisdom, grabbed the bat with both hands, held it in front of my face, and then stepped in front of the ball.

I did not bunt.

I took a fastball to the bat to my face and looked up from the flat of my back, my vision wet from tears streaming down my cheeks, a lump forming on my forehead, right in the center like a majestic unicorn of stupidity.

"No on the mahogany!" Sunshine called to our mother and stepped over me to hoist me back to my feet.

"I cannot. Sun, I'll finish later. That really rang my bell," I tried.

"You have to break the bat, Callie. Until you do, it's just going to get worse. Don't step in front of the ball. She can't walk you—this isn't a game. She's going to keep shotgunning hummers until you find a wand, so get over it and don't fart around on the ground." My sister handed me another bat and cleared the way.

"When I was your age, we had to throw our own softballs!" my mom taunted.

"Yeah, yeah, uphill, both ways?" I made a face and returned to my stance over the witches' pentagonal approximation of home base.

"In Allegra's day, they hit them with the boards..." Sunny reminded me.

"Technically, they broke them over their knees, settle down." I swung, failed, and flung the bat away.

"In Allegra's day..." My mom yelled since she didn't hear Sunny.

"Probably the only time besides Mom that the old witch got any wood," I murmured and stretched my neck, willing the next swing to be my last.

Poplar, oak, cedar, hickory, rosewood, cherry, apple, and pine all failed to produce any results. Pitch after pitch rang against my aching shoulders, lightning pain spreading to my wrists and fingers.

"Hawthorn's up next!" Sunshine called to our mother. Our father's wand was hawthorn. Perhaps there was a connection between us I'd failed to consider. Maybe our wands were linked, my magic green in the way his had always been.

What if I was getting a hawthorn wand because he wasn't going to make it?

Sweat poured off my upper lip, my hands inflamed and shredded from the wood. This was it. I was going to get a sign. What if our wands were twins? I couldn't remember if that was a thing, but why not? Maybe I could save him with a wand like his? Maybe I could look into his wand? Could I see who attacked my family? Or could I see what my father might need to recover from his coma?

I was so ready. My mother wound up and pitched and I was ready. I swung from the depths of my soul, hawthorn in my heart, heroism on my horizon.

The ball flopped off the bat as though I barely swung but the pain lit me up in neon colors, and I would have bet my car that my entire arm fell out of the socket, hit the ground, and rolled away.

I was not so lucky. Nobody even cared. Sunny was watching me suffer and just kept handing me bats, calling out woods, cracking wise with my mother. It'd been so easy for her. So easy for everyone else to get it right.

I snatched the bat Sunny offered and ignored her. I was going to swing myself into exhaustion before I strangled my family. They wouldn't be having nearly as good of a time if I ignored the ball and swung at their ignorant faces, would they? Foolish Callie. Silly Callie. Slow Callie. Irresponsible Callie. Unsportsmanlike Callie. Unathletic Callie.

Fat Callie!

I never even felt the impact. Never heard the crack. When the bat touched the ball they shattered against each other, the bat exploding around me. The pieces hung in the air and hovered before crashing, evaporating, and then disappearing. A plain wooden wand now clutched in my hands where the bat had been.

"Birch?" I asked, breathless.

"Magnolia," Sunny confirmed. "Learning from the past, finding your true self, and easing restlessness. Sounds about right."

My new wand looked like every other wand. I'd need to roll it back and forth between my hands, despite them being bloody and split, because that's how the bond formed. My blood, my sweat, her resin, her splinters, mixing, transferring, bonding. Later, I'd have to paint it, sealing it in with lacquer. I felt a warm comfort that was familiar to my hands, the same way it felt when I picked up a pen. It was slender, long, thin, sort of a pencil without grooves or ridges.

Each time I gripped the wand and rolled it between my palms, the pain receded, bleeding into the wood. Instead of aggravating the wounds, it was healing them quickly.

"Magnolia," my mother said, approaching us. "That's a solid gift, Callie." She slipped her arm around my shoulders, and I realized all the pain was gone.

There was no soreness. No ache making my muscles stiff or weak. I was actually invigorated. It was still early in the day, I had a wand, and only one question of note.

"Is Magnolia like…" I worried, but my mom kissed my temple.

"No, Callie, it's not the gray rock of wand woods. That would be petrified wood. Plenty of incredible witches have Magnolia wands. And none of the legends call them out in any way that's critical to the witch, so rest easy."

"See, Callie! You can't even manage to be the worst witch properly!" Sunny teased and yelped when Clue bit her right on the ass cheek. It wasn't enough to break the skin, but it was enough to know I needed to talk to my dear familiar about sibling ribaldry.

The three of us spilled out of the gates to the cages, passing families of witches needing wands and non-witches looking for actual batting practice. Set on the massive grounds of Harkness Park, a community recreation center that boasted baseball fields, tracks, swimming facilities, and both the batting cages and a broom track, it was positively thrumming with people in spring.

The early afternoon was considerably brighter than the morning, a bonus because it dried up some of the swelter, but also hotter as the sun warmed the grass. Walking across the field, I felt the heat emanating from the wet ground. Huge puddles in the park from the morning storms played host to dozens of kids dressed in their early summer play clothes but wearing oversized cartoonish rain boots. Squeals peeled from the groups as kids as they took running starts and splashed cannonballs of water onto their giggling friends.

The parking lot was packed, almost every space filled with cars or people standing around, talking, organizing kids, carriers and caddies, and teenagers hanging out in sporadic handfuls. My sister ducked down, as we passed a small family, stealing a kiss on the forehead of a bespectacled girl with a high ponytail and striped knee socks.

"Miss Sunny! We're playing soccer in the park!" The little one ran after us and pulled on my sister's shirt.

"Are you?" My sister scooped up the child and returned her back to her parents.

They wore the exhausted faces of two people who had a kid with more energy than they could imagine. Chattering with the child, my sister set her on the ground with a calm promise to see her at school.

"Do they just run you down everywhere you go?" I asked.

"They can smell me. They come out of nowhere. I can't wear skirts because I'm scared they'll pull them off in an attempt to get my attention."

"How do you get away from that?" I looked around the lot, noticing various little kids were standing around, practically breaking their wrists to wave at us.

"Direct attention. Pick them up, let them speak, listen, respond, and return to sender." My sister shrugged. "They just want to be heard, Callie."

Don't we all.

"There's a body! She's dead! Someone call 911!" A voice broke through the hum of families chattering in the parking lot. As the screaming erupted, the crowd fell silent for a single second before all hellfire broke loose. Children cried in fear, parents rushed across the lawn, and teens scattered in droves. Everyone tried to get somewhere different at the exact same moment. Bodies crashed together, non-witches fell to the ground, and my mother grabbed my upper arm so hard I cried out.

I never heard my voice leave my chest. The grip my mother had on my arm spread across my body and my vision went black as midnight. Every molecule of my being was compressed, a feeling of spaghettification mixed with suffocation threatened to start a panic in my chest.

The moment I realized I was dying, the sensation stopped instantly. My breath came back, my vision brightened, and the three of us now stood inside the park district building. We'd gotten here through some magic of my mother's I'd never experienced. Water poured from the faucets on the walls. Despite there being nobody in the pool showers, the water streamed full blast, pooling around our feet, and a familiar floral aroma leaned heavily on my senses.

"Sunny, go divert everyone from coming in here!" My mother pointed at the doors behind us before she scurried to the corner and hunched over a gray lump I didn't see at first.

"Did we teleport?" I spun around in a gentle circle, taking in the room. I'd never seen any witch move like that, let alone take two others with her.

"No, I panicked, I don't know. Callie, come help me!" My mother sat on the wet shower floor, pulling the gray lump into her lap.

I hurried, sliding across the water, skidding to the side of my mother, overshooting my stopping point, crashing into the tile wall, and coming to rest on my face under an inch of standing water.

"We're too late," she whispered. Her hand rested on my back as I pushed myself to crawl to my knees, my head aching and my bell appropriately rung. I needed to get checked for a concussion soon. I was treating my head like a soccer ball lately.

"What is that?" I pointed at the lump that rested in my mother's arms.

"It's Ginger. She was dead before we got here."

"What happened?" I expected the answer to be she slipped, hit her head, maybe drowned in the minuscule amount of water.

My mother raised a single finger and spun it around in a slow circular motion, intimating the air around us. I remembered the smell.

"Morning glory?"

"Belladonna."

It took hours before we were finished giving our statements and allowed to leave the park since we were the only people who had contact with Ginger after she expired. Teddy showed up with Declan, both of them channeling their shock into perfunctory, businesslike, Dragnet speak.

"And what did you see on your way into the locker room?" Declan asked without meeting my eyes.

"Nothing but blackness. I think my mother teleported us in a panic." I didn't have any reason to lie to him.

"Declan, Teddy said we could take off." My mother approached with her arm protectively around my sister.

"Okay, Mrs. A." Declan stood and hugged her as I gathered my things. "I'll bring Callie back to the store when we're finished taking her statement."

I dropped my stuff and flopped back down into the wooden chair, blowing a hard, exasperated breath up into my forehead to passive-aggressively show my disappointment.

"I'll take the puppy, Callie," my mother said as she scratched the back of Clue's head.

"*Ugh, I'm not a puppy!*" Clue complained as she followed my mom and Sunny out of the building.

"She's awfully young to have an identity crisis," I mused out loud after the door shut.

"I didn't know Ginger was having an identity crisis," Declan said. He leaned forward toward me with renewed interest.

"Oh, no. My familiar, she's... she's on this 'I'm not a puppy' kick. I don't know what she means."

"Maybe it means she's not a puppy?" Declan offered.

I smiled back weakly and with more than a bit of condescension.

"Well, whatever she is, she's not the reason I'm being detained here, is she?" I didn't know why my instinctual response to Declan was always so sharp, but I was exhausted in both body and heart.

"You're not being detained."

I looked around the Park Manager's office, noting the harsh white walls were covered in adolescent graffiti murals. It was cold and the air conditioner was running full blast, fighting the warmth of the late spring afternoon, gaining little ground against the thick beam of sunlight that poured over the desk. Declan and I sat in front of the desk where it was almost icy in the shade.

"Why am I locked in here, then?" I shot at him.

"The door isn't locked, Callie. Stop being dramatic."

"Yes, you do know what the hell I'm talking about!" I snapped. "Why am I still here?"

Reaching into his badge wallet, Declan pulled out a small vial of orange liquid swirled with white that glittered in the bottle. He set it gently on the desk next to us and sat back; his posture was kind, gentle, and very non-threatening.

"Is that re-Dew?" I'd heard about the memory potion, but it was advanced-level spellwork. It was a creamsicle-flavored memory spell that allowed a person to speak freely and have no recollection of it. Invented by the Witch Force to assist with PTSD recollections in soldiers, it was incredibly dangerous to have in a police situation.

"It is," Declan said, softly. "This is a one-time offer."

"What about me makes you think there's a chance in hell I'd want to pour my heart out to you and then forget I did it, Deck?" I was offended at the very thought.

"I'm offering to take it. I'll take it and you can have someone listen without worrying they're going to use it against you." Declan had a point, but still.

"Do you think I have nobody to confide in?" I reached for an arrogant tone but veered into an accusatory one.

"I think... in fact, Callie, I know, you haven't processed your feelings about your grandfather, and you just found a dead body. I know your tendency is to avoid anything that makes you feel even a little vulnerable, and you are loath to allow anyone to know you intimately. But I also know you and you are walking around like a shaken champagne bottle about to explode. If you don't let some of that out, you're going to tear yourself apart. I'm offering you a place to say whatever you want, and I will not take it out of this room. Help me, help you."

I pulled my face together. Erasing the frustration lines on my forehead from whining about being in the office, I grasped at a gentle smile. He'd understand I was okay if I looked magnanimous, charming, and a little indulgent. Pulling my magic to my chest, I leaned forward to place my hand over his, still smiling. In my mind, my countenance was in the process of beautification. Nobody struggling with grief could look as angelic as I did at that moment.

"I really appreciate your offer, but I don't think you know what you're talking about." I squeezed his hand, my inner monologue shouting, *"Look patient, calm, disaffected. No that's entitled, try distracted. Wait that's confused. Smile brightly, stupid, and he'll never know the difference."*

"Callie, can I tell you a secret?" Declan lifted his hand and my own rose with his.

I nodded gently. Every molecule in my body and mind was working with an adverb of gentility floating behind it.

"Resting angel face doesn't work on me." He slid out of the chair, kneeling next to me. Pressing my hand to his heart, his voice dropped so low I had to lean in to hear him.

"You've always thought your face is an enigma, a puzzle, your mask to the world. I don't know if it's because I've spent most of my life mesmerized by it, or if everyone can see you as clearly as I do, but I see the ache in your eyes." He sat up, his face just in front of mine. Swiping his thumb across my jaw, he held my face tight.

Shit.

He had me dead to rights.

"Declan, if you know me that well then you know there's no way I can do that. Not with anyone. Not even you. Not even temporarily."

"Callie…" He took a deep breath, exhausted with my shit.

"But," I put my hand up and stopped him. I wasn't finished. "I'll accept your offer without the spell. I can't have some kind of iocane powder moment where we finish, and you have managed to avoid the spell's intention. I'd rather know you're going to remember it and speak as freely as I can. If that's okay with you." My stomach turned twice, the idea he didn't want to remember the conversation popping into my mind. What if the spell was his way of leaving my baggage behind? Had I just told him I only want his conversation if he has to carry it with him into the future?

He reached for the vial, and I grabbed his wrist.

"Unless the forgetting is a feature and not a bug!"

"Callie," he shifted his hand, so we were holding each other by the forearm. "I just want to give you the safest place to unload that I can."

"Since the moment I got home, the world has proceeded to fall apart around me. I don't know what I'm doing wrong; I want to get my magic together, but every time I get close to it, something happens, and everyone gets hurt. I got my crystal ball and the next day my grandfather was killed, and my father went into a coma. I got my wand and thirty minutes later Ginger Arrietti was dead in a locker room shower. Everywhere I go, pain and death follow. I found out recently that if I fail to ascend then my family, at least the ones older than me, will lose their magic, putting my sister in the sole position to carry on. That, among other unpleasant surprises, has been pretty rough."

"You talk about pain like you're describing it happening to someone else."

"Right now, it feels like the pain happened to someone else. I can't even feel it. My logical brain knows Grandpa Ruari is gone and I should be sad, but I think the tragedy of it, the shock and surprise, just overloaded me and it's too much to take in. My sadness is usually like a pitcher of water, but instead of being poured down my throat, it's just sitting on my head, and I have to balance it every second, so it doesn't spill and drown everyone around me. And, not only that, but I have to be appropriately reverent about Ruari because if everyone around me knew how empty I felt, they'd hate me. Grandpa was the only one who really believed in me. He was the only one who thought I was special and valuable, and he's gone, and I can't even mourn him properly. I can't grieve. I can't even think about it when I'm alone because any examination threatens to drown me in my sadness, so I keep moving and keep moving and just wallow in things that don't matter, like figuring out how to move droplets around on a flower petal. I'm broken Declan."

I gasped for breath after my speech. I had to let it run until it was out. How I could say all of that to Declan shocked me. Maybe, possibly, he was non-threatening because he was no longer an option for me. His engagement to Beaux meant even knowing me intimately wouldn't matter. My mental health garbage wouldn't help or hinder him from being a good husband to her. And because he wouldn't be my husband, I wasn't handing him the keys to manipulate me. I could tell him anything without fear of repercussions or rejection.

"You've spent a long time feeling responsible for the whole world, Callie. It's okay to be overwhelmed," Declan reminded me.

I didn't understand why those words from his mouth made me feel so secure. His voice made me think it was normal to be overwhelmed. His eyes were empathetic and understanding. I felt heard for the first time in far too long.

"Every day there's so much pressure. Did you know they have families attend our ascensions so they can drown us if we fail?" I blurted out.

"What?" Declan shook his head and shivered as though my comment surprised him.

"Yeah, Allegra wants to drown me."

"Your grandmother said she wants to drown you?"

"Well, no. She didn't say it, but she does. Why wouldn't she? I'm a magnet for destruction."

"Callie," Declan chuckled. "When the Source gave you a familiar, nobody died. It's easy to see patterns if you cherry-pick your data. The Source has given you plenty of gifts in your life that didn't come with a catastrophic death attached. *Post hoc, ergo propter hoc*, right?"

Declan's ability to boil my fears down to a single, logical fallacy drove me wild in both the best and worst sense of the phrase. His voice carried the dead language in a visceral and sexually charged way that was entirely made up in my head.

But that didn't mean it didn't exist. Did he speak to Beaux in Latin? Did he threaten he would get his family crest tattooed across his back with the motto "No True Scotsman" every time she doubted her witchcraft?

I chuckled internally at Beaux having a moment of self-doubt—a situation that was indeed happening only in my head.

"It's only weird when it doesn't work, Declan." Just because something fit a logical fallacy didn't mean it wasn't true.

"Did you just counter Aristotle with a beer commercial?"

"I'm under duress, I found a dead body today."

"Callie, you are heartbroken. You can't see it but you're broadcasting loudly that you're in pain. How can I help?"

Something in the way he looked at me, his open kindness, his earnestness, just devastated me all over again. I hated how much I wanted him. Not even knowing he'd moved on was enough to stop me from wishing I could crawl into his lap and sob uncontrollably until I got it all out. How could I tell him my guilt came directly from every emotion in my heart, that the sadness and grief to fear and worry were silenced by the depth of my need for him? I couldn't stop aching for him long enough to even consider crying over my grandfather or Ginger.

"You don't have any Face Up To Your Feelings Fritters in your wallet, do you?" Even I was disappointed I pivoted to humor instead of to honesty. Humor that didn't register with my conversation partner.

"If your feelings aren't coming, don't force them. You have a lot on your plate, and you're allowed to partition things in a way that lets you handle them in your time, Callie. It doesn't have to be organized all at once."

"Exactly!" It was about time someone understood I was emotionally repressed to the point of dysfunction, and it was a good thing.

"But if you are having emotions and feelings and grief about anything, if you're not empty, you should probably talk to someone. Are you having any feelings at all or are you really just empty right now?"

It was a nice try, but there was no way I was going to tell him all of my feelings were about him. I knew he expected me to say something about being home and feeling like I should leave versus being gone and longing for home, but the truth was, the only thought I had was Declan, and until I put that in order, I'd suffer. It was the perfect time to tell him, sort through our bullshit, and move on in a healthy manner.

Somewhere in the back of my brain, there was another Callie, younger, brighter, more settled, and understanding, who screamed at me to tell him. Just get it off my chest. Admit I made more mistakes than choices and beg him to love me again. The voice wanted me to take back everything I'd said when we split and lean in hard to loving the only person on this planet I didn't want to live without.

I could have told him the emptiness came from the hole he left. It was too large to be filled and threatened to swallow me whole every second of my life.

I could have said, "Tao is an empty vessel."

I could have said anything.

I supposed a movie quote would work as a stronger tourniquet to stop the flow of conversation.

"God put that rock there for a purpose, and um, I'm not so sure you should move it."

I don't know if he could see I was cringing, but I could feel the shame tickle down my spine until it made my glutes clench. I wanted to fall through the floor and dissolve in a puddle of acid. While there were moments I wanted to be transparent and vulnerable, they were rapidly followed by the self-loathing that drove me to want to run away from my family.

When I returned to the store that afternoon, my anxiety roiled beneath my skin. I parked in the far corner of the lot, under the shade of a young oak tree, and tried to settle my mind enough to go inside.

Sitting in the shade, drawing in my breath through my nose for eight seconds, letting it flow out of my mouth for ten, focusing on my mantra, I was thrummingly unable to sit still. My right knee bounced with a violent rhythm, and I chewed mercilessly on my inner cheek.

I would come to my senses, stop biting myself, cross my ankles, and start over trying to settle down, but just as soon as I closed my eyes, the shiver returned, and my mantra went from a clear word, designed to reset my meditation, to a chant that drove me toward insanity.

"Things would be better if you left."
"You came home, and everything went wrong."
"Two weeks in Argentina could be enough."

My brain seized on the idea of running and I felt my anxiety melt into excitement. I could just get away for a short time. I could make up some excuse to just slide out of town, gather myself, and come back to set things right, couldn't I?

When I thought about coming back, the anxiety prickles climbed up my spine with fresh and icy-cold claws. The notion of leaving, just fading away into the margins of the world and living like a vagabond, was all that gave me any sense of peace.

"Your momma said no running off in disgrace," Clue said, popping up at my door. She leaned on her front paws, standing next to me, trying to crawl over the door and into the car.

I could hear the claws on her hind legs scratching the paint down my driver's side door as she scurried into my lap. Briefly, I wanted to open the door and save the paint, but I was frozen in stress. A quick vision of my car door opening with my familiar draped over the windowsill like a fuzzy black saddle broke through my horror and I caught myself snickering.

Soon, Clue was standing on my thigh, her front paws on the center console, her tail smacking my face.

"Sweetie, you're hitting me," I tried.

"*Yes, yes I am.*"

"Do you want to go on a trip?"

Clue leaned her head toward the windshield and whimpered. I leaned forward to see what she was whining about, and she crashed her head back, nailing me right in the cheekbone.

"Son of a banshee!"

"*I'm trying to knock some sense into you.*"

"What is that supposed to mean?"

"*If you leave, it will destroy your family.*"

"I'm talking two weeks, Clue. I'll come back and finish my ascension with a clear head and some new perspective." It even sounded weak to me.

"*You won't have a family to come back to.*"

Clue stepped off my lap and settled into the passenger seat, facing me, eyes locked to mine. Her voice echoed in my head.

"I just need to get my head straight."

"*And that's okay, but Callie, you need to know, if you leave this time, you will never come back. There will always be a reason to stay away. Your fear will never subside, the guilt will never let you go, and you* will *become the reason your line crumbles.*"

She sounded older, wiser, and tonally more advanced than the small puppy she appeared.

"I don't know how to live through this," I choked. My tears came fast, blasting out from where I'd been holding them back.

"Yes, you do. You figured it out in Cardiff."

"Why did you say that?" My stomach shivered under her intense gaze.

"You remember what happened in Wales."

I did. But how did she? I had never spoken of it to anyone, ever.

"I can hear your heart, Callie. Each and every time you think about that night, I can feel it."

"I haven't thought about that night in a long time."

"You've thought about it twenty-seven times since you woke up this morning. Yesterday you thought about it two hundred times and even had a dream about it. If you don't realize it, you're fixated on the solution."

"Solution?"

"How would you describe it?"

"Self-torture. It was a sleepless night. It wasn't the first or last."

"It was the night you realized that adventure was a checklist you were forcing yourself to complete so you could go home."

"I needed to experience the world, exhaust my wanderlust, and live my freedom before I came back here and…"

"No. That might have been your outlook in the beginning, but no. You realized it in Cardiff. The voice in your head said, and I quote: 'It's just you here, Callie. There's nobody to convince. There's nobody to impress. Your passion for exploration has deflated to become a thankless task you feel you must complete before you do what you truly want to do and go home.' You were ticking off boxes, desperate

to find places to go, hoping to find anything similar to the joy you felt when you went home. You were longing for the meaning you wanted travel to have, the meaning it had in the beginning. When you lay awake in Cardiff, you realized your life had become a series of passing through places to be able to say you'd seen it because once you saw everything you could go home. What you wanted to see was that Bay, those people in the store, but you put this gigantic mountain between yourself and your own happiness as though you had to earn it through suffering."

"Since the moment I got back, the world has spiraled into a trash tornado! I don't know if anyone is paying attention but there is a clear line of demarcation between everything is fine and everything is on fire. If I'm not here, then I can't screw up everything. I'm a sucking magnet of garbage that forces everyone around me to suffer. I'm cursed."

"Be that as it may, Callie. That's what family is. They're the people you're here to suffer alongside as you experience the universe. This is the setup that Cailleach Aigean has, and aren't you lucky for that?"

"My luck is my family's misfortune."

"Hogwash. I can tell you, unequivocally, that each and every person in your family feels lucky to have you."

"How can you possibly know that?"

"Callie, just the fact you feel fortunate to have them and worry so deeply about disappointing them is proof enough. Loving them so much, worrying about them so intensely, fighting through your fear to come back to them, and every single time you swallow your temper to protect their feelings... Callie. The only thing you don't seem willing to do for them is stay. Commit to being here. Get involved,

make a life with them, and take your place. Your grandfather never asked you for anything except that. Take your place. Own it. Be here now."

I knew better in my heart but my gut reaction to her words was to berate myself for needing the family pet to kick me in the ass. That was how I knew I needed to stop minimizing my love for my family and maybe learn what I could be capable of once I committed to being a part of something bigger than myself.

Chapter Ten

Rusty, razor-wired memories of the way we were...

PHEME: *This week, Blue Crab Bay After Dark has a special surprise for our listeners! We're announcing our first live event!*

ERIS: *Do you ever wonder how much you miss out on each month? Ever think about all the funny jokes we leave on the cutting room floor? Well, wonder no more!*

PHEME: *Join us for our Memorial Day Marathon! We'll be broadcasting live all day long as we celebrate Memorial Day and tell stories and read letters from you! Do you have a favorite holiday?*

ERIS: *We can't wait to hear about your favorite time of year as we celebrate... oh, for keening out loud... this is the worst script I've ever read. Nobody gives a short, sharp shit about favorite holidays!*

PHEME: *Eris! Just read the script! We're giving away a lot of fun sponsor prizes and having some special guests!*

ERIS: *I cannot say the words, 'Imagine being able to talk on the phone with your royal, magical misanthrope.' No matter how true they are.*

PHEME: *But it's the start of summer! This is an important holiday.*

ERIS: *Pheme, cut the shit. We celebrate every holiday. Every faith, every Holy day, every national special time of the year. We go from Commonwealth Day to the Fourth of July to Bastille Day with zero irony.*

PHEME: *You know why we do that?*

ERIS: *Yes, because if we have to support and serve the entire planet then we deserve to celebrate every holiday in existence. We are miserable appropriators.*

PHEME: *Which holiday do you want to give up in protest?*

ERIS: *Why should I give up any holidays?*

PHEME: *You could renounce Christmas and just save the money!*

ERIS: *I love Christmas! Why don't you give up Boxing Day?*

PHEME: *I'm not the one who has an issue with our deep, celebratory nature.*

ERIS: *You know what? That's why. That's why I'm doing the live show with you. I want the audience to hear my great lines; the lines you edit out so you can add them in and steal my sense of humor. Listeners! You're going to learn how you've been manipulated in believing Pheme is the good cop! I'm going to be vindicated!*

PHEME: *Or the whole world will understand the depth and breadth of the mission I'm on to try and present you as palatable to the world, my dear.*

ERIS: *I'm going to start working on my jokes right now.*

PHEME: *We have a few weeks before the live show.*

ERIS: *I need to be ready. Hand me that pen.*

PHEME: *Speaking of pens, our newest sponsor might be able to help you out.*

ERIS: *You're a rat. Did you plan the show for this one sponsor?!*

PHEME: *How many times have you been hard at work on a new spell...?*

ERIS: *Disgusting.*

PHEME: *On a new spell that's too complicated to finish without stopping over and over to write down your steps. Do you worry about the integrity of your spellwork, and the repetition required to improve every day?*

ERIS: *A sad sell-out...*

PHEME: *Try Grippy!*

ERIS: *Oh, that's clever!*

PHEME: *Are you trying to cast a complex spell? Do you need a buddy by your side to keep up with counts?*

ERIS: *I see you're trying to cast boils on your lying spouse again! Would you like some help with that?*

PHEME: *Grippy is the first wand cozy that helps you relax your grip and keeps a running tally of the spellwork when you need a helping hand! Available in twenty-four colors and twelve patterns—*

ERIS: *Is one of those patterns a set of googly-eyed, anthropomorphized paper clips?*

PHEME: *—for a fully customizable magical experience.*

ERIS: *Don't forget to join us on our live show where I make Pheme eat her own sellout words!*

PHEME: *Grippy is available at fine wand shops across the coast!*

I left my car at The Dove and set out on a walk that evening, not directed anywhere in particular. Following the curve of the beachwalk, I wandered slowly, letting Clue run like mad around in the surf where she could eat seagulls until she burst.

On the water's edge, it was cooler than the rest of the town. A gentle breeze carried on around us, more refreshing than I expected after the heat of the day. I wasn't paying attention to where we were until Clue barked frantically, running back to me from the waterline. I froze and realized I was about to walk over a section of seawall that was broken apart for hundreds of feet in front of me.

I could see damaged, upended, and jagged sections of concrete jutting from the water at strange, deadly angles to warn away pedestrians and pets. Razor-sharp barbed wire was wrapped around rusted metal poles sticking out of the water. A long-faded caution sign was zip-tied to the barbed wire. I would have turned back, but looking at the shattered seawall haunted me in a beautiful way. It shimmered in the fading light, as though the reflection off the water caused my vision to waver and waft around in the evening air.

Magic, not disaster. It had to be a painfully strong glamor to fool even my familiar. I checked the cross-street sign to confirm where we were and then walked off the edge of the seawall.

As I expected, there was no damage; instead, the area was a small, pristine beach, just a few feet into the water, fully submerged at high tide and foamy white with sea caps. Though the seawall wasn't broken, the area out past the beach was treacherously rocky where it dropped off, making it a sinking sentence for any boats that approached.

I was standing on a beautiful driftwood dock when Clue caught up to me.

"This is family magic!" she said. *"How did you know it was there? I couldn't see through the spell!"*

"I've been here before. Declan's family owns this land. They call it 'Friendship Shores of Happiness Beach'. I'm not even kidding a little bit." I pointed at the wooden bench at the edge of the dock, remembering the last time we sat there together. "This is where we broke up."

I'd avoided him for a week or so after I decided I wasn't leaving with him, but finally, we met here. I was ready to talk, to be heard, to try to listen and give him a place to speak and feel freely. He showed up loaded for romance and had already transfigured the white caps of the sea into millions of miniature unicorns running toward the beach, a huge bonfire sent off small crimson tornadoes that took the form of a fiery bull driving them back out into the water.

For so long I saw myself as the unicorn trying to get away from the mundane. Declan was the bull, constantly sending me back where I didn't want to be. But now I was the bull, stopping him from being happy, from following me to his doom. He was the light. I was an angry, red-heifer fire.

I had come upon him that evening so long ago before he turned to look at me. Bright red firelight reflected against his white button-down shirt, and he was positively glowing in the magic hour of sunset perfection. I wanted to run away with him. I had to run away from him.

"Schmendrick is the original unsung hero," I said to get his attention.

"I'd watch a thousand episodes of Mommy Fortuna's Midnight Carnival & Traveling Swamp Market," Declan answered. He stopped what he was doing (making unicorns create cheerleader-style pyramids) and smiled at me. I don't know if his smile actually glimmered in the sun or if I could see the small calcium spot on his tooth, but he pushed his hair off his face, and I swooned. Leaning onto the wooden bench for support, I tried to play it off as though I rolled my ankle.

"I know you're not coming to Texas, Callie. I saw it on your face at Mimi's on Easter," Declan got his words out first.

"What did you see on my face?"

"Forever."

"Please speak plainly."

"Callie, when you talk about forever, your face goes pale and almost a little green. You look lost and afraid, overwhelmed and anxious. When we lined up for the family photo, you looked like you'd seen a ghost." He put his arm around me, and we walked in the sand.

"Well, I mean, I ate a lot of very spicy crawfish. I wasn't weirded out or anything." This wasn't his fault, and I wasn't going to let him derail me.

"Okay, and then after the picture you said, 'Two people made all these people. They just made people who made people who are making people and it's going to go and on forever'."

"I was interested in how your family went from two to almost a hundred in four generations." I was going to feel bad enough today—I didn't want to insult his family on top of that.

"And then you threw up..."

"So, you want to mock me?" My fury shut down all my guilt.

"Oh, for keening out loud! I'm trying to tell you we don't need to have a difficult talk. If you want to go to college while I'm in the Witch Force, I'm all for that. We have centuries if we want them. I'm not here to hold you back!" He kept trying to look into my eyes, but I had to look away, turn my head, something to keep myself from falling apart.

I didn't want him to fight with me. I did not. I didn't want him to make it even harder for me. More than that, I slowly realized I wanted a little resistance. Couldn't he even try to negotiate?

I respected and appreciated the even-handed nature Declan played in situations of extreme emotions. I loved him because he wasn't a troglodyte, wasn't selfish or manipulative. Maybe it was proof that in my own way I was incapable of being happy. If I could have learned that lesson that very day, it would have been a very different seven years.

"I don't want you to wait for me!" I had to blurt it out. He needed to move on, find love, have his big, wonderful life and not sit, rotting in poisoned feelings for me.

"Callie, you don't get to make that choice. I won't ask you to wait. I don't want you to wait, actually. If you need to get out of the Bay and find joy someplace else, then I support you, but you don't get to leave and still dictate what my heart does in your absence."

"That's the point, Declan." I took a deep breath. "I don't know what I want, but I know I don't want this. I'm desperate to get out, get away, see other things, be in other places, know other people. I admit I don't know what I want, but I do know what I don't."

"And what you don't want is me?"

"Declan..." This was what I didn't want. "If there is a single part of any of this, I can see would make me happy, it's you. The rest of it isn't for me. Not now. But if it never becomes my path to come home and ascend, I can't have you torn between me and the coast." A small voice whispered to me that I should lie to him, tell him I didn't want him either, break his heart, and set him free, but I couldn't do it.

"I'm not in a rush to make any decisions, Callie." Declan sat on the bench and patted the seat next to him. "Granny Fianna told me there's a reason our kind won't force young people to make forever decisions about our magic. She said we can't know ourselves until we've really lived, and really living takes time. I know your family traditionally ascends on their twenty-fourth birthday, but my parents waited until the very last moment to ascend. They didn't marry until a decade later and they were both fifty when I was born."

"I could wait until I'm three hundred and still not want kids," I blurted. It was the first time in my life I'd spoken the words out loud in front of anyone else.

"Same," Declan chuckled.

He always said that. It drove me nuts because Declan was great with children, and they loved him. He was a walking amusement park, and as a witch with conjure powers to rival creation, he was a claw machine just spitting out toys, stuffed animals, and candy.

"So, do we officially break up?" I didn't know where to go from here. Would the magic of his family's land kick me out into the bay if we broke up and he decided that I was no longer welcome here? Maybe the happiness and friendship magic of the area was more than just a name? Was there some land magic or family spell that made everything between Declan and me so easy?

"I'd much rather just fade apart. That's the best idea we can hope for. We talk when we can, when we want, maybe write letters, send emails, or chat until we drift off into our own lives. Sure, we'll probably drift in and out as we walk through the future, but I don't think I can start acting like I hate you. And I know I can't just never talk to you again. Do you want to never speak to me again?"

Did I? I took a second, considered it, and rejected it instantly.

"No, I want to keep talking to you. You're my best friend and part of what's so hard is not being part of your life or having you in mine. I do think it's for the best if we agree to see other people," I admitted. Declan's happiness hinged on finding his perfect person. I needed to push him to be out there and open to it.

"Were we not seeing other people?" he asked in a simple voice.

My brain crashed right through my chest, stomach, uterus, and flew out of my asshole.

"I... uh, I wasn't... but I mean... we never talked about that, but I guess, I just assumed we, uh... it doesn't matter. Nope, that's great. No adjustments needed." It was the first time I intimately understood what it meant to choke on my words. I completely forgot how to breathe.

"Callie, I'm only kidding. I don't think we should discuss our relationship for a while. We don't have to talk about it. I couldn't tell you about someone who interests me right now. Maybe someday, if the world spins in a truly strange way... but I also don't want to be your sounding board if you develop a crush.

We shouldn't be that to each other. From now on, nothing but friendship."

Declan wanted to pretend we'd never been in love.

The idea pierced my heart like a spear. It was brilliant, cold perfection. We could just pretend we'd never been in love. Nothing had happened. Or even better? It happened but passed and didn't matter. I could outwardly pretend there were no feelings between us on my part. If his happiness, his future, depended on stuffing down my feelings, then I'd work the rest of my life to pack all of my pain into the smallest nugget of anguish I could manage and swallow whole.

"That nugget of anguish didn't sink down like a lead weight how you expected, huh? It's been more like a violently dying star that keeps shooting beams of light that are desperately trying to reach back to Declan, but they just keep throwing you into a herky-jerky, off-balanced, rage spasm."

Clue's soft, cheerful voice contradicted the razor edge of her truth. I'd surely get accustomed to our mental connection, but her insight would probably always set me on edge. Maybe she was my Slip-and-Slide into self-awareness?

"Yikes!" It didn't feel cruel but matter of fact. Clue's sage moments unnerved me.

"The most chaotic force in the universe is love withheld, restrained," Clue said. *"When you put it all out there, you get your heart broken once. When you try to hold it in, try to stop it from coming out each time it escapes, then your heart breaks over and over."*

"Better my heart than his." I made my choice. We wandered clear across the Bradley's land and passed through on the other side of the magic. Clue and I were coming up quick on a young black woman sitting on the seawall dragging her gold-painted toes through the water.

Bianca.

We had walked all the way down the street where Bianca's store sat, albeit several blocks inland from where we stood. I was momentarily frozen, unsure if I should make myself known or run away and give her privacy. I didn't want to bother her, but I could just imagine the pain she was in. Bianca came out here to be alone. I had no desire to bother her.

So, I walked up to her, sat down, put my arms around her, and cried with her. I don't know where I got the nerve or the direction, but I was drawn to her. With my blood rushing in my ears, I knew in my witch's heart if I were Bianca, this was what I'd want.

She held onto me with more strength than I expected, sobbing into my shoulder as I gently rubbed her back and rocked. She exhausted the various pitches of grief, swinging from high and shrill to low and guttural. There were animal cries of pain and heart-wrenching, broken sobs, and each time I leaned in harder.

I wasn't an expert on grief, but I knew when sadness needed to come out—despite being a champion grief bottler. One way or another, each tragedy had a certain number of tears associated with it and people couldn't start to heal until those tears were spent. I didn't have any proof of it, but I knew every time I tried to hold in tears, they came back around later, when it was more inconvenient, and shook me uncontrollably until I gave in and just had The Big Cry. I likened it to how I knew when I felt sick, throwing up would quickly help me get back to normal, but I still could not help myself but to fight the urge until the last minute, rather than just leaning in and getting it over with. Just because things would be better after the act didn't make the act any less painful.

Bianca didn't hold back, and her unspoken trust touched my heart. I wanted to be there for her. I wanted to be her friend and support her through the pain. I wanted to be with her when she needed me.

"She's been my best friend my whole life," Bianca said. They were the first fully formed words she'd spoken since I'd arrived. "I don't know how to be me without her."

I wanted to empathize out loud. I wanted to tell her how leaving Declan felt since his memory still swirled around me like a cape, but it wasn't about me. A few teen years and some on-and-off long-distance chatting seemed like dust compared to the lifetime Bianca and Ginger had spent side by side. In the end, I just listened.

"When we were babies—first grade? Maybe even younger—she'd tell me about how we'd own a bookstore one day and make tea and sandwiches and every day would be a grand party. We set up the store just like her bedroom. Bookshelves to the north, kitchen to the south, tea and fountains to the west, and the porches to the east. She stayed up for fifty hours straight with a compass and protractor making sure the positioning was exact enough to rival a palatial table setting. Precision. Ginger was the only precision witch I'd ever known."

Bianca let go of my shoulders and chuckled. We sat side by side on the seawall and my hand took hers, interlacing our fingers as we leaned against the other.

"I used to say her soulmate was a nanoscale. She had this deep, pure adoration for exactitude. Anytime she found something out of sorts in the store, she'd get so excited to reset it. You'd think someone so devoted to precision would go mad over things being a bubble out of plumb, but not Ginger. Anytime she had the chance to tweak things toward perfection, she lit up like the sun."

I was struck by the emptiness I felt in a small, hidden crevice of my heart. Someone I had known briefly was taken from us, and I'd never even truly known her. I would only ever know Ginger from others, seeing her through others' eyes that cried with her, watched her struggle, and winked with inside jokes.

But what about the things she hid away from those people who loved her? What about her hidden dreams and desires she didn't share? Her true self passed to the Source, taking her knowledge and secrets with her. I acutely felt her loss alongside my own longing to have known more of her. Would every shameful thought and feeling I had die with me? Would I spend my life pushing people away, fighting to keep everyone at arm's length, and die, leaving an amalgamation of thoughts to carry on as memories?

Briefly, the thought of nobody knowing me intimately was more horrifying than opening myself up to rejection, but then I stuffed that horror into the recesses of my mind and covered it in shame and regret. No point playing in that particularly painful sandbox.

Bianca stood, keeping hold of my hand.

"Can I walk you home?" I finally asked.

They were the first words that came out of my mouth since I'd arrived. I'd shushed and held her, but after speaking, I knew she'd know I was actually there with her, and it would disturb her emotional process.

"You don't have to," Bianca answered, kissing the side of my hand that held hers. "You look like you need some time here yourself."

"Not anymore." I shook my head. "It's dark, anyway. If we walk together to your place, then I can follow the boulevard back to the square. It's a long, dark road behind us if we split up." And also, honestly, I just wanted to see her store. The things she said about Ginger piqued my interest and I wanted to know more. I couldn't know her in the flesh, but maybe talking about her would help both Bianca and me feel less lost.

"Only if you promise to come in for tea?" Bianca asked.

"Only if you promise I can have cake and pay an accurate tab after?" I countered.

"Cake is on the house, full price for the tea, and a half-eaten Reuben sandwich for the pup?" Bianca tugged me up to my feet and we climbed over the seawall.

We spoke deliberately, trying to be clear over the cacophony of twilight creatures calling in the wooded area around us. Clue ran around us in a huge circle, searching for errant seagulls or intriguing smells.

"Her parents are still in Havana, so I'll be traveling with the body. I'm not looking forward to coming back to an empty house, but it will be nice to celebrate her life with her family." Just beneath her voice, I could hear the gentle tinkle of her bangles bouncing on her wrist, echoing off the crunchy gravel road under our feet.

"How long do you think you'll be gone for?" I didn't know how to contribute to the conversation except to ask questions and give her something to respond to.

"I should be back relatively soon. It's busy season right now at the store but it will fall off after the Fourth of July. It's too hot for people to be walking around here in the summer, so I might go back then for a longer stay."

"Cuba in July? That's the kinda weather that makes you try to set yourself on fire just to cool off," I mentioned.

"I hope to hellfire and back it is. Maybe I can sweat out the grief and pain; come back feeling a little less broken?" Bianca broke down again but shook it off hard. "I can't. I can't just sob for days. Ginger would be furious if I let her business falter because I was too soft. Say something else. Anything?"

I could see her cross streetlight in the distance, a giant yellow pool of light in a black curtain of wilderness. I was not going to do it. I was not going to be someone who talked about the weather at that moment.

"I always forget the untouched wetlands that come up back here." Bullfrogs screamed at us, and it was all I could grasp onto and mention at the moment.

"It's going to stay that way, too," Bianca sighed in a happier tone. "Witches have been buying up this property for decades, passing different ordinances and making sure nobody could develop anything in the area. From Coral Drive to the seawall is safe from developers."

"And to anyone with a drop of witch blood, land is the only thing that matters... Didn't someone say that?" The quote popped into my head, but I drew a blank. It sounded so much like my grandfather's wisdom, or maybe my dad?

"Yep!" Bianca snorted, laughing. "Scarlet O'Hara's dad said it in the movie. But it was Irish blood, not witch blood. But you're not wrong. All twelve families are devouring available areas and driving up prices."

"I need to start paying more attention," I whispered mostly to myself as we walked up to her small white picket fence. "I mean, it's

"You know, it's funny you said that about the gray flo[w]," Bianca said before disappearing back into the kitchen. "[The] morning you came home, Ginger was saying some of her [tea] blends were leaching color, turning gray on her."

"What does gray mean?" Everything else in our faith had symbolism. Colors could represent feelings, thoughts, emotions, dreams, elements, powers, etc., but gray wasn't really on that spectrum.

"Ginger said it meant mildew and scrapped the batch." Bianca offered me a small triangle of lemon cake with soft, white lace icing.

"Yeah, I'm sure that kind of thing happens all the time, right?" I took the plate and inhaled deeply so I could bask in the fresh scent.

"Does it? You're the eldest daughter of the most powerful plant witch on the coast. If there was a common reason everything turned gray, shouldn't you have at least heard about it?" She sat across from me at the small wooden table set between two overstuffed armchairs and took a bite of her own piece of cake.

"Bianca, I'm embarrassed at how often I didn't pay a bit of attention to his magic. I never showed any aptitude, so I left it to the experts." I did not want her thinking I had any insight at all, especially compared to someone like my father or Ginger.

"Ginger seemed unbothered," Bianca shrugged and retrieved the softly whistling kettle before it launched into a scream.

"Then again," I mused. "Gray mildew is powdery mildew, so that would turn tea and roses a little gray, but it didn't explain why she's pooping gray-petaled flowers whenever she eats the seagulls."

"It only happens when seagulls are dead before I eat them. There were dozens of dead ones in the woods between here and the beach

and I ate every last one of them!" Clue bragged as she licked around the carpet for Reuben crumbs.

Something stopped me from repeating her words to Bianca.

"It's probably because seagulls are rats with wings, and they make everything terrible and gray. I hope your puppy eats every last one of them and covers the coast in gray floral. It can be the latest fad at all the summer weddings!" Bianca laughed out loud. And she deserved to do so. It was funny. I'd have laughed if the word 'wedding' hadn't sent me crashing back into memories of Declan.

That was when I should have known my heart was too broken to think straight.

Chapter Eleven

I decide to show off and turn a swan dive into a belly flop...

PHEME: *This week on Blue Crab Bay After Dark, we're talking about our favorite spells. My partner Eris is an expert on entrepreneurial spell creation and is here to share her myriad of successes with our audience!*

ERIS: *Pixie Post-Its, probably. Or those Handy-Man Hags. Oh! Sweet Singing Sleep Assist Satyrs? Maybe Name Gnomes?*

PHEME: *You have definitely made lives easier for a lot of witches!*

ERIS: *I mean, how many times have we all been in a social situation and forgotten a name. Then you're too embarrassed to admit it. Then you have to hope someone says the name of the person you've forgotten. It's a hopeless feeling and I hate it. So, I fixed it.*

PHEME: *You touched on something so many of us struggle with. It's an inspired spell.*

ERIS: *I really was operating on all cylinders that day. I needed something small enough to be discreet but smart enough to remember names—or at least magical enough to be able to find out the names so they could tell us.*

PHEME: *Micro-gnomes who can telepathically communicate with you certainly fit that description.*

ERIS: *The spellwork just required a lot of coaxing and rewards. Gnomes really love little treats.*

PHEME: *So, like food, or beans, or flowers?*

ERIS: *Think more sparkle!*

PHEME: *Coins, gems, and crystals?*

ERIS: *Uh... sharper things. Useful, sharp things.*

PHEME: *Are you talking about weapons?*

ERIS: *They're tools. The gnomes use axes in their everyday life. Knives and shovels aren't just for violence.*

PHEME: *I feel a 'but' coming on?*

ERIS: *Maybe a butt-kicking?*

PHEME: *By a tiny army of weaponized gnomes who have been armed with a solid steel weapon set that would, hypothetically, allow them to declare war on goblins?*

ERIS: *Goblins aren't real, bro.*

PHEME: *But there are a number of goblins in popular culture. From yard decor to gargoyles, there is a bit of an issue.*

ERIS: *Yes, when mind-reading gnomes are bespelled to learn a name, they learn... THROUGH NO FAULT OF THEIR OWN, MIND YOU... uh, they learn every name the person ever had. So, you can't really hide any nicknames from them.*

PHEME: *That doesn't sound terrible.*

ERIS: *Well, it's not. What's terrible is when people use the term 'goblin' to describe their children, their decorations, their pets... Misnomers have consequences, people!*

PHEME: *And those misnomer consequences include random attacks by the magical gnome army?*

ERIS: *To be fair, actual goblins are terrible.*

PHEME: *Were terrible. They were terrible. There haven't been goblins around witches in centuries.*

ERIS: *Two hundred and twelve years if you want to be exact.*

PHEME: *And the outcome was?*

ERIS: *Bloody.*

PHEME: *I think that's the perfect way to talk about our newest sponsor!*

ERIS: *All of those tiny gnome hands stabbing away at anything and everything that's ever been called a goblin. So many went after cats, and they were just no match for the claws and the fangs...*

PHEME: *Do you have drama with pests of a preternatural sort? Are you tormented by tiny tyrants in your life? Evil elves? Fighting fairies? Hags haunting your home and breaking things just so they can fix them? Do you have serenading satyrs singing away your sleep because they weren't trained to ever shut up? Did you create a small army of war-obsessed, well-armed gnomes that are invading the local pet populace?*

ERIS: *You're damn right, I did.*

PHEME: *If your garden is going to hell in a Hag's handbasket, call Clover Clerios' Catch & Capture Creature Connection Co-op. Their around-the-clock staff of expert magical creature curators can come to your rescue no matter which magical malfeasance has manifested in your mansion! Don't suffer through another Satyr* *song! Forget fighting with Fey! Clover Clerios' CCCCC will see to it that you're safe or the visit is free.*

ERIS: *They really are a top-notch organization and far too reputable for this shambling podcast.*

PHEME: *Clover Clerios can be reached at 228-555-4357. That's right, just dial 555-HELP and Clover's crew will come to you! Magical plant menaces are not included in their service.*

ERIS: *Your mother drank heavily during her pregnancy.*

PHEME: *At least she didn't birth a baby who brought upon a mini-military massacre... GNOME' SAYIN'?*

ERIS: *So much blood...*

My mother and sister gave me a basic transfiguration/conjuring lesson at the back table in The Dove. It was covered in a fresh silk cloth, empty of all objects except a small China teapot hand-painted with pink and blue flowers and spindly green leaves. I knew it was China because I was going to have to turn that pot into a plate and the remedial lessons included objects in the same material and general family of items. It would be easier to turn China into China rather than ceramic or glass. It made no difference to me because this was the lesson for which I was ready. I had an ace up my sleeve.

I sat down and my mother sat across from me, my sister coming in and out as she handled customers and deliveries.

"We'll start with changing the structure of the teapot into a plate," my mother began. "You start by focusing, communicate with the heart and energy of the object, and coax it gently into another form."

She focused on the teapot, and I watched it melt into the plate almost instantly, the floral design on the belly becoming a beautiful border around the plate.

"This can be super helpful if you need to hide magical items as common, everyday household objects." She reset the pot back to itself and gestured for me to proceed.

I took my time, focusing, connecting with the Source, and within a few moments the pot sloppily melted into the plate. I had this feeling when I connected the teapot had started its journey as a plate and was transfigured by my mother. I wasn't so much changing it into something else as it was resetting it back to its original form, a far easier task than a total transformation. I didn't say anything. She wanted to give me an early win, set me up to feel successful and confident, get me to trust my magic, and hopefully, make the next lesson easier.

"That's great!" My mother looked so proud. She picked up a small teacup from a box on the floor and set it beside the plate. "Now, into the teacup, please."

This was harder and took more concentration, but eventually, the plate swirled and became the replica of the teacup. It was harder but not impossible; both objects were full of energy, and it was easy for me to tap into them.

"What else you got?" I felt like I was on fire with magic.

"Make tea," my mother said simply. I nodded. Conjure water—easy enough in theory; conjure tea—I could find tea from any of the myriad tins in the store; boil water—which would be tricky; and pour!

First, I transfigured a new plate that hadn't been transfigured before. I had to focus so hard my body shook, my mind locked on the object, my will easing it into the shape I needed. It took a few minutes, but soon it was a pretty cute little teapot, though empty.

The water was harder, and after fifteen minutes I was exhausted. I imagined drawing the water out of the sink, from the dew on the leaves outside, from the special spring that fed our house, everything I could think of, and nothing happened.

"Callie, you have to relax. I can feel you getting frantic," my mother warned.

"Hang on, Ma." I stood and reached for my bag; my wallet had my answer. It was a special spell I'd copied from Declan ages back when he was first learning to conjure. He said it was a surefire way to manifest something, but it could only be used once and then it would be powerless. I'd been saving it in case of an emergency. Actually, I'd forgotten I had it and just recently found it in my drawers, so I was going to use it to impress my mother.

"What do you have there?" She was skeptical but gestured for me to proceed.

"Callie, mon, Callie, mon, Bali Mangthi, Callie, mon, Shakthi degi Callie!" I tried and again nothing happened. I tried again, louder. "Callie mon!"

"What in the world are you doing?" My sister ran into the back room and grabbed the teapot off the table.

"Declan taught me this spell to conjure whatever I wanted, but I can only ever use it once," I explained. "I don't think it works."

My mother looked sympathetic but still like she was trying not to laugh.

"That's not a spell! That's from Indiana Jones and the Temple of Doom!" my sister cried, laughing, and doubled over, falling to the floor.

"That bastard," I fumed.

No wonder he said it only worked once. I hated him and his ridiculous sense of humor so much. I tried to wait until their laughter subsided and my irritation passed, but they went on for a while.

"Callie mon? That's not even the line in the movie," Sunny whooped.

The more they laughed the hotter under the collar I felt, my skin prickling, my body disquieted. They were allowed to enjoy my foibles, but I'd get Declan for this one. I'd find him, someday, when he was happy and content, when his life was right where he wanted it, and then I'd have my revenge. My revenge fantasy developed in my mind. Scorpions. I'd put them in his car, or his bed. Maybe snakes, or rats—he deserved rats. He was a rat. A damned rat, and I'd put his damned rat self in the teapot. I'd find the magic I needed to shrink him down and stuff him right in that pot.

As my rage reached its apex and the top of the teapot bubbled off, water overflowed the table and splashed onto Sunshine.

My mother sat up, a little shocked and proud. She clapped, genuinely clapped, and cleared the excess water with a wave, sending it back to wherever I drew it.

"There you go. Now, conjure the tea. Aim for something calming—you don't need any more caffeine, Callie."

I was able to master almost every step except boiling the water. I needed Sunny's help for that. My mother taught me to turn tea back into water, back into tea, and on and on until I couldn't remember where my magic started and ended.

By the end of the day, I was able to change various natural liquids into water, transfigure basic shapes, and conjure enough heat to light a candle. It wasn't the best start, but I made progress and was proud of myself.

I felt better until Declan arrived right around closing. The minute he walked into the store, I picked up a large pillar candle and hummed it right at the back of his head. I'd show him Callie Mon. The head injury I so wanted to give him was thwarted by my mother who transfigured the candle into tissue, and it flittered to the ground harmlessly.

"I worked your transfiguration spell today, you rotten son of a banshee…" I screeched but my mother interrupted me.

"This is a place of business, not a fight club, Callie."

"I mean, how should I know that? If it were a fight club, we couldn't talk about it." I made a face at her and glared at Declan.

"I mean, honestly? I didn't think it would take you two decades to try the spell." Declan sat his bag on the low table in the reading area and sat on a couch, stretching out his legs. "I figured someday we'd watch the movie together and you'd get the joke. I thought I had time to play the long game."

I wasn't going to let the fake, dejected look get to me. Granted, he seemed authentic, but as far as I was concerned, he could watch movies with someone else.

"I'd rather swallow a stalk of aloe," I huffed and marched in the back to get another candle.

"She seriously went for it?" I heard him ask my mom.

I didn't hear any response from her but figured she must have nodded because he chuckled and didn't stop until I walked out with an armload of pillars and a look in my eye that said, "Try me."

"Can you wait to bludgeon me after I tell you what we uncovered about the boat incident?"

I narrowed my eyes, my thirst for vengeance second only to my curiosity. I set the candles on the shelves where they belonged, picked up the biggest shillelagh we sold, and sat in the chair next to him. Once he was finished, I could swing the stick and wallop him.

"Forensics determined it was a thermite grenade, home-rigged in a thermos filled with diesel fuel. Whoever did this had a really clear timetable they wanted to use. They duct-taped a spoon and super glued the grenade to the top of the thermos. He or she must have left it teetering near the engine, knowing that when they accelerated the boat, the jerk forward would tip the thermos and likely knock it over, allowing the diesel to eat through the tape.

"There were bolts loosened on the propeller shaft, so as soon as one blew, the whole thing seized up, and that's why the engine would turn over, but they couldn't go anywhere. It also explains why Osian got in the water." Declan took my mother's hand, holding her tight in his grip.

"Didn't Aden say the electronics went out?" I vaguely remember him claiming the radio wasn't working.

"The radio and fish finder had a blown fuse. Simple fix." There was a weighty pause and Declan inhaled a deep, shivering breath. "But we found traces of brimstone and jellyfish tentacles near the electric panel. Someone wanted to keep them from calling ashore for help once stranded."

I felt sick. My mother looked horrified. Someone murdered my grandfather, tried to murder my brother, and almost murdered my father. Allegra's cryptic warning about a guardian echoed in my head.

"I swear to you, Mrs. A, we are going to find who did this and we're going to get justice for Ruari. By the Source, we will find them." His promise sounded so hollow you could hear the ocean behind it.

My lesson on tonic making with Aden was pretty straightforward potion work I never paid any attention to in the past. Because the men in my family were so talented it never fell to me to need to create anything like this. Sure, I could craft a quick pick-me-up or tonic for a sore throat, but my brother brought a laundry list of "basic" spells that were not basic at all.

We sat at my father's planting table in his greenhouse, nothing near us other than a mortar and pestle, scissors, scales, and a copper bowl of fresh water. I was a lot less arrogant about health crafting than conjuring, probably because I didn't have a pocketful of Declan's lies giving me false confidence.

"Are you even listening, Callie?" Aden waved his hand in front of my face.

"Sorry, I was thinking about murder. Maybe we could start with a potion to give someone warts? I think that would inspire me more than fopdoodles and mosquito repellant." Potions were tedious, nerdy magic, and although we'd been out here less than an hour, my eyes were already glazing over.

"First, we shall harm none... so no, you're not getting wart spells for Declan. Second, don't mess with the fopdoodle—that's some of the most advanced spellwork our family ever crafted and you ain't witch enough to try it yet." He was a drill sergeant.

Because his magic wasn't working, he was precise and meticulous with his potion crafting, relying on others to charge the items with magic and intention.

"Bad joke, I'm sorry. By all means, continue," I said. I'd get nowhere if I continued to clown around.

"The simple tonics and potions almost make themselves. They want to combine, flowing together almost naturally, and we only have to give them a little magical push, a little incentive. Sometimes that incentive is honey, sometimes it's wine, or sometimes it's wax, but there has to be pure intention behind the spell. For the time being, we're working with honey." He set a small jar on the table and licked his fingers.

"We're going to start with a simple meditation potion. We'll need lavender, chamomile, roots of a lily pad, a dozen morning glory seeds, and three drops of moon water." He stopped, waiting for me.

"Oh, right. Okay!" I hopped up and set out gathering ingredients all around the greenhouse, taking the small scissors and asking each plant for permission to take the bits I needed. "Humbly, I ask the Source, grant my leave to gather and receive, to heal the world and serve my community, as I harm none, so mote it be."

I didn't hear anything in response, but each time I chanted the prayer, I felt a sense of calm settle over me, a sort of peace in my path, reinforcing I was doing it right and nature was granting my request. It felt like acquiescence in my bones. Until I got to the lavender, where I found that no matter where I considered cutting, it didn't feel right. Something was off, and though I repeated the prayer until I was practically begging, I couldn't bring myself to cut it. I returned with the other ingredients and told Aden.

"The lavender—do I need to get it from the pot? Something feels off. The plant sort of shies away when I reach to cut. No matter where I try to snip, it doesn't feel like the plant is giving freely. What's wrong with me?" I wrung my hands with worry. Do I just have to go through life with plants disliking me?

"There's not a damn thing wrong with you!" Aden bellowed, looking shocked but incredibly pleased. "The spell calls for dried lavender, the jar on top of the third shelf! Hell yea! Feeling that is a great sign you're in tune, Cal!"

"Plants yearn for understanding. They aren't here for us to pillage. They're partners in our magic and by respecting them, by listening, we're giving them access to our spirit, and in return, they bring their power to us," Aden explained.

His joy was infectious, and I was energized by the praise. I had never been naturally good at any type of magic, but I felt a connection with that plant. Maybe lavender would be my key to successful potion crafting?

It was not.

I was not successful at potion crafting. My meditation tonic gave me a splitting headache. The healing draught made me vomit. Every tonic I crafted smelled like burnt hair and tasted like pennies.

The only success I had was with my grandfather's discovery potion, which was one of the more advanced spells we tried. A single drop on the corner of anything would grant a brief look inside any sealed, hidden, or erased secret. A drop on a wall safe would briefly reveal the contents, a drop on a door would reveal what was behind it, and a drop on the corner of a book cover would reveal the contents. It made me feel good to know I wasn't completely inept.

Aden gave me homework, explaining that the problem with making other potions was my intention. Had I wanted to create those tonics, I would have. My selfish desire to be nosy was what gave me the strength to craft the discovery potion and if I could channel that same level of focus, the easier tonics would manifest.

I took the homework he gave me, set it on my desk, and promptly forgot about it. I did make a dozen variants of the discovery potion and soon my whole room smelled like algae and Spanish moss. I dribbled it on every drawer, box, book, and opaque surface I could find. Aden called me "Sherlock Holmes and the Case of the Hidden Sock Drawer." But the joke was on him because now I knew where in the house he stashed Grandpa's cannabis candy.

Chapter Twelve

Let's talk about Decks, baby...

PHEME: *And we're back! You're listening to Blue Crab Bay After Dark. I'm your host, Pheme, and with me, as always, is my partner in podcasting Eris! Today we're going to talk about...*

ERIS: **ahem**

PHEME: *Um...*

ERIS: *Go on...*

PHEME: *The topic...*

ERIS: *Topic?*

PHEME: *I planned today's show around...*

ERIS: *NO.*

PHEME: *Can't we wait on that?*

ERIS: *Tell them.*

PHEME: *Today on our show, my partner will be...*

ERIS: *Tell. Them. The. Way. We. Agreed.*

PHEME: *Dear listeners, due to my previous confession where I admitted to attacking my dearest friend with a monsoon-like deluge* *of *ahem* filthy rainwater that represents my dirty addiction to practical jokes, today we're going to discuss funerals. That way I can think long and hard about how I'll feel when my dear podcast partner passes.*

ERIS: *Maybe we can touch on why there has yet to be a memorial for Ruari Aigean? He deserves better.*

PHEME: *You don't think maybe the family is waiting until his only son is out of his coma?*

ERIS: *And if he doesn't? Will they have just one big one?*

PHEME: *This is bordering on really morbid. Every witch has a special plan for their remains, a special way they want their families to celebrate them when they're gone.*

ERIS: *And it's none of my business how they do that…*

PHEME: *And it's none of your business how they do that… yes.*

ERIS: *To be honest, I've been hoping to find out they had the memorial and just didn't invite me. Spending all that time trying to chit-chat with people while the community mourns? It's exhausting.*

PHEME: *That's an interesting comment and really lines up perfectly with our newest sponsor.*

ERIS: *I WILL HEX YOUR ENTIRE LINE!*

PHEME: *Houser Mahmenem's Small Talk Fillin' Station, at the corner of Sandcastle and Island View, now offers a full refresh of your most precious resource! Do you worry that you're going to say the wrong thing? Are you too empathetic to spend large amounts of time in crowds? Fear no longer! Stop by Houser Mahmenem's Small Talk Fillin' Station to sample one of our premier vintages of Chit-Chat Wine. Do you want a delightful Bordeaux that brings brilliance to your conversation? What about a fine white to let you while away the hours talking about the weather? For more intimate gatherings,* *grab a bottle of Just Go With It Conversational Gin or Very Vapid Interaction Vodka! Must be twenty-one or over and have a valid Mississippi state ID.*

ERIS: *Nice job, asshole.*

My heart fluttered with anxiety and pride when my mother surprised me by having the chalk sign out in front of The Dove broadcasting my services.

Tarot Readings
1 p.m. until 3 p.m.
Free with a canned food donation for Pelican County Food Bank

Teddy showed up with a box of groceries, first in line for a reading.

"You really want a reading from me?"

"It's for a good cause. How bad can it be?" Teddy took great joy in tempting the universe.

"You do know what happened the last time I read?"

"I do. Declan told me. Maybe working together we can find clues?"

"You're the Chief of Police and you want my help finding clues?" Skepticism crawled across my skin. The idea he would be patronizing me, aware of my magical misfortune of late, and trying to make me feel better grossed me out.

"This case is the only thing I'm working on right now, Callie." Teddy's eyes turned dark and serious. "Anything that can give me an edge to find out what happened is worth a try, and a little birdie told me you seem to have the Source on speed dial lately."

That dumbfounded me. Granted, I'd had some interesting moments of comeuppance recently, but a puppy and a rock do not a connection make. But Teddy had a point, if anything could help him find out what happened to my grandpa, I couldn't turn him down.

I realized briefly, even if he was being cruel and waiting for me to do something worthy of ridicule, it would be worth it on the off chance something good came out of it. The possibility of the greater good meant more to me than my pride. Either I had grown up tremendously since I arrived home, or more likely, I'd been so slapped around by my own ineptitude that my pride was nonexistent.

"I'm asking for help, Callie," Teddy said quietly. There was a haunted look in his dark, gray eyes, fearful and pleading.

"Absolutely. Take a seat."

I handed him my tarot deck and told him to shuffle until he felt like stopping. "You can focus on a topic or consider a question, but the cards are going to tell you only what they want you to know, so don't try to shoehorn every message into prophecy."

Shuffling made Teddy uncomfortable. His fingers fumbled a bit with the oversized deck and more than once he smiled meekly as he tried to stuff them back together. The frustrated crinkle between his brows betrayed the sheepish smirk on his face.

"I think that pretty much does it."

Teddy was uncharacteristically uncoordinated with the cards. Didn't anyone get their cards read by anyone else while I was gone? Did other witches not use cards on their own?

"We have crystal balls, Callie," Teddy reminded me. Empath. So unsettling.

"Right, yeah." I gathered my cards and dealt a spread. I preferred to wait until all the cards had been dealt before I tried to really look at the story. A whole picture was safer than piecing together a narrative in stages. If I was wrong on a card earlier, I worried it could set off a domino effect of errors.

Despite my best efforts, Teddy's story spilled out in droplets, adding to a larger and more tightly woven narrative.

"The Star is for your intuition covered by The Devil. This tells me the worst mistake you can make is to only follow your intuition, but it might also mean the devil is in the details," I said.

"So, which is it?" Teddy asked.

"I don't know yet. There's probably something you're mishearing from your gut—like you have an unbalanced equation but you haven't noticed. The Page of Pentacles needs you to investigate the physical world. You might feel like it's time to look at motive, passion, or emotion, but no. Stay on the evidence." I stopped trying to get ahead of the cards and summarize his reading in a pithy rejoinder and let the words tumble out of me.

"Justice is behind you, which tells me you're going to reap as you have sown. The Seven of Swords means there's a theft hanging over you... Wait, is there something missing?" I lurched my attention off the cards.

"Your mother mentioned she can't find your grandfather's book," Teddy admitted with a shrug.

"His grimoire? With his spells and notes?" A sick feeling spread across my navel.

"No, the manual? She said it was white leather with gilded letters. She didn't seem worried and told me he must have set it down somewhere and she hadn't run across it yet."

"What made her tell you about it if it wasn't a big deal? I didn't even know it was gone." It sounded more challenging than I meant to.

"I asked if anything was missing. She said she hadn't thought about it, but his room was basically untouched since the accident. I asked her to let me know if she noticed something, even if it seemed trivial. Are we going to finish the reading?" Teddy sounded nervous.

I took a deep breath. I needed him calm.

"Yeah, the manual is like the Big Book of Dolphin House. Favorite recipes, general instructions on the infrastructure of the house, passages, pipes, wiring, and cleaning secrets for the antiques, but nothing valuable. It's more than likely he set it on a shelf, got distracted, and we'll trip over it the moment we forget about it." I tried to laugh.

"Makes sense. You seemed upset."

"Not for nothing, but I spilled juice on my comforter this morning and was reminding myself to find that book while I drove here. I was just... because it had been on my mind, I thought maybe it would have been a clue for us," I covered.

"It might be, but it's not like he would have taken it with him, right?"

I shook my head and continued, shushing my brain.

"The Hanged Man. Right in front of you. You have to face him. Indecision is death but Death, even though it's your true fear, is simply another transformation. The Nine of Swords is regret...." That wasn't about his work. That was family; it was in his family position of the reading. None of the other cards told me he had already made a bad choice, only that he could if he stayed on his path.

"I think you can avoid the regret if you regroup and step back before continuing, Teddy." I reached out and put my hand over his. "The Three of Pentacles shows you're unavoidably manifesting your goals and..." I didn't have any words. The Eight of Swords loomed large as the last card.

"And winding up in a prison made of swords and blindfolds?" Teddy smiled, breaking the tension I felt.

"The situation you're in is going to tie you up," I admitted. "It's going to be hard to get out of, but not impossible. I think this is more what you're afraid of happening, being blinded by the evidence, and unable to figure out the crime."

"Sounds like the cards have a lot of faith in me." The uncharacteristic smirk was gone from Teddy and the sheepishness overflowed from him.

"We all have faith in you. You wouldn't be Chief if you couldn't handle it."

"That's nice to hear, Callie."

"Now, I have a few questions for you." I didn't wait for him to accept and hit him out of left field with, "Ginger was murdered, too. Wasn't she?"

Teddy nodded and leaned back in his chair. Every word out of his mouth, every movement of his body, would be an empathic clue. I didn't care if he talked or not. He was going to react to my questions all the same.

"Are you investigating them as related?"

"We're considering it strongly, but the type and manner of the deaths do not point to a serial killer. Your grandfather was in an explosion. Ginger apparently suffered an overdose. It's going to be hard to find the connection." Teddy sighed.

I had a flashing vision of him trying to pound a puzzle piece with a mallet and make it work in a space that wasn't right.

"Was it an overdose?" I needed to confirm my fears. Teddy nodded again. "Belladonna?"

Another nod.

"Grandpa's tincture?"

Teddy shrugged. "We can't know that. All of the ingredients match, but it's the Tylenol PM of witch tea. Everyone has a tin of mix lying around. Some came from Ruari, some from other places. He didn't sign that spell because it wasn't really his creation."

"And the fact that he and she worked together?"

"I don't think they killed each other, Callie." Teddy took a page out of my book, mirroring how I had reached to cover his hand. His hands were ice cold and slick.

"He was in a boat, and she was in a shower? Any connection with the water?" I needed him to eliminate something. There was too much going on in our town and I wanted one theory to be discounted.

"I think we've helped each other as much as we can, for now, Callie."

Something hard flickered behind Teddy's eyes, and I felt like any further questions would be stonewalled. I was disappointed but had new information to process and a Big Book of Dolphin House to go find.

I hated to admit I wanted to see Declan find his way into The Dove for a reading, but he didn't. I had a whole vision board for our next interaction.

In my mind's eye, there I was—elegantly charming the handsome Dr. Noah with my sparkling smile and luxuriously shining hair, holding my father's hand with a gentle and beatific sense of compassion visible on my face, luxuriously shining hair, carrying the lunch orders out of the café while bouncing salutations at my friends and neighbors who remarked how lucky I was to never sweat and also have such shiny luxurious hair.

In my fantasy, my hair was very thick, but I wasn't sweating down my neck. I imagined I finally ran into Declan and Beaux huddled close in a booth and I smiled brilliantly, threw my glossy mane over my shoulder, and felt nothing but sisterly witchery and forgiveness for them. I tossed them a cheeky wink and swirled out the door, balancing paper containers in a ballerina strut as I giggled out tinkling melodic laughter.

I supposed it was why I took it so hard when the day finally came a week later and I ran into Declan, Beaux, and Dr. Hot Stuff and didn't quite have the grace I imagined.

I was tucked into my father's guest chair, lost in my daydream, when Dr. Noah strolled in, looking tired yet still handsome.

"I feel like every time I walk in here, I interrupt someone praying." He looked apologetic and I felt bad for how obsessive my family may have been the last few days.

"There's not much more to do while we're sitting with him. The conversation seems to be a bit one-sided."

"You don't find the same problem with talking to God?" Dr. Noah smiled, a little teasing curve to his lips.

"Not the God we pray to," I said, shrugging, and then felt like maybe it came out sharper than I intended. "We're big on meditation, so we try to see the difference in stillness and silence."

"Well, I sure hope if I'm ever in your dad's place, my people are as dedicated and consistent as your family. I see your sister before breakfast every day, then again late in the afternoon. Your mom is here from five to ten every night and your brother shows up a few minutes after you leave."

I tried to keep my face calm, but I had no idea there was someone every night, all day, constantly around my father. Dr. Noah was right: that was a lot of visitation time. It might look like devotion, but I knew my family was standing watch, making sure my father wasn't left alone.

Murder has that effect on people.

"He eats a lot of candy when he's left alone," I joked. "It's a family trait."

Dr. Noah laughed gently, glancing at me over the top of his clipboard. "Speaking of food, my rounds end at eleven and I'd like to try that outdoor café toward the shoreline. Will you join me?"

I sat there idiotically, waiting to see if he would clarify he had said something else, and I was actually having a stroke. "Lunch?" I croaked, my voice faltering. He nodded and mocked eating. "I'm not available for lunch today...." I was struggling. I'd only been attempting this new responsible behavior for a short while and didn't think my family would appreciate it if I skipped out with Dr. Hotness and left my mother soupless.

"Dinner on Friday?" He interrupted my thought, shrugging. He had the vague look in his eye of someone determined, and it made me feel good. I nodded in agreement.

"Same place, Friday night?" I confirmed.

He handed me a Post-It, his phone number written quite neatly across the top. "Unless you have a different preference, Callie." He said my name with his breath at the end, his tongue peeking between his lips at the center, pink and soft.

"No, that little café is excellent. I'll call you?" I gathered my bags and hurried out before he could come to his senses.

Do you know the roses-and-sunshine feeling when someone you're interested in shows an interest in you? That's so mild a description of how it feels, right? It was the sparkly and effervescent champagne coursing through my veins feeling that followed me to pick up lunch for my mother and me. It was my warm, wanton daydream that had me so distracted when I walked into the café, vision blurry with joy, I was paying zero attention to the cars in the parking lot, people in the booths, or anything else besides the butterflies of feeling beautiful.

The café was called THE WICKED COOKIE and offered a pretty diverse menu for our small town. I was met at the front counter by Psykhe Adelphos, who went by Kiki and was the oldest child of the café owners. She waved to me to hold on while she took a phone order, so I turned to find a seat in the packed restaurant but froze solid when my eyes landed on Declan. He sat next to Beaux in a booth because he's ridiculous and gross and she probably hung on him and cried dainty tears that didn't smear her eye makeup if he got too far away from her.

They whispered together, locked deep in conversation, her hand in his. My breath caught in my chest, and I smelled roses and brimstone. Turning back to Kiki, I hoped she could get me out without anyone noticing I was there.

"Callie!" I winced at Declan's voice, foiled again. I turned back, trying to remember my new mantra: *glossy hair, don't care.* He waved me over, and I pointed at my wrist because I couldn't go smell them in love and happiness.

He shook his head and curled his finger at me.

What did I have to lose? This was my chance to handle the situation seamlessly. I could walk over, be charming, strut away, and continue hating them from afar. My mind chanted *hips, hips, hips,* as I made my way toward them, concentrating on a naturally sparkling smile and not a tight, smug look of discomfort, not quite unlike constipation.

Effortlessly, I ran my hand through my hair, wanting to shake out my mane, but the knots caught on my fingers and my ring. I slowed my walk to give me time to detangle, but each movement tied my hand worse and soon I was frantically shaking my hand, my hair spider webbing between my head and scalp. Completely unwilling to ask for help, I ripped out the chunk of hair and kept going. Trying to be kinder to myself meant believing it couldn't look as bad as I expected. People probably weren't looking. If they were, they weren't paying attention.

"Hey you, two guys!" I was so loud the restaurant hushed a bit around me, unsure in the callithump if I was about to cause a scene. Which I most definitely was not.

"How are you?" Declan was calm and even. He'd let go of Beaux's hand and gestured to the bench across from them.

"I'm great, like, super great." Hellfire bunny nuts, why does this always happen to me? "I can't stay, picking up lunch for Mom, and taking it to the store. I'm working. At the store. With Mom. So, we need... uh, soup. And croissants. You know. For lunch. At the store." Charming. I felt my face flush and tried to picture having dinner with Dr. Noah. I'd be wearing a luxurious, slinky dress and holding a glass of wine, refined and not stuttering all over myself because Declan didn't look like he'd been kissed right since I left.

"Callie, your head is bleeding." Beaux handed me her napkin and pointed to the warm trickle starting to slip past my scalp line.

"Oh! Well, you know what they say: bloody head at lunch, best witch of the bunch!" I had to stop.

"Speaking of best witches," Beaux said, "how's the training? Town chatter is you're killing it with the tarot!" She looked so friendly I wanted to die.

"Oh, not really, but soon, I hope! I'm working hard every day to get there!"

"If I can ever help, I'm more than happy to. I'll be in this area more often now, so anything I can do. I'm so happy you're back."

"That's so sweet," I croaked again. What do I say? *I'm trying to be nice, but I want to scratch your eyes out and I hate myself for it so stop talking and let me leave with the small dignities I have left?*

"For now, I think we're covered. Mom, Sun, and Ade, they keep me busy. Like a Rocky montage. If you can catch a chicken, you can catch... never mind." I strongly considered jumping out the window.

"Well, if you don't mind, I'm going to come by after lunch. I have some questions for you and your mom," Declan said. He didn't look away while he talked and I was trapped in his eyes, warm and soft, tiny crinkles at the corners when he smiled.

If I said he was so handsome it made me nauseous and I hated him for it, it would be understandable, right? Casually handsome, smelling like a summer barbecue and fresh-cut grass, which is obviously the best thing you can smell like, and he only does it to spite me.

"Yeah, come on by!" I squeaked, sweat making my body clammy despite the climate control inside the restaurant. "Mom would love to see you. She'd be happy to have you come to the store. Bring her, it's fine! I mean, obviously, Beaux, you're more than likely to come. More than welcome. To come. In the store. To the store. With Declan, or even without him, come on by. Come on by and buy! Buy, store, by, bye." I laughed until I coughed, my panic rising. I looked back and forth between them.

Declan pointed behind me. Kiki was holding a paper shopping bag and waving. I turned to rush back, hurrying away from my stammering idiocy. My flip flop turned over under my toes and sent me ass over teakettle into Kiki's younger sister, Iphigenia, who we call Fifi.

Luckily for me, she was carrying a tray full of water glasses and a water pitcher; I got every drop of it poured on my head. I sat there, drenched, ego bruised, fuming at myself for several deep breaths.

I slowly climbed to my feet, strutted back to the counter like it never happened, took my bag, and turned, crashing right into Dr. Noah as he stepped into line behind me, knocking him into a chair.

I apologized profusely and yelled right in his face, "I have to go, or the soup won't be hot, and my mom will kill me!" And then I ran away, like an adult.

I pretty much crashed through the door of THE DOVE to get out of the public. My mother stared in disbelief.

"Did you go swimming?" Clue asked, bounding out of the back office. She'd been enjoying lazy mornings with my mother while I spent time with my father.

I struggled to catch my breath, dripping water across the floor.

"What happened?" My mom grabbed the shopping bag and handed me a large sheet of linen to dry off.

"I had a wobbler at the Cookie," I sighed, dabbing water out of my hair. "Dr. Cabotin asked me to lunch, but I'd already sent our order to Kiki, so I declined and was all dreamy when I ran into Declan and Beaux and lost my ability to talk and walk, ripped out a bunch of my hair, tripped, and sailed into Fifi and the seventy glasses of water she was carrying. Then Dr. Cabotin showed up in time to witness the sea hag rising off the floor—the sea hag who bashed right into him and knocked him on his keister before I could escape." I could see my mom trying to hold back her bubbling laughter. "Then I screamed in his face that you needed your soup and ran away."

Her face contorted and soon I couldn't hold it in, and we were both laughing hysterically at my foible.

"Momma, I went down like a tree, grabbed Fifi by the boob, and dragged her with me. I can never go back."

"Maybe you need to focus on getting to the store after the hospital and I'll handle lunch from now on. I don't want you taking out a wall like the Kool-Aid man because you can't resolve your feelings," my mom teased.

"I don't have any feelings. I was dreamy from the flirting and then seeing Declan and Beaux was a shock. I'm fine, really," I promised, lyingly, like a liar.

"Don't lie to your momma!" Clue chirped, looking up from the bone my mom had gifted her that morning.

I glared down at the devious little familiar. She had an angelic look on her face, enormously kind eyes gazing up at me.

"I can't hear her, but she's right," my mom corroborated.

"You'll see, Declan is coming by here later. I'll be fine." I was hoping I'd be fine. I couldn't keep losing my mind every time I saw him. Maybe seeing him alone would give me a chance to get back to normal around him?

"Did he mention why he's coming by?"

I shook my head. I hadn't given it much thought. "I figured he was coming to talk about the memorial service?"

"He's coming to talk about the explosion," Clue said. I repeated her words to my mom. Her face fell a bit, resigned to the discussion.

We ate nervously, waiting for him, each of our stomachs knotted for different reasons. Every emotion I had was heightened to an almost unhealthy degree where he was concerned.

I don't know what drove Declan to reach out to me in English class all those years ago, but one chilly winter afternoon our class was discussing a book that had bored me to tears and he handed me a folded note:

I can conjure a rockslide to end this torture

He wrote in a stocky, precise block script that had an angular beauty in its simplicity.

Violence isn't the answer. Violence is the question. And the answer is yes

I responded in my most fluid, looping, swirling script so he would see it and think about how incredible I was.

I handed him back the note and waited. He didn't conjure a rockslide or any other disaster, but he did slide a long, thin bookmark made of aqua sea glass onto my desk. Etched in the glass, in his perfect print, was my name and the epithet, "The girl with all the answers."

After class, I teased him the bookmark didn't look like a rock, and he spent the next three months conjuring pebbles I would find in my shoes, pockets, purse, and once even sitting in the center of my makeup compact when I opened it. I was sitting next to him in the same English class when I felt a crazy itch on my nose. I opened the small silver mirror (which, incidentally, I could use to make witch calls from school) to see if I had some kind of bug bite and saw the pebble.

Laughter bubbled up and out of me so fast and so loud that most of the class turned to see and caught me red-faced. I kept the deeply embarrassed blush for several minutes, unable to even look over at Declan because for some reason I was beaming with an unadulterated joy that only comes from that first crush flirting with you.

When the bell finally rang and we gathered our things, I spoke first.

"Why do you keep doing that?" I asked, fishing for some kind of compliment while letting him know I knew he was doing it, a lot, and on purpose. I should have been direct and asked why he was paying so much attention to me, but teenage flirting language was complicated.

"When you blush it's my favorite color." He smiled and winked at me, and I beamed so hard my face ached in the corners.

That was the current feeling in the pit of my stomach, the nervous excitement of knowing you're going to need to hide that unbridled joy from everyone or they'll know. They'll know there's someone in your life who makes you smile like that, that makes that smile poke its shy face out from under the hidden rock of self-control. They'll know that when someone does that, it's because nobody else ever has and it makes them special. Declan already knew he was special. I didn't need to add to that self-assurance.

When he finally got up the nerve to ask me to be his girlfriend, we were sitting in the courtyard gazebo at St. Tituba the Powerful after making googly eyes at each other during a church service that evening. It was still light out, but people had cleared from the grounds and left us, settled in silence, awkwardly enjoying each other's company.

Moments afterward, he sat next to me and spit his charming opening line, "Do you hear something?" There was a deep, angry growl coming from behind us, close enough to attack.

I jumped up and turned, stumbling back and crashing into Declan's chest. He closed his arms around me, protective and strong to defend me against the beast who looked to make us its lunch. It was a cat, solid white, the size of a young elephant, back arched in fury, paws the size of my torso shoving claws longer than my forearm into the grass. It would have been instant death in one swipe.

"What the hell is that?" I struggled to push him back, but he held me tight.

"Don't move. You don't want it to think you're prey," he growled in my ear. "I'll protect you, Callie. I need you to stay calm." We backed up slowly, both of us silent and terrified.

The monster towered over us but didn't move in for an attack. Instead, it curled in a circle, laying down and yawning deeply before purring. In my shock at the size of the cat, I didn't notice the look of it, not exactly; it wasn't a jungle animal or wild cat escaped from some exotic collection. This was an oversized kitten, a baby someone had enlarged past logical size.

"Declan, I don't think it's going to hurt us." I tried to move forward but he spun me around away from the cat.

"*Shhh*, you're in shock. This beast is fierce!" he promised.

"Did you enlarge a kitten to rescue me from it?" I asked, already knowing the answer.

"Callie, the terror has you confused!" he yelled, throwing me over his shoulder as I laughed uncontrollably. He carried me a few feet as my laughter built but stopped because his laughter caught up to him.

"Declan, the terror is looking for belly rubs." I pointed behind us where the kitten had rolled over, scratching her back against the grass. It was a great spell. I had to admit I was impressed with the witch who wanted my heart. Even young, he was crazy talented, probably because he never stopped practicing ways to get my attention.

"I knew I should have found a tabby!" Declan sank into the grass next to the kitten, beet red from laughing. He leaned over, resting against the kitten's massive, furry side. The kitten stretched out against him, crashed a behemoth paw down on his legs, pinning him to the ground below, and wetly groomed him. Declan tried to wiggle out from under the paw, but the kitten rolled, covering him in white fur as he struggled.

"Oh, sweet kitty, no..." I reached out and scratched behind her ear, gently urging her off Declan. I backed up and she followed me, pushing her head against me, knocking me back slightly. She lay down and looked at me expectantly. I scratched her again and backed up, luring her to follow, hoping Declan wouldn't suffocate.

"That's a sweet baby, follow Callie, come get scratches." Each time I scratched I moved further away, eventually hearing Declan gasping and coughing. "That's Callie's good kitty, good, sweet girl, follow me."

"I'm here to rescue you," Declan said, his voice small and weak, his body covered in white fur. He lay flat, panting, exhausted from fighting underneath the cat.

"I'm thankful for it. Can you breathe enough to shrink this cat back to normal?" I was now scratching her with both hands, hoping she didn't decide to groom me next.

"Can you reach in my back pocket and grab the parchment?" He groaned and rolled over, looking up at me adorably.

"I can," I said slowly. "I'm sure you're hurt, Deck, but if you make me leave this cat, come to you, dig in your pockets for jollies, and I get clawed while you get fondled, we're not going to fall in love."

He reached back without comment, grabbed the parchment from his pocket, and tore it in half. "Felis Catus Bastet Ailuros."

With a faint pop, the wooly white monster vanished, and a teeny baby kitten sat in my hands nuzzling my fingers.

"Now you have to fall in love with me," Declan groaned as he struggled to sit up.

"I said *we* would fall in love," I reminded him.

"You may not have noticed, Callie, but I've been here for a while." He was adorable on a level that drove me crazy. It's easier to deal with someone who didn't always say the right thing, and his way of verbally sweeping me off my feet never got old.

I sat next to him in the grass, pulling blades out of his hair as I handed him the kitten.

"Does she belong to you?" I asked, really hoping she wasn't stray or going back to a kennel after his scheme.

"My mom," he admitted. "When did you realize she wasn't a white tiger?"

"When I remembered there's no such thing as a seven-foot-tall white tiger who looks like an overgrown kitten and you quoted the Beastmaster," I confessed. I hadn't realized it then, but we had a deep mutual affection for eighties pop culture.

"Should I have gotten a boombox?" he offered.

"What song would you have played?" I wondered how far his creativity would stretch or if he'd follow the movie plot.

"Hungry Like the Wolf." And then he kissed me, full hand in my hair, arm around my back, pulling me into him completely. Even then, I loved him so much it terrified me.

Chapter Thirteen

There are books out there actually trying to kill me...

PHEME: *Welcome back to your favorite podcast for witches, by witches! As always, I'm your host, Pheme, the goddess of gossip, and with me, as always, is my partner, Eris, the goddess of discord!*

ERIS: *Golden apple and all right here!*

PHEME: *Speaking of magical objects, I heard you had a pretty wild weekend?*

ERIS: *Don't make this out like it was some hot witch party... I had a personal tragedy that required the services of a team of dedicated professionals and experts. I will not be shamed or treated as though my situation was my own fault—*

PHEME: *I mean... do you feel like it was someone else's fault?*

ERIS: *Why does someone have to be at fault?*

PHEME: *You're exactly right. Pray continue, my dear friend.*

ERIS: *After dealing with a high-stress, low-wage job that doesn't provide me any support or paid vacation, I decided to spend my* weekend in the country. I wanted to have a peaceful time back in the old world: ride horses, play a little chess, maybe do some painting.

PHEME: *Painting? That's an interesting idea...*

ERIS: *Do you want to tell the story since you know so much?*

PHEME: *My sincerest apologies. I truly wasn't aware your day job was as oppressive as that.*

ERIS: *My day job is fine, Pheme. It's this absolute nightmare I needed a break from!*

PHEME: *I'd like to let listeners know my partner is gesticulating wildly around the studio.*

ERIS: *So, I went on a short vacation and got stranded.*

PHEME: *Stranded where, exactly?*

ERIS: *Essex.*

PHEME: *That's a long flight for a weekend, Eris.*

ERIS: *You know damn well I didn't fly.*

PHEME: *Are you growling at me?*

ERIS: *Who is telling this story?*

PHEME: *Tell them what you did, please?*

ERIS: *I decided to spend a few days wandering around in a painting of the English countryside and I couldn't get back out.*

PHEME: *You magicked yourself in and couldn't magic yourself out?*

ERIS: *I was just going to climb out when my time was over. That way I didn't have to account for magical stability in a constructed environment. I left the window open between reality and the imaginary world so I could just wander around and return back through the canvas when I was ready. It was a very simple solution.*

PHEME: *It's surely a great idea. It's definitely a time saver. Could you see the window while you were in the countryside?*

ERIS: *Sure, off in the distance. I had a horse, a tiny little cottage, a beautiful sunny day, all of it only limited by my imagination.*

PHEME: *Sounds very What Dreams May—*

ERIS: *Yes! It was heavenly!*

PHEME: *So, the issue was?*

ERIS: *Icouldn'tfitbackthroughthewindow.*

PHEME: *I'm sorry, I didn't catch that?*

ERIS: *I couldn't fit back through the window. It was only a ten by twelve painting, and I couldn't fit through. I managed to get my head and shoulders back into the real world and then I was stuck. I was trapped. Half in and half out of reality.*

PHEME: *I imagine that was indescribably scary.*

ERIS: *It was actually pretty funny, until the goat showed up.*

PHEME: *The goat?*

ERIS: *There was a little goat, a baby calf, and some kittens. There were a number of animals in the painting, and they were all very docile on my trip! I didn't realize... I had my phone, my keys, and I'd brought a bunch of things in the pocket of my jeans. The goat ate everything from the waist down.*

PHEME: *Everything?*

ERIS: *Don't be repulsive! But yes, everything that wasn't my actual body was eaten by that evil goat. I kept trying to kick at it, but it pulled and pulled until my pants were gone and when the authorities arrived to assist me, there was no trace of my pants, phone, keys, ChapStick, nothing. Just a fat goat with a smug smile on its stupid goat face.*

PHEME: *That is quite a story. A goat pulled off your pants and ate your phone. The Magical Disposal Unit probably sees that all the time.*

ERIS: *I was unable to inquire as they were laughing so hard they couldn't really do that thing where you form words.*

PHEME: *Do you blame them?*

ERIS: *No. I blame you.*

PHEME: *ME?*

ERIS: *If I didn't have to deal with you, I wouldn't have needed an escape.*

PHEME: *How did you get out?*

ERIS: *You came to my place to drop off some sponsorship gifts and heard me yelling.*

PHEME: *Gifts as in free things we get for running commercials on this podcast that takes up just a few hours of your day a few days a week? Those gifts?*

ERIS: *Did you want another thank you?*

PHEME: *Not at all. I just wanted to give you a safe space to tell your story!*

ERIS: *A safe place?*

PHEME: *Speaking of safe places...*

ERIS: *You old cow, I should have just stayed in Essex!*

PHEME: *Have you ever wanted to take a temporary trip to an exotic location? Do you long to look at life in another time? Spectate in Spain? Lounge in Liechtenstein? Gad about in Ancient Greece? Salome's Safety Sheet Spaces are life-size paintings, bespelled to offer you a worry-free travel destination in your own home?*

ERIS: *This has got to be intellectual property theft!*

PHEME: *With their walk-in / walk-out service, you can slip into and out of any piece of art known to exist. Our designer replications will hang freely on your wall, adding space and security to your home without fear of intruders. Specially designed to only open to your* *personal magical signature, Salome's new show room at the Witches Museum of Modern Masterpieces offers a strolling gallery where you can sample different paintings to see where you belong!*

ERIS: *Absolutely vile.*

PHEME: *With Salome's subscription service, you can exchange your personal vacation painting every three, six, nine, twelve, or twenty-four months to keep the experience fresh and offer unlimited vistas for witches with a wanderlust. Visit the museum in the month of May for Masterpiece May, when admissions are minimized to maximize your moments inside the masterpieces.*

ERIS: *And people wondered why I wanted to wander into the woods forever!*

PHEME: *Through Midsomer, we're offering a buy one, get one free deal for Bob Ross paintings so you can bounce between glorious, vermillion autumns and crisp glacial winter scenes. Salome's! For witches with wanderlust.*

ERIS: *For agoraphobes with cabin fever!*

PHEME: *I got you one!*

ERIS: *I can't wait to see it.*

PHEME: *It's being delivered next week. Do you want to know the title?*

ERIS: *Not even a little teeny bit.*

PHEME: *The Great Grand Gargantuan Goat Parade! It has enhanced smell features so you're right in the thick of it.*

ERIS: *Someday I'll send you to meet our maker. Right when you least expect it.*

PHEME: *But not today, deary. Not today.*

I shook off my memories and took my seat at the small table where I read and reached for my cards, but my mom stopped me.

"You look a little bockety. I think you should try something different today. These books showed up earlier, and I'd like to see if you can read them." She dropped six enormous texts on the table, and I half expected the wood to groan under the weight. They were each more than a foot long and covered in worn leather with split pages swollen from years of reading. Each had an arcane symbol on the cover, some I recognized and others foreign to me.

I opened the cover on top and she closed it on me. "Not like that. Read them." She tapped me on the forehead and disappeared into the storeroom, leaving me alone with the books.

I took the top one into my lap, closed my eyes, and lay my hands on top of the cover, my thumbs resting on the ouroboros symbol in the center. I found my focus quickly, my practice paying off as I sunk deeper into meditation. It was easier to get into a magical headspace; I was still hit-or-miss to create any spells, but clearing the first hurdle of focus was a gift unto itself.

My mind drifted to the meaning of the ouroboros, the snake that eats itself, on the cover. The sign of the infinite, the whole of creation, and the full expression of time and self-discovery came into view. A representation of how we consume our earthly bodies, live feeding on tissue and health until we shrivel and die. I could make out how our pursuit of knowledge costs us the potential of our younger selves, how procreating fed on parents, imparting that knowledge cost them energy and power. For a moment, it was terrifying, how the body dwindles as the mind grows, how the spirit is enriched as the mind falters.

The next book on the pile was thinner and newer looking, but equally large. It bore a symbol I didn't recognize, the general shape, some form of sacred geometry, squares, triangles, circles all perfectly spaced.

The moment my hand touched the book, I felt myself falling, hard, and then suddenly jerked back. I felt the balance align as though someone had spiritually adjusted my spine to open up the energy in my body. The world around me went blue-white, blinding me to everything but the brightness.

My throat was closing, my breathing labored. I tried to reach my neck, but my hands were tied behind my back. Every inhale gargled with blood, and I could feel it aspirating into my lungs. The whiteness brightened to noonday sun, blistering my eyes. It was so hot, so chokingly menacing on my skin. I felt beaten, bruised.

Hot trickles of filth caressed my legs and body, my feet swelling with blood. I looked down, seeing my feet dangling over an open square on a wooden platform. I swung, violently jerking to try and free myself, the rope around my throat getting tighter with each spasmodic twist. The light fluttered, white sparks at the sides of my vision accompanied a pounding in my head I recognized as my slowing heartbeat. I lost control of my bodily functions and felt it drip from my toes, my body finally still. I was pinned at the moment between body death, brain death, and what we believe is the soul's vanishing.

The sound of the chimes at the front of the store shocked me out of the trance, and when I jumped up, I dropped the book, and my vision came back. I hurried over to welcome our shopper and crashed face-first into Declan's chest. He grabbed me by the biceps and moved me away, trying to get a look at my face.

"By the Source, Callie, what happened to you?" He was frantic, pulling me back toward the stockroom, crying for my mother.

Her face was just as shocked, but nowhere near as horrified. She turned me around to face an old ornate mirror she kept on the wall and said, "The Tree of Life had something to tell you."

My eyes glowed a golden amber within deep pools of red as blood vessels burst in my eyes. My hair was streaked through white amidst the dishwater blonde, reminding me of soap sud colored highlights.

"What the shit?!" I screamed.

"You had a vision, Callie." My mother handed me a pair of dark sunglasses to cover my bloody eyes.

"Will this fade?" I shivered and worried my life would be uncomfortable if I showed up everywhere looking like I had two amber flashlights in pools of blood on the front of my face.

"The blood will heal. I have some salve that will help. Your eyes will fade, and we can cover your hair," she promised. "What did you see?"

"I was being hung on the gallows. From the snap of my neck to the last beat of my heart, I hung there, struggling. It happened the moment I touched the book with the sacred geometry on the cover." I sank into a worn wingback chair where my mother relaxed during slow hours. Declan handed me a glass of water and I was thankful that this time my drama had broken the ice. Once more, I let him take care of me.

He pulled out a chair at the table where we had had lunch earlier and opened his beat-up messenger bag. "Did the Source tell you about this?" He pulled out a small bag the color of cream and lay it on the table. I shook my head.

"It's a hex bag," my mother admitted. A brief, disturbing flash of recognition flickered behind her eyes, invisible to the untrained senses. "Where'd you find it?" She took the bag in her hand and closed her eyes. She had an unrivaled clairsentience, an ability to know things about objects and their history through her magic. Her face softened as she centered herself and read. She looked so peaceful, she glowed.

"Among the remains. It must have been on Ruari's body at the time of the explosion," Declan admitted quietly.

"Declan, do you know why I can't see inside the bag?" My mother sounded briefly concerned.

"We can't figure it out. It looks like canvas, but it's something much stronger than that. We can't see into the bag, and we can't open it. We know it's magic, but we don't know anything about it. Even the scans from our lab came back unknown fibers."

"Tell them," Clue howled softly in my mind. *"You're right. Tell them."*

"It's woven from a hangman's rope. That's what the Book of Sacred Geometry was trying to show me before it blew my eyes out and prematurely aged me." I sat quietly, waiting for the laughter or dismissal, but nobody made a sound. My mother seemed to sink into herself at the thought.

The air around us grew hot and thick under suspicion. Hangman's rope couldn't be any rope used in an execution. It needed to be the execution of an innocent person. It acted as a lead box around powerful magic, preventing detection from scientific and arcane sources. If someone cursed my grandfather's boat, the bag woven from the rope of a hangman would act as both a calling card and mask for the murderer.

Cloth of a hangman's rope had to be magically woven from the fibers of the rope, normally silk, painstakingly separated into individual strands and then woven back together on a loom of solid silver. A single rope from a hanging would create only a small amount of fabric because the fibers could not be cut once the rope was removed from the neck of the executed. No matter how long the rope was when you started, you had a small, finite number of strands to use, and you couldn't weave more than one rope together.

It was a magic of furious attention—all weaving had to be done at the same time. The weaver couldn't leave the loom and return later to finish. Once the process had begun, it had to be completed, or the rope was ruined and any residual magic from the tragedy would unravel as the fibers did.

"If that's true, we'd need to know the caster and spell to get into the bag," Declan explained.

"Let me work with it for a while. Maybe I can get into it. I'll get Sunny or my mother to help," my mom offered.

"I saw Sunny on my way here. She was walking her class to the library. The costumes came out super cute," Declan said.

"Which costumes?" I asked.

"She and her class made huge, orange duckbill hats to wear on walking trips. Your sister also has an oversized Mother Goose bonnet that she wears, and they all carry a cord she blessed to keep them safe." My mother pointed out the window over my shoulder.

I turned and sure enough, my sister was walking toward the store, on the opposite side of the street, probably going back to the elementary school from the library. She was followed by at least fifteen tiny ducklings, each clinging to a navy cord. I'm pretty sure they were singing, too.

Declan jumped up and opened the door so we could watch them walk past. They clapped on cue and sang along with my sister who spun around at the front of the line. The song was familiar in a way that pricked tears in my eyes behind decades of memories and moments she and I had shared. It made me want to be a teenager with my darling sister, the greatest sidekick in history.

"So, let's cause a scene, clap our hands and stomp our feet, or something. Yeah, something. I just gotta get my class back to room Three B!" She'd taken "The First Single" by The Format and reworked it to suit her class trip and my heart caught in my throat.

There was unspoken knowledge at that moment. It was a happy baby sister, sitting in the front seat of my car, top-down, sun shining, and us singing together so many years ago. She took that, she kept those memories and replayed them with her students. I'm not going to say that's the key to being immortal, but it's the closest I've ever felt. I could hear the ringing of a bell I'd struck so long ago, still vibrating through lives to make little ones happy.

"You made that magic, Callie." Declan leaned in close and whispered in my ear. My skin tingled and I wanted to turn my head, lean into his chest, and love him with every fiber of my being.

He kissed my forehead and gave my mother a farewell I didn't hear, being too wrapped up in the golden memory. Knowing my life had made an impact, however small, inspired me. I wanted to be a better witch.

I found motivation for my studies in those children. That feeling of putting lasting kindness into the world had gripped me by the heart and pulled me toward whatever potential I could muster. I went back to the books, concentrating hard to center myself, connect with the universe, and develop the magic that bubbled so near to the surface.

That warm feeling slowly spread up my arms from the third book, the thickest and shortest of the stack. Magical symbols and Greek letters encircled a pentacle on the cover. This book spoke of the history of our magic, tried and tested beginner spells, and tips for casting and tapping into the vast power of the Source. I probably should have started here first; back to the basics, exactly what I needed.

I sat with the book for almost forty minutes with not a single moment of magic. I could have been meditating on a brick for all the inspiration it gave me. It wasn't even a hollow, pregnant silence I could enter to experience the stillness of whatever void held our magic before we accessed it. It was a dense, thick silence, brick-like, impenetrable, uncomfortable.

It hurt more because it was the simplest of books giving me the hardest time. My neck prickled with discomfort, the hot and damp fresh-from-the-shower and wearing a wool sweater feeling that made me slightly carsick.

I couldn't stop thinking about Declan. Here I was, a date set up with a doctor who didn't seem to have a tall girlfriend who didn't age or have her makeup smear. She didn't crash into a tray full of water and then break all of the blood vessels in her eyes because her magic hated her.

I don't think Beaux even broke a sweat doing magic. And our magic was made to manifest by hard work and dedication to our craft. We had power, yes, but without training and study and work, there was no craft. We needed to learn to hone and cultivate our abilities, and some of us made things worse while others stood there, looking perfect and calm, doing long division in her bitchy head.

The prickles got worse, and I felt bad for my parents and their shame. I spent my day floundering from self-induced crisis to self-induced crisis in public so the whole town could see the lame witch my parents wrought. I tried to center my thoughts, but I was sure Beaux didn't fall, and if she did, she had magic to clean herself up. She had magic she could control, and she had control over her feelings. I couldn't even control my thoughts.

"Center, focus," I told myself and took a deep breath, but instead of relaxing, I was seething, furious with myself. I shook with rage.

How dare everyone I love be so happy and healthy and proficient? Why did I have to be the one to bring up the rear in this parade? The warmth in my body shrank from my core, drawing down my arms, but it didn't flow back to the book. It centered in my palms, itching like white-hot needles, and I convulsed uncontrollably. My fingers felt swollen and sausage-like, but stronger than they'd ever been.

I gripped the book; almost sure I could rip it in half if my rage would channel deeper into my fingers. I opened my eyes when I felt my nails growing. For the briefest second, I fancied myself having enough magic to manicure beautiful nails that never chipped or cracked.

These nails were not beautiful. They didn't look human at all. They were long and curved to deadly points, my hands gray and shriveled.

I blinked in disbelief at the talons at the end of my arms and fear crushed my anger like an anvil from the heavens. When I stopped shaking, my hands were normal again, although gouges marred the book I'd been holding. Deep, angry scratches ran across the back from the center out.

I did not hallucinate the talons. They were real.

Chapter Fourteen

This probably doesn't even need to be its own section...

PHEME: *Welcome to today's special podcast, where we're taking your questions once again!*

ERIS: *You ran out of topics again, didn't you?*

PHEME: *I get eight hundred messages a day—more than that if we don't answer any on the show.*

ERIS: *I never thought you'd be one to cave to audience pressure!*

PHEME: *If you're finished?*

ERIS: *Proceed.*

PHEME: *Our first question comes from Galatea in Salem. Galatea writes, 'Dear BCBAD, I've been looking for a map or photos of Blue Crab Bay, but I can't find anything. There's almost nothing on the internet, no descriptions of the businesses or companies that sponsor your podcast, even when I use the addresses you give out. I really want to know what the most magical place in the South looks like. Can you tell me?*

ERIS: *Ahhh... Clever.*

PHEME: *I considered a sponsor named Iliana's Info-dumpers, but the audience has questions.*

ERIS: *I thought you drank some Tell Us What The Town Looks Like tonic.*

PHEME: *There's nowhere near enough alliteration in that to be a real sponsor.*

ERIS: *Tell them about the clock, then.*

PHEME: *Okay, listeners, because of our special magical residents, the town isn't readily available on map systems.*

ERIS: *Even when they are, they only show the illusions we've built to protect our area.*

PHEME: *So, the center of the City of Blue Crab Bay is set up like a piazza, a central square or circle that has a clock-like setup. If we look at it from the water's edge, going straight west, the twelve o'clock building is Llewellyn's General store, with the Wicked Cookie Cafe at the one o'clock point. Moving down to two o'clock there's a small bench and shaded sitting area before you reach Already Been Boughton, the finest consignment store in the central US time zone. Around four or five o'clock is Shorsey's Dive Bar, a SCUBA rental service where they also plan excursions into the bay and offer tableside cooking of the day's catches.*

ERIS: *It's more raw bar than beer bar!*

PHEME: *They sell drinks!*

ERIS: *Dive Bar is such false advertising.*

PHEME: *Do you want to take over?*

ERIS: *My bad.*

PHEME: *At five on the clock outside of the piazza, we have the Eastwick Hotel at Mayfair Point, the tallest building in the bay at* three stories. And at six o'clock, right on the waterline, is the Sunset Pub, owned by the mayor. It's the only establishment constructed on the east side of Bay Way, the boulevard that runs across the bottom end of the piazza. It's technically a drivable street, but it's been closed to vehicular traffic since the Sunset Pub was originally built right after Hurricane Katrina.

ERIS: *It's much more restaurant than pub nowadays. There really aren't any great drinking establishments around here.*

PHEME: *We're just talking about the square! At seven, maybe seven-thirty, is the Gallery Aesthetica, the finest art gallery in our state. Nine o'clock finds us at Papa Smile's Olde Fashioned Soda Fountain and Ice Cream Shoppe – who many of our listeners will remember is a sponsor!*

ERIS: *My favorite sponsor!*

PHEME: *Because of their dedication to the Apothecary Soda Fountain aesthetic?*

ERIS: *What? No! They'll put booze in the shakes after two o'clock in the afternoon.*

PHEME: *You're going to confuse people, Eris!*

ERIS: *Whoopsie!*

PHEME: *And at ten o'clock there's The Dove & Pearl Antiquities, Inspirational Gifts, and more. Further southwest is Anne Boleyn High School—*

ERIS: *Go Banshees!*

PHEME: *—and Harkness Park. Straight west is the Blue Crab Bugle and WBCB TV, our local affiliate. Northwest is Petronilla De Meathe Elementary School, The Secret Keeper's Bookstore, and Guardian Hospital. Continuing northwards you can find the Blue Crab Bay Yacht and Sailing Club—*

ERIS: *Pretentious fart sniffers...*

PHEME: *—and the Bay Marina and boat launch. Straight south, past the Sunset Pub, you can find St. Tituba the Powerful, the oldest church in the area.*

ERIS: *You left out a lot!*

PHEME: *How do you want me to explain the placement of Holland's Farm or The Law Firm of Balk, Hubble, Spellman, Weatherwax & Rosen?*

ERIS: *You left out the fountain.*

PHEME: *There's a fountain in the center of Pelican Square.*

ERIS: *It's much more than a fountain.*

PHEME: *It's an eighteen-foot-tall sea goddess holding a blue crab in one hand and a staff in another.*

ERIS: *It's a statement about the divine female, built on a solid marble foundation and surrounded by a hand-carved marble reservoir that features the golden apple that my namesake dropped into the wedding of the very same sea goddess to start a war.*

PHEME: *For the fairest, Eris.*

ERIS: *It's poetic, isn't it?*

PHEME: *Legendary.*

ERIS: *Thetis is the leader of the Nerieds. It's a special story to our area.*

PHEME: *And that's why we saved her fountain for last.*

ERIS: *You know, this might be our first full show where I don't actively hate you! Today was fun. Read the sponsor and let's get some lunch!*

PHEME: *Do you have a podcast partner who acts like a preteen with a particularly problematic personality? Portia Pebblebrooke Painted Protection, Punishment, and Prison Printings give parents* *a way to help their children find empathy in the everyday. Is your teen overly concerned with status and reputation? Let them spend a day inside a Dickens' drama or a Dostoyevski dystopia. Will your youngins not stop fighting with you about food? A minute in* Les Miserables *should cut that conflict. Escort them to empathy with Emily Dickenson or motivate them through the mischief with some memorable Mark Twain! Just a day in the life of a put-upon protagonist has been proven to provide plenty of perspective to even the most problematic preteens. Don't be shy! Send your horny hellion into a hot pot of sin with our Paradise Lover's package, where they can spend the morning with Lady Chatterly and the evening with John Milton. Read along as they learn their lesson and come back a whole new kid. Portia Pebblebrook! Providing parents a positive place to placate their preteens since 1899. Perfectly placed at the Pelican Piazza for your convenient shopping pleasure!*

ERIS: *All those P's and not one allusion to Practical Magic? Pathetic...*

PHEME: *Picky picky.*

Sunny arrived shortly after that, carrying a flask of discovery potion to see inside the hex bag. Every drop seemed to evaporate off the bag without working.

"Is that the potion I made? It might not be strong enough..." I tried to explain.

"Grandpa made this one," Sunny promised. "So, I know it's powerful, and unless he made the hex bag or worked the curse on himself, it should work instantly. He always said that with enough of this, he could see through time." She put her arm around my shoulder, and I leaned my head on her. There would be a million moments coming for us to remember his wisdom, humor, and love as the knife of grief slipped in and nicked our hearts.

"He also said that about Irish whiskey, mushroom tea, and flying ointment," I reminded Sunny. She sighed deeply and then choked. I bit my lips together and snorted. Soon we were both cracking up at the memory of my grandfather and his old sayings.

My mother was digging through old Grimoires and Books of Shadows to find any magic that would work on such a malevolent item. The problem was we couldn't determine if it was malevolent, dangerous, inept, or inert. It was a hollow void of information, cold and calculating. No good magic would be bound in cloth woven from a hangman's rope, but we couldn't pinpoint any details that would give us a jumping-off point. That level of protection of the contents also kept us from seeing for whom the hex bag was made.

We were looking for a wand in a sea of shillelaghs and having no luck. I didn't mind the time spent in the store. It was rare that all of us were able to be together and on the same side of a cause.

A nest of pages in a deep green, leather-bound book, no bigger than my hand, caught my eye. Beautiful drawings of trees, branches, entwining roots that spelled words encircled every page on both sides.

Walk. Run. Fly. Time. Each page had a single word header drawn in the brambles, a complicated list of ingredients, and rules for working the spell. The header word was English, but the rest of the page was written in Enochian, not Lineara. That alone was noteworthy but not entirely applicable to the hex bags.

"Momma, take a look at this." I handed her the book, my thumb marking the page.

"Is that Enochian?" Sunny asked, looking over our mother's shoulder. "Who wrote spells in Enochian?"

My mother stared at the page, running her fingertips over the parchment, her smile spreading gently.

"Your grandmother Aoife wrote these. I think she may have discovered them or invented them." My mother read the spells, careful and slow, respectful of the language of the angels, disputed as it was by both witch and non-witch academics.

My mother finished reading the first page and the book shot a bright green light out of the designs on the side of the page. She set the book down carefully on the table, not having expected the reaction.

"That's a portal." Sunny put her hand over the light, and it pushed straight through her and created a patchwork of leaves on the ceiling, unimpeded by her hand.

"A portal to where?" I'd never seen magic at this level before. My mom shook her head and shrugged. "Touch it, Sunny," I said.

"I'm not touching it—I've got parent-teacher conferences tonight." Sunny crossed her arms, defiant. I missed the sister from a decade back who did whatever I told her.

There wasn't a menacing feeling in the light at all, so I knew it wasn't fear that kept my sister away. She was being responsible, but I had little to do tonight. I reached out to touch the page with my hand, and instantly I slipped my arm through the page to my elbow, my hand no longer attached to my body, though all the feeling remained. I pulled my hand back, unhurt. I tried again, this time moving my hand, trying to see what I could grab.

"Do you feel anything?" my mother asked.

I shook my head and reached deeper. My hand grazed against something cold and smooth, and I tried to grab it.

"There's something there, I can feel it. It feels like a jar, maybe porcelain." Right as I reached around the item, it wobbled, and a huge crash sounded from the greenhouse. Each of us jumped and I jerked my hand out of the book.

"Is someone breaking in?" Sunny hurried around behind me, baby sister once again.

"What's on your hand?" my mother asked me, and I looked down. My fingers were gray at the tips. "Do they feel different?"

Panic burst to life in my chest, seizing my heart. "Am I dying, Momma?" I clutched my wrist and backed up. "Is this necrotizing fasciitis? My fingers are going to rot off, aren't they?"

"Callie, relax," Mom tried. "Let me see." She reached for me, but I backed off again, worried she'd find something terrible and irreversible. I was so stupid for reaching into that damn book.

"Why did you stick your hand in that book?" Sunny whined. She stumbled, backing away from me, her face a horror. "I'm going to check the greenhouse. I can't look at rotting flesh."

"Oh, is it rotting? Mom! Is it rotting!" I held it out and showed her my fingers, gray fingerprints that were surely soon to rot off. "Can you smell the rot? Ugh, it's decaying flesh, I know it! This is my writing hand, Mommy!!!"

She seized my wrist and dragged me toward the greenhouse while I struggled and cried.

"I'm gonna be the one-handed witch, aren't I? I'm going to be Callie the Lefty from now on. What if this happened to both hands and I can't pick my nose anymore? Momma, I can't lose my hands to flesh-eating magic bacteria. I know I have chubby little sausage fingers, but they're *my* little chubby sausage fingers and I don't want them to rot until they're putrid flesh and hollow bone! I feel sick. I think I'm getting a fever. Is it hot? Oh god, it's gray. Is it ashes? Am I getting ready to spontaneously combust? Sunny, get me the ice! How is my whole day so awful—almost blinded and now burned?! Oh Sunny, help! The heat is rising!"

In the greenhouse, my mother walked over to where Sunny was looking at a smashed amphora that held dried dill. She let me go and crouched to pick up the handle piece of the broken jar.

"That's what I thought." She stood and held out the handled shard. I couldn't look at it. I was concentrating on my slowly burning fingers. "Callie! You're not burning, you have dust on your fingertips, calm down!" She snatched my hand back and held it toward the shard which had five fingertip-shaped circles where the dust had transferred from the jar to my fingers before I knocked it off the ledge.

"How the...?" I didn't understand how I could have pushed the jar. My mother pointed up at the Magnolia tree that grew through the greenhouse. My grandfather had built the greenhouse around it more than half a century before. I'd never noticed that near the top, almost directly across from the clean circle where the amphorae had sat, was a carving identical to the one in the book.

"So, Grandmother Aoife could bend space-time?" Sunshine asked, reaching up the side of the tree.

"I think this is some sort of metaphysical secret passage. I bet there's a tree at our house that has the same symbol. There have been whispers about legends of witches who could escape through trees, hidden portals into the woods, but I've never known anyone who could do it or who knew how to learn." My mother returned to the table and grabbed the book.

"See, this is too small to pass a human through, unless it was a child. She would have needed other portals for adults," my mother explained.

"Why the Enochian?" Sunny asked.

"I have no idea, but I have a theory. I think someone told her the spell in Enochian with some sort of angelic interference maybe." My mom shut the book and moved it away from where I'd been sitting. "Let me work with this a little and see what I can find out. I don't want anyone getting hurt or lost."

Sunny put the amphorae I broke back together and collected the dill from where it had scattered, shaking it off before returning it to the shelf. I was briefly both proud and jealous her magic was so seemingly effortless. It renewed my conviction to learn to connect with my magic, no matter how hard it seemed.

My mother wanted to swing by Holland's Farm to pick up a case of eggs and the half cow Allegra would butcher for our summer dinners. Clue heard the word "farm" and immediately jumped into the bed of my brother's truck which my mother had borrowed for the haul. My dear familiar was sure she could convince my mother, non-verbally, to pick up a leg of lamb since it was technically after Easter, and they might be on sale. They offered to pick up Sunshine from the parent meetings when they swung back through the Bay.

I offered to lock up the store so I could practice casting protection wards that would wear off at a specific time. The spells were easy, but the intention I had to master was more complicated. I needed to essentially tell the magic when to turn off, when to dissipate back into the world and leave the building. I left through the back door and kneeled on the lavender sea glass stone that acted as a doormat and kept our magic protected while we worked inside. It also acted like a Slip-and-slide during even the lightest rainstorm—even a good, hard fog would render that rectangle a death trap.

I focused slowly, drawing my magic into me to protect the building and evaporate one minute before eight in the morning. Deeply inhaling, I concentrated on my mother's soft, lilac-scented protection spells until my breath sparkled in the evening light. Each exhalation cast more soft light around the building where it seeped in and created a web of light points. There was a gentle hum, a single short note from an angelic voice before the magic disappeared into the building. The magic felt good, simple, complete.

I stood to check the one addition I made to the old spell. Sure enough, the lavender sea glass was backlit by numbers counting down, exactly to the moment until the spell wore off. I had added a digital timer, visible only from directly above the glass rectangle to basically show my work and check my spelling math.

I wasn't totally sure what the phrase "high on the hog" meant, but if it meant I felt like my competency was a giant inflatable piggy I could ride around the parking lot of my mother's business, then I was "high on the hog" of magical arrogance. The spell was a flourish, obviously, but it was my first signature. I'd never added a twist before, and that it worked so flawlessly had me floating.

However, my glorious witch senses were nothing to write home about, because I was halfway into the driver seat of my car with something pointy digging into my temple before I noticed anything amiss. My instincts said, "Bat! Rabies! Run!" so I screamed and flailed around wildly, scratching myself across both hands and forearms fighting an invisible, and quite possibly, blood-sucking monster.

Launching myself out of the car and onto the gravel parking lot, I scurried away until my knees were bloody. I crawled until I was wedged completely under a Jeep Wrangler parked clear on the other side of the lot. It was the first car I saw and knew I could get out from under and not be stuck until the driver came out and ran over me.

Then, I felt ridiculous, and my knees were on fire. Inching myself forward on my toes as I tried to keep my knees elevated, I wormed out from under the Jeep and rolled onto my back. Several deep breaths later, I figured either the bat was gone, or it was just going to have to be the owner of a decade-old convertible for the twenty seconds it took for me to burn it to the ground. I didn't go into this experience with any known fear of bats, prior. I did have a problem with things that attacked my head and hands and forearms in tight spaces, so Batty had to pay.

Nicknaming my nemesis Batty reminded me of Bitty's Bat Shop, a guano supplier who advertised on the local witch podcast. Not that I could call them for assistance since my bag was still where I flung it on the passenger seat before the attack. If I could grab the bag without dying, I could call for help.

Making my way back across the gravel, I noted I was limping on a sore ankle that must have twisted wrong when I hit the ground. That was the point where I'd had it with myself. Crawling around in a parking lot terrified of a tiny flying mouse was an embarrassment even I couldn't fathom at this point. It didn't escape me that in our first encounter, the bat kicked the shit out of me, and I had no idea if I'd even dislodged it from my roof.

I shook myself straight, adjusted my clothes, cracked my neck, and stomped back to my car, taking care to avoid putting my full weight on my sore ankle. It took a minute to see there was another oblong figure on top of my car. For the briefest of seconds, I guessed the bat had left the interior and perched on the top to square off with me the moment I came back, but it was a smooth outline.

When I finally figured out it was not a bat, but instead an icepick someone stabbed through my ragtop, my fury extinguished all of my embarrassment. I didn't fight off a bat and run scared like an idiot. I fought with an inanimate icepick, hurt myself, left a dozen scratches on my arms, and then crawled away in a panic.

Flapping gently, pinned against my car with the icepick, was a note. That was certainly a way to get someone's attention. And if I found out who had just cost me the price of a new convertible top, I'd give them more than my cursory glance in exchange for that shit.

I almost grabbed the handle but wondered if there would be fingerprints to destroy, so instead I reached in the door and pressed upward on the sharp point to pop out the pick. I popped too hard and sent the pick sliding off the roof before it rolled down the windshield, skidded across the hood, and flopped handle-first in the mud beneath the bushes at the front of the car.

I stuffed the note in my pocket, prints be damned, and went to my trunk to grab an old shoebox so I could scoop the pick out of the mud without touching it. Taking half a pound of mud with the pick, I put it in my trunk, covered the box with the lid, grabbed a roll of duct tape from my emergency kit, and shut the trunk. I'd think about mud and fingerprints later.

Cautiously, I got myself into the driver's seat and tore off a small silver square of tape with my teeth to temporarily seal the hole in the roof and put on my seatbelt. My keys went into the ignition, I turned on the lights, turned off the air conditioner, and then removed the note. I wasn't about to chance having the note blow out of my hands and fly into the mud. It could be a love note from someone who had psychotic tendencies, but maybe they had warm brown eyes and just needed a Rubenesque disaster lady to help them find happiness and curb their crazy.

It wasn't a love note.

The handwriting—and I used that word with the loosest interpretation imaginable—was part scratched missive and part printed language that spidered across the page menacingly:

Stix & stones brake witch bones & u cain't catch me

That was pretty much exactly what I should have expected. I stuffed the note back in my pocket, turned off the lights, and pulled out of the parking lot, the words from the note echoing in my brain.

I took the long way home but still arrived before my mother and sister. Aden wasn't home so I went upstairs and sat on my bed, grabbing my cards to see if I could work a bit of magic to try and pinpoint anything of value in the note. I didn't plan to deal a full spread because I wasn't giving myself a reading. I just wanted a few cards to point me in a direction toward the note-scrawler's identity.

Shuffle. Cut. Hierophant. I smiled when the cards told me I was on the right track.

The note was related to Grandpa Ruari. I kept going.

Shuffle. Cut. Hierophant. That got a chuckle and a verbal moment of gratitude for the reinforcement.

Shuffle. Cut. Hierophant.

"I give thanks to the Source for confirming my path of seeking is headed in its intended direction. I beg for further clues or directions to help me bring Grandfather's killer to justice. Also, Ginger. And maybe a smidge of justice for the roof of my car?" I ended in a whisper but meant every word.

Two Hierophants later and I was screaming over the deck.

"My grandpa didn't leave the damn icepick in my roof! Now, you show me an answer that doesn't involve the Hierophant, or I will set you on fire in the yard!"

"Do they ever respond?" Aden had come home and found me in a one-sided screaming match with an inanimate object. It wasn't the first time. He towered in my doorway, broad and tall, leaning against the frame. He wore a pale yellow T-shirt and black basketball shorts; a drumstick twirled in the fingers of his good hand, his wand in disguise.

"The only response they have is The Hierophant. I don't get it. I've drawn it six times. Do you think it could possibly be chance?" I needed someone to tell me I wasn't insane.

"What about an icepick? Aden asked and took a seat in the floral wingback chair that sat against my wall.

I told him the story. When he finished wiping tears from his eyes and howling over the bat attack, he wandered into my bathroom and returned with an unmarked amber jar and some cotton wrap. Sitting back down in front of me, he patted his knee, and I gently set my heel on his thigh. Slowly and methodically, he dabbed a fragrant ointment on the swollen areas of my ankle and wrapped it in gauze, taking care to one-handedly leave the gauze loose enough to allow blood flow. I sighed deeply when I could feel the cold, wet poultice making magic against my sore ankle.

"Thank you so much," I sighed. Relief finally washed over me. "And one-handed at that."

I tried to return the favor, do something nice for him, and pulled the pencil out of my hair.

"I knew it was going to be a pencil," Aden said, nodding at my transfigured wand. "Sunny has a matchstick."

"She's really committed to that fire aesthetic, huh?" I asked and pointed my pencil wand at him, trying to conjure a can of seltzer from the kitchen fridge as a refreshment thank you. Instead, I shot a pop can at his face from twelve feet away. He dodged fast to the side and caught the can before it hit the wall behind him and exploded.

"You can just say 'thank you' next time," Aden said.

I put away my tarot cards, just in case my next magical malfunction would ruin them.

"Where's the icepick? I can take a look at it. See if it's salvageable?"

"In my trunk," I answered and handed him the note. "Anything familiar?"

"No, but did someone chew on this?" Aden held up the paper by a corner, and I noticed the chewed edges.

"What? Ew. Why?" I was so tired of insanity following me around.

"Maybe saliva magic?" Aden suggested.

"Maybe psychosis, you mean?" I shot back. I'd spoken sharply without meaning it. It wasn't Aden's fault he was calm and patient. Not everyone needed to flail around like a fool because I was good enough at it, I didn't need help.

"It smells like iodine," Aden said as he wafted the paper toward his face.

"Iodine? Iodine isn't magical!" I reminded him.

"Not necessarily, not magic like we practice, but it's pretty common non-witch magic. There are a lot of 'magic' tricks we learned in science class that included iodine." Aden stood and nodded at me to follow him down to my car.

I popped the trunk and pointed at nothing. The icepick was gone. The shoebox was gone, and there wasn't a single trace of mud anywhere on the trunk's tan carpeting.

"Did you bring it in?" Aden asked while moving my emergency bag.

"No. I did enough damage and didn't want to screw up any possible fingerprints." I promised. "You didn't see anything when you got home?"

"No. Maya dropped me off and I came straight inside." He shrugged.

I was frantically digging at the carpet, looking for a hole in the floor, a gap between the edge of the trunk, wondering how I could manage to lose something so important.

"Is there magic that can make something be someplace but then snap back to where it should be? Like, could someone conjure an icepick to stick the note to my car and make it vanish at the right time?" I didn't want to ask about the great conjure witch that Aden and I both knew could pull off a spell that complicated.

"Callie," Aden pulled me out of the trunk where I dug at the corner of the carpet, about to rip the back end of my vehicle apart to see if the icepick, box, box top, and mud all fell down the side of the car somehow. "Callie, time magic isn't that precise. It's really hard to make magic disappear at a certain moment, let alone an item. It's way more likely whoever did this just bespelled it out of your trunk when they saw you get in the car."

"They would have been watching me..." I froze. I'm ashamed to admit I was less afraid of a taunting psychopath watching me from close by than I was of someone, anyone, seeing the flailing mess I'd been. Would I rather be murdered than humiliated?

I sat in the driveway, giving up, and falling against my car, exhausted, disheartened, and deeply concerned I was hallucinating things. At least Aden had the note.

Aden's truck's headlights appeared at the far end of the property as my mother, sister, and Clue wound their way up the drive. My baby familiar soared out of the truck bed, a thick, sinewy, leg of lamb twice her size clenched in her strong jaws.

"*Look what I got! Cooter told me I could come get anything I want if you bring me there!*" Clue chirped and passed right by me, unconcerned with my hopeless exhaustion, trotting right into the house.

"You want to see if Mom can...?" Aden whispered, but I shot him a dark look. We stared wordlessly at each other until he nodded his understanding. Our mother was slowly getting out of his truck, moving like a woman who could barely balance on her legs. She didn't need any more stress.

"No. If they were watching and wanted to hurt me, they had plenty of chances. This is someone getting off on scaring me—I'm not letting them scare her too." I stood, brushed off, and vowed to seize control of my life once and for all.

Chapter Fifteen

Everyone around me has pretty much had it with my smart mouth...

PHEME: *Welcome back to Blue Crab Bay After Dark, your number-one local podcast by witches, for the witches of Blue Crab Bay! Joining me as always is my partner, Eris!*

ERIS: *Today we're talking about magical signatures!*

PHEME: *We are! We've been getting a lot of messages about the signatures we as witches find attached to spells and why they happen. We're going to start with love magic.*

ERIS: *Yeah, yeah, yeah, love magic smells like florals. Everyone already knows that. We need to talk about the smells we don't always recognize.*

PHEME: *Our readers are asking about all signatures! That includes the ones you think are boring, Eris.*

ERIS: *The important smells are always the scary ones: brimstone, Carrion flower, Lantana, Bradford Pear, and dung. Those are the smells that tell you bad magic is around.*

PHEME: *That is hardly an exhaustive list and those are insanely specific smells! Are you trying to scare our audience?*

ERIS: *I'm trying to prepare them! All five senses are critical in the craft, but none more so than smell. Smell is what alerts us to danger before the other senses kick in and young witches need to know...* **PHEME:** *And we are going to talk about all of them, right after a brief message.... Are you struggling to conjure correctly? Do you need lessons on channeling the inner sense of magic when casting older spells? Are you concerned you don't know the difference between sweaty and sweltering? Magic is about nuance and knowing the exact sensations you should expect, and the exact motivations you should invoke will help you cast cleaner, clearer, more clever spells with less exertion! Valkyrie's Voluminous Vocabularium is the premier, total imagination immersion into information. Fully tactile; experience the sensations of selcouth, serein or sonorous. Experience the elation of ecstasy as it evolves into Elysian effervescence! Overwhelmingly olfactory; smell-o-vision scents for every signature spell. Visually viscous; an overwhelming experiential viewing to cement your language and magical connection. Auditory awareness of calls, cries, and the different crunches that snap magic into success. Valkyrie's Voluminous Vocabularium is your single source for sensory understanding.*

ERIS: *Have you ever tried to make Hugmeum and found your spell flavored more like cotton candy than creme soda? Does your dog shit smell like dingleberries because you're a dipshit? Step into the v-v-v-vestibule of FLAVOR-TOWN!*

PHEME: *I SAID VALKYRIE'S VOLUMINOUS VOCAB-*

ERIS: *Does your fairy dust smell like sweat socks? Are you unsure of what sweat socks smell like because you're senseless and stupid?*

PHEME: *WE DON'T GET PAID IF YOU DON'T LET ME FINISH!* **ERIS:** *Voopy Volupiter's Va Va voom dictionary for dummies!*

PHEME: *I know you're trying to be funny, but some parents find that children with learning disabilities benefit from experiential learning techniques. It helps them cement the knowledge of words that describe ephemeral concepts in their brains. I'd just like to remind you they listen to this and hear your attempt at humor.*

ERIS: *I didn't really consider that.*

PHEME: *I understand.*

ERIS: *I'm just making a kerfuffle. I'll stop. It actually sounds like a useful tool, and I'm just jealous I didn't think of it. I hope our listeners know I'm not a monster deep down. I'm just a foolish clown who took it too far. Pray, continue.*

PHEME: *Valkyrie's Voluminous Vocabularum, available at fine grimoire dealers, antique magical bookstores, and now on sale at The Secret Keeper's!*

ERIS: *What's that fine print?*

PHEME: *Nothing, I'm sure...*

ERIS: *YOU OLD BAG OF FART!*

PHEME: *I just, I mean, Eris... I'm not wrong.*

ERIS: *No, no, you're going to read it. Now finish it!*

PHEME: *Not to be used as a tool for tutoring kids with standard elementary school vocabulary lessons due to the psychedelic nature of the magic. Not to be used by those under 18, those with processing issues, sensory and seizure disorders, or other classroom testing situations.*

ERIS: *So, all that sanctimonious lecturing...?*

PHEME: *Find out what sanctimonious means in Valkyrie's new Voluminous...*
ERIS: *Virago.*
PHEME: *Yeesh. Vicious.*

My mother seemed to wilt more, every day. I'd never seen her shrink away from life and friends so dramatically. Taking on the family's service to the community in the absence of my father's presence and Aden's magic still being unaccounted for left her drained and exhausted. Even when I tried to remind her one cannot pour from an empty vessel, her haunted eyes just gazed through me. She was adamant to continue with her work to keep her mind away from the fear of losing my father.

This woman who'd lived in a perennially ageless and beguiling state took on the exhausted countenance of a life-beaten crone. She developed Allegra's sharp tone and fast irritation. She did her best when around us, trying to stop herself from griping and snapping, but she wore her exhaustion like the death shroud of our grandfather. I should have confronted her more, but I felt like my magic ineptitude was another irritation she'd have to manage, and I didn't want to overload her.

If my mother was bad, Allegra was worse. I could rationalize my mother's feelings; her sadness had sucked the life out of her, her partner and love of her life was comatose, faltering at the edge of consciousness.

Allegra barely showed up to check on my mother, and on the brief occasions when she did, she was a dick to be around. When she wasn't complaining and demanding, she was perfunctory, pushing my mother to move on and keep busy. Despite her years of experience, she couldn't nail down the empathy over her pragmatism. She could barely be bothered to show up most days, even though her home and office were only about a half mile from The Dove, despite my father making no progress coming out of the coma and my mother being a shadow of her vibrant self. I begged the Source to give me back the black claws so I could gouge her eyes out. Sadly, as usual, the universe declined.

My only salvation during that time was my sweet puppy who demanded we no longer call her a puppy because she was growing up and preferred we call her Clue, or She-Ra, because she was a talking puppy who enjoyed cartoons and cold cereal.

Dr. Noah and I didn't see each other much after his schedule shifted and he wasn't on duty in the mornings. We made plans to have our date and compromised that he would pick me up at The Dove at seven. He offered to pick me up from home, but I wanted to meet there. There was plenty of time to explain Dolphin House to him if something special developed.

Sunshine, Aden, and his girlfriend Maya McDonough plotted behind my back to combine my pre-date glow-up with a lesson on illusion magic, a specialty I was actually eager to learn.

"Ohhhhh, I love a first date!" Maya swirled into the house carrying a small box carved with roses. "Aden and I had our first date at the Cookie, too! He wore a pink paisley tie, and I lost my mind. So stinking cute! You're gonna be cute too! Let's get cracking!" She dashed up the stairs and left Sunny and me standing at the door, exhausted by her exuberance.

"It's okay if I start drinking before the date, right Sun?" I grumbled into my sister's ear.

"She's vivacious, but she's really good at this. I promise, you won't be disappointed." Sunny looped her arm through mine, and I trundled up the stairs.

Maya stood in front of my mirror, twirling her dress into different colors. With a swirl to the right, her dress became the softest blush-cream color. When she turned to the left, a shimmer of green spread across and turned the dress emerald.

"Let's get this bibbity bobbity bullshit over with. Teach me how to fix—" I gestured wildly all around my body, "all of this. Let's turn the excess weight into balance or some fairy wings or something to distract the doctor from my miserable personality?"

"You weren't kidding when you called her impossible?" Maya turned to ask my sister.

"Not even a little..." My sister dove into my closet, shoving everything to one side and tossing my sad gray rock onto my bed before digging around in the hamper.

"You called me impossible?" I wasn't surprised. I know I'm impossible, but knowing she knew it rubbed me a little raw. I can think I'm a mess, but having confirmation from the outside still stings.

"Your date starts in two hours. I can tell by your voice you haven't practiced this at all, and if you try and completely remake yourself into an unrecognizable alien goddess, your date won't know who you are, or he'll guess you're a witch and you'll smell like rotten garlic."

Sunny jerked my favorite nightshirt from the back of my closet with other dirty clothes. She lay it on the back of my chair, grabbed a spray bottle from her bag, and drenched the dress in what I guessed was fabric refresher.

"*Coloro, temporo poro nobis.*" Sunshine let her wand hover over the dress, and I watched the stains fade away as the colors revived to bright aqua and coral.

"Sunshine, did you pull a temporal swap?" Maya asked, a slight horror on her face.

"No, seriously? I wish. The only witch around here who can pull off something like that is Dec..." Sunny's neck snapped back, and she looked at me like she'd run over my puppy. Thank goodness my puppy was snoring and sprawled over my bed.

"You can say his name," I sighed. "What's a temporal swap?"

"Where you bring the original forward and send the current one back, so the energy maintains balance. It's conjure magic, but that was only a cleaning spell I got out of Grandpa Ruari's cookbook," Sunny explained as she shook out my dress.

"I mean, that's the theory, but nobody has ever actually done it. Like, let alone for a date dress; that kind of magic takes a large group of witches working within really strict parameters." Maya pushed the mirror in front of me and smiled brightly. "You're gonna do great, Callie. Take all the time you need, okay?"

"No magic is impossible. I'm sure the right witches could do it," Sunshine replied and handed me a cloudy lavender drink swirling with what smelled like mint. "Drink that."

"Not everyone draws from the same well of power that you have," I reminded my sister. I held my nose and drank deep. Oh, the delightful surprise of imagining a mojito and getting liquid Good N Plenty candies. It wasn't necessarily bad, but it was cloying and thick down my throat. My body and face did an unknown move that felt half sneeze and half full body shiver. I shook like a wet golden retriever and honked like an irate Canadian goose.

My magic flared to life, tingling within my skin.

"I want you to focus on the mirror, really look deep into yourself, Callie," Maya said. "Focus on the change from inside. Believe you can change."

I stared into the mirror, waiting for the change to happen, then trying to keep it going. It turned out, changing an appearance wasn't too hard. Sustaining that change was… well, as impossible as I am. Staring at myself in the mirror for so long made me feel like I was hallucinating. My face went from familiar to perfect stranger before I managed the first transition.

I saw a flicker behind the eyes, a flash of green, then blue.

"There it is! Hold it!" Maya cheered.

I was hit with the smell of what I thought was rotten cabbage and lost the change. "Why's it smell so bad?" I gagged a little and shook again.

"Everything has a cost." My sister shrugged. "You have to learn to control the smell, the change, the way others perceive you, it's part enchantment, part masking."

"Can you smell that?" I asked Maya, who looked horrified. My embarrassment swelled, and I wanted to quit and do my best on my own for the date.

"It's fine, Callie." Maya shook off her disgusted face and smiled at me gently. "I promise it's barely noticeable and I'm watching for it. Don't get discouraged! Try again."

She threw her arms around me, and again the smell of decay and rot hit me. I hugged her back with all of the appreciation I could muster, but it still felt off. I didn't want to hurt her feelings, but if she was gonna be my sister someday, I'd have to get her to settle down with the cheerful, loving-kindness because it's exhausting, and I deeply hated it.

When she pulled away, I caught a glimpse of myself in the mirror and realized she did most of the work for me. My hair was less dishwater and more golden-blonde and bronze-colored and looked bouncy and full, with glittery highlights. My eyes were clear and bright, and I looked like myself but better—a weekend-at-the-spa level of vibrancy emanate from me.

"She can't maintain that." Sunshine warned.

"I'll maintain it!" Maya promised. "Instead of holding onto a glamour, I did a little bibbity bobbity spell. She'll be fine until it wears off as long as she doesn't get soaking wet."

"Can you smell anything?" I lifted my shirt off my head and shoved my armpit into my little sister's face. She wasn't paying attention and fell right for it.

"Hellfire help me, Callie! Why are you like this?!?" Sunny gagged and pushed me, glaring at Maya who laughed so hard her eyes watered.

"It's my job as the big sister!"

"Get all that ridiculousness out of your system now..." Maya collapsed on my bed.

"There's no chance you're going to make it through dinner without farting, is there?" Sunny tossed me the dress she transfigured, and I immediately threw it back at her.

"Shouldn't he get to know the real me?" I looked at my sister, waiting for her to argue.

"You know what? Sure." She threw the dress back at me and walked toward my door. "Dress how you want. Let's go, Maya."

The air cracked with heat around my sister, and I knew she was irritated. Maya scrambled off my bed and hurried out as Sunny spun on her heels to leave.

"I mean... I'm not a dress-up girl, and I think he knows that. He's watched me grieve in a hospital room. Showing up dressed to the nines would be proof I'm trying too hard." I needed my little sister to understand my reluctance. And terror.

Sunshine turned back on me with a raging fire behind her eyes.

"You don't want to try because if he doesn't like you then who cares, you didn't try. If you put in an effort and he doesn't like you, then you can't blame it on your appearance and you might have to look a little deeper and admit maybe he didn't like you because you're a miserable asshole," she spat at me.

"Okay, that escalated quickly..." I tried.

"We're all sitting here trying to help, and you're faffing around like always because you don't want to put any work into something if you don't know you'll be great at it. You're afraid to work hard at something and just settle for being only okay at it." Sunny's tone softened, but her words were still so sharp they slipped between my defenses and sliced at my self-control.

"I'm really trying here. You can't imagine what it has been like to come back a failure," I whispered.

"Then don't be a failure. You mope around acting like we treat you like a failure, like Mom harbors some weird grudge, but it is all on you, Callie. You are the one who can't get over it. You're not getting that time back. Don't waste what time you have grieving the past. Try something new. Choose joy. Love yourself. Find a platitude. Whatever it takes. But put that dress on and go have a good time or I swear to the Source I'll set you on fire where you stand." Sunny winked and left me to bite all my nails and pee thirty times.

Sunny convinced me to wear the dress, but I drew the line at heels. I hated them and never loved anyone enough to willingly let my feet hurt. I think they looked foolish on everyone, not only me, even though my feet were chubby and often spilled over the straps in bubbly puffs. Also, I didn't wear shoes that disabled my running ability. I didn't like to run, but if I was going to run, I was not going to run barefoot. Either way, flats were fine for a first date because I already wore a dress and makeup, and how much more was going to be expected of me?

I only have so much natural effort, and once that's exhausted, I'm going to be crabby. It was for Dr. Noah's own good. And he wasn't that tall, so I was doing him a favor. If it were Declan, I'd bring a milk crate to both stand on and hit him with, because I'm short compared to Beaux and apparently, she was his type.

Dr. Noah arrived fifteen minutes early that evening, looking adorable and well-rested for a doctor who worked crazy hours. He meandered around the store, looking at the antiques and statuary, cautious not to touch anything, and I wondered silently if he was a germaphobe. When I greeted him, he was gushing about the goods my mother had collected for sale.

"Does she do any interior decorating?" He gazed up at an ancient painting of a witch in a fairy circle.

I shook my head. "She doesn't do much of anything lately but worry about my dad. But no, she's never been much into decoration. She prefers to collect and pass on pieces that mean something to her and will go on to have a happy life with others. My mom is dedicated to re-homing joy for her customers." I sounded wistful talking about her with Dr. Noah. He'd seen her at her most vulnerable, and I knew he could understand that grief.

The Wicked Cookie was sparsely attended, dimly lit with candles on the tables and soft, flickering white strands of lights twinkling in the topiaries and shrubbery. We sat on the outside patio, a rare treat in the short months between a rainy winter and oppressively hot summer.

It was a blessing in disguise we had dinner at a place where Declan and I never spent much time. Granted, we frequented many places on the coast, but we hadn't made an imprint on such a romantic place. Honestly, traditional candlelight and rose-style romance made me very uncomfortable. All the focus on me, my words, my face, it made me feel self-conscious and under scrutiny. What was I supposed to say or do? Did we sit there talking, speaking sweet nothings into the night sky while maintaining eye contact while keeping our words low and soft?

I've never been delicate enough to maintain that ingenuine facade for more than a few moments. Bubbling under the surface was always a laugh, a big, barking, honk of a laugh at something Declan said or did. Worse, there could be a whooping disagreement as we batted around ideas and feelings. Our love tempered between heated and hilarious; we were children, not ready for adult expressions of romance. Typically, our dinner dates consisted of a trip to Waffle House so we could delight in breakfast food and finish up quickly to move on to a private beach or teenage gathering.

Momentarily, I was nostalgic for the time when the dinner wasn't a hurdle to be cleared but the whole of the interaction. Conversation suspended in play-acting; the adult masquerade told me nothing about the person sitting across the table except how their best behavior breathed in candlelight.

"Callie?" Noah held my chair away from the table, staring at me with only a shimmer of impatience in a sea of pleasantries.

I shook off the insecurity and tried to smile with a bloom of gentle embarrassment.

"Sorry, I was just trying to place the song..." I lied.

I sat and scooted as he shoved my chair forward. I didn't think it was intentional, but my insecure lady lizard brain told me Noah used extra force to push my heavier-than-average body to the table.

"*Clair de Lune*? Claude Debussy, 1890," Noah said, wrongly.

"Oh... they are similar, aren't they?" I laughed as gently as I could. "I think, if I'm not mistaken, this is Chopin's Nocturne Opus nine, movement number two."

"Sounds like Chopin was a fan of Debussy!" Noah laughed.

I didn't want to. I had no choice.

"Debussy was about sixty years later..." I waited for his countenance to change. The flicker of resentment would flash across his face at any moment. Declan's voice echoed in my heart quoting the movie Tombstone and making me ache for something I couldn't even put into words.

"Are you a big fan of classical music?" Noah smiled brightly, and my body relaxed.

Wouldn't a beautiful love story need to start with a misunderstanding of classical music? Maybe that could be our wedding song. Sometimes I hated myself.

"Not necessarily a big fan. I enjoy it and know the more common pieces, but I'm not crazy about the symphony. I went to Chicago a few times, and unless it's a particularly outstanding piece I've connected with, it wasn't really for me," I admitted.

"What's your favorite piece?" Noah asked, pouring me a glass of wine.

"Ode to Joy or maybe Canon in D." Where composers were concerned, I was a basic witch.

"You mean Beethoven's Ninth in D minor Opus one hundred and twenty-five?" he teased.

"I do, indeed. I saw a flash mob use that in a video, and it really made a huge impact. I got so homesick; there was a public square and people and birds..." I gestured out toward Pelican Square. "My own joy, right there."

Noah raised this glass to the square.

The Cookie didn't have a liquor license, but they allowed dinner guests to bring a bottle of wine and pay a decanting fee.

I'm not going to lie—I'm not a drinker. Witches drink wine with ceremony and dinner, but it's usually our family vintages, heavily mixed with mineral water and imbued with a communion spell to open us up to the divine and keep our senses somewhat sharp. I'm not saying witches don't drink to excess, but it's unsafe because it warps the magic we have and makes it dangerous.

I'd planned to drink a glass and enjoy myself until that moment. Something about the shimmer in the gold liquid turned my stomach and made me think of my wipe-out in the dining room. I wanted my wits sharp, my conversation sparkling, and my first date with such a well-matched man to be free of me drunk and obnoxious. I also, selfishly, wanted to test the first actual transfiguration I'd been practicing: turning wine back into water.

Imagine my great and joyous surprise when my trick worked. The water stayed the same pale golden color, but our initial toast was a sip of cool water with no wine.

"That's lovely!" I lied.

"Wine is something of a hobby for me." Dr. Noah seemed smugly flattered. He wanted to impress me, and he wanted to be adorable doing it. "Speaking of lovely, you really are pretty in this light."

I couldn't smile. Declan always called me radiant. I heard Noah's words as a reason to cringe at meeting him in the harsh hospital lighting.

He pulled out my chair and told me I looked beautiful. Why couldn't that be enough?

"That's pretentious," I muttered and coughed. I said the wrong word. I didn't mean it.

"Excuse me?" He hadn't quite heard me, and I felt relieved more than guilty. I had no reason to be salty with him. I could recover.

"I said, 'That's precious!' You don't see many people who understand wine around here. I have little knowledge of it myself." I covered it quickly.

"I'm a man of many interests, most of which are scientific. I became a doctor to take care of people, to draw a link between the sterility of science and the warmth of personal attention. I've found that people avoid real doctors because they're typically impersonal and cold. They'd rather take advice from someone to confirm their bias than listen to scientists and experts. 'I did my research' has become the rallying cry for dangerous and misinformed medical advice," he said.

There must have been a look on my face that bothered him because he stumbled to keep going.

"And I get it, doctors see a lot, and they can be callous, ignorant jerks, the real ones. I mean, they have to be because they see a lot of death and pain, so they're typically detached, but I try not to be. I want to be a different sort of doctor. I want to be more like the doctors who made house calls and worked for a glass of brandy and good conversation." His blue eyes glittered in the night; the excitement of discussing his passion lifted his color. I wanted to tell him he looked radiant, but I held back. His emphasis and repeated use of the word 'real' stuck in my craw.

"My father is a naturopath, and my brother is almost finished with his D.O. Do you consider them real doctors?" I was getting aggressive, and he wasn't going to like it.

I took several deep breaths and settled myself. I was under stress, and he didn't understand. Dr. Noah knew I was over-educated and was trying to impress me. For whatever reason, everything he said grated on me. I could hear the sparkling conversation I wanted to have, and yet everything out of my mouth was indescribably ignorant.

"What? Of course, I mean, real doctors? I meant people who prefer shamans or faith healers, woo medicine, and don't vaccinate their kids. I believe they turn to those pseudo-natural remedies because they get more compassion and understanding. You understand, right? Would you feel more comfortable if your father was under the care of a faith healer?" He spoke as if he knew it was the most naturally agreeable thing in the world.

"We're all fully vaccinated." It was all I could think to say in response. I couldn't tell him that if my grandfather were alive, my father wouldn't be under his care. He'd be home.

"Exactly!" he laughed in agreement.

We sat quietly for a moment, perusing the menu. Well, Noah perused the menu; I was too busy screaming at myself for being any and everything but sparkling.

"Do you have a recommendation? I know you're more familiar with this, uh, restaurant than I am." Noah didn't make eye contact.

"Branzino, hands down. A Greek family owns this place. It's outstanding." I debated telling him that the redfish was my favorite and the crabs, oysters, and shrimp came right from the Bay less than a thousand feet from our table, but he asked for a recommendation, and the Branzino was a renowned favorite by everyone who had it and was often voted the best dinner in the Bay.

He smiled and set down his menu. When Kiki arrived, Noah ordered for both of us. I was flattered he wanted to impress me, but despite the popularity of my suggestion, I wasn't among the fans. I didn't blame him. I should have spoken up. I just felt like discussing the food, and my favorites, would be cliche. Girls with curves had interests outside of calories. I'm saying, I didn't want to send a date home thinking I didn't get excited and animated until we discussed what I could stuff in my face. I snoozed and lost. Branzino it was.

I felt my chipper exterior failing and fantasized about a tornado hitting the restaurant. I tried to think of funny things, relaxing things, and concentrate on the delightful pilaf and seagrass stuffing that accompanied the main course—a favorite of mine at The Wicked Cookie. I didn't want my frustration to escalate into fury since my current furies were met with some kind of obvious disaster like claws, windstorms, and bloodshot eyes. My knee was bouncing away under the table, and when I slipped off my shoe, I could smell my own feet. My nerves were fried crispier than the shrimp on the po'boy I originally wanted to have for dinner.

I didn't want a disaster, only a diversion to make me stop feeling so claustrophobic and frantic.

I could have probably worded my prayer better, but the universe granted my wish in its typical dramatic flair.

Two bites into my fish and we were interrupted by a commotion around the corner from the café we couldn't see. I tried to be effortlessly nonchalant about it, I promise.

"I wonder what all that ruckus is all about?" I interrupted his talking with my most graceful and demure voice. My options were either fake gentleness or yelling, "My puppy can hear me melting down in my head and is on her way to wreck this joint and get me out of here, so... later!" I didn't have any other settings.

"Sounds like someone can't control their animal. I used to have a dog, but he was home alone too much, and I worked such demanding hours that I had to give him up." He shrugged and I threw up in my mouth. I no longer questioned my discomfort. Perhaps on a molecular level, I could see this coming? Maybe I wasn't just sick from wanting Declan and self-destructive?

Sure enough, right on cue, Clue came storming through the patio, dragging Sunny behind her.

"Callie, your damn puppy won't settle down!" Sunny was yelling over the other diners, seemingly drunk and obnoxiously loud.

"Tell her I'm not a puppy!!!" Clue jumped up on an empty table where diners had left scraps of beef Wellington and ate from the plates she hadn't knocked off the table.

Sunny was trying her best to pull Clue off the table, but it wasn't working. Her claws were dug in around the rim, and no matter how hard Sunny pulled, Clue was stronger.

"You have a puppy?" Noah asked, a little shocked and sheepish at his dismissive words earlier.

"She's not a puppy." I shrugged.

"See, Sunny. Not a puppy!" Clue garbled with her mouth full of beef and sarcasm.

"She's a demon!" Sunny said, grabbing an empty chair from the table Clue stood on and falling into it, the triangle point between Dr. Noah and me at our table. "Seriously, she's been impossible. She cried and barked and cried and barked until I walked her and then she came right here, ready to drag you home."

Sunny grabbed my wine and chugged it, giving me a dirty look when she realized it was water. "Well, that's bullshit!" My graceful sister tossed the empty glass over her shoulder, and Noah jumped visibly when it shattered on the patio.

Noah was definitely going to think she meant his choice of wine and not my keen ability to transfigure liquids.

Clue dove off the table, sailed over the couple seated next to us, and landed in my lap, far more gently than I would have guessed. She licked my face and wagged her tail in my dinner.

"That's my good girl," I told her and scratched her ears. She jumped up on our table and dove into the remaining food.

"You're telling her she's good?" Dr. Noah's face contorted, and he pushed away from the table fast, desperate to get away from Clue's flicking tail sweeping food into his lap.

"Yeah, I should probably handle this? Let me get them out of here." I set Clue on the concrete and took the end of her leash. Grabbing Sunny by the armpit to hoist her to her feet, I turned back to apologize to Dr. Noah. "Raincheck?" It was the best apology I could muster.

He nodded and smiled, waving me off. "Of course. One time I had..." He tried to relate, or at least turn the attention back to himself, but each time he spoke, Clue barked in a harsher tone than I was used to.

"Sorry, she's not usually like this—either of them." I rolled my eyes and pulled them off the patio, back toward the shop and my car. "I'll call you? I really am sorry!" I called over my shoulder as I tried to hurry away.

We were almost out of view, almost to safety, when Sunny stopped in the middle of the street, right at the center point of the intersection, threw her head back, and vomited thousands of salmon-colored, magical butterflies. They flitted around her as if in slow motion, glittering in the streetlights, before popping like a bottle rocket and drifting to the ground as a spark. She stood in that primal scream pose, her body sagging against the force of magic flowing outward.

This was a terrible sign.

"Magic poison!" Clue gasped. She sprinted so hard and fast that her leash jerked my arm and pulled me off my feet. I landed hard on my boobs, ripping my dress. Clue soared through the air and hit Sunny in the chest with her paws and knocked her to the ground. Ignoring the fact we were both lying in the street, Clue dragged my sister by the shirt to the curb. *"We need to feed her grass to get the poison out!"*

"Clue, I can carry her. Stop for a second. Grass doesn't work on people; it's a dog remedy. We have some antiemetic back at the shop. Come on." I tried to stand up, but she was still dragging us to the sidewalk, my wrist tangled up tight in her leash, and I couldn't get my legs under myself. I jerked back on the leash, but Clue barked at me and then growled.

"I am not kidding, Callie. She needs grass—trust me." Clue's voice was no longer sweet and girlish. There was a demonic growl that stopped me cold. Her momentary hesitation allowed me to untangle my wrist, and I dropped the leash entirely, fear swirling around my stomach like a flurry of winter. Her typical cheer and nonchalance were gone, replaced with a tiny tyrant who wanted to feed my sister grass.

Kiki Adelphos had been bussing a table when Sunny started purging papillons and jogged across the street, casting magic toward us, and pointed her wand (well-disguised as a long, slender eyeshadow brush) at the grass past the curb. "She's right—grass, Callie!"

I tried to help Clue drag her to the grass but couldn't keep up. Each time I'd grab onto my sister, she'd vomit another thousand butterflies and Clue would jerk her so hard my hands would slip. My familiar might say she isn't a puppy, but she pulled my sister like a Bernese Mountain Dog would have pulled a sleigh of kids in a blizzard.

Clue dragged Sunny into the grass and dug frantically.

"Callie, it's fine. My mom made everyone think a car hit the fire hydrant and it exploded. They think we're all sitting here drenched in the deluge." Kiki talked a mile a minute as she baseball-slid into the dirt and pulled up a handful of grass to drop it into a vial she had tucked in her pocket. It was half-full with a glowing yellow liquid that smelled like honeysuckle and charcoal. She took her time, the seriousness of the situation broken by Clue.

So frantic was my familiar that she was just tearing up grasses and dropping them onto my sister's face.

"Hold her up a little," Kiki commanded, and I got underneath my sister's head and boosted her by the shoulders. Kiki dumped the potion down her throat and had me hold her head back so it would go down.

"How will we know if it's working?" I patted Sunny's hair, kissing her brow. My sister lurched forward, threw up a fire hose worth of clear water into the hole Clue had dug, and then looked back at us, curious.

"How was your date?" She was a little confused but no longer slurred or wobbled. She leaned back against me, exhausted.

"Her date was a tragedy, and you rescued her from it." Kiki sat back on the grass, holding the back of her hand to Sunny's forehead.

"I mean, it wasn't that bad," I tried, but it was, and I was so happy it was over.

"I could hear you calling!" Clue chirped at me, her sargent-like demeanor gone and her child-like joy returned.

"Callie, that puppy knew you were looking to bail. We were closing up the shop and she went wild." Sunny spoke softly, but there was humor in her tone.

A foul and gagging smell erupted around us, and we noticed Clue had left a package to brown town in the hole where Sunny threw up.

"What are you doing?" I cried, jumping up. Clue sat next to the hole, a curious look on her face.

"Oh, that's bad!" Sunny stood and pulled Kiki to her feet. "That's gonna make me sick *again*."

"Did you need to poop right there?" I asked Clue who tilted her head and bowed her ears on top.

"What do I know? I'm just a puppy." And she took off in a strut toward my car.

The overwhelming smell faded and was replaced by the heavy floral scent of the chrysanthemums that had grown out of the hole where she pooped.

"What did she say?" Sunny asked, brushing grass off her shirt and shorts.

"She said it's your fault, Sunshine," Kiki responded, laughing.

"You can hear her?" I gasped.

Kiki shook her head, cracking up. "Nope, but the look on her face when Sunny said the 'p' word was unmistakable. Y'all need a ride home?"

We declined and took my car. Clue in the front seat, and Sunny lay in the back.

"Do you want to talk about what made you throw up chaos magic?" I tried to see my sister's face in the rearview mirror but couldn't.

"Not really," Sunny answered.

"Do you know what happened?" I asked Clue. She gazed up at me with her big eyes, and I swore I could see a smile.

"She tried to do magic where magic didn't want to be done," my familiar answered.

"Sunny, tell me what happened!"

"I have a headache. Can we talk about it another time? It's a long story, and for now, I need rest and sugar."

"Just tell me whether this was something someone did to you, or..." I pressed.

"I misjudged a spell trying to heal Mom and it backfired. I'm not sure where it went wrong, but I'll figure it out and fix it. I promise."

"I'm so glad you guys showed up. That was not unfolding like a love story at all," I sighed, but my sister cut my poetic waxing short.

"Where are the orange slices, Cal!" Sunny threw the old, empty bag from my first day back in town into the front seat.

"What orange slices, Sun?" I snatched the bag up and tucked it into my car door's side map pocket.

"I know you have candy hidden in here—where is it?" Sunny dug through my seat pockets, looking for contraband.

"I only had the one bag. Stop making a mess back there!"

"Since when do you only buy one bag? Are they in the house? I know you have a backup bag." Sunny sat up and leaned between the front seats. Clue licked her face.

"I didn't buy those, Sun. Pippy gave them to me when I got here."

"Okay, then swing by there so I can get something. I need sugar." Sunny pointed to Llewellyn's.

I was stopped at the corner and about to turn in when I saw Teddy filling up his cruiser at the gas pump again. I sat a long second, watching him replace the nozzle and gas cap before walking back to the diesel pump and filling the same small container as he had the first day I got home.

"Sun, didn't Declan say the explosive had been in a thermos filled with diesel?" Between the hanged man card and the hex bag and the diesel, my witchy senses were tingling.

"He did," Sunny agreed. "Why?"

I nodded toward Llewellyn's. "The day I got home, the day before the accident, I saw Teddy getting diesel."

"This is Mississippi, Callie. Everyone uses diesel for something. Even Ma has a container for particularly stubborn repair and cleanup work on metal. That's pretty weak." Sunny laughed at me as I slowly pulled away from the stop and coasted into the parking lot of Llewellyn's.

"Maybe if it was a reasonable amount of diesel, but that's a teeny container. It's actually about the size of a thermos, if you think about it." We locked eyes in the rearview mirror.

"I'll find out, but you have to keep yourself together. Teddy is a strong empath, and if you walk up broadcasting suspicion, it will tip him off. You want anything from inside?" Sunny offered.

"*Get me a dozen stuffed crabs?*" Clue asked sweetly.

"I'm good, but get the pu... pawed wonder a dozen stuffed crabs?" I caught myself this time and tried not to break my arm patting myself on the back for supporting my familiar in how she chose to self-identify.

"*Pawed Wonder!*" Clue cried and stood in the seat, pressing her paws against the window stripping. She howled, long and low. Millions of responses came from the creatures hidden around us in the night. Insects trilled, birds squawked, bats chittered, several canines howled in the distance, and an owl called back to her.

"Is that the reason we get so many calls on the full moon, Callie?" Teddy called from across the pumps.

"Everything else has been her fault all night, so it might as well be, Captain Mayhem!" I parked and sauntered over to him. My stomach knotted, twinging around my belly button as I desperately held down my nerves to avoid his empathetic antennae. Briefly, I thought about mentioning the icepick, but I didn't want to admit I'd lost it. I waited for him to speak.

"I'm Chief, Callie."

"I'm never going to know the difference. Consider it a throwback to the football days if you need to." I wasn't going to lie and pretend I'd remember. I'd been calling him Captain for way too long.

"Are you guys out making trouble tonight?"

"Nah, my sister wanted me to hunt you down so she could flirt with you," I told him. That was what happened when I tried to play it cool: The normal, obnoxious comments I keep in my head just pop out. If I concentrate on not saying the wrong thing, I'd for sure say the ridiculous thing.

He froze, diesel overflowing from his container onto his shoes. I couldn't tell if he was scared or thrilled.

"Seriously?" He got up fast and fumbled with the nozzle.

"No! We were at dinner. What's the diesel for?" I was so nonchalant I should've gotten an award.

"Mower. That small field behind the old station is overgrown, so I've been cutting it in stages. Ma's old riding mower doesn't have the mpg we had with the backhoe," Teddy explained as he wiped the diesel on a rag and placed the container in his trunk.

"What happened to the backhoe?"

"Too big to get behind the station now that they built those houses on the south end. The mower is fine. I can spend five hours one week and have it done for a month with the backhoe, or I can spend five hours every week with the rider. We make the rookies do it." Teddy shrugged and closed his trunk.

"Well, if it isn't the most handsome police officer south of the Mason-Dixon!" My sister practically skipped down the steps of the store to join us. Tossing a huge, wet paper bag into the front seat, she leaned back against the door and gave Teddy her best come-hither smile.

"When we get home," I whispered to Clue, who immediately tore into the bag like she couldn't hear me and ate the stuffed crabs, shell, bag, sauce, and all as we stood there. "Or right now, in my front seat. That's cool too."

"How's school, Sun?" Teddy asked. They'd both forgotten I was around.

"I can see summer break from here," she sighed, looking down and back up at him through her lashes. He stood a little taller under her gaze.

"Plans for the summer?" he asked

"Nothing yet. You?"

"Protecting and serving. Same as every day."

"What's the diesel for?" she asked, and I groaned.

"Oh, oh I see..." Teddy shook his head. "The thermos?"

"What thermos?" both Sunshine and I said at the exact same time in the exact same inflection. Damn empaths.

"I wish it were that easy." Teddy stepped forward and hugged us both, one arm over each shoulder. "I really loved him too, and I'm going to get to the bottom of it." He grabbed Sunny's hand and held it out, locking eyes with her as he traced the triquetra symbol on her palm. "I promise." He sealed it.

"We don't want to keep you," Sunny spoke in barely a whisper.

"Two minutes ago, you wanted to torture me for information." Teddy stared at her; his magic told him exactly what mood she was in at all moments. He had a key to the psyche I couldn't begin to fathom.

"Two minutes is a long time."

"I'll see you Wednesday?" Teddy asked.

"Oh, yeah!" Sunny seemed to snap out of whatever concentration she had been in. "Yeah, the kids all made cards for you and the department. Cal, Teddy here is coming to talk about road safety with twenty bloodthirsty six-year-olds!"

"Bloodthirsty?" I laughed.

"Yeah?" Clue answered.

"Not you!" I replied. "Not this time, anyway."

"Last time I went there, I was in the room thirty seconds before one of the kids asked to see my gun. Children want the COPS version of my stories. They don't want to talk about looking both ways before crossing a street." Teddy laughed, never looking away from my sister.

I couldn't tell who was in whose head between them.

"Okay, well we'll see you around!" I said far too loudly after we stood in silence for a full minute. My sister and Teddy were locked in something, some silent battle or dance to which I wasn't privy.

"You ladies get home safe," Teddy said softly, and I could swear he blushed just a little under his collar.

"What was that?" I asked my sister when he pulled away.

"I searched his psyche. We locked eyes and I went in." My sister's tone was far too casual for what she was saying.

"You searched his psyche? What is that? What were you looking for? What did you find?"

"I was looking for guilt, but there is none. He feels bad he hasn't solved the case, but he didn't hurt anyone. His heart can't handle that pain. When I saw that, I looked for clues he might not have mentioned to us…" Sunshine stopped, stared after him, and then got in the car.

"AND WHAT DID YOU SEE?!" I couldn't stand her stalling.

"Ginger wasn't killed by Belladonna. She was poisoned by cyanide. No magical signatures whatsoever. He's looking into two separate killers at this point." Sunny sighed and lay down in the back seat.

"Do you believe him?"

"No, but I believe the evidence, and he has proof of the cyanide."

"Who would use cyanide?" I speculated, confused.

"Humans, Callie. Non-witches would use cyanide." My sister said, blowing a hole in every theory I had. The suspect pool just got forty percent wider. "Or a talented witch with no plant magic who wanted to make something look like a non-witch."

"So, everyone?"

"Yes. Everyone."

Chapter Sixteen

My master plan has always been to be wrong about everything...

PHEME: *Since we began spellcasting out this in-depth look at the sometimes-seedy underbelly of witchery gossip and lore in Blue Crab Bay, my partner Eris and I have received a tsunami of gossip from our tip line...*

ERIS: *Every single damn bit of which is a story about "Some no-good man doing things he ought not be doing!"*

PHEME: *You know they can't see the air quotes, right?*

ERIS: *They can get there by the tone of disdain, don't you worry!*

PHEME: *Is the disdain for the men or...*

ERIS: *Well, certainly, but it's also for the lack of self-awareness witches seem to have in this day and age. We live in one of the few societies that are almost entirely dominated by the matriarchy.*

PHEME: *Witches shouldn't have these problems?*

ERIS: *Not these insipid, teenage dramas. If your partner isn't behaving in a way that makes you happy, go find another partner.*

PHEME: *So, infidelity is a good thing?*

ERIS: *It's a non-issue. Witches don't weigh purity or suffering in our favor. If someone isn't the right partner, it means the right partner is out there and just haven't been found yet.*

PHEME: *So, we should thank our unfaithful partner and move on?*

ERIS: *If we could get out of our own way long enough, yes!*

PHEME: *Eris, we still face emotional attachment, feelings of betrayal, and pain when we split from someone we love.*

ERIS: *So? However much you loved the wrong one, however happy you felt and content your life was with the wrong one, it will be even better with the right one. That's the point.*

PHEME: *So, love that's not a true soulmate-level connection is pointless?*

ERIS: *Yes, exactly what I said. For keening out loud... no! Experience is valuable, but it's temporary. It's valuable because it's temporary. We're gonna make mistakes. We're going to hurt each other. It's how we learn how to treat others. We learn to be kind by understanding how much it hurts when others are unkind to us.*

PHEME: *So the essential and most critical moment of our faith, the actual pillar of belief in witchkind is basically boiled down to—and hear me out here—"Find your soulmate by process of elimination"?*

ERIS: *You are the worst person I have ever met.*

PHEME: *Then explain it better!*

ERIS: *We are a single soul experiencing the world subjectively over every lifetime ever lived to learn to experience it objectively, right?*

PHEME: *We are all one, yes?*

ERIS: *That's the macro view. Zoomed out wide to see the whole universe.*

PHEME: *Proceed...*

ERIS: *The micro view? We relate to people, friends, family, enemies, and acquaintances, all to learn how we impact others. We make mistakes and revise. Witches don't treat their adult friends the way they treated their childhood classmates.*

PHEME: *But...*

ERIS: *Listen, the point is they shouldn't. When you find your true partner, we want to do better. It's an internal shift in perspective. In the moment we see them as someone only deserving of our best and feel them treating us with only their best, we evolve into a partner worth having.*

PHEME: *So, anything short of perfection is pointless?*

ERIS: *Perfection is the destination. The point is the journey.*

PHEME: *So, we know it when we get there?*

ERIS: *Witches have instincts for a reason.*

PHEME: *We certainly can sense danger...*

ERIS: *You're not... you didn't set up another awful commercial segue?*

PHEME: *Do you worry that even your best protection might not be enough? Are you trying to reset your danger meter after a difficult breakup? At Waiola Wardwell's Wards and Warnings for the Wellness of Women Witches, you can relax in our wellness wards as our akashic practitioners work to clear your subconscious of confusion and rebuild your internal instincts.*

ERIS: *That's a lot of words to say bunk.*

PHEME: *May I finish?*

ERIS: *Not until you explain what a wellness ward is and where the hellfire I can find a definition for akashic practitioner.*

PHEME: **ahem* Our wellness wards are set up as a luxury theater, where you'll be treated to an old favorite film that's been bespelled to eliminate thought toxins and return your power to your subconscious.*

ERIS: *Subliminal messaging?*

PHEME: *No, Eris. Magic!*

ERIS: *Well, in this one and only specific case, I think we should go.*

PHEME: *You what?*

ERIS: *Oh, absolutely. Is there a discount code we can use? It's my treat. You and me.*

PHEME: *You're not serious.*

ERIS: *I've never been more serious about anything in my whole life. Let's get an appointment. My treat.*

PHEME: *My danger-tickles are crawling up my back, Eris. What's the catch?*

ERIS: *Oh! So, you do get the creeps on occasion? Good. I want Wardwells to have something to work with when we walk in...*

PHEME: *What?*

ERIS: *Why not? It's become obvious, to me at least, that your judgment is non-existent based on the commercials you run. Maybe a movie at Wardwell's will wake you up to the hucksters and weird claims you're spellcasting across the coast?*

PHEME: *Perhaps it's one of those services where only the people who use it are the ones who really need it.*

ERIS: *As my great-grandkids would tell you, my beloved, boneheaded compatriot... that isn't really the flex you think it is.*

PHEME: *Guess I shouldn't cash the check on that sponsor, huh? My instincts tell me we just got fired.*

ERIS: *See! I didn't even need a full movie to fix you. Maybe I'll see if Wardwell's is hiring?*

PHEME: *Until next time, when I'm sure we'll announce our subsequent cancellation and lawsuit, I'm your host Pheme and this has been Blue Crab Bay After Dark! Thank you for listening, and until next time, stay wild, witches.*

"Mother, just call Allegra and see if she can help you do research!" I didn't want to yell at the specter of a woman standing before me, but I was scared.

"She'll only make it worse and go on and on about how she saw this coming and warned me. I can't take that right now, Callie. Her craft isn't suited for healing and comfort. I'm only a little tired. I'll get some extra rest tonight, and I'm sure I'll feel better tomorrow," she promised.

"At least let me handle the shop?" I offered. "You can do everything else you normally do, and I can manage deliveries and keep the greenhouse alive for a couple of days."

She looked irritated, but I insisted, promising not to say anything else if she'd give in this one time.

"If you promise you will not keep reminding me I look tired, I'll agree," she acquiesced, and I hugged her. "Eh, seal it, Callie."

She put her hand up, and I sealed my promise with the triquetra symbol. Now I'd have to get creative with my henpecking, but creative wordsmithing was my superpower, so I figured I had the better end of the deal.

I loved working in the store. Sunny and I carpooled to see our father at the hospital before her school day started. Then I'd park my car at Petronilla de Meath Elementary and walk to The Dove, passing by and grabbing food from Kiki for my mother and me. Sunny would drive back to The Dove after school and stay with us until closing, helping me train and my mother research.

For a few days, no matter how tumultuous it was at home or how sad it was at the hospital, the store kept me going. Kiki would come eat lunch with me, chatting about gossip and filling me in on the tea among magical families, but she was taken back hard when I mentioned Beaux and Declan. They'd been keeping their relationship tightly under wraps.

"I know they're close friends and do some work together, but they are not a couple," she said matter-of-factly. Something flickered behind her eyes, but it wasn't curiosity. I had enough intuition to know what I disclosed bothered her.

She sat back and wound her mess of dark curls around her hand and pinned it up on her head, the ever-growing heat making the world stickier as the day went on.

"Every time I see her, she's with him. Every time I see them together, I smell roses." The more I talked, the more I sounded like a bitter ex-girlfriend, which I loathed. Being home without being Declan's was like trying on a comfortable old suit that no longer fit. Better yet, the jacket fit, but the pants were nowhere to be found.

You could slip into the sleeves, remember how much you loved the feeling, but still be exposed from the waist down.

"You should try asking Beaux about it. She would most likely want to clear the air." Kiki put her hand over mine and gave me the most reassuring smile she could muster. "I'd really love to be there with you, to support you when you talk to her, Callie."

"If Beaux wants to talk to me, she knows where to find me," I shrugged.

"Beaux also knows your grandpa recently died, your brother has been sick, your dad's in a coma, you're freshly home and maybe a little overwhelmed... what if she doesn't want to add to your plate?"

Kiki made a lot of sense. I didn't like anything she had to say, but it was rational. I'd give her that. It had been so long since I had a close girlfriend that I forgot how quickly time could pass when we chatted.

I hemmed and hawed a lot, talking myself into and out of taking Kiki's advice, but I knew I could ask Beaux for help with the Sacred Geometry book I had. Then I wouldn't feel like I was inviting her over for a confrontation. She did offer to help, and she seemed completely genuine.

When I connected with her, she sounded thrilled to meet me at the store and talk. She offered to help with whatever I needed and said she'd bring food and wine. Witches show love by feeding—or, more precisely, overfeeding—each other. Community and bread-breaking were sacred to us. Sharing a meal with Beaux would smooth away some of the rough edges, I hoped.

She arrived in pristine condition. Her nails were flawless, likely because she wanted to show off the massive diamond ring she sported on her wedding finger. This wasn't going to make my conversation any easier. Everything about her made me feel sick and sad. She didn't look like she'd ever broken a sweat, like she did Pilates three times a day like she didn't read fiction, like she moonlighted as a lawyer who evicted little old ladies from senior assisted living facilities.

Ice cold.

After setting down bags of food, she grabbed me in an impossible hug that recalled my first seeing her when I returned to Blue Crab Bay.

"I'm so glad you called, Callie. I've wanted to reach out and offer my help, but I know things have been hectic, and I didn't want to bother you. Your mother is one of my role models, and your family has always treated me like one of your own, despite my past mistakes. I want to know that you and I can move ahead together as friends. If you want to, that is."

She was so genuine, so earnest, that it became hard to hate her. It was hard but not impossible.

"I want to put the Declan elephant to rest," I said calmly.

She looked baffled and kept unpacking the food.

"What about Declan?" She pretended to be surprised, but I was not going to absolve her from this discussion.

"I know you are a couple. I want you to know it did bother me at first, but I thought about it, and I want you guys to be happy. I hope you'll invite me to the wedding." I patted her ring hand, and her eyes widened until I was pretty sure they would fall out of her skull and hit the table. I wouldn't hate to see that.

"Callie, Declan, and I aren't a couple. Declan's mom is making my wedding dress. I'm gay. I'm engaged to Kiki, and Declan is helping me with the wedding set-up logistics while I'm trying to move back from New Orleans." She abandoned the food and sat next to me.

"But the memorial service, the smell of roses, you and him sat together, the café, he kissed your hand—?" I was stuttering.

"I smelled like roses because I was proposing to Kiki after the service. And I sat with my people who had wedding fever right with me, but there's nothing romantic between Deck and me. Did you think I could do that to you?" She put her hand up, stopping me. "Don't answer that; it was stupid. Do you think Declan could do that? Callie, he hasn't been with anyone since you left. I don't know what he gets up to privately, but he hasn't had anyone worth bringing home, or taking out in public, since you left." Beaux put her hand over mine and gently squeezed, lowering her voice even though we were alone. "Since you got home, every time I've seen him, he's brought you up in conversation. I don't want to say he's preoccupied, but he definitely has you on his mind all the time."

I was speechless, stuck in limbo, unable to form words. Everything I'd built up as a wall and a protective coating against was falling apart and I was... *furious* at Declan. If he held that torch for so long, why not tell me? Why let me live feeling like I'd broken him? Why not rationally explain his feelings and ask if I felt the same? This wasn't a misunderstanding. This was a misdirection.

"Callie, Declan believes he was told by the Source that he'd never love another woman again. He was broken when he learned you went on the date with Doctor Debonair."

The laughs erupted out of me, hot like lava, and loud like a jet engine. I couldn't stop laughing, I couldn't talk, and I couldn't even breathe at the thought of Declan being jealous. Of course, I was wrong about everything. They'd put that on my tombstone. *Here lies Cailleach Aigean—she always got it all wrong*. I polished off the watery wine in my glass and sat, sputtering laughs and odd noises that sounded like the beginning of a sentence but didn't form words.

For the first time since I came home, Beaux wore a smug, satisfied face that didn't make me hate her. There was a teensy part of me that appreciated her candor.

"He talks about you *a lot*," Beaux teased me, her eyes glinting with mischief.

"How so?" I didn't want to pump her for information, but I did.

"Mostly he just worries about you, wonders about you, asks me how I think you're doing even though I haven't seen you much. When you got hurt from the vision, he was beside himself. Blamed himself, blamed me—the world was completely on fire."

"Speaking of Sacred Geometry, do you know what happened?" I'd serve Declan his head on a platter later. His investigations were taking too long for my liking, and my only leads on any part of this were from my visions—visions that still pointed a strong conjuring finger in his direction.

"I don't." She shook her head, and I felt crestfallen. "But I'm here to help you figure it out. I can stay as long as you need me, if you're cool with Kiki meeting me here after work. She said she'd bring cake and some tea." Beaux looked hopeful.

"I can be bought with cake," I agreed and grabbed the Sacred Geometry book that had given me the vision.

Looking back, Beaux was a gift. She was a painful, difficult, but important gift. Because of her, I'd learned to ignore and avoid unkind people. I'd learned to try to be kind to everyone, how to persevere in facing my bullies because I dealt with her betrayal. Because I'd been betrayed, I'd learned to be loyal; because I'd been hurt, I'd learned to be kind. I got a firsthand look at how cruelty felt and never wanted anyone to feel the way I did when the girls in my class chanted Haggy at me in the locker room.

What bothers me most about holding a grudge was that I honestly couldn't say I wouldn't have taken part in the bullying if it were another girl and not me. Was I capable of that? I don't remember caring as much about people's feelings until after the experience.

"If the Source is our home, this is the phone number," she explained. "You can look at a blueprint and understand it's a house and where the general rooms are, but without practice, you can't see the foundation, the nuance, and the important parts hidden behind walls. These symbols are like a tuning fork, and they can translate those vibrations into something measurable and rational."

The symbol on the book's cover was an icosahedron called the Tree of Life, and it represented a mathematical equation for how the Source impacted the physical world. It was the ground beneath the witch who stood with a foot in each realm.

"Imagine the Source is a heat map of color and light, swirling and changing, remaking existence with every moment," Beaux continued. "Seeing wouldn't make you immediately understand because the concept of the Source itself is foreign. That's how people see these symbols: only half of the picture. The complete image is only visible when you lay the symbols over the Source and see scientific perfection of the whole story."

Sunny arrived before Kiki and froze at the door, glaring back and forth between Beaux and me. I waved her into the room. "It's fine. We cleared the air—I was wrong about everything. Tell Beaux congratulations on her engagement to Kiki Adelphos."

"Get this one," Sunny rolled her eyes at me. "Kiki Adelphos, like we know so many Kikis?" She hugged Beaux and settled in, picking at the food left we couldn't feed Clue, who had fallen asleep on my feet after I promised I didn't need her to chew Beaux's face off.

"How are you feeling, Sunshine?" Beaux asked, likely hearing about the fluttering fountain.

"Peachy keen now, and that's why I'm here. I need to tell my sister something. I think I made a mistake. You know how Mom looks wrung-out lately?" Sunny leaned forward, elbows on the table, speaking softly.

I could only nod my agreement because my promise forbade me from speaking of it, and with the way my magic was going, I didn't want to make my face explode, or my feet triple in size for breaking that vow.

"Well, I've been trying to work healing spells on her, but she keeps rejecting them," Sunny admitted.

"Of course, she rejected them. Have you met our mother? She's fine, thanks, she'll handle it," I mocked.

"I waited until she fell asleep. I'm not a novice." Sunny breathed a deep, sad sigh.

That was the confession. I opened my mouth to speak, and her eyes threw daggers at me.

"I know, we don't force healing on people who don't want it. We don't subject other witches to magic without consent. I KNOW! But you've seen her; she's fading fast. I can't watch it, so if the

Source curses me with rebounding poison, so damn be it." She tossed her purse on the table and leaned back, crossing one golden leg over the other, ready for a lecture.

"I understand." She gaped at my response. Beaux nodded in surprising agreement. "If I had your magic, I'd have tried it," I admitted.

"Sunny, we all can't consent to everything all the time," Beaux said. "We don't shout at a witch in the street, 'Is it cool if I stop that truck from hitting you, or...? *splat* We react and help. If your mother is sick, it's not a sin to help her the best way you can." Beaux had a pragmatic way of simplifying our somewhat difficult rules into digestible parts.

"If you knew how adamant my mom is, Beaux... She won't even let our grandma come help." Sunny rolled her eyes again. I felt bad. It was no easy task to shine sunlight through a brick wall.

"You said it didn't work?" I didn't want Sunny to get off on a rant about stubbornness.

"No. Like, not at all. Instant regret," Sunny snorted. "I've never had magic rebound so fast. I have no idea what I did wrong. I tried to get in and see what was exhausting her, but it wasn't gonna happen. I got sick to my stomach right away. And my magic didn't cover her like it usually does during a healing. It sort of sank into her and through her and came back to me, rotten and wrong."

"That sounds like a curse." Beaux flipped through the book and found a section she thought could help as the chimes on the door alerted us to Kiki's arrival. "Use this." Beaux drew the image in free form on a piece of parchment, and I was enthralled she didn't need to trace it. "It will at least uncover any malevolent magic at work in her."

It was a swirling pattern I didn't recognize, but it was indescribably comforting to look at. I felt hypnotized and a little tipsy staring at it. Kiki snapped her fingers in my face.

"Hey, we don't stare at the secret magic symbols unless we're doing magic, so wake up outta that trance!" Kiki snatched the paper and folded it, breaking my thrall.

"And now we're gonna study together every day until you learn never to do that again." Beaux pointed at me and chuckled. It was a genuinely joyful sound, bells, and birds chirping. She was joined by my sister and Kiki until I couldn't hold back and joined in their laughter.

Nobody could tell me laughter wasn't magic.

Beaux was also patient and clinical, finally explaining our magic in a way that made sense.

"Every witch has internal power, and it manifests differently for everyone. The idea some of our elders have, the theory that peerage determines power, is bunk. Practice determines power. There's no exponential quickening when a witch dies, thus channeling their power to their offspring or descendants. Every one of us has a channel directly to the Source—we simply need to learn the language it speaks and tune in. You have to be dedicated, you have to be diligent, and you have to want it. The universe doesn't have time for people who aren't committed to learning her secrets."

Have you ever felt like everything clicked perfectly into place? I wasn't lacking in power; I was lacking in practice and motivation. Okay, granted, that's basically what my mother and brother had always said to me, but for some reason, I finally understood when Beaux said it.

The only lingering doubt I had was the family legend that my grandfather inherited his mother's power when she died. Perhaps that was the way they justified having a kitchen witch as a son during a time it was almost unheard of. Maybe he followed in her footsteps, practicing her craft to be closer to her, becoming a self-fulfilling prophecy?

My phone buzzed away on the table, but I was far too intrigued to answer it.

"It's your Dr. Hotness," Beaux teased me.

"If something were wrong with my dad, my mother would call. I'm not in the mood for distractions." I'd have to have a serious talk with him soon. He was overly nice and patient when we ran into each other at the hospital, but with Sunny around, we hadn't resolved anything. For all I knew he was calling to say he wasn't interested, and I shouldn't expect a call from him or something equally unnecessary.

By now, one would think I'd learn to stop pretending I could predict the future and saying stupid things like that. Of course something was wrong. He called back every minute until I answered on the fourth try.

"Hi, Dr. Cabotin. Sorry, I was..." I tried to sound cheerful, but he cut me off.

"Callie, your mother has collapsed. We think it's from exhaustion and dehydration, but..." I didn't hear anything else.

It felt like I blinked and went from The Dove to the emergency room where I stood, mind blank, holding my familiar like a toddler on my hip.

"Callie?!" I heard Dr. Noah shouting from inside the bay doors, but I didn't want to look at him. I didn't want to see his expression; if something serious was wrong I'd know and I'd break. Reading my thoughts, Clue did the dirty work.

"I was right outside." I lied.

"He doesn't look like he's sad, Callie. He looks concerned but a little happy to see you?" Clue whispered though I was the only one who could hear her. I turned to face him, and he faltered when he saw Clue in my arms.

"You can't have her in here!" he barked, jumping back. "Callie, she's not trained, and if she destroys something, people could die. How can you be so...?" He softened. "It's fine. I'll take you to your mom. Just put her down and pretend she's a service dog if anyone asks, okay?"

I followed him, not putting down my dog and not looking at anything but the curved hall ahead of us.

"Your mother collapsed a few minutes before I called you. We weren't sure if she stood up too fast or if she had any blood sugar issues, so I ran a full panel. We're giving her fluids, and she's resting comfortably. She has been suffering for a while and I have no idea how she's kept going." He paused by a door and ushered me in. I sat in a metal chair next to my sleeping mother and set Clue on the floor.

Dr. Noah kept talking, but I'd gone elsewhere, deep into myself, trying to connect with my mother. I was not going to be an orphan. Not today. I was going to walk straight into the Source, find her, and drag her back to her body if it killed me.

It didn't kill me, I didn't find her wandering the ether, but sleeping soundly and softly, her energy slightly glowing as it healed. She didn't look small and shrunken like my father. She looked better resting peacefully in the hospital bed than she had in weeks.

"We brought her into this room because I know she likes direct sunlight. She sits in the sun when it's coming into your father's room." When it was clear I wasn't capable of responding, Dr. Noah finally stopped talking and left.

"Check ya later, Captain Thinksy-Science," Clue said as the door closed behind me.

Sunny arrived a little later, storming through the door, a furnace of concern and worry emanating from her chest, but she stopped short.

"She looks fine." Sunny was whispering as though any sound could shatter the illusion and render our mother a desiccated husk in a hospital bed.

I nodded. "She is fine. They tested her: dehydration and exhaustion. Could we have been that wrong? That obtuse?" I felt guilty for ascribing a supernatural reason for her fading when all she needed was some rest and hydration.

"Callie, I'm not saying this isn't helping, but I can do this, and I couldn't heal her," Sunny reminded me, her voice trembling. "I tried that symbol Beaux gave us, and it faded into nothing. This isn't normal. She's not just tired and thirsty, she's sick—deeply, magically sick. And I can't help her…"

"Can you not get frantic? Not now, please, not now." I was begging, tears threatening to fall from my eyes and expose the worry I had in my heart. "Let's take it moment by moment, Sun."

She nodded in agreement and deeply swallowed her fear as she moved to the window. She faced directly toward the sun and raised her arms slowly. There was nothing to notice, but she was ramping up, the heat coming off her body raised the temperature in the room. When her hands were directly over her head, she took a deep breath, looked back at me, and smiled.

"Do you want to see something cool?" Sunny offered.

I wanted to explain that nothing about her was any temperature but sweltering, but my humor bone was broken.

As her arms lowered, I heard a soft and distant pop as a beam of sunlight swirled down from the Source and hit her forehead, brighter than expected for the partly cloudy day we were having. It looked like she was being filled with solar energy from the top down. Her face and shoulders glowed, and it moved past her torso, through her legs until she looked so full of light it radiated out of her, a force field that hummed gently on her skin.

Sunny returned to my mother, stood silently at the opposite side of her bed from me, and rose off the floor about a foot high. She put her hands together in prayer, and a swirl of energy formed around her hands. As she shaped it, edges would bend and swirl, like she was forming wet dough made of joy. The shape got longer, thinner, and more defined, until I realized it was taking the shape of my mother, turning to match her prone body. The energy sank into the bed, and I held my breath that the energy wouldn't fall through, corrupted again.

This time, it settled and sizzled over our mother, her body lighting up, bioluminescent, and honey-scented. Slowly, my sister settled back onto the floor, taking a few deep breaths, looking slightly wobbly. The energy sizzled and snapped, sparkling around the room before dissipating back to the Source.

"What was that?" I was stunned. I've never seen that level of power come directly from the sun for any person before.

"I call it the corkscrew," Sunny said. Her voice tinkled like a bell. "I've been perfecting it while Mom has been sick, but that's the first time it's ever worked like that." She pointed at our mother who was starting to gently stir.

My mother's eyes fluttered and she woke up, smiling.

When Dr. Noah returned, he was shocked to see the three of us laughing and talking. My mother thanked him for his help and concern. He wasn't so quick to let her go, though she seemed like she was better than she'd been in weeks.

"Mrs. Aigean, your potassium levels were incredibly high, higher than they can usually get from your diet. Are you taking any supplements? Are there any strange new foods in your diet?" He sounded gentle with her, less the pretentious man I went on a date with and more the concerned and kind doctor I agreed to have the date with.

My mother shook her head. "No, I don't take anything like that."

"I understand your husband is an herbalist," he persisted. "Perhaps he concocted a potion or supplement that's problematic?"

"He doesn't grow potassium, and if he did, he's been here for weeks and not home 'concocting potions'."

"Perhaps his absence has caused some trouble?" Dr. Noah offered.

"Perhaps I was poisoned by the terrible dead plants you serve as tea in this wretched building?" My mother was typically polite to a fault, preferring to get angry with my sister and I for voicing any displeasure no matter how serious the mistake, but something in her had changed.

This wasn't the same woman who gave me a deadly look for pointing out I'd received chicken noodle soup instead of the cream of chicken soup I had ordered. For the bulk of my life, I thought it was a diet issue. It felt like she was criticizing me for asking for a higher-calorie dish than the lower-calorie mistake I'd been given. It wasn't. I only noticed it when I was looking for fat-shaming. It was rude-shaming. My mother's theory was "What you got is fine, don't be a pain in the ass to service people."

Her ultra-sharp tone with the doctor was well past anything I'd heard from her. That struck me as strange since, as her daughter, I always thought she reserved her harshest tones for me and my siblings.

Dr. Noah sagged dejectedly with insult and gently set her chart in the bed holder.

"We will be moving you to the dialysis center for the rest of your treatment, Mrs. Aigean."

"I won't be staying, Dr. Cabotin. I'll be leaving here shortly with my daughters." My mother swiftly peeled the sensors off of her chest.

"Mother, stop pulling at those!" My sister tried to reach for our mother's hand but got slapped away.

"Do not touch me, daughter."

"Mrs. Aigean, I really must insist," Dr. Cabotin urged. "Please consider staying for the treatment." He turned, quiet, his feelings obviously hurt at my mother's refusal to listen to his opinion clearly in his bedside manner.

"Do you think someone poisoned you?" Sunny asked.

"I don't think he knows his ass from a hole in the wall. I know what happened, and I'm fine." Her eyes glittered with rage and venom.

"What happened?" I asked her. Her eyes settled, clouding over, hiding her secrets.

"I was tired and thirsty. I had a nap, got some fluids, and now I'm ready to go home. You're going back to that store, Callie. I don't want it closed during the day, and I don't want to hear any arguments. I'm infirm, so do what I say." She wasn't asking.

I couldn't fight with her or otherwise, the boils would be upon me, but something in her tone enraged me. For weeks, I'd been begging her to take care of herself. Here we were, verifiable proof she wasn't just tired and dehydrated. Damn the boils. She wasn't going to bully her way out of this. Just because my father wasn't around to take care of her didn't mean she didn't have to take care of herself. I couldn't argue, but I didn't have to agree.

I shook my head.

"Callie!" She snapped at me with a fury I rarely saw from her. The undercurrent of desperation was exacerbated by her visible exhaustion.

"One of us is staying here and getting the treatment. If it's not you, then it's going to be me." I crossed my arms over my chest and looked away. Making eye contact was likely to break my resolve.

"Don't be ridiculous. You're going back to that store right now. You have a responsibility, you promised me." My mother's voice was getting higher, more concerned, and I wasn't going to give in.

"If you want to leave so bad, then you can go to the store and work," I said.

My mother swung her legs over the side of the bed but faltered when she tried to stand. I reached out, pressing my sister backward with my forearm as my mother clutched at the bed rail to stay on her feet.

"Callie, help her up!" Sunny's voice was a low growl as she watched our mother struggle. I understood where she was coming from, but I was infuriated and would make my point no matter how much it pissed her off.

"What's it going to be, Mother?" I could feel my sister becoming inflamed behind me.

Our mother struggled to pull herself onto the hospital bed, obviously out of breath and unable to storm off.

"Just agree with me, and I'll go. The longer it takes you, the longer the store stays closed." I didn't want to push too hard, but I wasn't going to budge.

"Fine." She finally relented, laying over on the bed, pulling the blanket up to her waist.

I let go of my sister and directed her to stay with our mother until the treatments were finished. As much as I wanted my mother to have the medical treatment she needed, I didn't especially want to leave her alone.

Declan, Beaux, Kiki, and Wren Llewellyn, a witch nurse in the same hospital, sat in a prayer circle in the waiting room. Of course,

Declan was there. He was exactly what I needed for the frustration bubbling inside of me—a target for my ire.

"She's okay, dehydrated, and needs rest, but awake and aware. Now I'm in trouble for leaving the store unattended," I said. I didn't bother to lie—they knew how she was.

Wren stood first to catch me in a hug, and she was carrying a flour sack that was stuffed to the brim with what smelled like lavender.

"I came as fast as I could, but that doctor wouldn't let me in to see you. I'm going to complain when I get off tonight." Wren's sweet Southern drawl crawled out of her like maple syrup. "Bless his heart, he's only been here about a year, but he needs to learn what family means in this Bay."

I hugged her, laughing at her colorful and gentle temper. For Wren, blessing someone's heart was a raging river of swearing and a kick in the ass for anyone else.

"Also, these were in my locker. I'd planned to drop 'em at Allegra's house, but I can't get her to answer the phone," Wren said softly.

It is indescribably embarrassing to have a grandmother who was ultimately out of commission when her daughter is in the hospital.

I took the bag of dried, blessed lavender branches from Wren and promised I'd deliver them to Allegra. And I would. Eventually.

"Sunny is in the back with her, but my momma doesn't need any help managing that doctor. We've convinced her to stay for treatments even though he wanted to keep her overnight," I explained.

"Can we send anything to the house?" Declan asked, and I shrugged, not ready to make nice with him even though he smelled like sandalwood and ocean breezes. How dare he make my heart flutter when my mother was infirm?

"Wait and ask her. I need to get back to the store before she sees me and loses her temper." I shrugged at him and pulled Clue toward the doors.

Beaux left with Kiki, Wren returned to her floor, and Declan's handsome self followed me to my car.

"Are you not talking to me?" he asked as I got Clue situated.

"What do you want me to say?" I turned on the air conditioner and got back out of the car.

"You can admit you still care, because I know you thought Beaux and I…" he drifted off, laughing.

"Oh! This is a healthy conversation. I'm for sure gonna talk to you if you make fun of me. Smart call, Deck." I got back in the car and drove off in a fury, but feeling less stressed than I had in days. My mother would be okay, Declan wasn't engaged, and he watched my car longer than I watched him as I pulled out of the parking lot.

"He loves when you storm off," Clue told me. *"I can smell it."*

"I think he's just used to it, my love." I scratched her ears as I made my way back to the store.

Chapter Seventeen

When I finally start spontaneously manifesting real magic and pay zero attention to it...

PHEME: *Welcome back to Blue Crab Bay After Dark. With me, as always, is Eris and all that, but today we're throwing out the topics and ditching the plans we made. Eris! I noticed you brought your broom to the studio today!*

ERIS: *I did. I was running late and remembered I hadn't taken it out for a ride in a while.*

PHEME: *Like a car?*

ERIS: *They're nothing like a car.*

PHEME: *You run a car to keep the battery... uh, going? I'm realizing I don't know exactly how cars work.*

ERIS: *And you're not too clear on brooms either, huh?*

PHEME: *I understand magic wants to move and flow; brooms are magic that's made to move.*

ERIS: *But a witch doesn't need a broom to move. There are plenty of cases where a witch has left one point in space-time and arrived in another by no knowable means or magic. Instinct.*

PHEME: *That's almost always a situation of extreme danger or fear.*

ERIS: *But not for the witch herself. Danger to others. Service.*

PHEME: *So, they don't need the object.*

ERIS: *Brooms, like wands and orbs, are focal points witches use to condense and channel their magical energy. They're neither necessary nor special. They work because they help us focus in certain areas. Brooms focus on movement. Orbs focus vision. Wands focus intention and help us scratch our backs and pin up our hair. The instinct to serve and protect is so ingrained that we simply get there. By magic.*

PHEME: *Why do you think the witches and broomsticks and wands legend is so tightly woven if they aren't critical to our magic?*

ERIS: *They were critical at one time. The most critical. For millennia, witches believed we harnessed the power out of magical objects, crystals, wands, ingredients. As we evolved, we learned the magic was inside us, and objects help channel the magic in whichever way we need it.*

PHEME: *Wait. I don't know who learned this because I never knew it. It sounds to me like you're saying a potion to cure a broken heart is made up of ingredients because those ingredients channel the required magic to create a formula to do a specific task and not because the herbs combined have magic? That's the most bananas theory I've heard in my life.*

ERIS: *I'm not wrong. If the magic was in the materials, anyone could combine them into magic.*

PHEME: *If you're going that way, then any witch can do any magic with any ingredients or objects so long as those things channel the right facet of the witch's magic. The end of that slope is that witches don't need anything to do magic however they choose.*

ERIS: *That is absolutely correct.*

PHEME: *So, you can spontaneously do magic whenever you want to achieve whatever you want?*

ERIS: *Yes, of course, and so can you. We all can. We do instinctual magic over and over. That's what our training is. Learning where to tap into which magic by using clues and reminders to channel. I don't need a wand to untie my shoes because I've done it so much it is instinctual.*

PHEME: *You still take tinctures and medicines. You scrye in your crystal ball. What are you talking about?*

ERIS: *I haven't gotten there yet.*

PHEME: *You're old as shit. If you haven't gotten there yet, how could anyone hope to?*

ERIS: *Slowly, Pheme. Slowly. Evolution doesn't happen in centuries, even for witches.*

PHEME: *You believe we're evolving into...*

ERIS: *Spontaneous creation.*

PHEME: *What?!*

ERIS: *Why do we have to live every single lifetime that has ever been lived? Why is the Source systematically sending us back over and over to learn everything there is to know? We feel every feeling. We face every fate. We make every mistake that will ever be made and win every game that will ever be played. Why?*

PHEME: *To perform spontaneous creation?*

ERIS: *To become God. The Source is an egg.*

PHEME: *Speaking of eggs! Our newest sponsor, the Aurora Borealis Bed & Breakfast, is offering a complimentary champagne brunch with every weekend booked! Do you long to wake up under the soft flicker of the northern lights? Dream of seeing the lights without spending months in the cold northern climate? Don't gamble with your vacation. At the Aurora Borealis, you can choose from any number of settings, from the rugged tundra to the opulent open-ceiling lodge, where you can channel the magic of a sky on fire! Room rates based on occupancy, but there's no limit on group sizes.*

ERIS: *I'm not even mad at that transition this time. I'm just impressed.*

PHEME: *I've known you a long time. I know where you're going before you even get on the road, my compadre.*

ERIS: *And also before I take to the air, apparently?*

PHEME: *I don't follow...*

ERIS: *The broom?*

PHEME: *Ah, yes! The broom! I'm glad you reminded me, because uh.... Speaking of brooms, our sponsor, Bronte Broom Outdoor Escape Rooms, wants to remind you of their sale this week on the haunted manor themed experience! Spend the day investigating how the love between Catherine and Heathcliff destroys everyone around them and try to get away before you're swept up in the story and stranded in our Late Regency Recovery Room to gently live through the soft story of Jane Eyre until the vertigo passes. Current proof of accidental death and dismemberment insurance is required.*

ERIS: *Can't complain, because even if I did, who'd believe this horseshit.*

I reopened the store as fast as I could and settled in with Clue and my cards. I'd need to get in touch with my grandmother, but I wasn't looking forward to it. She could wait as far as I was concerned. I sat shuffling the deck, fuming at Declan in my mind, and feeling a little bad for Dr. Noah after my mom was so tough on him. He wasn't terrible—he just wasn't for me.

I deeply respected his dedication to modern medicine, and I'm the first person to decry anyone who ignores a doctor, but I believe there's room enough for all of us. You can't have too many people trying to care for others.

I made a note to send him something generic as a thank you but not to encourage him. It couldn't be easy for him to deal with a never-ending parade of witches and their medical needs. We tend to second-guess a lot, and we're naturally distrustful of outsiders.

The longer I shuffled, the less my mind raced. The cards had a way of calming me down, helping me focus, and drawing my attention inward. There's a comfort to me that only comes from this magic. Perhaps my magic is drawn directly from the tarot? Maybe the way my sister drew power from the sun was my way of drawing strength from the tarot?

The first card was the Ten of Wands, meaning obligation, a good idea, or an interesting project that has become a burden. It was a bit on the nose, but my emotions were heightened, so, of course, the cards came out swinging. I took a deep breath and turned over the Knight of Swords.

The Knight of Swords was one of those cards that always looked like it moved. If you stared at it long enough, it came to life, and you could see the knight racing on horseback toward a destination of violence and war. It was a card of a man on a mission, and I didn't have to think hard to find a man in my life who didn't fit the description.

I knew it was Declan. If everything around me was the burden of my return, the card crossing me was Declan. Even the cards knew he was a pain in my ass.

For the third position, I drew the Four of Swords, the card of distance and time apart. That was under me, moving away in the reading.

The fourth position was The Moon, a card of hidden mysteries that came to light under darkness. It was behind me, and it gave me an uneasy feeling.

In the fifth position was the Nine of Wands: anxiety and struggle. I'd like to drive the point home here that the cards tend to state the obvious, and when my cards beat a dead horse, there was probably a reason.

Of course, I'm anxious.

I'd been waiting for the sixth position as it represented what was coming. I turned over the Five of Wands, reversed in the layout.

Whatever fight I was in wasn't over, and I wasn't winning.

I swallowed hard and sighed.

Trying to determine what to do about it, I turned the seventh position card over. The Ten of Cups sat upside down before me, representing my fears and worries. While normally it was one of the luckiest cards in the deck, this meant upheaval and discontent in the home life, a lack of prosperity, and deep troubling strife.

The eighth position was family, and I drew the Seven of Wands, which meant defense, perseverance, and hard work.

The Star showed up in the ninth position as my deepest desire. The Star represented intuition, divination, and for my coven, it was the symbol of the tidal pool in the caves where we took our baptism and then the sacred bath of ascension.

I'd never drawn this card in a reading of my own. It represented an end to my studies, and although the date wasn't clear, I could tell it was coming up quickly, and that boosted my confidence.

The final card, the outcome, was The High Priestess. There was a strong wind through the store, and it sent a shiver down my spine. That was my grandmother, Allegra, the matriarch, the materfamilias, and the wench who abandoned us in my family's darkest time.

The High Priestess sat on her throne, snug between two pillars, one white, one black. I recalled my first vision, the horses, the light and the dark, the figure in green. It was a harsh, milky green, the color of infection and sickness, surgery and bile. I'd known it in so many names, but I knew it best as the color of Allegra's eyes.

I reached for the High Priestess first to gather the cards and shuffle them back into the deck. The moment my palm hit the card, I saw her, kneeling in her small apartment, chanting over candles. The vision was choked with brimstone and dark magic, her hair wild around her, evil darkness in her eyes.

"Darkest calling, the curse of life, break his magic, Source of strife. Twisted spines, eyes of glass, torn out heart, circumvent the past." Allegra's sonorous voice crackled with dark power.

"Run!" She turned and looked right at me, her eyes solid white and glowing.

I jumped back from the table, knocking my chair to the ground. For years, Allegra warned us not to work dark magic or call on pain and anguish to get vengeance. Watching her work a hex was heartbreaking, her spirit poisoned by whatever malice she held in her heart. I had to stop her.

"Stay here for me, okay?" I told Clue and grabbed the lavender.

I'd use it as an excuse to catch her in her hex and expose her to the family, but I couldn't risk my familiar if Allegra found me. She'd killed Grandpa Ruari; I was sure of it. I could smell the brimstone, feel the salt air, and hear the disappointment in her tone that my father didn't die alongside him. She was still trying to take his life, but if I could break her concentration and shatter her spell, there was a chance he could come back. If I couldn't, Clue would find a way to tell my family where I went and what happened.

Clue yawned and rolled over, showing me her downy belly.

Declan was outside when I opened the door. He was standing by his car, sunglasses on, calm.

Apparently, the motion I saw in the Knight of Swords represented Declan's *actual* drive over here to fight with me in real time.

"No, I do not have time to do this with you," I shouted and bounded down the stairs. But I did have time. If I was going to my death, I wanted to unburden myself on the man who held my heart in his hands. I didn't want to waste time-fighting with him, but I knew I was going to.

"Callie, what did you want me to do?" He jogged over toward me. "You can't expect me to lay my heart at your feet and heap the responsibility on you? We broke up. I was leaving for Air Force Basic Training, and you didn't want to go with me. I understood. I could have chosen to go with you, and I didn't. You take this burden so seriously."

"I'm a burden?" I turned on him and glared. I knew what he was saying, and I understood he wasn't calling me a burden, but his choice of phrasing made me irate.

"Oh, for keening out loud, Callie! That's not what I said, and you know it!"

"I don't know what you're saying, Declan. Since I got home, I haven't had a clue what to think about you," I admitted. "I didn't expect to come home and go back to the way things were. I never even expected to come back here, but I did, and you're still here. Part of me was relieved you and Beaux could be together. You deserve a normal witch-wife. Someone who will give you kids and a home, a lineage to carry on. You should have that. I can't give you that." No tears came; the words didn't cut me like they used to.

Sometimes I felt like my attraction and love for Declan was so heavy and all-encompassing that it made me numb out of self-preservation. I wanted him so badly that to have any of him, in any way, without having all of him, was too much to handle.

"You never asked me what I wanted, and still, you don't care that I don't want kids. I've only ever wanted you, Callie." Declan crossed his arms and tilted his head back.

"You're going to tell me you don't care, that you love me, that it doesn't matter. I know everything you'll say, Declan, and I don't believe a word of it. You might not care now, but you will, and you'll resent me, and I can't live with that." I was talking without listening because I knew that if I listened, he would ensorcell me with his words.

"There's nothing I can say to convince you I agree with you?" He looked crushed, saddened, and I tried to stop feeling so sympathetic to him. I wasn't wrong.

"Of course not. I know I've always felt like this, but you're just acquiescing to my wants. It's not worth the risk. You'll change your mind. You'll never be happy without the traditional family, Deck."

"You know, if anyone said that to you after you stated your wants, you'd have a fit about their misogyny and small-mindedness. How could you turn that on me? How many people have told you that you'd grow into your maternal instincts, change your mind about having kids, feel different when you had a partner who wanted a family," he challenged, and he was right. I had a humongous chip on my shoulder over how everyone treated women who didn't want kids.

"That's not fair, Declan. I've always known about this deformity in my spirit. I will not drag you with me."

"Oh, with the drama, Callie. Drag me into spiritual deformity, already! I couldn't be more ready! Have I ever doubted that commitment? Have I ever, in all the time we've known each other, ever once tried to dissuade you? Have I ever minimized this feeling of yours?"

I shook my head. He'd always been supportive of me, but Declan was that type. He agreed with me, supported me, and understood I had to do things my way.

"Never once have I done that, and I don't appreciate you treating me like a wolf in sheep's clothing, like I'm only waiting to trap you and guilt you into motherhood. I don't minimize it, I don't even bring it up, because I'm with you. I've always felt the same. I didn't think I needed to convince the only person who agreed with me! Why can't both of us not want kids simultaneously?" He wasn't shouting, but he was hurt and angry. His voice was loud but pleading more than accusing. "Why can't you admit we're perfect for each other?"

"I don't care." I hurried, but he blocked my car door, fully aware I was only struggling to escape him because it felt good when he stopped me. "If only you were this adamant about stopping me from leaving years ago." I crossed my arms, staring him down.

"Is that what you wanted? Is that the bitterness you held onto? That I didn't stop you? Take only that which is given, Callie. You know better!" He was pleased with himself. Pleased he'd gotten me to admit to some form of regret.

"Yes! No! I don't know! Would it have helped if you showed any emotion at all? Maybe, but now's not the time." I pushed at him with my shoulder and hip, trying to get him to move, inhaling deeply when I was closest to him. Oh, hellfire bunny nuts, he smelled incredible. I wanted to grab two fistfuls of his shirt, bury my face against his chest, and just breathe.

My body repeatedly crashed against him, pressing for longer and longer intervals, confusing my rage with how languid and intimate his body, which I was loathed to admit I desperately longed for, felt against mine. I was afraid to leave, and part of me wished he'd throw me to the ground and prevent me from rushing off to my demise.

Every time I tried to move him, he stood steadfast. I was practically bouncing off of him, and my anger was pricking like spiders crawling between my shoulder blades.

I squared off with him. I wanted to catch his eyes, make him slip off the sunglasses, and see how deeply I loathed him.

When he finally removed his sunglasses, the fear I wanted him to have, the horror that should have driven him away from me, was invisible under his smile. Slowly, and probably more wetly than necessary, he licked his lips, biting his bottom lip gently, and cleared his throat.

My rage burned and spread out like lava in my chest, pooling in my thighs, and aching in my insincere and deceitful honey pot. I didn't have time to let my better sense fight it out with my needy, two-faced, disloyal, desperate desire to have Declan.

I hated everything about him. His smug smile, his soft pink lips, the ignorant little white calcium deposit on his front tooth that gleamed in the spring sun—I couldn't stand him. His sparkle tooth enraged me, and I wondered how I'd ever thought it was adorable enough to give it that nickname. Briefly, I considered wrapping my hands around his neck, but unconsciously, I waited for the talons to return so I could puncture his jugular.

Declan reached up and ran a soft-skinned hand through his messy, chestnut mane of hair, all that natural body and volume wasted on his stupid face. He absently scratched at the small patch of skin beneath his earlobe. That skin patch was the single hairless point between his beard stubble and his hairline.

He damn well knew how I loved that spot. He knew I spent hours snuggling into it, running the tip of my nose along the baby-soft patch, inhaling his scent, dry-humping him into a teenage frenzy. In a split second, the fiery rage in my chest turned ice cold, and I realized that if I was right if Allegra was murdering my family, then I was effectively walking into my death.

It was the last time that I, Callie Aigean, would see the beautiful, soft, angel-skinned, full-lipped, thick-haired, hazel-eyed nightmare who was always too good for me. My only consolation was that if I didn't make it back if this were the end, I'd avoid what I'd always considered a fate worse than death: I'd never lose Declan. He'd never wake up to the fact I didn't deserve him and leave me.

This was what I was supposed to do. This was what my life was leading up to the whole time. I'd seen the world, known the young, passionate love of the virile, towering hero of a man against whom all other men fell short. I wasn't going to touch heaven and have it snatched away from me when I least expected it. He would go on. He'd remember me... well, that wasn't my business, but I hoped it would be fondly. I would win our battle. He would be fine. It would be the best-case scenario.

The ice in my chest instantly turned to water, and tears burned white-hot behind my eyes. In a moment, everything I knew, every firmly held belief, was threatening to spill out from me in tears. Twenty-five years, five months, four days, and a handful of hours wasn't enough. It couldn't be enough with him, even if I'd spent every moment by his side. Knowing I'd thrown away seven years was too much. Leaving him didn't make losing him easier.

It should have.

It was supposed to.

It didn't.

Without my knowledge or consent, my own body betrayed me. Whatever lizard brain drove my instincts snatched control away from my rational mind, and I jumped on him, wrapping my legs around his waist, and my arms around his neck, as my mouth sealed against his. This time, he didn't pull away. His arms came around and under me, turning to pin me between him and the car, his reaction as fervent and determined as I was. Thunder crashed hard in the distance, and the air crackled around us.

I got my hands into that thick, coarse hair, pulling his head back to nibble on his bottom lip, desperate to remember the texture of his mouth, the strawberry sweetness of his favorite soda, the velvet texture of his tongue. Declan was a big kisser, and I wanted to inhale him.

I wanted to devour him.

"Declan, I hate you. I hate you so much. You know that right? You know I hate you more than anything on this planet?" My voice choked out in deep, ragged breaths.

He pushed me harder against the car window and reached up, somehow holding my buxom rear end with one hand as the other grabbed my face, palm damp against my chin. Slowly, but with rock-solid determination, Declan tilted my head back and ran the same cursed pink tongue from the hollow of my throat across to my collarbone.

"It sure doesn't feel like hate, my orphic little raconteuse." His voice was liquid, silk chocolate against my skin.

"It will take more than a fancy nickname for an enchanting storyteller..." I was cut off in a yelp as his hand covered my mouth. I took his hand, holding it more gently than he deserved, and briefly considered biting him until he bled, but instead, I licked the pad of his palm. Salty, musky, smooth as sea glass, his flavor was familiar and intoxicating, a return to the forbidden fruit.

"Stop fighting with me and let me love you, my furious little hellcat."

"I can't be tamed. I can't let you chain me down..."

He leaned harder against me, pinning me hard between him and the car as he let go of me and reached up with both hands to grab two fistfuls of hair at the back of my head so he could pull my neck back and tilt my face to look directly in his eyes.

I wanted to shiver against his gaze, but I still truly felt like I couldn't give too much away, just in case he hadn't noticed I was practically on fire in want of him.

I was going to give myself an aneurysm trying to play it cool.

"I don't want to control you. I want to unleash you. I want the world to see the absolute violence and destruction of the only force of nature I've ever worshiped, Callie."

I was never going to make it to Allegra's.

The memory of her, chanting, drawing in evil and power, haunted me, broke me of the lusty spell that Declan's lips cast.

I shoved him, hard. Stumbling back, he tilted off-kilter and stumbled to regain his balance. Twisting and scurrying away from his hands, he wasn't able to grab onto me again.

"What did I say?" He looked shocked, hurt, but still flushed and sexy.

"It's not you. Not like 'it's not you, it's me'. But, it's just, not right now. I can't talk about this right now. I have a thing—I have to... I'll be back," I growled.

Every fiber of my being was screaming at me to get back in there and take him down to the pavement in rapture, public be damned. But Allegra.

I grabbed him by the chest of his shirt and pulled him into another kiss. A screaming tone came out of my throat as I struggled against the inescapable force of attraction.

"Like, five minutes, maybe an hour? I might not even come back, but I have to go, Declan…" I pushed him away again, my lips sore from attacking him.

"Are you okay?" He stuttered a little and looked a little shaken at my wildly swinging mood.

"I really fucking love you, Declan. Stay with my familiar. She's inside. You know I'll return for her, but you must let me go right now." And then I kissed him again, pushed him away, and just ran.

Of course, I ran the wrong way and had to double back, right in front of him, back and forth. I wasn't thinking right. Rational Callie would have just run the few blocks out of her way and not let Declan see I was so twitterpated I'd been turned around in my hometown and couldn't remember which way my grandmother lived.

Then again, when I ran back the other way, I did get one more kiss. Not that I planned it, of course.

Chapter Eighteen

Where I find out how woefully unprepared I am to face anything...

PHEME: *This time my esteemed partner has decided we're going to be covering that gentle and simple topic of "What happens when we die?" Apparently, we haven't had enough threats of lawsuits and ass-kickings to satisfy the old wench.*

ERIS: *If you knew the number of people I've heard talking about how we are each a single life in the collective and they're running simultaneously, then you'd know how badly we need to cover this.*

PHEME: *I'm fine with it. Proceed with your thesis.*

ERIS: *Our point on this planet is to live each and every life that has ever been lived to learn each and every lesson there is to learn. Those lives are not all running concurrently.*

PHEME: *So, time is a construct?*

ERIS: *Time is a misdirect. At the Source, there is exactly one soul. That soul will live every life and then, only then, can that soul move on to the next plane of existence. It's infinite.*

PHEME: *Does time pass at the Source?*

ERIS: *Bahhh, what does that matter?*

PHEME: *If time doesn't pass at the Source, we could be living those lives simultaneously and then bouncing back to the Source after we're done.*

ERIS: *Your soul is my soul, cherub. The order is inconsequential. Our belief is to be the person we would need if we were living the life of the person who needs us. Be the parent you would need if you were a teenager in trouble. Be the friend you would need if you were broken-hearted. That is simply yourself in another incarnation. They're not a separate piece of the whole.*

PHEME: *But if there is no time, as you said, then all things happen at the same time.*

ERIS: *You really put the Pheme in Blasphemy.*

PHEME: *If you insist! This edition of Blue Crab Bay After Dark has been sponsored in part by Bubble Town Magic Funtime Center in the Spanish Moss Woods off Coral Drive and Sunfish Blvd. School is going to be letting kids out for the break in only a few days—are you prepared for childcare all summer? At Bubble Town Magic Funtime Center, we offer a special summer program for baby and toddler witches. Imagine spending the day afloat in your own bubble, free to explore an ample section of the forest in absolute safety? Either take advantage of our playdate, multi-child camp for six hours a day or rent your own home bubble, where your baby can be safe and secure when you can't have eyes on them. No magic in, no magic out, full diffusion of all energies. Imagine a sweet, floating baby, safe for the summer! Spaces are unlimited, drop by anytime! Proof of accidental disability insurance required.*

ERIS: *Did you know I practically grew up in one of those bubbles? Excellent babysitters.*

PHEME: *Everything about you tells me you spent your youth in a bubble. Everything. Every. Single. Thing.*

I've never been a runner, which shouldn't come as a shock. The jog to my grandmother's should have taken all the energy I had, and it did, and more. When I arrived, I was panting, breathless, with my legs and back on fire, my hands pulsing with blood from swinging my arms to maintain my speed. I was lightheaded and sweating but still had enough sense to creep slowly up the back steps to her apartment. That's where I stood, gasping for breath and trying to straighten out from the huge cramp that was either in my stomach or my lung.

The door was open slightly, the scent of brimstone, diesel fuel, and blood heavy in the air that wafted out. I planned to sneak in, grab her, and drag her back to Declan so he could arrest her. Granted, she was a powerful witch with almost a century of magic behind her, but she was still an old woman, and I was pretty sure I would come out on top.

I crept in, thankful her home was only two small rooms. She was as I'd seen in the card, kneeling before her alter, lost in her chant, her body frozen. She looked like any other old woman in prayer if you didn't notice the plumes of brimstone smoke swirling around her. The air in her apartment crackled with life, a high-pitched snapping rang around her as her magic snapped and flew out to create havoc and hurt.

"Allegra!" I shouted to get her attention, but my voice was lost in the noise and chaos surrounding her. I tried kicking the door shut, but she didn't react. I needed to break her out of that trance. Stopping her was the only chance my father had. I raced to the front of her and knocked over her altar, but she wasn't praying to the Source. That was a foolish thought. The Source wouldn't imbue power on those who tried to work harm.

Her altar crashed to the floor, candles flying everywhere, crystals, charms, various magical detritus flew across the apartment, skittering on tiles. I knew it was serious, but I was emboldened by the knowledge she was kneeling on hardwood floors, which would give me an advantage when the sensation came back to her ancient joints.

The scattered altar didn't mean anything to her. Her trance was solid, disconnected from the altar, apart from the Source. Any witch worth her salt would be horrified to see her altar, a symbol of her dedication to the Source, knocked over. When Allegra didn't notice her altar in shambles, I realized she was channeling chaos, darkness, evil.

She was hunched over a small carved table. Four small white bags sat there, bound in what looked like canvas, but what I now knew was a fabric made of four separate hangman's ropes, four innocent lives lost. They were laid at the corners of a picture of my brother, his image outlined in black salt, nothing of my father anywhere near the magic. She had taken my brother's magic, kept him lame, and disenchanted him through her evil casting, but why? If I could disrupt that image, get the bags, then maybe I could temporarily break the spell.

I gagged at the smell, and the smoke stinging my eyes as I reached for the bags. My fingers barely brushed across the fabric of that first evil bag when she looked up, her eyes glowing white, rolled back far enough she could be scanning her brain. Her face contorted in pain as a piercing screech left her body.

Slowly, she levitated in front of me. Her body stayed kneeling, but her arms spread out from the prayer pose and she spun in a slow circle.

I know I should have grabbed the bags, but the raw display of chaos magic, the fury who levitated in front of me, had me frozen in terror.

She screamed in my face, "Go!" but it wasn't her voice. It was a demon screech, painful to hear as it vibrated in my bones.

I tried to turn my fear into anger, to fight back, to draw the wind, but I could not move. I was wildly outmatched, unprepared, and in grave danger.

She floated closer to me, and the ozone smell of chaos all-encompassing. My breath came in ragged gasps, and I could feel her drawing power off of me as the wind swirled, but it worked with her, making it harder for me to stand against it.

We were locked in a standoff that I couldn't hold, and she broke me faster than I imagined possible. I dropped to my knees in front of her shaking, weak and cold. Confusion came swiftly as my thoughts swirled, lost in a tornado of my own making. She was drawing magic out of me too fast, and I could feel my heart flutter under the chaos of her power.

It felt like she was ripping out my throat, clawing through my body to find my heart so she could crush it under her intense grip. I fell forward, onto my hands and knees, my vision darkening at the edges. My free will, my consciousness, slipped away into her, and Allegra grew stronger every moment. She loomed large over me, four feet above the ground, hovering like the goddess of lightning and pain, ripping the life from my very being.

I tried to blink, to make a fist, move my fingers, find some deep well of energy that might save me, but every burst of movement fed her more, and forced me against the ground harder. The pain and restriction weren't even the worst part.

The creeping silence rising inside of me was devastating. It was the small voice telling me to give in, to close my eyes and let the darkness take me. It sounded like the quiet of the universe beckoning me to come and take a nap. The sweet sound of the lies, the false hope of rest, and that deceptive sense all would be well if I gave up, squeezing my heart and lungs, making me cry out.

I wrenched out a deep and primal scream, my vision coming back in small flashes until I saw my only chance at salvation, of survival. She hadn't been kneeling on the hardwood floor. Under her knees had been a neatly folded square of the same thick fabric she used to make those infernal hex bags.

I tried to focus, to keep my eyes open and stop panicking. If I could find my center, summon a burst of energy, I could kick against the wall and launch myself toward the door, but I had to grab that wad of fabric on my way. If I could get out, I could get back to Declan, and he could help me. He could find a way to conjure enough power to stop her. He could tell people what happened. Declan wouldn't let everyone think I'd disappeared into the ether.

I stopped fighting the pain and crushing squeeze of her power and gave in to the burning feeling in my skin. Being ripped apart by chaos magic doesn't hurt as much when you give in, and for a moment I could think. Wits gathered about me, I focused on channeling the wind swirling around Allegra as I launched myself forward as hard as I could, pushing my legs against the wall and sliding underneath her, fabric in my hand, going right out the door and through the railing.

I landed hard in the grass at the back of her building, the breath struck from my lungs. A few ribs felt broken, and a massive head wound poured blood into the soil underneath me. I dragged myself to my feet, stumbling as my senses slowly came back. I made it to the curb and across the sidewalk, officially off her property, and lay there a moment, panting, pained, terrified, and barely but blessedly alive.

She beat the shit out of me without ever lifting a finger. Lesson learned.

The fabric in my fist was dark with dirt and streaked with my blood and grass stains, but I couldn't loosen my grip. I had proof. I had hope. All I needed now was help.

I didn't move for several minutes, praying to the Source she wouldn't follow me outside and finish me off. Every part of my body ached, my heart banging against my chest, and each breath was a stab in my back. Whenever I could, I'd crawl a bit, moving at a snail's pace back to the store, willing myself to cry out to Declan, praying he could hear me.

A car pulled up to the curb, braking hard into a shuddering halt. I heard the door open and slam, but I couldn't turn my head back to look.

"Callie, what happened? Lord have mercy! Were you hit by a car?" Dr. Noah's terrified voice was gentle and reassuring. He dove into the grass and was cautious to avoid grabbing me. "Lay back. You need an ambulance." He pulled out his cell phone.

"Get me out of here, please," I gasped, clutching his shirt, unsure if it was already torn or if I'd ripped it in my frenzy. He looked terrified and wild-eyed, I noted before my eyes closed, and I finally gave in, letting the darkness take me.

Chapter Nineteen

I sure can take a punch...

P**HEME:** *I've noticed that a lot of the letters we're getting include the pejorative "Lillim" when talking about....*

ERIS: *When talking about the actual Lillim?*

PHEME: *You know how ignorant it is to use that word. I'd rather you use muggle! Perish the damn thought!*

ERIS: *What would you call non-witches?*

PHEME: *People who aren't witches! They don't need a name!*

ERIS: *Too long, and Lillim isn't bad, necessarily.*

PHEME: *How do you go about calling non-witches Lillim anyways? The Children of Lillith are either demons or witches throughout history, so I don't get it.*

ERIS: *If you don't think people are demons, then you haven't been paying attention.*

PHEME: *Before my partner gets us canceled, let's hear from our sponsor! Lillim Lie-Detectors... Oh, for keening out loud, did you sell this?*

ERIS: *Are you curious about your non-witch associates? Believe they're being untruthful? Well, at Lillim Lie-Detectors, they make the best non-witch untraceable and budget-priced lie-detecting spells—perfectly crafted to mine the mind of the mindless!*

PHEME: *I sometimes fantasize we recorded this at the airport so I could push you into a jet prop...*

I expected to wake up in the hospital, connected to machines, injuries patched up, maybe a blissful pain reliever numbing me to the contusions bubbling blue-green under my skin, but I was still in blinding pain.

I could hear, but the sounds around me were so loud that nothing else existed. Nothing in Blue Crab Bay could sustain this level of noise but the falls in front of our sacred caves. It echoed off the stone walls and drowned out the sound of me being dragged across the flat, lumpy rocks that separated the tidal pool from the Bay. For the briefest moment, I was in a nightmare. I knew I passed out, and I was dreaming of the caves, my psyche calling me to a place of pure power and magic, where I could recharge and ascend before going back to fight Allegra and save my family. It didn't register that the pain I felt in every inch of my body would have been lost in a dream-state. I lost consciousness again before my wits came back.

"Wake up, witch." Noah slapped my cheek with enough force to wake me, but not hard enough to add more pain to my already broken body.

I blinked awake, shocked at his face, merely inches from my own, his green eyes wild and raging. Moss green. Acid green. Surgical scrubs green. They were similar to Allegra's eyes, but where hers were clear and sparkling, his looked swirled with white, like pus on gangrene. They looked poisoned.

"There she is!" He laughed and pulled me up by my shoulders, putting my body against the rocks at the far end of the tidal pool. My knees were bent oddly under me, creating more pain in my hips.

I was hog-tied.

"What are you doing?" I whispered, confused and afraid.

"I'm ridding this world of another menacing witch!" he cackled in my face.

"Dude, your breath is terrible."

It was all I could think to say to get him away from me. He slapped me again, still not hard enough to hurt but enough to let me know he was in charge.

"I'm going to show you something terrible," he said, rising and walking over to a paramedic bag he'd stashed in the corner. Dragging it back to me, he unzipped it and pulled out my grandfather's book; the missing, muddy ice pick; a metal bowl; and a plastic bottle filled with water.

"You're a witch hunter?" I snorted at him, derisively.

I always wanted to snort at someone derisively, and if he was going to kill me, he was going to listen to me berate him while he did it. We hadn't had witch hunters in the United States for well over a century. We were cautious and gentle with the magic, preferring to stay out of sight and keep our magic to the good side, to the small side, the local side.

He scoffed at me. The recycled water bottle was bothersome. Witches and magic workers of all shades are often loath to use plastics because there's no life force left after the process. Any hunter worth his salt would have a decent bag of gear, and this was more serial killer than witch hunter.

"No, you're no hunter—you're a psychopath, Noah." I tried to move, but my hands were bound to my ankles. My options were to sit and wait for him to kill me or throw myself into the tidal pool and drown. I'd keep the latter in mind just in case.

"Shut up, you filthy charlatan! I'm a man of science. I've spent my life dedicated to healing, to medicine, to science. I've given everything to help people in this community, and all anyone talks about is your evil warlock grandfather. 'Oh, I have strep throat? Ruari Aigean probably has a cure.' Your family is a curse on this world and a stain on good doctors who trained and suffered for years to help people. He wasn't much better than a sous chef for those people. His palatable placebos were nothing compared to the real medicine I offer!" The more Noah screamed, the more his mouth foamed, raining spittle down on me.

"Okay, you're big mad. I get it. I was a salty witch when I felt like a failure and a loser. Toss the book in the water, stab me, and put me out of my misery. It's better than listening to you."

I did not give a single fuck anymore. There's a quiet clarity that hits when you know you are going to die. I'd had it. He could have my life, but I'd spend my last breath reading him for filth and take his self-esteem with me.

"I'm not a failure," he screeched, his voice echoing around the cave. "Could a failure murder the most powerful witch in your family? Could a failure keep the great Osian Aigean comatose for weeks so I could infiltrate your family? Could a failure kill a witch like Ginger? She was going to find a way to make your kind immortal! It was so easy to poison her. People visiting the hospital will accept anything to drink from a doctor... Your mother even downed gallons of tea at my hand and never questioned it! I tried to show you. I tried to bring you to your senses. I poisoned your mother, and still, you gave your whore sister the credit for opening a set of blinds and letting the sun into the room!" He bent over the tide pool and filled the bottle with water.

"Twelve years of college and you were defeated by window dressings. I get it—you suck. I'd be pissed too." I know it's not smart to provoke an armed man while bound in a cave, but I couldn't stop. He could have the satisfaction of taking my life, but he wouldn't break my heart or my spirit. I'd be back by the grace of the Source, and he'd still be a turd.

I knew my only chance was to try and save myself, keep him talking, and focus on untying my body. Frantically, I tried to rub the ropes against the rock wall, but the stones were smooth from years of algae and salt water.

"Bianca will continue Ginger's work. You gained a year, tops, before she finds the right mix of spells. Then you'll be crazy *and* unemployed."

He must have decided those baby slaps weren't working, because when he struck me this time, he connected with a closed fist against my eye socket that rang my mouthy, rude bell. It helped take the focus off my ribs and knees because all I could feel was my face exploding as I fell to the side. He jerked me up by the armpit and set me back on my knees, leaning against the cave wall. I wasn't sitting on my feet anymore and hoped the feeling in my legs would come back now, if I lasted long enough. I hoped he didn't notice because for some reason, at that moment, it was crucial I die comfortably, if not quickly.

"I'm going to eradicate this world of witchcraft and fake science. I killed your grandfather, the supposedly strongest witch in the state. I killed Ginger, who was practically immortal with her concoctions, and you're next."

"Oh, for keening out loud, I barely have any magic. Why are you wasting time with me? If you were smart, you'd let me live. I'm likely as not to fail my ascension and strip all the magic out of the family that way. You'd be smarter to go after my sister," I struggled to talk but I couldn't stay quiet.

"Unfortunately, your sister didn't give me the time of day. *You*, however, seemed to light up under the slightest bit of attention. I found the path of least resistance." Noah reached down and grabbed the inside of my thigh, squeezing hard. "As long as I got one of you, I knew I could get the other. Imagine how thankful sweet, pretty little Sunny will be when I do everything in my power to save you from the injuries of your attacker and fail. She's going to have a lot of grief. I'll be sure to help her work through it."

"There are twelve original families, why are you so obsessed with mine?" I tried to hold in a scream while his nails clawed into my thigh.

He shrugged, a creepy smile flickering in his eyes before he just winked at me, digging in tighter with his nails on my thigh.

"My father died because a charlatan masquerading as a doctor convinced him he could treat cancer with turmeric and that he didn't need chemotherapy! Do you know what it's like to grow up without a father? I will destroy your magic if it's the last thing I do." He was quiet now, more terrifying. He set the bottle down and grabbed the icepick, slicing across my skin. A ragged, thick line of bright red blood snaked down my thigh. He'd positioned me specifically to be able to prop the metal bowl under my leg to catch the blood.

"I don't know what that's like, but I also don't know what it's like to have a naïve father either. Did he maybe want to get away from you because you're the actual worst?" I wanted to provoke him, make him make a mistake. The low tone in his voice was menacing and methodical, and I needed to shake him out of that before he put that icepick through my forehead and killed me. "Wait, are you using a dog bowl? This *is* your first time, isn't it?"

The pain was making me pant.

I squeezed my eyes shut and tried to draw his scalpel to my hands, or to his throat. Either was perfectly fine with me.

"If you'd have given blood at the hospital when I first suggested it, this wouldn't need to hurt. Now, stop talking or I will keep you alive and make you watch me strip the magic out of each and every one of you damn blasted Aigeans."

He grabbed my face by the cheeks with one hand and held me still. I was terrified he was going to kiss me, but instead, he ripped out a handful of my hair, jerking my head to the side and racking it against the rocks. Warm, sticky blood trickled down my scalp, and I strangely wondered if he pulled out some of the new white and gray hairs I'd developed in my studies.

My vision wobbled from the pain, and I understood woozy on a deep and profound level.

"This should do it."

He dangled the roots in front of me, my skin still stuck in patches at the ends, and dropped the hair in the bowl and moved back out of range. He cracked open the book and chanted. He sounded ridiculous, and I laughed. He ignored me and got louder, more forceful with his chanting.

"*Coloris, tempo, nox, domini, oro poro nobis*, Calpurnia." He chanted over and over, trying different inflections. There was something so familiar in his chant, but I couldn't place it. It was a spell I'd heard before, but the pounding water was still loud, even this far back in the cave, that I couldn't quite get what he was saying.

"You took an oath to do no harm," I tried reminding him.

He didn't even look at me.

I tried to conjure a rockslide, something to stop him, but the only spell I could remember was the fake one Declan gave me. I doubted screaming movie quotes would help streamline my power.

His voice boomed, he poured the water into the bowl and screamed the same nine words, bad Latin pronunciations and all. *Coloris* was the word that threw me off because it was so familiar but so odd. The problem was that the word doesn't mean anything, not in magic, and not in the context he was using it. It was difficult to think with my head throbbing and my scalp aching. My chest pinched each time I tried to breathe, my position putting excessive pressure on my broken ribs.

He was getting frantic as nothing happened, no matter how he tried to work the spell. I was safe from any magical retribution for now, but if he had something, and I didn't figure out a way to avoid it, he was going to keep going until he found something. The Big Book of Dolphin House. Why was that with him? What was in it? I couldn't remember anything with my head throbbing.

"I'm coming to rescue you!" Clue screamed in my head out of nowhere. I sat up, flopping forward onto my stomach, smashing my chin, and landing face first in a tiny tide pool.

No, stay away. I'm fine—stay away. I tried to deter her with my thoughts, but she laughed in my head. *"I won't let him hurt you, Callie!!"* she shouted in my head, and I knew I had to either get away or kill him before she found me and got herself hurt.

My only hope was that Declan would be with her, armed and sensible. Someone had to let her out of the store, and from the way she'd hijacked my sister on my date, I was sure she'd figured out how to make Declan understand her.

"*Coloris, tempo, nox, domini, oro poro nobis,* Calpurnia." He was on a roll with this, the definition of insanity.

"It's not working, dummy," I yelled at him and rolled onto my back against the cave wall.

He turned to face me and threw the bloody water and hair at me, splashing it across my face and clothes. Everything went red, and the dripping made me desperate to wipe myself. When I looked down, I expected to see a Stephen King-like scene of gore, my body drenched in bloody water, hair stuck everywhere, but only my skin was red. My clothes were clean, fresh as when I put them on that morning. The dirt and grass were gone, the blood from my fall, the sweat from my run—it was all missing, and I was... spotless.

He froze, unsure of what had happened. His folly was my luck, and I finally figured out what he'd done. He had managed to work a simple spell with massively supercharged ingredients.

"Oh, oh honey, you're gonna hate me for sure," I said.

I couldn't help it; I was laughing at him, again. I knew it would be better for me if I could get angry, but he was pitiful, all rage and impotence in the cave.

"Where'd you find that book? Somewhere special, hidden with a lot of spells and magic items? Made you think it was the secret to destroying our kind? It's a cookbook. Here, let me take a guess. You stole the book, found a spell named "magic remover" or something equally important to your cause, and figured it would remove my magic? You didn't think the cookie recipes and dusting tips were a hint? You've hit me with a stain removal spell, jackass. You would have done more damage if you stole Ginger's Calami-Tea, for keening out loud!" I didn't care how hard he hit me—that was worth it.

"SHUT UP!" he screamed and kicked at me, rifling through the book.

I was howling. Part of me hoped the sound of my joy would drive Clue away, keep her out of this. Noah was starting to unravel, and if I could concentrate, he might be susceptible to my little bit of magic.

"This isn't going to end well for you. You can't cure the world of her ails with tea and cookies without consequences, Calpurnia!" he screamed so loud that I felt my hair blow back despite his distance.

"Oh, for fairy's sake, you don't even have the name right! Calpurnia isn't my name; I didn't want to tell you my name. And the spell doesn't end with a name; it ends with *nomine*, which is why it didn't clean the rest of me. Do you think magic simply happens? That you can lie and murder and steal and work real witchcraft? The only magic in that potion is from my blood, my life. Magic isn't yours, and even if you had all the blood from all the witches who ever lived, you couldn't make magic happen. Plus, it takes practice and time and dedication. Magic is a way of life, which you'd have seen if that gigantic chip on your shoulder wasn't obstructing your vision!"

He was finally quiet, stunned, I suppose, by his own obtuse stupidity. I heard two soft barks and then two deep and frightening barks from the front of the cave. Clue was here to rescue me, exactly as she promised. Noah heard her too, galloping across the flat rocks, running as fast as she could.

He bent and picked up the icepick, and I felt something in my spine crack. My fury broke through the pain, and I felt like I was on fire. I shivered uncontrollably, and my fingers tingled and swelled.

Rockslide, I chanted silently, praying. I imagined my grandfather and tried to think of the things he taught me, simple safety tips I could use to bring the cave down around us, but there was nothing but a tingling sensation in my body and rage boiling in my veins.

In the Source's own completely useless way, the rockslide manifested, offering me zero help. Instead of the cave collapsing, my pointless rock ball, the crystal ball for rejected witches, dropped from the ceiling, landed on my thigh, and rolled uselessly about two feet.

Wand slide, I tried again. *Police slide, help slide, fucking Declan slide—something!*

My familiar, a literal baby in the world, was the only creature who came for me, and I knew in my heart she wouldn't survive.

My only other option was to try and throw myself backward to break a wrist to try and escape, but I'd run out of time.

Clue leaped over the tower of flat rocks that separated the pool from the sandy beach and soared through the air, her body shimmering with light. She sparkled, but it wasn't light-on-the-water sparkles. A swirl of colored lights sparked around her as though she was riding on a gaudy, sparkling Christmas tree. Her barks got deeper and louder, and soon she was roaring, her puppy withers elongating to accommodate inky black wings, her hair growing around her neck to protect her throat. Gone was my baby familiar, and in her place was an actual, full-sized, flying, black lion.

"I'm not a puppy! I am THE LAMASSU, Goddess of Assyria, Protector of the Storm! And I'm here to fuck you up, Dr. Dickbag!" she roared in my ear and landed right on his chest, knocking him back into the rocks. As she tried to bite him in the face, he caught her with the icepick in her left side.

She yelped in pain, and I felt my body explode. The familiar tingle of transformation buzzed in my hands as the talons returned, shredding the bindings around my wrist.

My claws cut clean through the ropes that bound me, and I scrambled forward to grab my rock ball, throwing it with everything I had left right at Noah's head.

For all the magic I didn't possess, my aim was absolutely true. The stone hit him smack in the middle of his forehead and ricocheted off before smashing against the cave. It shattered, the rock parts falling away, revealing a smaller-than-normal blue apatite crystal ball, the stone of transformation.

Noah went down hard, but only briefly. It invigorated me. I would have accepted taking him out of commission without much more than a well-placed pitch, but I really wanted a reason to fuck him up. Seeing the small trickle of dark purple blood coming from Clue's haunch demanded nothing less.

I didn't have to stand. I levitated three feet off the ground, my muscles jerking and twitching. A strong wind whipped through the cave, the water in the tidal pool a swirling vortex of magic that rose from the pool in a pillar, lifting me mid-transformation. Blinding light exploded out of me, shoving my Lamassu to the side.

"Oh... Momma's mad," Clue said, satisfied.

I wasn't mad. Mad was a passing emotion. I was fury personified. I was the living embodiment of rage and vengeance and hatred. I was the darkness. My familiar had said it. I was the storm. The pain in my shoulders I thought was from the binding of my hands turned white-hot as six-foot wings burst from my back and I took the form of the harpy.

I had razor-sharp claws, thick ropey muscles, and zero patience. I screamed out a sonic wave of power that shook the cave, blowing the water back and making Noah seize in front of me. His ears oozed, blood dripped down his nose and eyes as he tried to protect his head. I caught him in my claws before he could drop. My talons dug into his shoulders on both sides as I towered over him. My vengeance would be legendary.

I screamed until I couldn't breathe and dropped his broken body in a heap of tears and watched him beg at my feet. Clue wound herself around my legs, her fur bringing me back from the brink of losing myself in the transition. Slowly, I felt my body start to reset. Declan was behind me, silent, gun poised but unnecessary.

The wind slowed and settled around us, and I turned back to Declan.

"Allegra!" I growled. I could stop her now. I could save my father.

"Oh, honey, no!" Clue roared and jumped up on her back paws. Her front paws hit me in the shoulders, knocking me off my feet and into the tidal pool.

I felt the cold water envelop me and heard my grandfather's voice calling from the Source. I swam down, following the sound of his voice into the bright aqua light that flickered at the bottom of the pool. I swam for long strokes before I realized I wasn't in the salt water any longer.

I was at peace for the first time in a long time: my mind wasn't racing, my body didn't ache, and my fears didn't press on my heart. I felt like I was floating in a warm vat of gooey caramel, cradled in love by the Mother Goddess, my turmoil soon to be forgotten.

"This isn't even the good part!" Grandpa Ruari manifested in front of me, coming into focus, standing tall, young, and so much stronger than I ever knew him to be.

"Have I passed?" I was confused, unsure if the scene in the cave was real or a fever dream my brain had as I died. "Is Clue okay? Tell me Noah didn't hurt..."

"Everything is fine. Mr. Bradley is taking Dr. Cabotin in for questioning in your kidnapping. Clue is perfectly fine, though I don't think you'll ever call her a puppy again!" Grandpa's laughter erupted, his cheeks pink with joy. "I was so pleased when she was assigned to you."

"She was from you?"

"She was from us, the Source." He gestured around the gold light where we stood, or floated—it was hard to tell what happened as my physical senses were muted. "This is all of us, Callie. Past, present, and future lives spring from here, and here is where all knowledge awaits. If you stay long enough, you'll develop memories for every journey you've taken, but once that knowledge comes, you can't return."

"I can't stay. I have to stop Allegra!" I felt the panic rising. "She's cursed Aden, bound his magic; she's an evil, vicious, and thieving witch. I have to go back. Someone has to stop her!"

He shushed me, pulling me into his embrace. Everything again settled, and I was at peace, although I was trying to stay upset, remember where she was, what she was doing, how she was breaking my family.

"Cailleach, your grandmother isn't evil. On the contrary, she's dedicated her life to vanquishing evil from the world. Your grandmother is a legendary curse breaker. That's how we met. When my father was a young witch, he was employed by an evil man in his town. Krithik Humgruffin was obsessed with magic, obsessed with finding a way to obtain magic for himself. He'd stolen a young witch bride from the old country and brought her here to be his wife and steal her power. When she refused, he tried to force her, bribe her, brainwash her, starve her—everything short of pure violence.

"My father loved her immediately and promised Krithik he'd find a way into her heart, and he kept his promise. They fell madly in love, and when Dad had all of Krithik's trust, they fled but found nowhere to go. In his rage, Krithik cursed my father and my family line that our wives would die in childbirth, bearing a single son, always carrying on the pain of their betrayal. He struck a dark bargain with something powerful to spin that generational curse, and it took my mother Aoife, it took my beloved Cordelia, and it would have taken your mother when Aden was born had Allegra not intervened.

"It took our whole coven, all the magic we had, every ounce of power, but we managed to reset the curse into those hex bags, one of which I carried until I died. That bag took my ability to walk, twisted, and gnarled my body into the decrepit old man you knew. I could do no magic beyond cooking and basic charms, but it worked. The five bags went to the leaders of our coven, all of whom are dead now except Allegra. They took the death curse placed on the Aigean line and spread it, holding the magic themselves until they died. They didn't have to.

Your grandmother, she never even considered telling Aggie to stay away from Osian. She took the bag and left her old self behind. Her curse was the hardest to manage; her magic still intact, her mind sharp as a wip, even her cheerful countenance was untouched, but around her always, everyone shrank away in horror. Even your family, even I couldn't be around her for long without feeling the rage and anger she carried from that spell.

"When I died, the curse would have passed to Aden, back to full force, but as long as she stays focused, stays diligent, and invokes the guardians six times a day, she can stop the curse from moving on and taking you girls and your mother. The curse doesn't want you or Sunshine to ever have been born."

My mouth sat gaping, my heart aching for the bitterness I'd always had toward Allegra, the disrespect and apathy I'd shown her.

"That's why I'm trapped here, in this between place, unable to reincarnate and continue to the next life, because once I do, the curse will return and take your mother. It's already wearing on her, weakening her, making her vulnerable to poison and almost invulnerable to healing. We don't know if the curse will take you and Sunshine too. According to the rules we know, neither of you were supposed to be born, because Agrippa should have died as she birthed Aden."

"I saw her, Grandpa. I saw Allegra's spell. It's the darkest magic I've ever known. It's so foreign to who we are, our faith, it feels like it could rot the Source from the inside."

"Callie, we try to use magic to impart lessons to our progeny, give them the tools to bring good into the world, but dark magic, all magic, has a place. You've been off-kilter because nobody ever told you that rage is as magical as love and equally as valid. You and your sister are two sides of the same coin: You're the North Wind, and she is the Sun, and both sides will have to come together and break this curse."

"Grandpa, the North Wind is the villain in that story, and I don't want to be the villain. Our calling is to be the person we would need..." I didn't understand how I could honor our ways as something as cold and callous as the North Wind in the fable.

"Sometimes, what we need is someone to give us tough love and not gentle kindness. Sometimes, we need blunt honesty and a kick in the ass. I'm not talking about cruelty—I'm talking about the times in your life you need to take your power back. Kindness isn't spineless; it's knowing when to extend a hand and when to step away. The Source wants only our best, not our nicest. Stop being afraid to take up space, Callie." His words hung in the air, obvious but foreign. He smashed every excuse I'd been using to hold myself back.

"How did Noah get that icepick out of my trunk?" I asked him. Everything else made sense except for that one trick.

"He had help, Callie..." Grandpa Ruari's voice flickered out, his loving tone turning worried as it drifted away.

He faded, and the air around me got colder, wetter, the golden tones fleeting, and the aqua ascension lights coming back strong. I reached to touch him, and he faded, his final words, "I believe in you... find the truth and tell our story," softly drifted to me as he vanished completely.

I shot out of the water, panting, breathless, but tingling with power all over. Everything felt heightened, colors were brighter, I could see better in the dim light, and my familiar sat grooming herself at the edge of the pool. She'd returned to puppy form.

"Did you see the Source?" She paused, one leg in the air so she could lick her tail.

"I saw Grandpa," I whispered, his words still echoing in my mind.

"I wish he would have met me. I think he would have gotten a kick out of me." Clue trotted over and nuzzled my face.

"We're going to have to break a curse, Clue." I climbed out of the pool, looking for Declan, for Dr. Dickbag. The magic worked like Novocain, aware my injuries existed but didn't feel them as my pain.

"It's pronounced Kahlu," she remarked. *"Or it was until you said Clue. I like Clue better. Games are better than coffee liquor."*

"It's fine with me to call you whatever you prefer, my little lion. What about Lambert or Tiffany?" I offered.

"What about if I bite your face while you sleep, hagfish?" Clue responded.

"Clue and Callie work for me." I stood up by using the cave wall that was smeared with my blood and tested my weight on my leg. "Declan?"

"He took in the perp," Clue explained. *"Said to tell you that you can wait here, and they'll be an ambulance by shortly to retrieve you... or I can fly us out?"*

"I can walk, but I think I could fly us out too! I mean, I did turn into a harpy," I reminded my familiar as we climbed the narrow path to the street. I could hear the sirens in the distance. A hundred years ago, this was all rocky coastline and dirt paths, but as the town grew, the coastal roads were paved to this point.

"You better practice first; I've heard how many times you had to take the driver's test," Clue teased, leaping over the last boulder blocking the path from sight. I crawled over, the pain starting to fade back into my periphery.

"You're just jealous my wings and claws are bigger," I grunted and collapsed onto the grass next to the street.

"Let's sit on the curb and wait for the ambulance. I don't want you to run off the road like you did on your first driver's test."

Chapter Twenty

Epilogue

I accepted the first aid offered by the paramedics but refused to go to the hospital. My family could handle a slash in my thigh, a few broken ribs, and a rainbow of assorted bruises, Next time I set foot in a medical institution would be way too soon. I compromised by returning to the police department for pictures and a statement under the condition that Clue come with me.

When I walked into the precinct, Declan swept me up in his arms and held me until the sobbing stopped. If any of the officers around us even started to cough, clear their throats, or try to hurry us along, Teddy was there to kick them away until I was spent and empty of grief and fear.

"I thought I lost you. I've never seen anything like that. I can't lose you again." Declan cried into my shoulder, kissing my forehead, and apologizing for letting me go without him. I wanted to point out that I was pretty much in pieces and didn't have a lot of energy to absolve him, but I did. I took what strength I had and held him until Teddy asked if I was ready to make a statement.

Declan listened intently as I explained the family curse while he drove me home. I was going to need all the help I could get to break that curse, and Declan was nothing if not a strong, smart, irritatingly handsome witch. He helped me into the house, where everyone except Allegra waited to hear my story. When I was done, he helped me to bed, tucking me in and promising to visit every day. I told him I loved him, and he told me he knew that, so I snatched my new blue apatite crystal ball and threw it right at his foolish, arrogant, adorable face.

He caught it one-handed and tossed it like a baseball into the air, again snatching it just before it flopped to the floor.

"Crystal balls as weapons? What would the Source say, Callie?" Declan teased, returning toward my bed and gently setting my shame stone on my nightstand.

"If the Source didn't want me to use it for violence, they wouldn't have given me this one," I explained. "It's not a crystal ball—it's a banishing rock. I'm supposed to throw it at anyone who displeases me."

"Is that what the Source told you?"

I nodded, spinning the crystal in my hand.

"And how many displeasing persons have gotten the banishing rock treatment?" Declan tried to hide a smile, but he was positively twinkling with amusement.

"You're the only person I've hated enough to use the banishing rock." I shrugged at him but had to keep my eyes focused away from him because there was a bubble of joy threatening to pop into a smile on my face. Our banter was an elixir I couldn't live without.

"And for how long do you plan on hating me?"

"Forever," I decided.

"If it's forever with you, I'm happy."

"Stop it right now, Declan Bradley!" I broke open, my smile exploding across my face, and I had to turn my head to try and prevent him from seeing the blush that swept across my skin in a heat of love and flattery.

"I'll see you tomorrow, Callie," he whispered, leaning in to kiss me so softly my skin bubbled with gooseflesh. "And every tomorrow until there are no more tomorrows?"

"I mean… I don't really have any plans that can't be immediately and forever canceled." I gave in and sighed against him, content.

He came back to visit every day. Some days we sat, him reading to me or helping me practice the small enchantments my grandfather had so delighted in doing. Some days my house was packed with well-wishers, and he'd wait until they left and hold me as I cried for the years I missed and the love I didn't know I had from my community.

I healed quickly, remaining sore for a few weeks but back on my feet to greet my father when he got home a week later. Dr. Demented had been keeping him comatose to make sure my mother showed up for her daily dose of poison; a poison that wouldn't have bothered her if we weren't a family weakened by dark magic. She wasn't the only one who suffered—since he poisoned the water cooler near my father's floor, there was an influx of issues from quite a few guests Noah must have considered collateral damage in his witch hunt.

The story of my transformation swept through the witch community, but luckily, the regular folks only thought "harpy" was the insult of a man who had his brains scrambled when a puppy tried to rescue me and knocked him into the cave wall. Declan and my sister did a lot of memory magic and transfiguration to hide the gory details from the general public.

Clue was a local hero and had her picture taken for the paper. "Town pup comes in like a lion, goes out like a lamb," the headline read, which satisfied her ego and managed her disdain for the "p" word. For a solid month, she sat, holding court on a couch in my mother's store, sucking up ear scratches and treats from locals who'd heard about her heroics. By my third day back at work, I threatened to drown the next person who walked in with another bag of chicken livers, because the smell got so pungent and lingered so long, I was starting to dream about them at night.

My mother made me go outside and think about my selfishness while she conjured several pounds of my familiar's favorite snack to "teach me a lesson about gratitude."

I accepted the punishment and hightailed it to Allegra's apartment. Now that I knew her story, I wanted to help. We had a curse to break, and it would take all of us, as a family and a community, together again, to bring balance back into the world.

About the Author

Airie Avant is a Chicago-born, Mississippi-raised international trade expert and Gulf Coast enthusiast. She spends her days ghostwriting logistics news and opinions for C-suite executives. A writer from the start, she launched the creative side of her career as a live concert photographer but pivoted away from visual media when her concert recaps got more attention than her pictures.

Since the pandemic, she's been working from home alongside her husband and an eighty-pound Bernese Mountain Dog, who tries desperately to climb into her lap. She's obsessed with the color aqua, summertime, roasting the people she loves to show affection, and she's not above burning her baby sister's hair off in a book to deal with her real-life attitude.

www.ingramcontent.com/pod-product-compliance
Lightning Source LLC
Chambersburg PA
CBHW031634110225
21778CB00002B/2